Praise for the Rama novels of
Arthur C. Clarke and Gentry Lee

RAMA II
"This is a space trip that no reader will want to miss."
—*Playboy*

"Offers one surprise after another."
—*The New York Times*

THE GARDEN OF RAMA
"A fascinating mix of technology and humanity, soaring
high into the mysteries of the universe and far into the
depths of the soul."
—*Chicago Tribune*

RAMA REVEALED
"Breathtaking."
—*The New York Times Book Review*

"More than fulfills the awesome scale of size, alien
presence and spiritual exploration that were introduced in
[*Rendezvous with Rama*] 20 years ago."
—*The Indianapolis Star*

DOUBLE

FULL MOON NIGHT

GENTRY LEE

BANTAM BOOKS

NEW YORK TORONTO LONDON SYDNEY AUCKLAND

DOUBLE FULL MOON NIGHT

A Bantam Spectra Book

PUBLISHING HISTORY
Bantam hardcover edition published March 1999
Bantam paperback edition published February 2000

ISBN 0-553-57336-5

Published simultaneously in the United States and Canada

Bantam Books are published by Bantam Books, a division of Random
House, Inc. Its trademark, consisting of the words "Bantam Books" and
the portrayal of a rooster, is Registered in U.S. Patent and Trademark
Office and in other countries. Marca Registrada. Bantam Books, 1540
Broadway, New York, New York 10036.

PRINTED IN THE UNITED STATES OF AMERICA

OPM   10   9   8   7   6   5   4   3   2   1

TO MY SEVEN SONS,
Hunter, Travis, Michael, Patrick, Robert, Austin, and *Cooper,*
WHO HAVE ENRICHED MY LIFE BEYOND MEASURE

DOUBLE FULL MOON NIGHT

PROLOGUE

IN THE THIRD decade of the twenty-second century a global stock market crash precipitated a devastating world-wide depression known as the Great Chaos. Throughout the world, the destitute flocked in thousands to metropolitan areas, desperately searching for work and creating a homeless problem that overwhelmed the infrastructures of the great cities.

In London, fear of uncontrolled anarchy prompted the city fathers to accept an extraordinary proposal to care for the homeless. The Michaelites, a new religious order dedicated to serving humanity following the precepts of the charismatic Franciscan novitiate Michael Balatresi, martyred in June 2138, converted Hyde Park into a tent city. There, under the leadership of a twenty-four-year-old woman ordained as Sister Beatrice, the unpaid, energetic sect members provided hope, training, and sustenance to as many as ten thousand of the temporarily downtrodden.

During the bitterly cold winter of 2141, both Sister Beatrice and her Michaelite apprentice Sister Vivien, a former high-class call girl who had experienced a life-changing epiphany during a chance late-night meeting with Beatrice on the streets of London, had eerie encounters with glowing clouds of sparkling, dancing particles of unknown origin. Later, after Sister Beatrice was appointed Bishop of Mars and the two women had moved to the red planet, they would convince themselves that the astonishing particle apparitions they had seen were angels sent by God to strengthen their faith and dedication.

During that same winter of 2141, Johann Eberhardt, a thirty-year-old system engineer responsible for water distribution and allocation throughout greater Berlin, also had a startling encounter with a similar apparition of the sparkling, dancing particles that always drifted about, seemingly at random, inside a glowing cloud of constantly changing shape. Even though his busy life was burdened both by the dire financial straits of his parents and an ugly resurgence of racist nationalism in Germany, Johann was nevertheless fascinated by the apparition and expended considerable effort to understand it. He was certain that there was an explanation for the phenomenon he had witnessed that was consistent with the laws of science.

When Johann moved to Mars, he became the director of the Valhalla Outpost, a facility located near the northern Martian polar caps whose function was to provide water to the other human habitations on the planet. On Mars Johann and Sister Beatrice both had additional encounters with the clouds of enigmatic, sparkling, dancing particles. For each of them, the new apparitions only reinforced their earlier conclusions about the true nature of these experiences.

The Great Chaos resulted in substantial reductions in funding for the Martian colonies. Although the lack of money undermined the essential infrastructure on the planet and triggered a mass emigration back to Earth, Johann and Sisters Beatrice and Vivien steadfastly remained in their jobs on Mars, eventually becoming acquainted with one another and sharing stories of their unusual apparitions. When a giant global dust storm swept across Mars, threatening to deliver a deathblow to all human habitation, Beatrice and Vivien were at Valhalla with Johann. The three of them, along with eight other human beings, had the courage and faith to enter a strange, hatbox-shaped structure that had been built by bizarre alien robots just before the dust storm reached the outpost. To their astonishment, the structure turned out to be a vehicle. This vehicle blasted off and orbited Mars for several hours before being swallowed by a gigantic spherical white spacecraft with a red polar hood and red linear markings around its equator.

Once inside this amazing extraterrestrial spaceship, Johann and Sister Beatrice were separated from the other nine humans. They were guided toward a small boat, which took them on an incredible voyage, a magical mystery tour that suggested whoever or whatever had created the giant sphere not only had thorough knowledge of recent human history, but also had somehow accumulated intimate personal information about Johann and Beatrice.

At the end of the voyage Johann and Sister Beatrice were deposited near an uninhabited island paradise somewhere inside the sphere. They lived together on the island in harmony, arguing only about whether their hosts were God's angels or an extraterrestrial species with unbelievable technological capability. During this period they also fell in love. However, the strength of Beatrice's vow of chastity, taken when she was ordained as a Michaelite priestess, prevented the physical consummation of their affair.

Johann and Beatrice were visited by a glowing ribbon of the sparkling, dancing particles, which performed a complex display that each of them interpreted differently. Immediately thereafter, their almost perfect island existence was irrevocably altered by the arrival of a third person who had left Mars with them, Yasin al Kharif. Johann and Beatrice found Yasin unconscious and near death, clinging to a floating piece of debris in the lake that surrounded their island. The good and gentle Beatrice exerted her considerable energies to nurse Yasin back to health.

Yasin had worked for Johann at Valhalla. Johann knew that his former employee, although extraordinarily intelligent, had a history of sexual assault and other sociopathic behavior. Johann brooded about what life would be like when Yasin was again healthy. He also shared his knowledge of Yasin's past with Sister Beatrice, but she essentially ignored his warnings.

In the days that followed, Johann's worst fears were realized. Yasin, after first being rebuked by the outraged Johann for suggesting that the two of them should subdue Beatrice and together enjoy her sexually, seized the first available opportunity to attack Sister Beatrice. Johann stopped the rape before it was successful, and was going to kill Yasin, but Beatrice interceded. Later, after a period of uneasy peace, Yasin trapped and imprisoned Johann. Leaving Johann to die in his cave prison, Yasin repeatedly raped and humiliated Beatrice in many additional ways.

The particle beings, however, kept Johann alive in his prison by providing food and water. When Yasin entered the cave to confirm that Johann was indeed dead, Johann's righteous anger erupted and he murdered his adversary. Unfortunately, Yasin had already impregnated Beatrice, and she refused to even consider aborting the child. Johann and Beatrice lived together as husband and wife while Yasin's child grew inside her womb. She died shortly after giving birth to a daughter, but not before she extracted a promise from Johann that he would care for Maria as if she were his own.

Johann dug a grave for Beatrice and buried her. Soon thereafter, a glowing white hovercraft, accompanied by many dazzling ribbons of the sparkling, dancing particles, appeared at the island site where he was struggling to care for the infant Maria. To Johann's astonishment, a ramp descended from the hovercraft to the surface and a white being, looking and sounding exactly like the woman he had just buried, beckoned for Johann to ascend. After a moment's hesitation, he picked up Maria and climbed up the ramp.

JOHANN

AND

MARIA

ONE

JOHANN CAREFULLY PLACED eight thin twigs in the cake. He inspected his creation a final time, gently chastising himself for the messiness of the inscription, and then lit the makeshift candles with a small hand torch.

"You may open your eyes now," Johann said to Maria as he carried the cake into their cave.

The girl's face broke into a dazzling smile. She rose from the chair where she had been sitting and bounded toward Johann. He bent down and held the cake, which he had made from the fruits and berries on the island, directly in front of her eyes.

"Happy Birthday to you . . . Happy Birthday to you," Johann sang. In the flickering light from the candles he could see Maria beaming with joy.

When the song was over, the little girl blew vigorously across the top of the cake. All but two of the twigs stopped burning immediately. The sudden burst of smoke, however, made Johann cough. Laughing, and moving away from the smoke, he put the cake down on the small table next to their mats. Maria ran over and threw her arms around his waist.

"Thank you, Johann," she said.

He picked her up and hugged her. "You're eight years old now," he said. "You're a big girl."

"You don't really know how old I am," she said in a teasing voice, kissing him lightly on the forehead. "You're just guessing."

Johann dropped her to the floor of the cave and stared at his little companion. The light from the torches standing just outside the cave entrance caught the deep blue of her eyes, suddenly reminding Johann of Maria's mother. There was a powerful rush of memory and emotion that left him momentarily speechless.

"What is it, Johann?" Maria said, noticing his change of expression.

"Nothing," he replied. "You're right, of course, about your age . . . It's impossible to determine without any true frame of reference." Johann suddenly brightened. "But it doesn't matter if today is *really* your birthday, or not," he said. "Because *we* are going to celebrate anyway. . . . Wait here for a moment, I'll be right back."

Johann dashed out of the main cave and turned left, into the plaza where the perpetual fire burned. Around behind the fire, in a barricaded alcove beside one of the smaller caves, he had hidden all of Maria's birthday presents in a decorated wheelbarrow. He removed the barricade, grabbed the handles of the wheelbarrow, and drove it back to the entrance to the cave.

"All right, young lady," he said. "It's time for your presents."

Maria stepped out into the artificial daylight. She removed the decorative fabric from the top of the wheelbarrow and began rummaging through her new toys. Each of them had been painstakingly created by Johann during the weeks before her birthday from materials that he had collected from the island and the lake. There was a new, larger abacus, several pieces of furniture for the tiny houses in their make-believe city on the sand beside the lake, a pair of small carved dogs, new costumes for both the Siegfried and Brunhild marionettes that Johann used to illustrate his Wagnerian stories, and three human figurines, about twenty centimeters high, two men and a woman, wearing robes that covered their bodies from just below the neck down to their ankles.

The delighted little girl held the three figurines close to her face, so that she could see them more clearly. "This must be Brother Ravi," she said after a moment's examination. Johann nodded. "And these two are Sister Nuba and Brother Jose."

Maria carried the figurines into the cave and placed them on a shelf that had been built against the wall behind her bed. On that same shelf were eight other human figurines, the tallest of which bore a striking resemblance to Johann. Maria surveyed her collection with satisfaction.

"I have them all now," she said. "You, Mother, Father, Sister Vivien, Kwame, Anna, Fernando, and Satoko, and now these three." She spun around and ran back toward Johann, literally jumping into his arms this time. "Thanks again, Johann," she said. "I could not have asked for better presents."

In a few seconds she wriggled out of his arms and returned to the wheelbarrow to pull out the carved dogs and the doll furniture. "Come on," she said, running off toward the lake. "Let's go play—we can eat the cake later, after lunch."

Johann followed her down the path toward the water.

ON THE SAND beside the lake what had originally been built as a small town, named Potsdam after Johann's boyhood home, had now grown into an extended city. Construction on their city in the sand had been ongoing for over a year by the time Johann and Maria celebrated her eighth birthday. Their play together in Potsdam offered Johann a perfect means of introducing the girl to a wide range of human endeavors and activities that would have been utterly foreign to her otherwise. The concepts of family, marriage, divorce, school, work, money, and other items that would have been familiar to any normal eight-year-old on Earth meant nothing to Maria, who had never seen any human beings other than Johann. She was fascinated by his descriptions of the daily lives of the people in their tiny houses, descriptions which Johann, who lacked a fertile imagination, drew completely from his own childhood memories of the people who lived on his block in Kiezstrasse in Potsdam.

Potsdam was Maria's favorite play activity, and time with Johann on the sand in and around their city was often her reward for outstanding performance during the morning school lessons that the girl tolerated only because they were so important to Johann. Maria had little or no interest in spelling, or multiplication tables, or Earth geography, but she did her lessons brilliantly so that she could spend more time sitting beside Johann on the beach and creating a new school complex, or a shopping center, or a residential housing development.

What thrilled Maria the most during their play were the details of daily life in Potsdam for the people who inhabited their buildings and worked in their offices. Constantly prodded by his young companion for more minutiae about the lives of the citizens in their city, Johann began to recall events from his childhood that he had long since forgotten. Maria took these vignettes from his memory and expanded and embellished them. Thus the day that Johann's friend Otto temporarily disappeared (in reality there had been a new film that Otto had risked the wrath of his parents to see) became, in Maria's mind, a family soap opera that ended with Otto's unconscious body being dragged from the Havel River and miraculously resuscitated.

Maria's precocious imagination, which Johann only fettered when her lack of life experience caused her to concoct a scene or situation that could not possibly have happened, eventually became the driving factor behind their play. It was as much a source of delight for him as it was for her.

"Mr. Kleinschmidt has made another ten million marks," she would say, "and wants to build a new Wagnerian theatre out by the lake. . . . But he insists that the audiences must have good restaurants available in the immediate vicinity." She would sketch the general design of the buildings on the sand and then, with Johann's counsel and engineering advice, choose the building materials and the sites for the new complex. Maria did not do any of the actual construction. That was Johann's task. But she would regale him with tales about Mr. Kleinschmidt, or his daughter Katya who wanted to be an actress but had a speech impediment, while Johann was adding the new buildings, roads, and trolley tracks to their make-believe city.

Several months before her eighth birthday, Johann and Maria's imaginary abode had changed, at her insistence, to a brand-new house in their Potsdam on the sand. They had moved from Kiezstrasse to a housing development close to the Schloss Cecilienhof and its magnificent lakeside park. In this new neighborhood Johann no longer had his childhood memories to help him recall who lived in what houses. Maria, of course, knew not only the names of the imaginary people who inhabited every one of the little houses spread out on the beach, but also all the details of their lives. She chided Johann when he forgot that Ulrike was the daughter of the Muellers, not the Heinrichs. The play in their city had by this time become completely hers. Johann was only a willing acolyte.

According to Maria, one of the most recent families to move into their housing development was from Egypt, like Maria's father. Both of the parents in the family worked all day. Their only daughter, Tetrethe, was lonely. She had not yet become friends with the other children in the neighborhood. Tetrethe wanted a pet. On the day of her birthday, by the time that Johann reached their re-created city on the sand, Maria had already placed the two carved dogs outside a specific new house at the edge of the city.

"Tetrethe is happy now," she shouted as Johann approached. "When she comes home from school she'll have someone to play with."

She looked up at him innocently and a quizzical look spread across her face. "But she wants to know what kind of dogs these are, and I can't tell her."

"The lighter, long skinny one is a dachshund," Johann answered. "The other is a schnauzer."

Maria explained what she had just learned to the make-believe Tetrethe and then began placing the other pieces of birthday furniture in houses in the same neighborhood. One of the homes had to have its walls torn down to accommodate a fancy entertainment/communications system. Maria explained to the Offenbachs that now they would be able to have "full-screen, interactive entertainment on demand" as a result of their purchase. Johann smiled to himself while he was reconstructing the Offenbachs' house and listening to Maria's banter. *She has learned my words well,* he thought, *even though she has absolutely no idea what they really mean.*

When Johann was finished, Maria looked troubled. "While I was talking to Mrs. Offenbach," she said, "she told me that her husband, Fritz, has not been feeling well. He is over at the doctor's office now. Let's go see what's the matter with him."

Johann and Maria took several steps to the right and Maria dropped down on her knees next to the building marked with a red cross on the top. "Oh no, Johann," she said after several seconds. "Mr. Offenbach has a brain tumor that must be treated immediately or he will die. What a terrible tragedy that would be for Mrs. Offenbach and their two daughters. . . ."

• • •

JOHANN WAS STANDING in the placid lake, the water just below his knees, holding the large net beside him. From time to time he would bend down and retrieve one of the fishlike creatures trapped in the net and drop it in the bucket dangling from his left shoulder. Behind him, fifty meters away, Maria had moved across Potsdam to the small pond that represented the Havel in their imaginary city. She was kneeling next to the only mosque in the miniature town, talking to Tetrethe and her family. Tetrethe's mother was explaining to her daughter (Maria was, as usual, speaking for everybody) that most of the people in Germany were Christians, not Muslims as they were. From the distance Johann could hear many of the same words he had often used in explaining to Maria the differences between her mother's and her father's religion. *I have kept my promise, Beatrice,* he thought idly as he dropped a long, slithering, eellike being into the bucket. *She has learned about God and Christ and Saint Michael. She knows what an essential role religion played in your life. . . . I have even taught her the basic tenets of Yasin's religion.*

Even after all these years Johann could not mention Yasin's name to himself without a surge of antipathy. Pushing these negative feelings aside, he recalled an evening a few months earlier when Maria had asked if the real St. Michael had had curly hair like the carved image of the young man on the amulet on her necklace. Johann had answered that although he had not personally known St. Michael, other people, Maria's mother among them, had assured him that St. Michael's hair had indeed been very curly. Johann had then explained the rest of the imagery on the amulet, including the nuclear fireball behind St. Michael's head, and had taken advantage of the opportunity to remind Maria once again of her mother's priesthood and her devotion to both Jesus and St. Michael. For once, the girl had not peppered him with questions. In fact, she had been so quiet that Johann had worried that something might be bothering her. During a particularly long pause in what had essentially been a monologue, Johann had looked across at Maria and in the reflected torchlight she had appeared far older than her years.

"You always tell me," the girl had then said, "what my mother believed, and how important her religion was to her. But you have never told me what *you* believe, Johann. Are you a Michaelite too, like my mother? Or something else altogether?"

Johann had turned away for a second, astonished by the directness of the question. "I was raised a Lutheran, like most Northern Germans," he had said after some reflection. "It's a slightly different religion from your mother's, but it is Christian and accepts the concept that Jesus Christ was the divine son of the one true God and appeared on Earth both to show us how to live and to save us from our sins."

Johann had smiled. "If your mother were here, Maria," he had continued, "she would justifiably have claimed that what I just said was a gross oversimplification. But it will suffice for now. . . . Anyway, what do I believe? I believe there is a magnificent order in nature that may be the result of a master designer. I believe human beings are an incredible miracle, a collection of chemicals manufactured in stars that have somehow evolved into consciousness and awareness. . . . But, as far as I can tell, none of these beliefs has anything to do with the divinity of Jesus Christ or the personal Gods of Christianity and Islam. . . ."

Standing in the lake deep inside the spherical extraterrestrial spaceship of unknown origin and purpose, Johann could remember vividly the puzzled, almost bewildered look on the girl's face after their discussion about religion had concluded. *It's not enough that I force her to learn about a planet she has never seen,* he thought, criticizing himself. *I even confuse her with the illogic of the religions of our species. . . . Of what possible importance is the concept of God here, in this alien world of ours? Of what significance are the lives of Jesus*

Christ, Muhammad, and Saint Michael? If I had not made that promise to Beatrice, I doubt if I ever would have mentioned the subject of religion to Maria.

Johann's contemplation was broken by the sound of splashing in the water. He turned to his left and saw Maria cavorting with her aquatic friends, Hansel and Gretel, a mated pair of creatures whose physical appearance and behavior both suggested a cross between sea lions and dolphins. Most afternoons, before the artificial daylight disappeared, the pair would approach the shore and squeal for their human playmate to join them. Maria loved to wrestle with Hansel and Gretel. She also rode on their backs, or tossed a light wooden ball back and forth with them. The sea creatures were Maria's only real friends other than Johann.

Johann smiled as he listened to her laughter. *I'm virtually certain,* he thought, *that this lake contained no life of any kind when Beatrice and I first came here. Our hosts stocked it for us while Maria and I were away. Now it would be difficult for us to live without the food it provides.*

Maria was swimming a speed sprint beside Hansel. She lost, but just barely, and playfully whacked the creature's flipperlike arm. Hansel feigned indignation and Maria laughed uninhibitedly. *She needs their friendship,* Johann said to himself. *I am certainly not much of a playmate.*

He felt a tug on his net and looked down into the clear water. Johann could not recognize what was caught in the net. He reached down and picked up something he had never seen before, a long, light blue tentacle, resembling a very thick garden hose, at the end of which was a large and powerful claw the size of a human hand. The edges of the claw were as sharp as a knife. Johann dropped the tentacle with the claw in the bucket without thinking. The water in the bucket suddenly exploded as those creatures who were still alive scrambled to move away from the new arrival.

• • •

MARIA WAS STRETCHED out on her bed a couple of meters to his left. Johann had dimmed the torches, as he always did at bedtime. He could barely see her face, but he could tell that her eyes were still open.

"Did you have a good birthday, Maria?" he asked.

"Oh yes, Johann," she said quickly. "Dinner was great, the cake delicious—and I loved the presents." She held up Sister Nuba so that Johann could see her. "See, I'm sleeping with one of the new figurines. . . . Tell me, what was Sister Nuba like?"

"I never knew her that well," Johann answered. "The first time I really talked with her was when she came to Valhalla with your mother, right after Kwame Hassan and I explored those subterranean ice caverns beneath the Martian north pole. Sister Nuba was from Tunisia, if I remember correctly, and was one of the most devoted priestesses on Mars. She was quiet and shy, but had a beautiful smile. I'll never forget how terrified she looked when that snowman-like thing wheeled into the large waiting room shortly after we entered this sphere. . . ."

Maria had heard all Johann's major stories several times. She knew the names and personalities of all ten of the other humans who had, along with Johann, departed from Mars in a bizarre, hatbox-shaped spacecraft that had been engulfed hours later by the gigantic sphere in which Johann and Maria were still residing. She was well aware that her mother, Beatrice, had been the first bishop assigned to Mars by the Order of St. Michael, that Johann had been the director of the Valhalla Outpost (the northernmost habitation on the red planet), and that the two of them had each separately seen, both on Earth and later on Mars, several astonishing apparitions of enigmatic, sparkling clouds of particles that had never been explained. Maria also knew that Johann and her mother had significantly different opinions about the likely origin and nature of these apparitions.

From time to time Johann reminded Maria that her

mother never once wavered from her belief that the particles, whose manifestation inside the sphere had been as glowing, flying ribbons of light, were messenger angels sent from God. For his part, Johann explained his reasons for believing that the sparkling particles were some kind of extraterrestrial being, or at least an alien creation of some kind, and represented a species so advanced that to us they would seem to possess magical attributes.

Many of their late-night discussions were about the other people who had accompanied Johann into the sphere. In general, Johann told Maria the truth about everything. There were one or two exceptions to his rule of truth. The girl knew, for example, that Johann and Beatrice had been alone on the island for a long time before her father arrived, and that they had essentially lived together after her father's death; however, Maria did not know the true nature of the relationship that had existed between Johann and her mother. She thought that they had only been the best of friends, like a brother and a sister, and that Johann had consoled Beatrice after the death of Yasin. Of course Maria knew nothing at all about the way her father actually died. She believed, because that is what Johann told her, that Yasin had fallen from one of the high cliffs on the opposite side of the island during the first trimester of her mother's pregnancy.

On the night of Maria's eighth-birthday celebration, after Johann finished telling his story about Sister Nuba, the girl rose from her bed and went over to the shelf where she kept all her human figurines. She pulled down three, Johann, her father, and her mother. Then she turned around and looked at Johann.

"What is it, Maria?" Johann asked.

For a moment she was silent. "You know, Johann," she then said matter-of-factly, "I really don't have a very clear picture in my mind of my father. But it doesn't really bother me. Would you like to know why?" She skipped across the cave until she was beside him. "My father couldn't possibly have told me any more about my mother than you have, or, for that matter, cared about her any more than you did." Maria grinned. "And even if he had lived, my father couldn't have been any nicer to me than you have been."

She kissed him on the forehead and returned to her mat. Johann did not fight the tears that came into his eyes. "Good night, Maria," he said. "And Happy Birthday again."

TWO

JOHANN LAY AWAKE on his mat a few meters away from the sleeping girl. Despite the fact that he was tired, his mind would not let him sleep. It kept jumping from one topic to another. For a while he thought mostly about Maria, worrying about the kind of future she would have. Then the focus of his anxiety changed and Johann found himself asking the overwhelming questions for the umpteenth time since they had returned to the island. *Why are we here? Who are our hosts? What is going to happen to us?*

Unable to sleep, at length Johann rose quietly, pulled on the new trousers that Maria and he had made the previous month, and walked to the front of the cave. He stood beside one of the two torches on either side of the entrance, idly staring out at the rocks, the plants, and the dirt pathways surrounding the cave. It seemed to Johann that he had been in this place forever. His childhood and university days in Germany, his years on Mars at Valhalla, and even the six months Maria and he had spent, just after her birth, in that strange place Johann called Whiteland, all seemed to be part of another lifetime.

As his eyes searched the darkness beyond the areas illuminated by the torches, memories of his first days on the island flooded into Johann's consciousness. Again he could see Beatrice's lovely face and hear her incredible voice, soaring majestically while singing one of her favorite songs. He had a vivid recollection also of the intensity of his love for her, and how happy he had been during those first hundred days, before Johann and his angel Beatrice lost the paradise offered to them by their unknown hosts. *That was all here,* Johann thought, *in this same cave.* He was unable to quell his feelings of sorrow.

Thoughts of Beatrice always pulled him toward her grave. He glanced back at the sleeping child before trudging up the pathway. Along the way he stopped to gather a bouquet of the red and white flowers that she had liked so much. Beatrice had always told him that those particular flowers reminded her of the amaryllis, one of the Earth's most beautiful creations.

When Johann turned the corner in the path next to her gravesite, he looked up into the darkened interior of their mammoth alien spaceship and invoked Beatrice's name. He asked her to give him a sign that Maria and he had not been abandoned by her altogether. For just a moment he thought he saw a light in the far distance. But the surge of hope quickly waned. There was nothing unusual in the sky.

He laid the bouquet of flowers beside Beatrice's grave. *Eight years ago you died,* Johann thought. *You gave me your daughter to raise.* He leaned back and stared at the exact place above the gravesite that had been filled with glowing ribbons on the night he had buried Beatrice. *Or did you really die?* he asked himself. *Maybe transformed, or transfigured, would be a better word.*

On that amazing night Johann had been astonished to see Beatrice again, apparently alive, only minutes after he had covered her lifeless body with dirt. In his emotional distress, he had been certain that the glowing white figure beckoning to him from the top of the ramp that dropped out of the white hovercraft had indeed been his Beatrice. Only later, after he had carried Maria with him up the ramp and they had been transported to some other location in the starship, did the idea occur to Johann that perhaps the white being who was beside him was not really Beatrice at all, but just an amazingly accurate reproduction of her.

This person was his regular companion in Whiteland for the next six months. Slowly, surely, Johann realized that the woman nursing the child Maria was not really *his* Beatrice, but some other kind of creature or being altogether. She was so perfect that only someone who had studied Beatrice as closely as Johann had could possibly have noticed the subtle mistakes. A wrong gesture here or there, an occasional facial expression that was not correct, a speech pattern that she would never have used—these were the only differences between the Beatrice in white who was caring for the infant Maria and the woman who had died in Johann's arms after childbirth.

Johann had yearned to touch this beautiful white Beatrice, not just because he wanted the comfort and pleasure, but also because he knew that if he could hold her in his arms for even a moment he would know for certain if she was really *his* Beatrice or simply a superb copy. She always told him gently that no physical contact between them could be permitted. The Beatrice in white explained that her body had "undergone a change" that might cause him distress if he touched her. "Maybe someday, Brother Johann," she had said consolingly, "but not yet."

But even a fake Beatrice was better than nothing, Johann thought. He recalled the morning when the Beatrice in white had announced, with no prior warning, that it was time for Johann and Maria to return to their island. During their flight back to the island in the hovercraft, Beatrice had explained to Johann that Maria now had enough teeth that she could eat solid food. She had then told him that Maria and he were to stay on the island until they received an unmistakable sign that it was time for them to leave. When they arrived at the island and disembarked, the white Beatrice had said only a brief good-bye and had then departed.

Suddenly she was gone, Johann recalled, somewhat surprised by the strength of his bitterness, *without either explanation or preparation. It was abrupt and insensitive, both for Maria and for me. Since that time we have had no interaction with either Beatrice or the glowing ribbons.*

Johann detested self-pity, especially in himself. To force a change in his thoughts, he walked away from the gravesite, up the side of the mountain, and stared out toward the lake. In the total silence of the island he thought he could hear the water lapping gently on the shore. *I am lonely for an adult companion,* he thought to himself. *But it could be much worse. I have someone to love and cherish, which makes me . . .*

His reverie was broken by Maria's shout. Johann bolted down the pathway toward the caves, hurrying past the gravesite, and reaching Maria's side in no more than a minute. Her beautiful blue eyes were wide open and a look of amazement was on her face.

"It was here, Johann," she said excitedly. "Over there, against the wall. . . . One of those ribbon things you told me about. Its light woke me up. As soon as I opened my eyes, it zoomed out the cave entrance."

Johann pulled the girl to him. "That's all right, Maria," he said soothingly. "You've just had another of your vivid dreams."

"It was *not* a dream, Johann," Maria insisted. "I *did* see the glowing ribbon. Right there, in our cave. Only a few minutes ago."

To placate her Johann toured the entire cave with the girl, searching for any evidence there had been a visitor. They found nothing. When Johann suggested that Maria should return to her mat and go back to sleep, the girl was indignant.

"Whether you believe me or not," she said angrily, "I *know* what I saw." Maria stomped over to the entrance. "It disappeared right . . ."

The child interrupted herself to bend down and pick

up an object that was leaning against the bottom of the torch holder on the right side of the cave entrance. "See," Maria said, turning to Johann with a satisfied smile on her face and holding up the object, "I told you so. That ribbon left me a birthday present."

Johann was thunderstruck by what he saw in Maria's hand. It was a doll, a perfect likeness of her mother, Beatrice, dressed in shimmering white exactly like the person or being that had accompanied them during the first six months of Maria's life.

MARIA WAS NOT interested in the geography lesson. She ignored Johann's lecture about the Arabs and the Mediterranean. She continued to chatter about the glowing ribbon that had visited their cave. In the intervening four days, Maria had embellished the story of the ribbon's visit with details from her hyperactive imagination.

"It did such a wonderful dance, Johann," she said, interrupting his lecture while they were standing on top of Egypt on the flat world map that Johann had laboriously drawn on the beach sand. "Its tail bounced up and down quickly, the particles drifted back and forth, and then whoosh, it was gone."

"You told me that night that you barely saw the ribbon at all," Johann said crossly. "And besides, Maria, we are presently in the middle of our geography lesson."

"But it's *boring*, Johann," Maria said petulantly, switching the Beatrice doll rapidly from one hand to the other. "I don't care about Egypt, or China, or Germany, or America. What difference do any of those places make to *me*?"

"Someday, Maria," Johann said, "we may meet other human beings. Who knows, maybe you and I will even be returned to Earth. Then all this geography will be important. You may meet members of your family. . . ."

"All right," Maria said playfully, sensing that he was

going to be stubborn. "I'll show you what I know." She jumped across the outline of the Atlantic Ocean that was drawn on the sand. "My mother grew up here in Minnesota, in America," she said. "And Fernando Gomez lived here, in Mexico, until his assignment to Mars."

She came back over beside Johann. "You were born in Germany, just behind your left foot, and Anna Kasper came from nearby Switzerland. My father lived in both Egypt and Saudi Arabia, here and there. The only other person in your group from that part of the world was Kwame Hassan, a man with very black skin who came from . . . I've forgotten the name of his place, but it was down here somewhere."

Maria glanced up at Johann. "See, I know enough already about the geography of the Earth. What I don't know is what's on the other side of this lake. That seems much more important to me. You promised me long ago, Johann, that you would build us a boat, and that we would go exploring."

Johann looked down at the beautiful little girl beside him. *She's right, of course,* a voice inside him said. *Earth geography is completely irrelevant. And you did promise her once, in a weak moment, that the two of you would see what was on the other side of the lake.*

But what about the white Beatrice's insistence that we stay on the island until we receive a sign, another of Johann's inner voices answered. *Her statement was perfectly clear.*

That was over seven years ago, the first voice now said. *Are you just going to languish here forever? The girl deserves some adventure and excitement. And so do you.*

He felt her touch his arm. "Can I, Johann?" she was asking. "Please?"

"I'm sorry, Maria," he said, "I was thinking about something else. What did you say?"

"I want to go swimming," she said. "I'm tired of school. And my Beatrice doll needs a bath."

"All right," he said after a brief hesitation. "But tomorrow . . ."

She was gone before Johann finished his sentence. Maria sprinted across the sand and plunged exuberantly i ᷄ ᷄ water.

THREE

OVER THE YEARS Johann had learned the characteristics of virtually all the plant materials available in their island domain. To build the bottom of the boat, he chose the strong but flexible long strips that were part of the tubular connections among the disparate clumps of the strange network bush that grew near the top of the mountain. It was difficult work to cut the tubes from the bush and then remove the strips. Johann's hand tools, the same ones that Beatrice and he had first discovered in the supply cave years before, were barely adequate for the task. It took him most of a day to harvest enough of the strips for the bottom of the boat.

Johann, the strips wrapped in a bundle on the ground beside him, wiped the sweat from his forehead and took a drink of water from the pool created by the two springs at the top of the mountain. It was late afternoon in their world. In two more hours the artificial sunlight coming from far above their heads would abruptly vanish, as it did each night. Below him, down the slope of the mountain covered with green growth, Johann could see Maria playing in the lake with her two aquatic friends, Hansel and Gretel. She had spent most of the morning beside him, chattering away about what they would likely find on their voyage of adventure in the new boat.

Johann hoisted the bundle onto his shoulders and began the climb down the path that ran beside the stream. He had misgivings about setting forth in the boat. It was not for himself that he was concerned—Johann would have readily admitted that he was definitely eager for a break in their routine. But what if he exposed Maria to some kind of danger? He would never forgive himself if he were responsible for something terrible happening to the girl.

He heard the first of the unusual cries when he was several hundred meters from the beach. A few seconds later the cry repeated and Johann stopped to listen. The aquatic creatures often squealed with delight while they were playing with Maria, but this was a different sound, almost certainly a cry of fear or pain, and it frightened Johann.

"Maria," he called out. "Are you all right?"

There was no answer. Johann stepped up his pace, emerging from the brush onto the sandy beach at the moment when a cacophony of animal yells exploded in the air. In the middle of the din Johann could hear Maria screaming, "Help, Johann, help."

He dropped the bundle on the beach and raced into the water. Hansel, Gretel, and Maria were fifty meters offshore. Johann sped toward them with huge, powerful strokes of his long arms. When he reached Maria, the girl draped herself around his neck and wept hysterically. Beside them, Gretel was swimming circles around the lifeless, torn body of her mate, Hansel. The animal stopped periodically to emit a mournful wail.

Johann carried Maria back into the shallow water, attempting without success to calm her enough that she could tell him what had happened. Every time Maria tried to speak, she would just cough and tremble, and then start sobbing again.

At length Johann managed to soothe and comfort her. "There was this horrible *thing*," Maria said eventually, "with three eyes and an ugly gray head floating on the water. . . . And long blue wriggly arms with claws on the end. It was churning up the water not far from where we were playing. When it looked at us, Gretel squealed with fright.

"Hansel swam over to protect us. When he jumped out

of the water and made a threatening sound, the thing attacked immediately, ripping into Hansel's skin with its claws. It was awful. Hansel didn't have a chance."

Maria started to cry again. Then she abruptly stopped and motioned to Gretel. "Come over here," she shouted. "We'll take care of you." Gretel must have understood Maria's words and gestures, for the creature started swimming in her direction.

"We can't leave her out in the lake with that thing, Johann," Maria said. "We must take her to our big pond, behind the grove." The girl ran over and hugged Gretel as the animal approached them.

Johann escorted the pair into shallower water. "Stay here with Gretel for a moment," Johann said softly. He swam out to where Hansel's body was floating on the surface of the water. Johann rolled the animal over and examined its other side. Hansel had been ripped apart. Chunks of his flesh had been completely torn away, and in other places the attacker's claws had sliced halfway through his body. Treading water, Johann carefully scanned the lake as far as he could see. At the limit of his vision he saw six or eight tentacles waving in the air, many with fish in their claws. They appeared to be dropping the fish into a large object floating on the water.

"THE DRAGON FAFNER roared and aimed a terrible burst of fire at the man who dared to challenge him. The fearless Siegfried, protected by his magnificent shield, was unharmed. When the fire was no longer a threat, Siegfried stepped out from behind his shield and raised his magic sword Nothung."

Johann, on his knees behind the marionette theatre, pulled the strings that controlled Siegfried's right arm. "With quick and powerful strokes our hero struck the dragon. Once, twice, three times. Then, when the dragon was off balance and its vulnerable spot exposed, Siegfried shouted and lunged, plunging Nothung deep into the heart of the loathsome creature."

With his other hand Johann made the dragon recoil and then crumple into a heap. He waited for the praise and applause that usually followed this part of the story, but he heard nothing from Maria. At length, instead of continuing with the next scene in the show, Johann stuck his head around the corner of the theatre. The girl was crying.

"What's the matter?" Johann said.

Maria wiped her eyes with the back of her hand. In the reflected torchlight Johann could see that her eyes were swollen again; she had probably been crying during the entire performance.

"What's the matter, Maria?" Johann repeated.

"I'm sorry," she said in a sad, little-girl voice. "It's not your fault, Johann. It's just that Fafner the dragon reminded me of that nozzler, and I can still see it attacking Hansel as if the whole thing happened only a few minutes ago."

Johann lifted the marionettes over the back of the theatre and placed them in their boxes. Then he crossed the cave to where Maria was sitting, picking her up in his arms. "What you're experiencing is normal," he said gently. "You've had what's called a traumatic experience, and it's natural for you to remember it very clearly. In time, the horror of that attack will fade away. But it may take many more days."

The girl buried her face in Johann's neck and held him very tightly. "Can we go down to the pond again and make sure that Gretel is all right?"

"No, Maria," Johann responded. "It's past your bedtime and we just checked on Gretel only two hours ago."

"But what if one of those nozzler things comes out of the lake and attacks her? Gretel is such a gentle creature, Johann. She wouldn't know how to fight."

Johann sighed and carried Maria over to her mat against the wall. "I will check on Gretel," he said. "You brush your teeth and finish getting ready for bed."

Maria smiled. "Thank you, Johann," she said.

He bent down beside her. "Darling Maria," he said, "you can't continue to worry about Gretel all the time. She is in no danger now. Whatever it was that killed Hansel has gone away."

She didn't respond. Johann had made basically the same comments to her every evening since Hansel had been killed. Nevertheless, each morning Maria had been in such a state of frenzy and hysteria that she could not be calmed until she had seen with her own eyes that Gretel was still all right.

Johann slipped on his moccasins and left the cave. He returned about five minutes later. Maria was already on her mat, lying on her back.

"Gretel was fine," Johann said as he started preparing for bed. "She squealed thank you at me when I fed her some fish from the bucket."

"Thank you, Johann," Maria replied.

"I was thinking about Siegfried while you were gone," the girl said a little later in the serious voice that made her seem much older. "He was not afraid of anything. I bet he would have searched the lake, found that nozzler, and killed it with his magic sword."

Johann recognized the challenge in her tone and understood immediately the thrust of her remarks. He stood beside his mat, cleaning his face with one of their well-worn pieces of fabric. *She's disappointed in me,* he thought while he was considering how he should respond. *She expects me to be her hero.*

"Siegfried *might* have gone off in search of the nozzler," Johann said slowly. He sat down beside Maria. "I can't say one way or the other. But Siegfried was not a real person. He was a make-believe, mythological character, with abilities far beyond those possessed by ordinary human beings."

The girl propped herself up on an elbow on her mat. "Was Siegfried bigger, stronger, or smarter than you, Johann?" she asked defiantly, fixing him with her gaze. "You told me once, while we were playing together in Potsdam, that almost every *real* person was smaller than you. Are heroes smaller than you too?"

This is really serious, flashed through his mind. *She's been preparing for this conversation.* "Maria," he said at length, "I'm sorry that you're so upset. Believe me, I would love to wave my arms, like a magician, and make that nozzler go away."

She wasn't impressed. "But Maria," he continued, "real life is not like the fairy tales and legends in our bedtime stories or marionette shows. In real life, when people try to accomplish heroic deeds, they are sometimes hurt, or even killed. If I were to be killed or disabled, there would be nobody to take care of you."

She did not back down. "You told me that heroes," Maria said stubbornly, "protect women and children from the monsters or bad people who terrify them. Heroes are never afraid of anything, and they don't let themselves get hurt or killed."

This is amazing, Johann thought. He didn't know what else he could say to comfort her. He released her hands and stretched out on his own mat. "We can talk about this subject again tomorrow," he said uncomfortably, "when you may be more willing to listen to what I'm telling you."

Maria did not reply. "By the way," Johann added several seconds later, "I have not been taking my regular morning swim since Hansel was killed, because I knew that you didn't want to be left alone. You know how important that swim is to me. Starting tomorrow, I will be swimming again every morning just after dawn."

IT WAS A terrible night. Johann stayed awake for over an hour, going over all his conversations with Maria since

Hansel had been killed. Was there anything else he could do? He felt inept and inadequate. In one internal monologue he entreated Beatrice to reappear and give him some advice on how to handle the situation. Johann even seriously considered Maria's suggestion that he should hunt and kill the nozzler. *At least I would regain my lost stature in her eyes,* he thought, before dismissing such a venture as foolhardy.

When Johann finally fell asleep, he was awakened only a few minutes later by a bloodcurdling scream from the mat beside him. His heart pumping furiously and adrenaline pouring into his body, Johann was immediately alert and ready to protect his ward.

The girl had had a nightmare. She crawled over on Johann's mat and snuggled into his arms, still whimpering from fright. All Maria would say about the dream was that a nozzler had attacked Gretel and her while they were swimming.

Maria managed to fall asleep again quickly but Johann remained awake for another hour. Later, not long before morning, he had a dream so vivid that it took Johann a long time, even after he was awake, to convince himself that it was not real.

Johann had been in a deep green forest in the dream, following a yellow and black bird with a beautiful voice who was leading him to a magic mountain. The top of the magic mountain was hidden behind a barrier of flames. Johann understood in the dream that he needed to wade through the flames to reach the sleeping Brunhild, who would fall madly in love with him as soon as he awakened her with his kiss. But the sleeping woman on the mountaintop was not Brunhild; she was Beatrice, whose kisses after waking stirred Johann's sexual ardor. In the dream, as he tried to remove her clothes, Beatrice whispered "Not yet," and pointed off to her right. There, coming up the side of the mountain, was a huge, bizarre monster breathing fire. The monster vaguely resembled a dragon, but instead of hands this creature had hundreds of long blue tentacles with claws on the ends. Most of these tentacles were extended in Johann's direction. When he felt the first sharp touches on his neck Johann awakened with a shudder.

He did not sleep again. When the artificial daylight first lit the front of the cave, Johann checked the sleeping Maria and then jogged down toward the lake. He plunged into the water and began to swim. Within minutes, as his long body eased through the water, stroke after stroke, Johann felt his frustration and anxiety begin to lessen. Years of competitive swimming had made Johann completely comfortable in the water. After the initial release of pent-up energy, his body moved into an effortless rhythm so natural that it seemed to be totally disconnected from Johann's volition.

During these periods Johann's mind sometimes focused on a specific topic, but more often it drifted idly, serving up a potpourri of unrelated thoughts and images. Later, after fifteen to twenty minutes of steady swimming, Johann usually entered a slightly altered state of consciousness, one which a friend of his had once called "exercise nirvana." A sense of peace, harmony, and communion with the world around him pervaded Johann during this portion of his swim. This feeling of contentment, and the residual sense of well-being that often lasted the rest of the day, were the primary reasons that Johann swam every morning.

Johann was well into the nirvanic phase of his morning swim when he began to feel an unsettling disquiet whose origin he could not pinpoint. When it would not go away, he opened his eyes during his breathing. There was nothing unusual about the island landscape that greeted his eyes on the right side. On the other side, the lake extended to the horizon in an unbroken line. What was disturbing him, then? Johann was miffed at this intrusion into his most peaceful sanctuary and was about to dismiss his disquiet altogether when he happened to look more closely at the water. It was discolored.

Johann stopped swimming and examined the water around him. On an impulse he decided to taste it. The taste seemed familiar, but Johann could not identify it. Looking around, he could see that the discoloration increased off to his right, away from the island. Johann began swimming in that direction.

Just after Johann positively identified the strange taste as blood, he saw an unusual object about two hundred meters in the distance. The object was bobbing up and down in the small waves of the lake. At first Johann was wary of possible danger, but as he drew closer he became certain, from the object's lack of movement, that it was not alive.

When he first recognized Kwame's body, Johann could not believe what his eyes were telling him. But what in the world was that thing *with* Kwame? Johann continued to approach, swimming breaststroke so that he could keep the scene in view. Both surprise and horror swept through him moments later when he realized that Kwame was floating on the water, locked in a death embrace with one of the nozzler creatures who had attacked Hansel.

Kwame's knife was embedded deep in the frontal underbelly of the nozzler. Both of the creature's blue tentacles were wrapped around Kwame's back. One of its vicious claws, which was still affixed to the side of Kwame's neck, had obviously sliced through the jugular vein. The fight to the death had occurred not many hours earlier, probably sometime during the night. Blood was still oozing out of the many wounds in both Kwame and the nozzler (its blood was bright purple), and there were not yet any signs of rigor mortis in Kwame's body. Johann's feelings of grief were accompanied by a thousand questions that rushed into his mind. *What was Kwame doing here?* Johann asked himself. *Where did he come from? Where are the others?*

Johann swam in an ever-widening circle around the two corpses, searching for clues that might provide answers to his questions. He found nothing. When he returned to Kwame and the nozzler, he carefully inspected the alien creature.

The nozzler's body was long and thin, approximately as tall as Kwame, and consisted of ten identical middle segments with hard black carapaces that were connected to a broader head-and-chest segment in the front and a fanlike tail at the rear. Three oval, bulbous gray eyes were distributed uniformly in a line along the top of the turquoise-colored head-and-chest segment. The front two of these eyes were placed at an angle that suggested their primary look direction was forward; the third eye was positioned so that its natural field of view was to the rear. Along the sides of this front segment were three symmetrical pairs of attachments, the first pair being the long blue tentacles with the terrifying claws that could reach a full meter in front of the head, the second resembling a pair of circular washboards built against the side of the head next to the middle eye, and the back pair looking like clusters of tiny pearls on either side of the rear of the head.

The body of the nozzler narrowed slightly behind the frontal region, tapering into a centipedelike arrangement of the ten middle segments, each with the hard black carapace (above the body and partially around the sides) and a soft, fleshy underbelly with hundreds of flexible cilia extending below. The fanlike tail, which looked solid from a distance, was actually thirty or forty individual strips of textured material attached to a central nexus or ganglion located at the rear of the last of the middle segments.

Johann was fascinated by the nozzler. Although he was horrified by the sight of Kwame, the astonishing biology of the alien corpse piqued his curiosity. Surveying the entwined pair while continuing to tread the water, Johann decided that he would tow them together to the island so that he could study the nozzler more closely.

He heard Maria's frantic cries while he was still well

offshore. When Johann had not returned to the cave at his normal time, the girl had panicked. Fortunately, she had had the good sense to search the water for him, and her keen eyes had located him far out in the lake. After first verifying that the local currents were insignificant, Johann left his discovery a hundred meters from the beach and swam into shore so that he could reassure the girl.

Johann's description of the dead pair was sufficient to send Maria into another bout of hysteria. No matter what he said, she insisted that the nozzler corpse should not, under any circumstances, ever touch their island.

"What if its friends or family should find it here," she said, "and somehow decide that we were responsible for its death? What would happen to us then?"

Johann's biological assessment that a nozzler was not a land animal was of no importance to Maria. She adamantly repeated that she never wanted to see "one of those things" again, dead or alive. There was no way that Johann could mitigate her fear.

He reluctantly swam back out to where he had left the pair of corpses and began the process of disconnecting Kwame from his foe. It was not an easy procedure. The tentacles around Kwame's back were still tight and Johann could not muster much strength while he was treading water. Eventually he separated the pair. Remembering his lifeguard training in Berlin, Johann swam back to the island with Kwame in tow.

Maria was pointing outward with a terrified look on her face when Johann finally reached the shore with Kwame. She did not scream. She did not say anything at all. Out where he had left the nozzler corpse, Johann saw churning water and as many as a dozen blue tentacles wafting through the air. After depositing Kwame's body on the sand near a grove of trees, Johann picked up Maria and carried her back to their cave.

FOUR

LATER THAT MORNING Johann dug a grave for Kwame not far from where he had buried Beatrice eight years earlier. Maria did not help. The girl was still in a state of shock and was incapable of doing anything. While Johann was depositing Kwame's body in its permanent resting place, Maria was sitting with her back against the trunk of a large tree, gently rocking back and forth. She was holding the Beatrice figurine with one hand and clutching the Saint Michael amulet around her neck with the other.

Afterward, Maria showed no interest when Johann suggested that they go down to the pond and check on Gretel. She did not touch her lunch, nor did she respond to any of Johann's attempts to cheer her up. Throughout the afternoon Maria sat by herself in the cave, over against one of the walls, with her eyes open but expressionless. Once her face contorted in fear, and she screamed. When Johann rushed over and asked her what was wrong, Maria ignored him. Instead she stared straight ahead, and mumbled to herself.

Johann prepared all her favorite foods for dinner and spread them out in front of her in the cave. The child managed to say "Thank you but I'm not hungry" in a tiny, faraway voice before retreating again into her inner, private world.

Maria did not object or resist when Johann picked her up that evening, moving her from the cave wall to her mat. She lay there on her back, her eyes staring fixedly at the ceiling. Occasionally tears would form in her eyes, roll out sideways, and run down her cheeks into her ears.

Johann's grief over Kwame and his natural questions about the meaning of his friend's appearance, after all these years, in their island realm, were pushed aside by his concern for Maria. At first he told himself that her total withdrawal was probably not that unusual a reaction for a child, that she was simply protecting herself until she could deal rationally with all the horrible events of the last few days. But when she showed no signs of improvement by evening, Johann's concern changed to alarm.

Lying beside her on their mats, hours after they both would normally have been asleep, Johann periodically cast furtive glances in Maria's direction, verifying that she was still awake. In between the glances, Johann thought pessimistically about their future life together, wondering how he would cope with Maria if she were permanently damaged psychologically by what had happened. It was not a comforting vision. Despite his attempts to force himself to focus on more pleasant subjects, Johann became more and more depressed and angry as the hours passed and Maria still did not fall asleep.

Finally, a few hours before daybreak, Maria's eyes closed and her body relaxed into the rhythmic breathing of sleep. An exhausted and frustrated Johann rose from his mat and left the cave. He walked over to where he had buried Kwame that morning, allowed himself some fond memories and a few tears of grief beside the grave of his friend, and then proceeded across the small open area to Beatrice's grave.

Johann knelt down on the ground and clasped his hands in front of him. "I do not know to whom I should address this plea," he said out loud, "but I need some help. So God, or alien host, or quasi-Beatrice, or whoever might be listening, please hear what I have to say. . . . I do not know what I'm supposed to do with Maria. I have no experience with children in situations like this. But I *do* know that I can't raise a mentally disturbed child, by myself, all alone on this alien island. I'm not Job, nor do I have any desire to be. Life, in order to be worth living, must have some happiness. And some hope. Otherwise, it makes no sense at all."

Johann stopped, looked up at the dark ceiling far above him, and then stood up. He spread out his arms. "Does anyone hear me?" he shouted. "Does anyone even care about us? I am Johann, the girl is Maria. We are here together on this island, not knowing where we are or what we are doing here. . . . We can't go on forever like this. And I can't bear Maria's pain. . . . Help me, oh please, help me *now*!"

His shouts died out in the darkness of the night. Johann searched the sky for more than a minute for some kind of a sign. He saw nothing. Then he shrugged and turned around.

"Johann?" he heard a little girl's voice say. "Are you all right?"

Maria's silhouette was standing on the path that led to their cave. He hurried over to her and they embraced. "Your shouting woke me up," she said. "I came out to see what was going on."

"Are you feeling better?" he asked, astonished at both her presence and her demeanor.

"A little," she said with a yawn. "I'm really tired. . . . But I don't dare think about either Hansel or that man Kwame. His body was absolutely—"

Maria stopped in mid-sentence. She was staring at something on the other side of Johann. "Look, Johann," she said. "There's a light coming this way."

Johann spun around and looked where Maria was pointing. High in the spacecraft sky a ribbon of light was approaching their island. When it drew close enough that Johann and Maria could just barely make out the tiny, sparkling, dancing particles inside its structure, the ribbon suddenly plummeted, landing somewhere close to the beach.

At first Johann was disappointed. "Our boat," Maria said. "I think it landed near our boat."

They walked carefully down the pathway and then along the beach toward the grove where Johann had been building the boat. The ribbon of light rose in the air a minute or so before their arrival. It hovered twenty meters above them for only a few seconds, and then zoomed off in the direction from which it had come. Johann stared at the ribbon as it grew smaller and smaller. Maria kept walking toward the boat.

"Come here, Johann," he heard her yell exultantly. "The ribbon has painted our boat."

She was correct. When Johann burst into the clearing, he saw that their large rowboat had been painted white, with a rich red stripe decorating the edges. *Now this is an unmistakable sign,* Johann said to himself, holding the excited girl in his arms.

THEY SPENT THREE days preparing to depart. Maria was totally consumed by the activity. She behaved normally during the days. Only at night did the child show any residual signs of the terror that had overwhelmed her following their discovery of Kwame's body. She asked that Johann move his mat over to where she could hold his hand while she was sleeping. He complied willingly.

Johann was busy planning their voyage. He surveyed all their possessions, making mental notes about what was essential, what would be useful, et cetera. He also estimated the amount of gravity in their worldlet by measuring the length of time it took for objects to reach the lake when dropped from the cliffs on the far side of their island. He then calculated how much weight the boat would be able to carry and shared his results with Maria.

She did not like what he told her. From the beginning Maria had insisted that Gretel should ride with them, in the boat, so that her aquatic friend would not be in any danger from the nozzlers. Johann argued that Gretel could swim beside them, and that he could protect her, if necessary, by using his oars as weapons. "Otherwise," Johann told Maria, "we will not be able to take enough food or other necessities. Gretel is very heavy."

When Johann told Maria that she would be forced to leave behind all her toys to make room for Gretel, the girl simply refused to accept Johann's engineering judgment. She told Johann instead that *she* had looked at the boat and that, in her opinion, there was plenty of room inside for everything on their list, including Gretel.

Johann carefully explained to Maria that it was total weight he was worried about, not the volume of material that the boat could contain. She remained intransigent. The exasperated Johann decided that he would conduct an engineering experiment to prove his case to the child. *Besides,* he rationalized to himself, *she'll learn something from all this.*

After simulating the weight of all their provisions and necessary equipment, including the "minimum list" of Maria's toys, by stacking dirt and rocks in the boat (Maria carefully supervised the process to make certain that Johann was not biasing the results), he then took Gretel out of the pond and carried her to the boat. Once Gretel was inside, Johann pushed the boat into deeper water and then climbed in himself. The boat sank almost immediately. Gretel thought the entire experiment was a game and tried to frolic in the water with Maria. The girl was angry and disappointed, but at least she understood the point that Johann had been making. She helped him bail the water out of the boat and reluctantly agreed that Gretel could swim beside them while they traveled.

The day before they were scheduled to leave, Johann and Maria toured their island one final time, staring out at the lake from every coign of vantage and attempting to discover some kind of landmark that they might have missed previously. There was nothing but unbroken water in every direction.

They had no idea what direction to go in the boat. Maria favored rowing along a line perpendicular to Potsdam on the beach, primarily because she had concluded that Kwame must have come from that direction. Johann, standing beside his ward on the top of the island's summit and seeing nothing as he looked around, admitted to himself that he had no reason to favor any particular direction.

Toward the end of the day they took everything that was going with them except for their sleeping mats and carefully packed the boat. Back in the near empty cave, Johann and Maria chatted excitedly, both wondering if their lives would be irrevocably changed by the events of the following day.

"We may end up returning to this island after all," Johann said just before they stretched out on the mats. "That's what happened to your father. He built a boat and took off one morning, but he came back the next day."

Johann had never mentioned Yasin's brief attempt to depart from the island to Maria before, and he was not completely prepared to merge this new story with his fabricated history of the life that Yasin, Beatrice, and he had shared. Nevertheless, he stumbled through Maria's questions without too many inconsistencies. What he wanted her to understand was that they were not necessarily leaving the island forever.

"If we reach a place where we have eaten half our food," he said, "and still have no possible destination in sight, it will be prudent for us to return to our island. We have no guarantee that there exists any other place in this sphere where we can survive."

Johann remained awake for an hour or so after Maria fell asleep. He found himself having mixed emotions about their departure. *This island has provided a good life for us for many years,* he thought. *We have created a comfortable existence for ourselves.*

As he lay there, reflecting, Johann recalled the other great transitions in his life—his decision to move from Earth to Mars, his departure from Valhalla, the death of Beatrice and the birth of Maria, and his return to the island from Whiteland with the infant Maria. *I guess change is the only certainty in life,* he thought. *We resist change, but it comes anyway, sometimes in overwhelming bursts. We struggle to achieve stability between the major upheavals. Yet we know that some future change will utterly destroy any equilibrium we establish.*

FIVE

MARIA WAS UP before dawn. She had already rolled up her mat, and bound it with their makeshift twine, before Johann even opened his eyes.

"Come on, lazybones," she said to him. "You said yourself that we wanted to have an early start so that we could increase our chances of finding something before nightfall."

Johann and Maria ate fruit and grain for breakfast and were down beside Gretel's pond before the day was even one hour old. Maria fed Gretel the last of the fish in the bucket beside the pond and then motioned for her to come over to them. Johann waded into the pond and picked the aquatic creature up in his arms.

Since the boat had been packed the previous day, there was not much that needed to be done before they left. Johann dropped Gretel in the lake, placed Maria in her spot in the boat, and pushed it off the sand. Once the boat was floating in the water Johann lit the small torch he had carefully constructed on the prow. Then he climbed into the boat and started rowing with the larger pair of oars.

Gretel swam circles around the boat. "I had a long talk with her yesterday," Maria said, "while you were packing everything. I told her that we were going on a *big* trip. . . . I think she understood."

Johann's strong, regular strokes with the oars propelled them swiftly through the water. The island receded behind them. After a couple of hours, when Johann declared a snack break, they could still see the outline of the island, but could no longer distinguish any of its features.

Maria glanced in every direction while taking a bite of the brown carrotlike tuber that was her favorite vegetable from the island. "I don't see anything else out there," she said to Johann. "I thought that by now we would find something."

Up until this point Gretel had been swimming either behind or beside their boat. While Johann and Maria were snacking, Gretel began jumping out of the water, looking at them and squealing with each leap. She circled the boat twice and then took off to the left, making a sixty-degree angle with the direction the boat had been traveling before the break. When Gretel was about fifty meters away, she breached the water again with a vertical jump that carried her completely out of the lake.

"Gretel is signaling to us, Johann," Maria said. "She wants us to follow her."

Johann did not argue. He thought it was extremely unlikely that this alien aquacreature actually had any idea why Maria and he were taking this voyage. He was willing to follow Gretel, however, because he didn't have any preferred direction in mind.

Gretel kept the same general heading for most of the next hour. As the island became a speck and then disappeared from his view altogether, Johann attempted to track their position using both Maria's superb eyes and the stationary artificial light source above them as references. He marked their estimated path with his knife on a roll of thin bark that he had prepared before they departed. When Maria admitted that the island was approaching the limit of even her vision, Johann stopped rowing and pulled his oars back into the boat.

"Maria," Johann said in a serious voice, "we have reached a very important decision point in our journey." He motioned for her to come over beside him to look at the map. "This map shows the approximate positions of our boat, the island, and the light above us. I could navigate back to the island from any point near where we are at the present. However, once we are out of sight of the island, our ability to return there will depend upon how accurately I have assessed the direction and distance of our additional travel. There will then be some risk that we might not be able to find our way back to the island."

The girl glanced at the map Johann was holding and checked the placement of both the artificial light and the island. "You mean we could be lost?" she asked.

Johann nodded. "So far we have seen nothing out here but more water. We have no evidence yet that there even exists a possible destination for us. Our most prudent course of action would be to keep the island in sight at all times, and make a wide circle around it, like this, while searching for a possible place to go. That way we could guarantee that we would always be able to return to our island."

Maria watched his knife make a circular motion on the crude map. Then she turned and looked at Gretel. The aquatic creature, who had noticed that the boat had stopped and was now bounding in and out of the water about thirty meters in front of them, squealed when she saw Maria looking in her direction.

"Gretel knows where we are going," Maria said. "And she would be able to take us back to our island if we asked her."

Johann sighed. "Maria," he said, "I don't think you understand fully the seriousness of our situation. We have only a limited amount of food, and can't be certain that we can find more. We don't know where Gretel is leading us, or even if she is taking us anywhere at all. I think we should change our direction now, before we lose sight of the island completely."

Maria glanced back and forth between Gretel and Johann. "I don't agree, Johann," she said in her most adult tone. "You yourself said that Gretel has been heading in the same direction since we started following her. Why else would she be doing that unless she was going somewhere specific? It wouldn't make any sense otherwise."

"You *may* be right, Maria," Johann said, "but *may* is not sufficient in our current situation. In my engineering training, I learned to consider all the possibilities." He paused for a moment. "Suppose Gretel is *not* taking us someplace where we can survive," he then continued. "Then we will become lost and/or run out of food. In my opinion, the probability of this occurring is high enough that we shouldn't risk it."

Maria, deep in thought, stared at Johann for a long time. "I'm not sure I really understand what you just told me, Johann," she said at length. "But my point of view is very simple. I don't want to return to our island, and I'm not afraid of what might happen if we continue to follow Gretel. I *know* that Gretel is leading us someplace. She is my friend, and I have faith in her."

Maria's words and her facial expression both struck a resonant chord in Johann. For a brief instant he thought he was listening to Beatrice again. *You are too analytical, Johann,* Maria's mother had said to him on more than one occasion. *You must have more faith. Otherwise you will never be happy.*

"All right, Maria," Johann was surprised to hear himself say. "We will follow Gretel. But I want you to know that I am not completely comfortable with that decision."

"Thank you, Johann," the girl said excitedly. She hugged him and then raised her oar to signal to Gretel. "We're ready," Maria shouted.

JOHANN DID NOT become seriously worried until late in the afternoon. During lunch, and immediately thereafter, he was in a great mood and joked with Maria about the possibility of their seeing sea monsters, or mermaids, or even more fantastic creatures. Gretel continued on the same course and Johann updated his map periodically by making new incisions with his knife. When night began to approach, however, and Maria and he had still not seen a single landmark, Johann began chastising himself for having acquiesced to Maria's desire to follow Gretel. His arms were also growing tired from all the rowing.

With a heavy sigh, Johann retrieved the oars and placed them where they belonged in the boat. "That's enough for today," he said. "You'd better signal to your friend."

Maria waved an oar at Gretel. The aquacreature swam back beside them while Johann replenished the fuel for the torch and found the supper he had packed the day before.

"Here," he said harshly, handing Maria her meal. "Try to eat it quickly, so you'll finish before dark." His comment was purposely intended to remind her of his dislike of her normal eating habits. Maria often dallied with her food, eating only a little at a time.

"You don't need to be mean, Johann," she said, taking a big bite out of a piece of fruit. "It's not my fault that we haven't seen anything."

Johann forced a smile. "You're right, of course," he said. "I guess I'm upset with myself. We should have stayed within sight of the island. . . . Now we could really be in trouble. During the night we will drift with whatever current there may be here, and I will have no idea where we are when morning comes."

The girl leaned over the side of the boat and stuck her hand in the water. "It doesn't feel as if there's any current at all," she said hopefully. "And besides, as I told you before, Gretel knows where we are, and where we're going."

Johann didn't respond. "We'll head back in the morning," he announced brusquely when he had finished eating. "With or without Gretel . . . and there will be no discussion about the decision."

Night came abruptly in their world. The artificial sunlight simply vanished in a moment, without a warning.

Dark fell only moments after Johann had pulled the pillows out of their temporary storage bins. Gretel chirped beside them to acknowledge the night.

The torch was behind and above Johann's head when he was sitting in his normal seat in the boat. A few minutes after dark, Maria came over beside him on the bench. "Talk to me about my mother," the girl said. "That always seems to cheer you up."

Johann restabilized the weight in the boat and then looked down at the beautiful little girl beside him. He marveled once more at her spectacular blue eyes. How could he possibly remain irritated when confronted by such an innocent and adoring smile?

"Your mother was the most amazing human being I ever met," he began. He closed his eyes and leaned back, suddenly remembering that one special night when Beatrice had sung love songs to him on the beach. The power of his instant heartache took Johann aback and he was momentarily speechless.

"Go on," Maria urged. "Tell me what was so amazing about her."

"So many things," Johann said, shaking his head. "Her singing voice had to be heard to be believed. She was also beautiful. . . . But I think it was her goodness that made her so extraordinary. I never even heard a story about someone who was as good a person as your mother. She not only preached the words of Christ and Saint Michael, she actually lived by them. . . ."

BEFORE THEY FELL asleep, Gretel had a couple of visitors. Judging from her initial reactions, Gretel had not met the other two members of her species before. At first she stayed close to Johann and Maria in the boat, but later on she ventured away from the boat, even out of sight, to play with her friends.

Johann and Maria could still hear Gretel and her play-mates an hour later, but they could no longer see them. Maria yawned and then curled up to sleep sideways in the boat. Johann attempted to sleep sitting up, with his head resting in one hand and that elbow planted firmly on his thigh. He managed to sleep for periods of an hour or so, each time being awakened by aches in stiff joints that were not accustomed to the unusual position.

A few hours before daylight, frantic, high-pitched cries from Gretel and her friends woke Johann abruptly from a dreamless sleep. Before he had time to survey the situation, Gretel leaped over the boat to escape the oncoming rush of a solitary nozzler, whose blue, lofted tentacles with their fearsome claws were a terrifying sight in the torchlight. The tentacles had smacked the water only a few centimeters behind Gretel just moments before she jumped.

His heart pumping furiously, Johann grabbed one of the oars, shaking Maria awake in the process, and swung at one of the tentacles, now up in the air again, with all his might. He scored a direct hit, nearly severing the tentacle structure, and leaving its front portion with the vicious claw dangling helplessly aloft.

The damaged tentacle drooped into the water. Johann swung again, aiming for the other tentacle, but the nozzler had already retracted it a safe distance away from the boat. Maria, who was sitting on her knees in the boat, watching the battle in speechless fright, now began to scream. Johann, still brandishing the oar and not taking his eyes off the nozzler, put one of his hands on Maria's left forearm and squeezed. "Stop," he ordered. "Stop now!"

She obeyed. Maria sat quietly, her body trembling, as Johann and she watched the nozzler draw closer to the boat. The one good tentacle remained elevated, half a meter or so above the water, poised and ready for a possible attack. There was movement inside the two forward nozzler eyes, as if it were looking at them carefully, assessing the probability that an attack would be successful.

The nozzler turned and swam parallel to the boat, allowing Johann and Maria a clear view of its side. The circular washboard organ facing them was open, exposing a nasty set of sharp teeth around its perimeter. The hard carapaces were the only part of the middle segment that was above the water line while the nozzler swam. The fanlike tail moved in and out of the water with ease and grace, acting as both an accelerator and a brake for the alien creature.

Gretel and her playmates, meanwhile, had disappeared. They had doubtless been the nozzler's original prey. Now though, as the alien continued to swim beside them just out of reach of the oar, it was obvious to Johann that Maria and he had replaced Gretel and her friends as the primary object of the nozzler's attention.

Suddenly the nozzler vanished. It was a second or two before Johann realized that it had gone underwater. Turning his body so that he could fend off an attack coming from either side of the boat, Johann tensed his muscles and waited.

It wasn't a long wait. The nozzler struck from the opposite side, its tentacle bursting out of the water and into the boat in an instant. The end of the claw snapped shut, catching Maria's dress, and began pulling the child toward the water. She screamed in terror. Johann swung the oar hard, narrowly missing Maria and smashing it against both the back end of the claw and the side of the boat. The claw was torn from the tentacle and the oar shattered into two pieces. The tentacle slithered back into the water as Johann grabbed Maria.

"Are you all right?" he asked.

The girl nodded her head up and down. The end of the claw was still affixed to her dress, just above her stomach. Johann was unable to pry it open. With one eye on the nozzler, who remained beside the boat, watching them, Johann tore off the part of Maria's dress containing the claw. She had a long, thin flesh wound that was fortunately not too deep. It was barely bleeding.

Johann picked up Maria with one hand, and the second oar with the other. He set her down at the opposite end of the boat, where he had packed their medicine kit, while he kept a wary eye on the nozzler. "Rub the greenish stuff on it," he said, after explaining to her where to look. "It will reduce the pain."

Maria followed his instructions. Slowly she was regaining control of herself. After she had applied the herbal medicine, she glanced again at the nozzler.

"Why won't it go away, Johann?" she asked in a frightened voice.

"I don't know," Johann answered. "But I don't think it can hurt us anymore. It has lost both its claws."

The nozzler now rolled over on its side, exposing part of its underbelly. The region around the clusters of tiny pearls, which were now aimed directly toward the spacecraft sky, began to pulsate and undulate. A few seconds later a loud, long bass sound, like an extended blast from a tuba, emanated from the temporary hole that had formed among the pearls. The sound repeated twice more, at approximately five-second intervals.

Almost immediately the call was answered, first faintly off in the distance to the left of the boat, and then, much louder, from in front of them. In both cases the answer consisted of five blasts, the last two at a slightly higher pitch.

Johann and Maria looked at each other. "It's calling others," the girl said, her eyes wide open with fear. "What are we going to do?"

When the nozzler started preparing to call again, Johann lunged at it with his remaining oar, nearly falling out of the boat. His stroke fell short of its mark, but he did distract the alien. The nozzler quickly swam several more meters away and repeated its three-part call.

This time there were three responses, one now coming

from directly behind the boat. "Sit down and pick up your oars," Johann said to Maria. He turned the boat so that it was headed to the right. "Now row," he said, "as hard as you can."

With Johann using only a solitary oar, it was difficult to control the direction of the boat. Eventually he settled into a routine of three strokes on one side, followed by three on the other. Maria rowed fiercely, timing her strokes to coincide with Johann's as he had shown her during the day. Within minutes they were both sweating and breathing heavily.

Their nozzler swam along with them, dropping behind when it issued another call, and then catching up effortlessly with a few rapid motions of its tail. The answering sounds were becoming louder and more numerous. Johann and Maria were not escaping.

A loud, five-part nozzler blast from their right indicated that a second nozzler had almost reached them. "Are they going to kill us, Johann?" Maria asked.

"Not if I can prevent it," he said. He pulled his long oar into the boat and turned to face the direction from which the answering nozzler blast had come. Less than a minute later, Johann and Maria saw their new adversary. This nozzler was huge, maybe four meters in length, by far the largest one they had seen. Its elevated tentacles towered above its swimming body almost as high as Johann's head.

"Try to stay calm," Johann said to Maria, sensing her redoubled fear. "And use your oars to protect yourself."

The new nozzler swam completely around their boat, the fluid in its eyes in constant activity. Then, to Johann's astonishment, it retracted its tentacles and appeared to be treading water just off the prow of the boat. After several seconds the nozzler lifted its powerful tail out of the lake and smacked it down hard, sending an enormous burst of water toward Johann. He reacted quickly, grabbing the side of the boat just before the wave struck. Johann was drenched, and knocked down, but he managed both to hold on to the oar and to stay in the boat.

"Johann, Johann," he heard Maria's desperate call in the darkness. He looked around, unable to see the girl, and realized that the torch had been extinguished by the wave.

"I'm here, Maria," he said. "Crawl over in this direction."

They somehow found each other in the center of the boat. Maria held tightly to Johann as they both listened to the new nozzler's deeper, louder, three-part call that was followed by a flurry of responses.

"What is it waiting for?" Maria asked.

"I don't know," Johann replied. *Maybe it wants to kill us in the light,* he thought. He briefly considered trying to make a stealthy escape in the darkness, but he rejected such an action as useless. Johann hugged Maria against his chest and tried not to think about death. "I love you, Maria," he said. "I'm sorry. . . ."

"It's not your fault, Johann," she said. "And I love you too."

There were soon four nozzlers in the water around them. Johann and Maria could not see their bodies, but they could hear the alien sounds, now shorter, and more clipped, and occasional splashing on all sides. Then they became aware that their boat was moving. Johann crawled in the direction of their movement and verified that four nozzler claws were attached to the front of their boat, one pair on each side. The powerful, extended tentacles of the nozzlers were pulling the boat through the water.

They are taking us somewhere, Johann thought. *We are their captives.* He tried to calm his own fears as he crawled back to where he had left Maria. He was planning to attempt to reassure her, to relieve her of some of her terror, when he suddenly noticed that it was no longer pitch-black around them. *What the . . . ?* the confused Johann was thinking when Maria stood up in the boat.

"Look, Johann," the girl shouted. "The ribbons are coming!"

Johann barely had time to look up into the spacecraft

sky before there was a blinding explosion of light just above them. The next several seconds were complete chaos. Frenzied nozzler sounds and thrashing in the water surrounded Johann and Maria. The ribbons were everywhere, even under the water, as the nozzlers scattered in all directions. Then, just as quickly, the ribbons zoomed up into the sky and disappeared in the direction from which they had come.

Johann and Maria held each other in the center of the boat. They were too exhausted to talk. The nozzlers did not return.

GRETEL'S FRIENDLY SQUEAL awakened them. Johann and Maria opened their eyes almost simultaneously. It was already light in their world.

Maria reached into the lake to pat her friend. "And where have your friends gone, Gretel?" she said. "I hope they escaped from those nasty nozzlers."

Gretel chirped and began cavorting in the water. "She's inviting me in for a swim, Johann," Maria said. "Is that all right?"

Johann, who was already attempting to make some sense out of what had happened to them the previous night, nodded affirmatively. "But stay close to the boat and come quickly if I call." The girl dove overboard and within seconds was swimming and laughing with Gretel.

Johann did not think about the fact that he had absolutely no idea where they were, and that their meager remaining food supply was soggy from the water inside the boat. He also pushed aside thoughts about how easily Maria and he could have been killed. For once, he suspended all his analyses, and simply watched with delight as his ward frolicked with her special friend.

When their play was done, and Maria was back in the boat, Gretel again began swimming in front of them. Johann, now using Maria's two small oars to propel the boat, followed the aquacreature. Much to his surprise, Maria actually seemed to be in a happy mood, and showed no outward ill effects from the previous night's harrowing experience.

"I don't understand," Johann said to her while Maria was struggling to make a decent meal out of soggy grain and berries. "You were totally devastated by Hansel and Kwame's deaths. How can you be so carefree and nonchalant after what happened to us last night?"

She offered him one of the few dry bites she had found among their provisions. "Last night I was absolutely certain we were going to die, Johann," Maria said. "My fear seemed to last forever, and then poof, it was gone. I don't know why."

Johann stared at her while continuing to row. He didn't know what to say. *She's remarkable,* he said to himself. *And I am still learning something new from her every day.*

An hour later Maria spotted a feature on the horizon in front of them. Johann could not yet see anything. When Maria could definitely assert that what she was seeing was a land form, she shouted "Land ho," as Johann had told her seafaring explorers had done years before.

At first Johann thought that perhaps they had returned to their own island. However, as they drew closer, and saw unfamiliar landscapes, Johann realized that they were indeed approaching a new place. The new island was larger, and more mountainous, than their home of eight years. As Johann guided the boat past white cliffs that dropped precipitously to the water, he could see tall, stately trees on the ridges above. There had been no trees that tall on their island.

"See," Maria said for the umpteenth time, unable to contain either her delight or her excitement, "I told you that Gretel knew where she was going. Look, Johann. Look how beautiful it is."

Johann too was excited. He had never imagined that there might be more than one Earth-like habitat inside their alien sphere. Years before, when Beatrice and he had reached the island they called Paradise, they had both believed that their island was unique, and created especially for them.

Now, as his eyes surveyed a handsome, forested hill that sloped down toward the shore, Johann's amazement continued to grow. *Who or what has built this?* he wondered again. *And for what purpose?*

"Look there, Johann." Maria interrupted his thoughts. "Something is moving through the trees. . . . Look, there's four of them."

He followed her pointing finger with his eyes. Emerging from the trees and staring at them from a ridge several hundred meters above the lake were four large brown animals of the same species, each with six muscular legs. Two of them had an enormous, bizarre white protuberance growing on what must have been the forehead, just above a wide, dark rectangle that appeared to contain the visual sensors. One of the animals turned its head and issued a plaintive bellow, allowing Johann and Maria to see the thick white growth on its forehead. Close to the head, the tusk was a single branch, like the trunk of a tree, but as it moved outward and upward, away from the animal's body, the tusk spread out into three separate branches, each with its own complicated design.

Johann was fascinated. He stopped rowing and stared up at the alien animals. He had just remarked to Maria that the two tusks on the animals they could see were clearly different, when something caused the alien ungulates to retreat into the trees.

Maria and he tried to follow their movement but could not. At length Johann began to row again, following the impatient Gretel, who had been squealing at them during the entire time they had been stopped. Soon the gentle, verdant mountain slopes disappeared and harsh new cliffs, with brownish rock faces, towered over their rowboat. After several kilometers of these cliffs, Johann began to wonder if there was going to be any place for them to land.

Then suddenly, as they rounded a sharp corner in the cliffs, Johann and Maria encountered a deep, beautiful half-moon bay with a long stretch of sandy beach and lush green vegetation everywhere. Johann saw the smoke before Maria. It was rising slowly from a spot a few hundred meters behind an expanse of beach on the opposite side of the bay.

Gretel now increased her speed toward the land and left the boat behind. She was heading directly for the rising smoke, jumping out of the water every twenty meters or so. A few minutes later two half-naked children, a boy and a girl, both brownish-black in color, came out of the brush. They laughed and pointed at Gretel. The boy had started to walk into the water when he was stopped by the girl. She grabbed his hand, pointed at Johann and Maria's approaching boat, and hustled quickly back into the bushes.

Johann continued to row toward the shore. Maria, thrilled by the prospect of meeting other children, jabbered ceaselessly. When the water became shallow, Johann jumped out of the boat and pulled it onto the sand with the rope that was attached to the torch stanchion on the prow. Maria helped him. As they were beaching the boat Johann heard a voice call his name.

"Johann?" the voice said. "Is that really you, giant Johann?"

Coming down a narrow path through the brush was a tall, thin, copper-skinned woman wearing only a loincloth. Her face was alive with laughter and happiness. The two children Johann and Maria had seen before were following close behind the woman.

"Come here, giant Johann," Sister Vivien said, pushing her long, thick hair out of her face. "Come here and give me a hug."

SISTER

VIVIEN'S

TALE

ONE

"LET ME LOOK at you," Vivien said. She pulled away from Johann, and shook her head quickly back and forth. "You are even larger and grander than my memories, giant Johann," she said with an easy laugh. "How long has it been? Nine years . . . ? It doesn't seem possible that it's really you. . . . But where's Sister Beatrice? Why didn't she come with you?"

"Beatrice . . . Jomo . . . where are you?" a child called from farther up the path before Johann could answer.

"Down here, Keiko," the girl answered. "With Mother . . . and the strangers."

A brown-skinned girl, seven or so, with exotic facial features, stopped immediately when she saw Johann and Maria. "Who are *they*?" she demanded of Vivien with a worried look on her face.

Vivien laughed again. "It's all right, Keiko," she said. "Johann is a very dear old friend."

Keiko joined the group hesitantly and stood behind Vivien with the other two children. "I guess introductions are in order," Vivien then said, moving over toward Johann and Maria. "This charming girl is Keiko, the daughter of Fernando and Satoko. That pair over there are God's gifts to Kwame and me. My daughter is Beatrice, named, unless my eyes are mistaken, after this young lady's beautiful mother, who was my very best friend for several years."

Vivien gestured toward Maria. The girl, who was still overwhelmed by everything that was happening, tightened her grip on Johann's hand. "Her name is Maria. Her mother was indeed Beatrice," Johann said. "And her father was Yasin," he added awkwardly. "They both died many years ago."

Vivien's eyes widened immediately and her brow knitted into wrinkles. She stared at Johann and started to say something. "Later," he said softly.

It took the flustered Vivien several seconds to regain her composure. Her son helped her. Staring continuously at Johann and Maria, he walked over and put both arms around Vivien's left leg. "And this urchin," Vivien said fondly, "who makes me crazy, is little Jomo."

"Maria is pretty," the boy said.

Everybody laughed, diffusing some of the tension. "Thank you, Jomo," Maria said, proving to the other children that she could speak.

Keiko and Beatrice took Maria's comment as a cue and came over beside her for a closer inspection. "I have a dress too," Beatrice said, fingering the material Maria was wearing. "But I don't wear it very often."

"So tell me, giant Johann," Vivien said in a more somber tone, putting her arm through his and turning toward the path, "what brings you to this shore? Is it pure chance or did you know we were here?"

Johann smiled. "Sister Beatrice," he said, "would probably have insisted it was divine intervention. We had no idea—" He stopped in mid-sentence. For a split second, as Johann glanced up the hill, he thought he had entered a time warp and returned to the Earth or Mars. There, standing above him on the path, was a woman dressed in the blue robe and headpiece of the Michaelites.

Vivien saw the astonished look on Johann's face and laughed heartily. "Oh, I'm sorry," she said, "I completely forgot. Sister Nuba is also here with us, helping me with the children while we wait for Kwame to return with the others."

The shy Nuba came down the path with her hand extended. "It is delightful to see you again, Brother Johann," she said softly. "When the children said that a boat was coming with some people onboard, I thought our prayers had been answered and that Kwame had finally returned."

Johann shook Sister Nuba's hand and almost said something about Kwame. Reflecting quickly, he turned around. Maria and the other children were playing together on the beach. Beatrice and Keiko were pointing toward the lake where Gretel was bounding out of the water. While the children exclaimed and applauded, Johann excused himself from Vivien and Nuba and walked swiftly toward the children.

When he reached them, Maria was showing the others the carved wooden amulet around her neck. "Sister Nuba wears one of these," Keiko said, turning the amulet over in her fingers. "And Brother Jose too."

"Mom has one in her box of important things," Beatrice added. "But there's nothing written on hers."

"Maria," Johann said, touching her lightly on the arm. "May I speak with you for a moment?"

He led her down the shore until they were several meters away from the other children. "What is it, Johann?" Maria asked, a worried look on her face. "Have I done something wrong?"

"No, Maria," he said, touching her shoulder reassuringly. "I just have something important to discuss with you."

As Johann bent down to talk to Maria at her level, Gretel suddenly started squealing at a high pitch and clapping her flippers with each leap out of the water.

"That's the way she says good-bye," Maria said sadly.

He took Maria's hand and they walked together to the edge of the shore. Gretel's display continued as she moved away from them, out toward the open water of the lake.

"She's probably going to look for her new friends," Johann said.

"Good-bye, Gretel," Maria shouted. She waved. Her eyes were brimming with tears.

"Good-bye," Johann yelled. "And thank you."

He dried Maria's tears and gave her a long silent hug. At length Johann broke from the hug and bent down again to talk to her. "Maria," he said, "nobody here knows what happened to Kwame. He was Vivien's husband, and the father of Beatrice and Jomo. They will be very upset when they find out that he is dead, and I want to wait until the proper time to tell them. Will you promise not to say anything about Kwame, at least until I tell you it's all right?"

Maria thought for a moment. "Sure, Johann," she said. "I can do that."

He kissed her on the forehead. "You're a good girl, Maria," he said.

A FEW MINUTES after Johann and Maria rejoined the others, Vivien invited him to come with her to their "home." Sister Nuba graciously volunteered to remain on the beach with the children. Jomo insisted that he was going to accompany his mother, and a struggle of wills ensued. Jomo adamantly refused to stay with Nuba and eventually threw a temper tantrum of the first order. Vivien reacted swiftly, smacking him firmly on the behind and then handing him, kicking, to Sister Nuba.

"I'm sorry," Vivien said to Johann as they started up the path that she, Sister Nuba, and the children had worn through the calf-high vegetation. "Jomo can be really difficult at times. It's his age. . . ."

"There's no need to apologize," Johann said, interrupting her gently. "I know what it's like. . . . I have raised Maria since she was an infant."

It was not easy for Vivien to restrain her many questions until they were out of earshot of the others. "All right, giant Johann," she said, spinning around in the middle of the path, "you can't keep me waiting any longer. How did that bastard Yasin happen to be the father of this beautiful child? We all thought he was dead. He was thrown into a deep chasm during a fight with Fernando and Kwame. How did he . . . ?"

"Hold it," Johann said with a laugh. "One question at a time." He glanced over his shoulder in the direction of Maria, who was still playing with the other children on the beach. "Maria never knew her father," Johann said. "Yasin died before she was born. . . . And I have purposely never told her what he was *really* like. I didn't see any reason to tell the child that her father was a . . ."

Johann didn't finish his sentence. Vivien reached over and touched him lightly on the forearm. "I understand," she said. "You are a very kind and generous man, Johann. You can rest assured that neither Sister Nuba nor I will destroy the girl's illusions about her father."

Johann was now looking in the other direction, gazing out at the lake. His mind was full of memories of another beach, at another time. He could almost hear Beatrice's voice calling to him from the lake.

Vivien must have been reading his mind. "And how did dear, sweet, perfect Sister Beatrice die?" she said. "That's even harder to believe. She was so *alive*, and so healthy. . . ."

"She died soon after childbirth," Johann said with difficulty. He didn't turn toward Vivien. He couldn't. The terrible heartache had returned, as it always did when he thought of Beatrice's final moments.

After a long while Johann slowly turned to face Vivien again. Her arms were open and extended. Johann accepted the comfort of her embrace and allowed himself to grieve.

"I couldn't save her," Johann said, his body trembling as he spoke.

"I'm certain you did your best," Vivien said quietly.

At length they separated and Johann followed Vivien

up the remainder of the path. They didn't talk. Nor did Johann even notice the numerous new and different species of flowering bushes and exotic grasses that surrounded them as they climbed. He was deep in thought, and still recovering from the outburst of emotion that had accompanied his telling Vivien about Beatrice's death. *That was the first time I have ever shared her death with someone else who knew and loved her,* Johann realized.

But another subject was also disturbing him. How was he going to tell Vivien about Kwame? From the inflections in her voice when she mentioned his name, Johann knew that the two of them had had a good marriage. *She will be devastated,* Johann thought. *I must tell her at the right moment, and give her comfort during her sorrow.*

At the end of the path was a rock overhang, underneath which Vivien, Sister Nuba, and the children had created a temporary home. "It's adequate for now," Vivien said, chatting idly and offering Johann a hot herbal drink from the pot hanging above the fire, "at least until Kwame and the others arrive. Then we'll build some real houses. Kwame says that the wood here is much better for construction than it was where we were living before."

Johann's internal struggles must have shown in his face. "Are you all right, Johann?" Vivien asked with concern. "Do you want to talk some more about Beatrice?"

Now, a voice inside Johann said. *Tell her now.* Johann leaned forward and took both of Vivien's hands in his. "There's something that I must tell you, Vivien," he said.

He paused. "What is it, Johann?" she said.

"Kwame is dead," he said simply. "I found his body and buried him a week ago."

Vivien sat opposite Johann, her eyes blinking occasionally, looking at him with profound disbelief. Seconds passed. Tears wedged into Vivien's eyes and her breathing became more and more labored.

"Kwame is dead," she said twice to herself. "How did he die, Johann?" she finally managed to ask.

"I'm not completely certain," Johann said. "I found him in the lake, wrapped around a dead alien creature we call a nozzler. It appeared that Kwame and the nozzler had been fighting, and that they had killed each other."

Vivien looked down at the ground for almost a minute, shaking her head mechanically. The gray tinges in her hair were more apparent from the top. "Hold me please, Johann," she then said, her body starting to shake. "I think I'm going to cry."

For the second time in an hour, the two friends held one another in sorrow. Vivien wept. "He was such a good man, Johann," she said, between bursts of tears. "So tender and patient with the children. And kinder to me than anyone has ever been."

After her long cry, Vivien pulled away from Johann and stood up straight. "Will you kneel with me, Johann?" she said. "I need to pray."

Johann dropped down beside Sister Vivien, recalling the times he had knelt beside Beatrice while she prayed. "Dear God," Vivien said, "I ask you to help me to be strong in the hours and days ahead. Help me to guide my children through this terrible loss, and to be thankful for the wonderful years we all shared with Kwame as our husband and our father." Her voice broke for a moment. "And dear God," she then continued, "thank you for having the compassion to send Johann here with this news, so that I have a good friend to comfort me in my hour of loss."

JOHANN WAS SURPRISED that Vivien was as concerned about Keiko's reaction to the news of Kwame's death as she was about her own children's responses. "Keiko has not yet completely recovered from losing her own parents," Sister Nuba told Johann in a soft voice while Vivien and Keiko were off on their long walk and Jomo was napping. "Vivien and Kwame had essentially adopted her. . . . And Keiko absolutely adored Kwame."

Before Johann could ask Nuba any more questions, Beatrice came over and interrupted them. The little girl looked miserable. "Is Mommy not back *yet*?" Beatrice asked petulantly. "I need her *now*."

Johann and Vivien did not have another chance to talk together until late that night, after she finished putting the children to bed. Mindful of the strong emotions of the day, both Vivien and Nuba had spent extra time with the children after dinner. They had encouraged Maria to place her mat alongside the other two girls, and Nuba had told a long and entertaining story about Carthage and Hannibal. Finally, while Vivien was nursing Jomo, the last of the girls had fallen asleep.

When Vivien sat down on the flat rock beside Johann, and accepted the cup of herbal tea that Sister Nuba offered her, she admitted that she was exhausted. "It's not every day you find out that your husband is dead," she said, forcing herself to smile.

"How were your talks with the children?" Johann asked.

"Terrible," Vivien replied. "Jomo couldn't understand what I was telling him, and the two girls both cried hysterically. I had wonderful feelings of ineptitude and inadequacy—just what a mother needs." She shook her head and took a drink of her tea. "Nuba," she then said, "would you hand me one of my cigarettes, please. They're in that skinny brown pouch."

Johann watched with amusement as Vivien leaned forward and lit her makeshift cigarette with the fire. She inhaled deeply and blew the smoke out both her nose and mouth.

"I found this stuff growing wild out beside the chasm

where we used to live," Vivien said, answering Johann's unspoken question. "It's not tobacco, and there's not much of a buzz, but hey, it makes me feel good to watch the smoke coming out of my mouth."

Vivien sighed. "Memories of another life, on another world," she said. She forced a laugh. "It used to drive Kwame crazy when I smoked in front of the children. So we compromised—the essence of any successful marriage in my opinion—and I agreed to smoke only at night, after the children had gone to bed."

She took a sip of her drink and inhaled again. This time she blew four perfect smoke rings and admiringly watched them rise to the underside of the rock overhang. "But enough of this idle prattle, giant Johann. What Nuba and I are both dying to know is how did Yasin conceive a child with the woman we all loved? I can't accept for a moment that she was a willing partner."

"It's a long story," Johann said. "Are you certain you want to listen to it tonight? Wouldn't it be better to wait until some other time, when you—"

"If I go to bed now," Vivien interrupted him, "I'll just think about Kwame and feel sorry for myself. I need to be distracted, to forget my own concerns." She took another drag off her cigarette and flicked it into the fire. "By the way," she added, with a fond gaze in Sister Nuba's direction, "isn't she impressive, still wearing that shit after all these years? She makes a new costume every few months from whatever she can find. And she is still true to all her vows—service to others, no possessions, no sex. Now that's some kind of devotion. There had better be a special room in heaven for people like Nuba, or God is missing the boat. . . ."

JOHANN STARTED HIS story at the beginning, when Sister Beatrice and he departed from the nine others soon after they had entered the gigantic alien sphere in which they were still living. He told the tale in chronological order, without inordinate detail, highlighting all the major events. He fairly summarized his running debate with Beatrice about whether their hosts here were God's angels or aliens of extraordinary technological capability. Johann omitted only those things that were intensely personal, such as his specific arguments with Beatrice about the physical consummation of their love, or embarrassing, like his bizarre encounter with the simulated Amanda in the reconstructed Mutchville beside the canal. Johann was forthright about both the strength of his love for Beatrice, and his disappointment that she was unwilling to forsake her Michaelite vows to become his wife.

Vivien and Nuba listened for a long time without interruption. When Johann fell silent, struggling to find the proper words to express the happiness he had felt during his first hundred days with Beatrice, both women offered him understanding and encouragement with gestures and short comments.

Johann's summary of Yasin's story about his life with Kwame, Vivien, and the others caused an angry outburst. "What a liar!" Vivien said, taking advantage of the break in the story to light another cigarette. "We gave him every possible opportunity to be part of the group. We even had special meetings, which Kwame called Yasin discussions, to try to figure out some way to include him in our activities in a positive way. . . . And his description of his relationship with Satoko is so ludicrous that it's comical. She was terrified of him. Yasin took advantage of Satoko's mental confusion and abused her completely. He was utterly despicable. Can you imagine any human being so low that he would rape, several times, a woman who was both mentally disturbed and pregnant?"

Vivien blew out jets of smoke and her eyes narrowed. "When we suspected that Yasin was returning to the village and having sex with Satoko, but could not confirm anything because Satoko wouldn't implicate him, I told Kwame that we should catch Yasin in the act and then dismember him. Well, we did catch him all right, but we gave him his freedom by error."

Johann continued his story, describing Yasin's first attack on Beatrice, Johann's own imprisonment, Yasin's outrageous suggestion that they should share Beatrice, and her eventual sexual humiliation and total denigration.

"Why does God let people like that exist?" Vivien exploded at one point. When Johann told of his escape from prison and Yasin's death, Vivien applauded. "Good for you, giant Johann," she said. "You finally gave that bastard what he deserved."

"You're not being very charitable, Sister Vivien," Sister Nuba said softly. It was one of the few times that she had spoken during Johann's story. "Remember the long discussions we had in the village after Yasin—"

"Yes, yes, Nuba," Vivien said. "Thank you for reminding me . . . My feelings about Yasin are still so negative that it's difficult for me to understand that he too is one of God's creatures. There are aspects of Christian charity that are sometimes beyond my comprehension."

There was a brief silence and then Vivien yawned. "Johann, I don't want to be rude, but I also don't want to miss any part of your amazing story. I'm really tired, and Jomo will be up at daylight. If this is a good stopping point, can we continue again tomorrow night?"

AS REQUESTED, JOHANN finished his story the following evening. Both women wept with him as he described Maria's birth and Beatrice's death. Sister Nuba was fascinated by Whiteland. She interrupted several times, asking Johann to supply more details. When Johann admitted being confused and somewhat bitter about being returned to the island, Sister Nuba made an uncharacteristically long speech.

"Whiteland was a part of heaven, Brother Johann," she said. "And Beatrice and all the other glowing figures you encountered were angels. There's no other possible explanation that makes sense. . . . You are a most fortunate man, Brother Johann, to have made a visit to heaven during your lifetime, while your soul is still inside the limitations of your body. What a rare privilege you have had. God must still have some extraordinary work for you to accomplish. Do not feel sorrow because you were returned to what we call the real world. Rejoice that you have been granted a glimpse of heaven."

Johann summarized quickly his years of life on the island with Maria, but then gave a fairly detailed account both of finding Kwame's body and his subsequent encounters with the nozzlers. Both Vivien and Sister Nuba were intrigued by the intervention of the ribbons and asked many specific questions about their appearance and behavior. Johann's responses stimulated a long and lively conversation about the ribbons, the nature of the spaceship in which they were living, and the source of the unusual apparitions that had occurred on Earth and Mars. The discussion reminded Johann of the many hours Beatrice and he had spent talking about similar subjects, and thinking about her forced him again to struggle with his feelings of loss. Sister Nuba, not surprisingly, was extremely active in the discussion. She adhered to the explanation that their spaceship was part of the domain of God's angels, and only they, or He, understood the grand scheme of what was occurring.

"We have been chosen by God, all of us, for some special purpose that we will probably never comprehend," Sister Nuba said.

Johann reiterated his reasons for believing that the ribbons were representatives of a technologically advanced alien culture. He also acknowledged, however, that nothing that had happened to any of them thus far was irrefutable proof of either point of view. Vivien's comments suggested that she could accept either explanation of the true nature of their hosts. Sometimes she agreed with Johann, sometimes with Sister Nuba.

"Besides," Vivien said near the end of their discussion, "as a mother these infinite issues do not occupy much of my energy. I am more interested in *how* we are going to live, on a day-to-day basis, than in what power is controlling our microcosm."

Johann hugged both Vivien and Sister Nuba before going to bed. "Now it's our turn to tell a story," Vivien said, "although I suspect I'll do all the talking. I think you'll find our tale equally fascinating, even though I probably won't be nearly as orderly in the telling of it as you were. . . . So until tomorrow night, good night and sleep well, giant Johann."

Vivien reached up and kissed Johann on the cheek. Then she turned and headed for her mat near the children.

TWO

"EXCEPT FOR THE events involving Yasin," Vivien said the next evening as the three adults gathered to talk and sip herbal tea around the fire for the third night in a row, "his description of what happened to us after your departure with Beatrice was reasonably accurate. Two of those peculiar snowmen creatures and a ribbon came for us in that waiting room two hours later. We followed the ribbon up the helical slide and then across a long, dark plateau of some kind until we came to a lake. After a four-hour boat ride we landed on a forested shore, where we walked for hours on a narrow path through the trees. Eventually we reached the clearing with the continuous fire and the tepees that became our village home. We lived there until a month ago.

"At first we *did* have difficulty organizing ourselves into any kind of a coherent community. In those early days life in our new village was chaotic and stressful. Everybody seemed to be in everyone else's way. Brother Jose and Sister Nuba were both outspokenly critical of me for renouncing my Michaelite vows so quickly and becoming Kwame's sexual partner and wife, Yasin fomented controversy and argument in his own unique way, and poor pregnant Satoko, who could not cope with anything that was happening, was a total mess. After a while, however, when everyone but Yasin began to accept Kwame's leadership, the required tasks were divided up among the members of our group and we settled into an acceptable daily rhythm."

Vivien lit one of her cigarettes and smiled at Sister Nuba across the fire. "Nuba and Jose even apologized to me for having given me so much grief about Kwame. . . . Soon thereafter, Ravi announced that he too was going to renounce his vows and marry Anna Kasper. All in all, our life was fairly good for a couple of months, and all of us except Yasin were making the necessary adjustments to live together in our unusual environment.

"Then, when it seemed that Satoko's improved mental condition had finally stabilized, she suddenly took a dramatic turn for the worse. At first none of us suspected that her breakdown might have been caused by a specific event, for Satoko never told us of anything untoward that might have been responsible for her alienation and depression. As time passed, however, we began to notice that her terror and heightened nervousness were always more pronounced when Yasin was around. One evening, while we were talking, none of us could account for Yasin's whereabouts for several hours on the day that Satoko's breakdown occurred. On subsequent days when Satoko was left by herself in the village and Yasin was assigned solitary work tasks, her condition was always markedly worse when the rest of us returned from our hunting and gathering."

Vivien finished her cigarette and shook her head. "It was stupid of us not to realize earlier what was going on. It just didn't seem possible to us that any human being could be *that* depraved. Of course, when Yasin was actually caught in the act of raping Satoko, all of us except Sister Nuba exploded in rage. Our primary concern after Yasin was thrown into the chasm was *not* what a terrible sin we had collectively committed; we were all worried that the bastard might somehow have survived the fall because of the low gravity here."

Vivien was silent for a long time. "Eventually, of course, each of us realized that we had all participated in what we believed at the time to have been a murder. Especially to those of us who had spent part of our lives in formal religious training, such a deliberate act of violence seemed unforgivable. Our small village became pervaded by an overwhelming gloom. With all that guilt upon our shoulders, life was very difficult for many weeks. Several of us, including Ravi and me, both of whom had vocally encouraged Kwame and Fernando to kill Yasin, had sustained bouts of terrible depression.

"Without Brother Jose and Sister Nuba," Vivien said, reaching over and touching Nuba's hand fondly, "we might never have been able to forgive ourselves. But after they both publicly reaffirmed their Michaelite vows, Nuba and Jose declared that we were going to atone for our misdeed by collectively sharing all our feelings about what had happened. For weeks they were towers of strength, eventually managing to convince us that God does not demand perfection, just recognition of sin and then expiation."

A sound from where the children were sleeping at the opposite end of the cave caused Vivien to turn her head in that direction. She listened intently for a few seconds before taking another sip of her tea. "A mother's senses are so keen, Johann," she then said. "I never would have believed it if I hadn't experienced it myself. No matter what we're doing, we hear every cough, every sleeping moan that our children make. It's another of God's miracles."

Vivien smiled and looked momentarily puzzled. "Now where was I?" she said with a short laugh. "I'm becoming forgetful in my old age."

"The period of atonement after Yasin's death," Sister Nuba reminded her.

"Oh, yes," Vivien continued. "Gradually we all returned to our former selves and laughter again rang out regularly in our village. I resumed my role as the comic relief for the group, occasionally sharing some of my more hilarious experiences from my pre-Michaelite days as an escort in London. Sister Nuba and Brother Jose often acted as if they were scandalized by my tales, but more than once I caught them laughing out loud. . . . Satoko gave birth to Keiko without difficulty, and we all joined with Fernando and her in the celebration of the first addition to our community. Our existence then became very orderly. Each of us had a prescribed set of duties.

"After a while, I'll admit that I started becoming bored by the predictability of our daily routines. Kwame even referred to me as a 'bitch' a few times during this period. However, he and the others were saved from my compulsive hunger for variety by a natural event. I became pregnant, and then a mother, and found an infinite outlet for my curiosity and energy.

"Motherhood transformed me, Johann. After little Beatrice's birth, I often laughed at the strange odyssey of my life, from high-class whore on Earth to doting mother in an alien sphere. I had never imagined myself being the enthusiastic parent, but there I was, day after day, regaling everyone with the newest achievements of my darling daughter. . . . Meanwhile, Ravi and Anna had a son, Eric, a year younger than Beatrice, and then Anna became pregnant with Serentha less than two months after Kwame and I conceived Jomo.

"Anna and I became very good friends during our pregnancy together. We would often compare observations on how our thoughts, feelings, and even our dreams changed during pregnancy. At night I would sometimes exult, while rubbing my stomach and feeling my son inside my belly, on the astonishing miracle that is human life. I was happier than I could ever remember being. . . . But Anna and I had to be somewhat circumspect about our joy, for poor Satoko had only recently had her second miscarriage and any overheard comments about the delights of pregnancy were virtually certain to send her spiraling off into another depression.

"Satoko's mental health was the only significant problem in our community during those years. She knew that Fernando wanted to have a son and obsessively blamed herself for both of the miscarriages. Satoko was so focused on the son she had not yet had that she paid very little attention to her daughter. Since Keiko and Beatrice were playmates and friends, it was natural that I became Keiko's acting mother. Fernando didn't mind. In fact, he was grateful that I was willing to take some of the parenting burden off his shoulders.

"When Satoko became pregnant again, and made it successfully through the first trimester—which was when her earlier miscarriages had occurred—we all rejoiced. For the first extended time period since we left Mars, Satoko seemed normal and rational. Fernando was deliriously happy. The whole community, including Beatrice, Keiko, and Eric, all of whom were now old enough to understand what was happening, participated in the almost daily discussions about how Satoko was carrying the child, and what the implications were for the baby's sex.

"Sister Nuba had worked extensively with pregnant women at the church in Mutchville and was our resident expert on the sex of unborn children. She had correctly called each of the previous five births. Although she cautioned us that she could be wrong, the day Sister Nuba indicated that she thought the next Gomez would be a boychild, an impromptu party occurred. Kwame and I talked that night, before we fell asleep, about how disappointed Fernando and Satoko would be if the baby turned out to be a girl. We never even considered a more unpleasant scenario."

Vivien stopped and grimaced. She reached for a cigarette and lit it before continuing. "There are moments in each of our lives that profoundly impact everything that happens from that time forward. Sometimes the significance of these moments is clearly understood at the time, such as when I decided to become a Michaelite priestess, or when we all boarded that hatbox waiting on the Martian plateau. But none of us knew, as we looked in sorrow at Satoko and Fernando's stillborn son, that all of our lives would be irrevocably changed by the child's death.

"I have never seen any human being as utterly devastated as Satoko was by the stillbirth. She emitted a terrifying wail when she realized that she had delivered a dead baby, and even five hours later, when darkness came, her body was still convulsing with her sobs. We attempted to sit up with her during the night, but she kept screaming for all of us, even Fernando, to go away and leave her alone. We finally left her. It was a terrible mistake. The next morning she was gone."

Vivien took a final drag on her cigarette and then stubbed it out on a nearby rock. "That first morning," she said, "we all volunteered to help Fernando with the search. . . ."

THREE

EVERYONE EXCEPT SISTER Nuba, who stayed in the village with the children, left the village to search for Satoko within an hour after Fernando informed them that she had disappeared. Vivien and Kwame followed the path through the forest that led eventually back to the lake. Ravi and Anna headed one way along the rim of the chasm, while Brother Jose went with Fernando in the opposite direction.

They gathered back at the village late that afternoon. Nobody had found any clue that suggested where Satoko might have gone. Fernando was beside himself with grief. He asked the group to help him look for her again the next day, and they all assented. But the second day, with everyone searching a new and different area around their village, was equally fruitless. There were no signs of Satoko anywhere.

By this time everyone except Fernando had come to the same conclusion. "The only explanation that makes any sense," Vivien said softly to Kwame as they were strolling along the path with their children, "is that Satoko jumped into the chasm very soon after she departed. Otherwise we would have found something. She wasn't in the frame of mind that she would deliberately have concealed her route."

"I agree," Kwame answered. "I've been thinking about it all day. But how do we tell Fernando to give up hope? He is obviously expecting us to continue the search yet another day. Meanwhile, it is time for us to harvest the grain from the northwestern farms."

Fernando was not pleased the next morning when Kwame informed him that only Brother Jose was available to continue looking for Satoko. His eyes glazed from weeping and lack of sleep, Fernando announced that he would *never* give up searching for Satoko and that he intended personally to cover every square meter of their domain. He was true to his word. In the month that followed Fernando was rarely present in the village. He would stay away for two days, then three, as his search for Satoko covered territory more and more distant from the village.

To keep Keiko from feeling completely abandoned, Vivien and Kwame essentially adopted her during this period. Keiko and Beatrice became inseparable. When Fernando did return to the village, he was usually too exhausted or distraught to pay much attention to his daughter. After her father's brief visits, Keiko would crawl silently into Kwame's comforting arms.

Late one evening Fernando came back, after having been gone for almost four days, with some surprising news. He had worked his way through the thick, nearly impenetrable forest on the far side of their domain. On the other end of that forest, he had discovered a spot where the chasm was so narrow that Fernando had been able to jump across to the other side. He had explored over there for two days. Fernando reported that it was an exciting and wonderful paradise full of fruit trees, vines, bubbling streams, and cascading waterfalls. He even brought back a large, new, purple fruit, the size of a basketball, that was absolutely delicious.

In spite of Kwame's suggestion that they should be cautious, and ask themselves why this other land had so deliberately been hidden from them, the village consensus was that an expedition should be sent immediately to explore this new realm across the chasm, both to see if perhaps Satoko might be there and to learn more about it. Brother Jose was selected to go with Fernando.

They were gone for six days. During their absence a euphoric optimism swept through the community. Vivien especially was carried away by her own fantasies of a more interesting place to live. After eight years, she told herself, there were finally going to be some real changes in their lives. Vivien couldn't wait for Fernando and Brother Jose to return.

The men came back with baskets overflowing with fruits, vegetables, grains, and vines that were unlike any that grew in their territory on this side of the chasm. They were followed into the village by two friendly little six-legged animals that looked like a mixture of a squirrel and a rabbit. Anna Kasper called them squibbits and the name stuck. Fernando and Brother Jose said that these animals were "all over" the other side of the chasm, living in warrens underneath the ground.

The two men mentioned that they had built a small bridge across the chasm so that the group would be able to move their supplies and equipment across in the event a relocation was considered desirable. In the excitement of the descriptions of the exotic flora and fauna of the new land, nobody paid much attention when Kwame commented that the presence of the bridge also meant that whoever lived "over there" now had access to their territory as well.

The village feasted on the new food for several days. It was unanimously proclaimed to be far superior to their standard fare of the last eight years. The friendly squibbits scampered around the village for a couple of hours and then disappeared. At the weekly council meeting Fernando recommended that the group move permanently across the chasm. The response was enthusiastic. Sensing that the others were ready for a change, Kwame put aside his misgivings and agreed to participate in the planning of the move.

•   •   •

THE VILLAGE WAS infused with a new vitality by the thought of moving to the new location. Even the five children were swept up in the excitement. Beatrice and Keiko were thrilled at the prospect of having the cute squibbits as pets. Little Jomo gathered up his favorite toys, put them in one of the small pouches, and announced ceremoniously to his mother that *he* was now ready to go.

Vivien's primary task was matching the inventory of items they would need to take with them against the available number of wagons, packs, baskets, and pouches. She quickly concluded that there were not enough carrying devices. Vivien and Anna started working immediately to make new packs from the strong, supple bark of the "broom" trees that grew in a grove near the lake. Kwame and Brother Jose, meanwhile, were busy building a large wagon to carry the tepees.

Fernando and Ravi were dispatched, as preparations proceeded, to cut a wide path through the thick forest in front of the bridge, and to reconfirm that the village site tentatively selected by Brother Jose and Fernando on their previous visit was the best available location. When the two men left, it was expected that they would be gone for several days. It was a surprise, therefore, when Fernando and Ravi returned to the village only four hours after they departed.

"What's up?" Kwame said, temporarily stopping his work on the wagon when the two men stepped into the clearing from the forest.

"This is something I think you'd better see for yourself," Ravi said, his furrowed brow showing his concern. "And we'll need at least one extra torch. It will be dark before we come back here to the village."

When Kwame returned and called a council meeting to report what they had seen, it was well after dark and all the children, except little Jomo who never went to bed without his mother, were already asleep. "The northeastern farm, the closest one to the thick forest," he said, "has been overrun and completely destroyed by the squibbits. We will not be able to harvest any grain at all from the farm. At least a hundred or so of the squibbits are now living underneath where the farm was, and they are decidedly territorial. When Ravi and I walked on to the farm, to see if any of the grain could be salvaged, the squibbits immediately formed into several large groups of twenty or so each, and made menacing noises at us. I believe they might have attacked if we had not promptly left the area.

"What I want the council to consider, based on this latest information, is whether our decision to move might have been a bit hasty. Given what I saw this evening, and Fernando's report on the number of squibbits living on the other side of the chasm, it seems unlikely that we will be able to farm over there. Besides, although the squibbits may be a manageable nuisance, do we know for certain that there are not other larger, more dangerous creatures living in our chosen area? Maybe we should do some more careful exploration before making any final decisions."

Kwame's impeccable logic carried the meeting. The group decided that the move would be postponed at least until more information was available about the fauna that lived on the other side of the chasm. Kwame was selected to go with Fernando on the next exploratory expedition.

THE MORNING THAT Kwame and Fernando were scheduled to leave, Fernando woke up with a debilitating headache. The normal herbs that usually provided headache relief had no impact on his pain. In fact, his pain seemed to intensify after he ingested the herbs and the water in which they had been mixed. By mid-morning Fernando complained that he could no longer see, and his body broke into a profuse sweat. The cold, wet compresses that were laid against his forehead and other parts of his body only made Fernando more uncomfortable. By lunchtime he was delirious and unaware of his surroundings. He died two hours later.

The entire community was in shock. As they mourned together, gathered around Fernando's lifeless body lying on a mat in front of what had been his tepee, little Eric pointed at the dead man's face and began to scream uncontrollably. A trio of round, pulsating, brightly colored blobs, two red and one blue, the size of pearls on a necklace, were oozing out of Fernando's right nostril. They crawled a centimeter or two and then stopped just above his upper lip. A few seconds later, with everyone watching in horror, these three blobs lifted their translucent gossamer wings that had been folded tightly against their bodies, and then flew away in the direction of the land across the chasm.

Soon after the first three departed, streams of brightly colored blobs began to flow out of each nostril. A few even crawled out through the ears. Altogether more than a hundred poured out of Fernando's head, each disappearing in flight only a few seconds after its appearance.

Anna Kasper fainted. Everyone else was frozen in terror. Brother Jose and Sister Nuba made an effort to comfort the hysterical children, but their own obvious fear only frightened the youngsters more. After a protracted silence, everyone started talking at once. Kwame was the first one to suggest that Fernando's body should be thrown over the chasm, in case whatever had killed him was contagious and any disease agents still remained in his body. Since none of the other three men wanted to touch Fernando for longer than a split second, ropes were wound around his body and he was dragged the two hundred meters to the edge of the chasm. Less than ten minutes after he was pronounced dead by Sister Nuba, Fernando dropped into the darkness.

There were no more excited discussions about how life would be improved in their new locale. In fact, there was very little talk at all, not even by the children. Each of the remaining three families (the two Michaelites, who were

like brother and sister, were essentially a family unit) retreated into the privacy of their own tepees, and dealt with
their fears in the company of their closest loved ones. Sister
Nuba and Brother Jose eventually emerged to lead everyone
in a long, heartfelt prayer just before dark.

Vivien prayed that evening with an earnestness that
had been missing since the first days of her arrival in the
giant sphere. The horror of Fernando's death still fresh in
her mind, she beseeched God to spare her children another
sight like the one they had witnessed. She told God that
she was not afraid to die, if that was His plan, but that she
hoped that He, in his infinite wisdom, would realize that
the children could be permanently traumatized by watching
others repeatedly die in such an awful manner. Vivien also
asked God to help her be a worthy mother for the now-or-
phaned Keiko.

During the days that immediately followed Fernando's
horrible death, fear held an iron grip on the village. In spite
of the daily prayers offered by the Michaelites, the adults
moved through their tasks like zombies, trying to avoid
saying anything that might disturb the children. Kwame
sent Brother Jose and Ravi to destroy the bridge across the
chasm, even though he admitted privately to Vivien that
the action was mostly for psychological relief, for the
damage had probably already been done.

In the middle of the fifth night after Fernando's death,
Brother Jose and Sister Nuba woke Kwame and Vivien
from a sound sleep and asked them both to step outside. "I
have had a steadily worsening headache now for over an
hour," Brother Jose said, his body trembling with fright and
nervousness. He was carrying his sleeping mat. "Sister
Nuba and I have talked and prayed together. We have decided that if I have contracted the same disease that killed
Fernando, it would be better for everyone, especially the
children, if I went away from the village until the malady
has run its course. There is another small clearing near the

chasm, almost half a kilometer from here, where I propose to stay. Sister Nuba has volunteered to come with me."

"I will go with you also," Vivien said. The trio gathered some food and water and wandered through the trees to Brother Jose's selected spot. By the time daylight arrived Jose's pain was so severe that he could no longer see. He prayed fervently, holding both women's hands, and asked God to be merciful. Two hours later he didn't recognize his own name. Shortly after he died colored blobs oozed out of his nose and ears and flew away toward the land across the chasm. Vivien and Sister Nuba pushed Brother Jose's body over the edge of the chasm and then wept together. When they returned to the village, there was no need for them to say anything. The five remaining adults hugged one another, shared their sorrow, and asked Sister Nuba to lead them in prayer.

FOUR

JOHANN WAS STUNNED by the story of Brother Jose's death. "How terrible for everybody," he managed to say. He extended a hand to each woman.

"It wasn't bad enough that we had lost two of our small group in such an awful way in a period of less than a week," Vivien continued after she composed herself. "What everyone was wondering was, what happens now? Who else is going to die? We all lived in absolute horror for the next ten days or so."

Vivien was visibly struggling with the memories. Johann stood up. "Come now," he said, "it's late and we have all had a busy day. Let's go to sleep and you can finish the story tomorrow."

Vivien motioned for him to sit down. "Not yet, giant Johann," she said. "I'm nearly done and besides, I've decided to have one more cigarette before I go to bed." She laughed. "I tell myself it will make me feel better."

She lit the funny brown cigarette and blew the smoke out into the darkness opposite their cave. "By the way," Vivien said, addressing Sister Nuba, "you've been unusually quiet all evening, even for you. Is there anything you want to add?"

Nuba smiled. "Not really," she said. "You're doing a fine job with the basic story. . . . I can supply Brother Johann with a slightly more spiritual version at another time."

Vivien laughed again and winked at Johann. "A slightly more spiritual version," Vivien repeated. "Unless I am mistaken, giant Johann, I have just been reproached, albeit gently, by the good Sister Nuba. . . . In fact, I believe I have just had a déjà vu of sorts. I can recall when Sister Beatrice made similar comments to me about what she called my 'Earthbound' point of view."

Vivien inhaled deeply on her cigarette and blew the smoke out with gusto. "For a few years of my life I was actually Sister Vivien, a priestess of the Order of St. Michael, dedicated to the service of my fellow humans. It always seemed an impossible miracle to me that I, with my love for jewelry and parties and fancy clothing," she said, flicking her ashes into the fire, "could possibly have been willing to forsake sex and material possessions, forever, so that I could spend my life helping others. Sister Beatrice must have hypnotized me."

"God works in strange ways sometimes," Sister Nuba commented.

"Oh yes, that He does," Vivien replied. She stifled a yawn. "Well, Johann," she then began, "you can well imagine the mood in our little village after Brother Jose's death. Each day we waited for someone else to develop a ferocious headache, the first symptom of what we called 'blob disease.' But fortunately, no one ever did. After several weeks, we concluded that Brother Jose and Fernando must have contracted it on the other side of the chasm, and that it was apparently not contagious.

"I had already decided by this time that we should pull up stakes and leave where we were living. Kwame was not convinced. He questioned whether there was any other place in this entire worldlet that was suitable for human beings. When I reminded him that Sister Beatrice and you must have been taken *somewhere*, he acknowledged the logic of my argument, but said that trying to find you would be like looking for a needle in a haystack.

"He swung over to my point of view, however, as our harassment by the pesky squibbits continued to increase.

By this time they had spread throughout what we had previously considered to be our domain. They had destroyed most of our farms and regularly made themselves a nuisance when one of us went out to gather fruit or grain. Eventually the men had to take clubs with them when they foraged, and inevitably several of the squibbits were killed one day when Kwame lost his patience and bashed a pair of them with his club.

"From that day forward our tepee village was always surrounded by several hundred of the little furry creatures. They never did anything overtly hostile, they just sat there and watched us. Whenever someone left the village proper, several dozen of the squibbits would follow. It was a tense situation and we were worried, of course, about what might happen if one of the children were left unprotected.

"Several years earlier, we had built a small boat and had searched unsuccessfully along the lakeshore for any possible fish or seafood. Kwame and Ravi found the boat again after we made a tentative decision to leave. They spent a couple of weeks refurbishing it while we worked out our plan. Since the boat would hold a maximum of five people, maybe six if three of them were children, we decided that Kwame, Sister Nuba, our three children, and I would make the first trip. If we found a suitable home, Kwame would return for Ravi, Anna, and their two children.

"We set out about a month ago and found this place in only a couple of days. We did not see any other land or sea creatures en route. Kwame stayed with us here for about ten days, until he had convinced himself that we would be safe, and then he returned for the others."

Vivien was quiet for a long time. Then she stood up and stretched. "And that, giant Johann," she said slowly, "is *our* tale, such as it is."

Johann and Sister Nuba stood up as well. "Thank you, Vivien," Johann said after a brief yawn. "The story was fascinating."

"You are very welcome, Johann," Vivien replied. She took his hand and held it tightly while Sister Nuba excused herself and headed for her sleeping mat.

"Could I interest you in a short walk?" Vivien then asked Johann.

"That's not necessary," Johann said. "I can see that you are absolutely exhausted."

Vivien pulled him away from the cave and the fire, out along the path in the darkness, and put her arm around his waist. "I have not been sleeping well, Johann," she said. "My thoughts go back and forth from Kwame to the children's uncertain future. . . ." She stopped and turned toward him. "Would you be willing to hold me tonight? I think it would help me sleep."

"Sure, if you want," Johann said. He was going to add something but didn't know exactly how to say it.

"We're not going to do anything either of us would regret," Vivien said. She laughed. "At least not now. . . ." She took Johann's hand and led him toward the beach.

THE
MASKETS

ONE

KEIKO, WEARING HER finest, freshly cleaned dress, emerged from the trees and ran toward where all the others were standing together on a bluff that overlooked the water. "She won't come," the little girl said. She looked up at Johann and Vivien. "She told me to go away."

Johann sighed and shook his head. Vivien reached over and took his hand. "Maybe I should talk to her, darling," she said gently. "After all, in Maria's mind, I am the one who is displacing her. Maybe if I explained to her again—"

"Thank you, but no," Johann interrupted. "Maria is *my* responsibility."

He addressed Sister Nuba, Vivien, and the three children. "I'll be right back," Johann said. "With or without Maria. Please give me a few minutes."

Little Jomo had already lost interest in the ceremony. "Can I go to the beach now?" he asked Vivien.

Johann found Maria playing with her figurines of Beatrice and Yasin a few meters in front of the cave. "Maria," Johann called as he approached. "Let's go. Everyone is waiting."

Maria glanced briefly at Johann and then returned to her play without saying anything. He came over and bent down beside her. "Everyone is up on the bluff," Johann said. "We're ready to start the ceremony. But we don't want to begin without you."

"I'm not coming," Maria said. She did not take her eyes off her figurines.

"And why not?" Johann asked, his impatience showing.

"I don't want you to marry Vivien," the girl said.

"But we have discussed this issue many times," Johann said in an exasperated tone. "I have explained to you repeatedly that Vivien and I are adults, and that we love each other, and that we will all be one big, happy family. . . . Last night you said you understood, and you agreed to participate in the wedding."

"I've changed my mind," Maria said stubbornly, still refusing to look at Johann.

Johann put his huge hand under the girl's chin and turned her face toward his. "Look, Maria," he said, "I love you completely, and so does Vivien, and we both want very much for you to be happy, but we are going to be married whether you like it or not. Now I'm asking you for the last time, as a favor to me, will you please come with me now and be a part of this ceremony?"

Her blue eyes were full of defiance. "No," she said crisply.

Johann's first frustrated impulse was to seize the girl and carry her forcefully to where the others were gathered. Muttering to himself, he resisted the temptation to use physical force. "All right," he said angrily, "have it your way. . . . But I will remember this the next time you ask me to do something special for you."

Maria was now ignoring him and appeared to be totally absorbed in whatever game she was playing with her figurines. Johann walked away in disgust.

FOR THEIR WEDDING night, Johann and Vivien chose to spread their mats only a few meters away from a beautiful pool at the bottom of a waterfall. Because of the lower gravity in their worldlet, the water appeared to glide gently over the rocks on its descent, and fell more softly into the pool at the bottom.

They decided to swim together after making love.

"You're still worried about Maria, aren't you?" Vivien said as she swam to Johann and put her arms around his neck.

"Yes," he said, pulling her body closer. "I'm sorry, Vivien, you deserve better on your wedding night. I shouldn't let her bother me so much."

Vivien kissed him tenderly. "Don't give yourself such a hard time, Johann," she said. "Your concerns about Maria are perfectly understandable. You have spent the last eight years of your life caring for the girl and fulfilling your promise to Beatrice. . . . And I must say your strong sense of responsibility is an attribute that I find very attractive."

"But it's so damn frustrating," Johann said. "We have waited all this time just to let Maria adjust to the idea of our being together. We might as well have married three or four months ago."

"She's still a child, Johann," Vivien said, "with very limited experience. You are the only security that she has ever known. She's never had to contemplate sharing you before."

"I know, I know," he said. "You and I have had variations of this same discussion at least once a day for the past two weeks." Johann sighed and leaned down to kiss Vivien. "I don't want to hear Maria's name mentioned again until morning," he said after the kiss.

Vivien pressed herself tightly against Johann and bit him playfully on the neck. "Your wish is my command, giant Johann," she said.

"NOTHING EITHER VIVIEN or I say makes any impression on her, Sister Nuba," Johann said. "Would you please try to talk to her?"

"Yes," Nuba replied, "but in my opinion it won't help the situation any. In Maria's eyes we adults have all betrayed her. I'm as guilty as Vivien or you because I performed the wedding ceremony. . . . No, Johann, as difficult as it may be for you to accept, I think there's nothing we can do to speed up this process. Maria will adjust, or she won't, according to her own timetable."

Johann reached up to the next set of branches and plucked three more pieces of the round yellow fruit. He placed them in the basket that Sister Nuba was holding. "What if—" he had just said, when they were interrupted by the sound of a child's wail coming from the cave area almost one hundred meters away.

"Uh-oh," Sister Nuba said, "it sounds as if Beatrice has been hurt."

Johann and Sister Nuba walked briskly back to the cave. Beatrice was no longer crying when they arrived. "But there must have been some other reason, B," Vivien was saying, "surely Maria didn't punch you just because you picked up one of her figurines from the sand. Did you say something to provoke her?"

"No, Mother, I didn't," the girl said. Her left eye was already beginning to swell. "Ask Keiko. Maria came over to me, jerked her stupid toy out of my hand, and then hit me as hard as she could."

Keiko verified that what Beatrice had said was true. Johann felt his anger rising. "Where is Maria now?" he asked.

Keiko shook her head. "I don't know, Uncle Johann," she said. "We left her down on the beach."

Johann started down the path. "Remember," he heard Sister Nuba say behind him, "she's only a child."

Maria was not playing on the wide beach down the path from the front of their cave. Johann called her name but there was no response. After searching for a few minutes, Johann finally found her in an isolated cove farther up the shore, near where the bay spread out into the lake.

"Maria," he said, "didn't you hear me calling you? Why didn't you answer?"

Five figurines were spread out on the ground in front of the girl. The one representing Vivien had her head nearly twisted off and looked grotesque. "Ah, friends,"

Maria said, "the *real* Johann has arrived, just as I said he would." She picked up the Johann figurine. "Say hello to Johann, Johann."

Maria laughed at her own witticism. Johann was not amused. He moved into the space where she was playing with the figurines. "Did you hit Beatrice?" Johann asked.

Maria nodded.

"And *why* did you hit her?" he said.

"Because she was interfering with my game," Maria replied nonchalantly, her eyes still focused on the figurines in front of her.

Johann was having difficulty controlling his anger. He jerked the Johann figurine out of Maria's hand and then reached down on the ground and swooped up the others. Her response was immediate. "Give them back," Maria shouted, struggling uselessly with Johann's closed fist. "They're mine!"

He bent down directly in front of her face. She had already started to cry. "Now you listen to me, young lady," Johann said in a voice louder than he intended. "You will *not* hit the other children. Under any circumstances. Is that *clear*?"

Maria had become frantic. She was now tearing wildly at his hands. "They're mine!" she shouted again through her tears.

"If you *ever* hit Beatrice or Keiko or Jomo again," Johann said, "then I will take all these figurines away from you. *Permanently.* Do you understand?"

Maria nodded her head vigorously up and down. "Please, Johann," she then managed to compose herself enough to say, "may I have them back now?"

Johann dropped all the figurines on the ground. Maria picked them up, one at a time, inspecting each carefully. "There now," she said in her play voice, "it's all over. Everybody's all right."

TWO

JOHANN WHISTLED TO himself as he picked the flowers. When he felt that he had enough of the royal blue bulbs with the creamy white centers, he wandered across the meadow to where the long, skinny red-orange flowers were growing. He picked three or four, and then tried several different ways of mixing them in the bouquet he was carrying in his arms.

He was in a great mood. That morning Vivien had risen from their bed at dawn, taken five or six steps toward the bay, and thrown up their dinner from the previous evening. "That's the final confirmation," she had said to Johann with a broad smile when she had returned a few minutes later. "Twelve days late, swollen breasts, and morning sickness can only mean one thing."

Vivien had plopped down beside him and then leaned across his chest. "You, giant Johann, are going to be a father," she had said.

Johann had been surprised that he was so excited. As he had lain there in the early morning hours, cuddling Vivien who was again fast asleep, he had felt a surge of joy that he had not anticipated. *I'm going to be a father,* he had said to himself. *For the very first time. At the age of forty or so.*

All day long Johann had allowed himself to delight in fantasies of the future. Earlier, he had imagined that he was out in the bay with his son (always in his mind's eye the unborn child was a boy, *never* a girl), teaching young Siegfried to swim almost before he could walk. Now, as he finished gathering the flowers, Johann was conjuring up a vision of an overnight camping trip with the boy, some four or five years hence, to show Siegfried the bizarre giant insects that lived in the bushes with the huge leaves on the far side of their island.

The bouquet completed, Johann decided to wander back toward their cave. By his own reckoning, he was about a kilometer away. Instead of taking the normal route home, Johann decided he would try to find a shortcut through a small, dense wood of tall, stately trees with white trunks and very large red leaves.

It was slow going through the woods. Johann had only taken a few steps into the thick undergrowth before he decided to turn around and return to the meadow. Just as he turned, however, he heard a peculiar, high-pitched yelp only a few meters away. Johann bent down, holding the bouquet in one hand and parting the plants with the other, and found what appeared at first glance to be a large, oval brown fruit, roughly the size of Johann's fist. Sticking out of one end of this apparent piece of fruit was an unusual animal face that had been the source of the peculiar yelp.

Johann picked up the object so that he could examine it. The dark little face squirmed, and yelped again. Its toothless mouth was just below its pair of widely separated eyes, which were outlined in a raccoonlike mask of pure white. Everything else on the face was a dark brownish-black. Above the white eye mask, arranged in a row across the forehead, were three small indentations, each containing a different structure unlike anything Johann had ever seen on a living creature before.

Johann brought the fruit up closer to his eyes so that he could inspect the extraordinary tiny structures on the animal's forehead. The frightened creature writhed and pulled itself back inside the fruit, out of Johann's sight. He heard a guttural growl only an instant before something with sharp claws landed on his back, knocking him forward into the trunk of one of the bigger trees. Johann remembered dropping both his bouquet and the unusual fruit just as he lost consciousness.

WHEN HE WOKE up Johann had a headache and a large knot on the upper right side of his forehead. As he rose and stumbled back into the meadow, he felt the pain from the scratches on his back. Johann reached around to check himself and realized, from the wetness of his shirt, that he had been bleeding. Remembering what he had been doing in the first place, Johann then retraced his steps back into the forest and retrieved the bouquet that he had dropped. The unusual fruit was nowhere to be seen.

He heard Vivien calling him when he was about half-way back to their living area. Eventually they met in a glade near the stream from which they drew their drinking water. "Where have you been?" Vivien shouted when she first saw Johann. "We have had another crisis—"

She stopped in mid-sentence when she was close enough to see Johann's condition. "Good grief," she said, running up and immediately examining his head and back, "what happened to you?"

"That's a good question," Johann replied, wincing from the touch of her fingers on his back. "I'm not alto-gether certain."

He forced a smile. "Here, mother-to-be," he said, handing Vivien the bouquet. "These are for you."

"Our baby and I thank you," Vivien said, accepting his gift. "But you may have paid too dear a price for these, giant Johann," she added. "Your back is a total disaster."

Johann laughed. "I wasn't attacked until *after* I finished picking the flowers," he said. He quickly summarized for Vivien what had happened to him in the woods, spending most of his time describing the strange animal with the white mask and forehead indentations.

"Your attacker may have been a mother protecting its child," Vivien said. "Sometimes, Johann, your curiosity needs to be tempered by a little judgment."

"You're probably right," he said. Johann changed the subject. "Now what were you saying about another crisis?"

Vivien sniffed the flowers and looked up at Johann as they walked along. "After what you've been through already today," Vivien said, "I don't think you want to hear about it."

"Is it Maria again?" Johann asked.

"Yes." Vivien nodded. "But we can wait until tonight to talk about it."

Johann stopped walking. "I'd rather know now," he said.

Vivien turned to face her husband. "Maria and Beatrice have had a terrible brawl, Johann," she said. "I think that Beatrice's nose is broken."

"Shit," Johann muttered angrily. "I told Maria if she *ever* hit—"

"Wait," Vivien interrupted. "There's more to the story. . . . I'm very sorry, Johann, but when I was interrogating Beatrice about the cause of the fight, she confessed that she had told Maria that her father, Yasin, was a very bad man who liked to hurt women. When Keiko corroborated the story, Maria apparently went berserk."

"What?" Johann exclaimed. "How do Beatrice and Keiko know about Yasin?"

"They must have heard his name mentioned many times in the village," Vivien said. "Children often know much more about what is going on around them than we adults give them credit for."

Johann was experiencing a tumult of emotions. His anger toward Maria was being overwhelmed by his concern about what she had heard about her father. *There could not have been a worse way for her to find out,* Johann was thinking.

He tore away from Vivien and started running toward their cave. "I must talk to Maria," Johann shouted.

"I understand," Vivien shouted back.

NO ONE HAD seen Maria since the incident. Johann at first assumed that she had gone off to be by herself, as she often did, but after looking in all Maria's favorite places, Johann began to panic. "She has run away," he said to Vivien when she arrived.

"Don't be silly, Johann," Vivien said. "Maria's only eight years old. . . . Besides, where would she go?"

Darkness fell and there was still no sign of the child. Johann could not eat. He interrogated Sister Nuba, Keiko, and Beatrice over and over, searching for anything that Maria might have said, even in anger, that could provide a clue to her whereabouts.

He took a torch and revisited all the places he had searched in the late afternoon. At the isolated cove where Johann had confronted Maria after she had struck Beatrice the first time, Johann found her figurines, in two pouches, underneath a bush beside the rock on which Maria usually sat. Had the pouches been there that afternoon? Johann couldn't say for certain. His only concern at that time had been locating the girl.

Dejected and depressed, Johann sat down on Maria's rock with the pouches in his hands. Idly counting the figurines with his fingers, he realized that only seven of the eleven were inside the pouches. Curious, he opened the pouches and removed their contents.

The missing figurines were Johann, Beatrice, Yasin, and Vivien. Using his torch to look around, Johann noticed that off to the right a few meters, on a flat piece of sandy ground, a kind of crude village had been built with sticks and grass. In the middle of this village was a circular hole, into which two figurines had been stuffed.

Johann extracted the figurines from the hole with some difficulty. When he pulled them up beside his torch for a closer look, he saw that both were headless. The two had once been Johann and Vivien.

THREE

JOHANN HARDLY SLEPT that night. Whenever he heard any sound that he did not immediately recognize, he rose from his mat to look around. Each time he was awake Johann checked the other end of the cave, where the children were sleeping, to see if perhaps Maria had slipped home unnoticed. Her mat was always empty.

By daybreak Johann had formulated a plan to search for the child. In his mind there were only two possible places Maria might have gone. One, the closest, was the pool below the waterfall where Johann had spent his wedding night with Vivien. The family had gone there together several times on outings, and Maria was quite familiar with the route from the pool to their cave and back.

The second location was farther away. Three weeks earlier, while they were swimming together in the bay, Johann and Maria had been recalling the first sights of their new island home, after their harrowing escape from the nozzlers. Maria had wondered out loud why they had never again seen the sturdy, six-legged brown animals with the unusual antlers or tusks that had gazed down on their boat from the cliffs.

"Perhaps there aren't very many of them," Johann had said at the time. "Or their territory is comparatively small. After all, it was almost an hour after we saw them before we came into the bay."

Without thinking, Johann had then asked Maria if she would like to take an exploratory expedition with him, to see if they could find the "tuskers," as Maria called them, again. She had immediately and enthusiastically replied, "Oh yes, Johann. I would *love* that!"

Those three days together, Maria and I were very close, Johann thought as he put everything he might need during his search into his pack. *It was the only time since we came here that I have really seen her laugh.*

"I don't think I'll be gone long," Johann said to Vivien, after reviewing with Sister Nuba and the girls exactly what Maria was wearing when she left. "I don't imagine that she's very far away."

"Try to check in periodically," Vivien said. "My guess is that Maria will be lonely and hungry and home before much longer."

"Will you be all right?" Johann asked, feeling awkward about leaving his pregnant wife to look for Maria.

"I'll be fine," Vivien laughed. "I've done this twice before, and never had any trouble. . . . Maria should be your primary concern."

Before Johann set out, Vivien insisted on rubbing a soothing herbal unguent on the scratches on his back. "This is what wives are for," she said with a grin when Johann complained about the delay.

He reached the pool in less than an hour. Maria had been there, probably the previous afternoon. There were fresh little footprints all over the soft dirt right next to the water, and two neat fresh stacks of yellow fruit rind beside the flat rock to the left of the waterfall. Johann spent a long time studying the tracks away from the pool. He concluded that Maria had headed in the direction they called west, toward the region where the tuskers lived.

Johann was able to follow Maria's footprints for only a few minutes. Then the grass and the undergrowth thickened and he was forced to guess which way Maria would have gone if she was trying to duplicate their earlier trek. This was not a modus operandi with which Johann was comfortable. He much preferred using deductive processes that eliminated uncertainty and constrained the possibilities.

But it was not just the uncertainty about whether he was going in the right direction that was bothering Johann as he walked along at his normally brisk pace. He was also concerned about Maria's safety. Three weeks before on their trip together they had indeed encountered the tuskers. Maria and he had come upon a dozen of the animals grazing contentedly in a meadow. Their response had certainly not been friendly. The tuskers had quickly moved closer together, into a defensive formation. While the others had continued to graze, the large leader had kept a wary eye on the two strange beings who were observing them from the edge of the woods. When Maria had come out of the trees making gestures of friendship, it appeared to Johann that the lead tusker had shifted to a charging stance. What might have happened to Maria then if Johann had not stopped her advance? How would the tuskers, or any other large, unknown animals that might live in the area, react upon finding a solitary, defenseless eight-year-old girl in their domain?

Johann continually looked on both sides, searching for any sign that Maria might have come in this direction. At length he began to sweat, and to feel the sting of the sweat on the fresh scratches on his back. Johann stopped and drank briefly from his water pouch, wondering what Maria would have done when she became thirsty. Imagining that she would have searched for something to drink, Johann turned to his left when he heard the sound of running water. He ate lunch beside a brook at the bottom of a steep bank.

Before proceeding, Johann tried to recall in detail all the major landmarks along the route Maria and he had followed three weeks before. Could she have found the way? he asked himself again. Or was it more likely that by the time she reached this brook, Maria would have become confused and unsure of her directions? He knew that Maria was an intelligent, practical child who would have realized, by the time she came this far, that she should not have left home without her water pouch.

She would have stayed close to the water, Johann convinced himself. *She might even have followed this brook. Maria would have known that eventually it would lead her to the lake or the bay.*

He decided to follow the brook downstream. Johann was now in territory he had never explored before. The brook meandered this way and that, the steep, tree-lined bank giving way to a grassy meadow with thousands of beautiful purple flowers. On one side of the meadow was a large dirt mound, almost as tall as Johann and eight to ten meters wide. As he approached the mound through the flowers, Johann saw hundreds of long, skinny, multilegged creatures, each the size of an ordinary nail, filing in and out of the mound. Pairs of the incoming creatures were carrying parts of the purple flowers.

Johann paused briefly to have another drink and to watch the bustling activity. When he walked around to the other side of the mound, he found Maria's footprints in the dirt. Relieved by the evidence of her recent presence, Johann carefully examined Maria's tracks. Eventually he spotted another stack of yellow fruit rind, not far away among the flowers. Johann smiled to himself, seeing the girl in his mind's eye, and conjectured that she had most likely returned to the brook after visiting the mound.

Suddenly he heard a weird shriek from far above his head. Two small, sparrow-sized creatures were circling the meadow at an altitude of thirty meters or so. Keiko and Maria had once reported seeing a similar pair of flying beings, off in the distance, but this was the first time that Johann had seen anything other than the ribbons flying in the alien sphere. He watched the creatures circle, punctuating their flight with an occasional shrill call, for a few minutes.

When Johann glanced down at the mound again, he was astonished. All the mound dwellers had disappeared. In addition, the several exits and entrances, all of which had been clearly accessible just a few minutes earlier, were now plugged with some kind of white material. Momentarily distracted by the natural spectacle, Johann stepped back, away from the mound, and watched the two flying creatures dive to the surface.

Their attack was too late. The element of surprise was gone. Johann's presence had deterred the fliers just long enough to allow the mound dwellers to establish their defenses.

Mindful that dark was approaching, and that he had brought only a limited amount of fuel for his hand torch, Johann returned to the brook and continued downstream. The brook soon entered a deep, dark wood not unlike the one where Johann had been attacked the previous day. Johann was uncomfortable, and had almost decided to turn around, when he noticed the fresh footprints in the mud beside the brook. *So she returned to the brook when it entered the trees,* Johann thought. *That makes sense. The easiest way through the forest would be to follow the brook.*

As it always did, the artificial daylight vanished in a moment. Johann lit his hand torch and bent down to inspect the footprints more closely. He followed Maria's tracks downstream for several more meters, until he came to a break in the trees where the ground was covered with a short, tundra-like grass right up to the edge of the water. Johann could not find any footprints on the other side of this grassy area.

Johann yawned and realized he was tired. Except for this small section of grass, and the gurgling brook at his back, he was surrounded by a thick forest. "Maria," he called out in a loud voice. His shout echoed through the dark woods on both sides of the stream. There was no answer. Johann spread his sleeping mat on the grass beside the brook and sat down upon it. "Maria," he shouted again. After waiting a few moments, Johann extinguished his torch and went to sleep.

• • •

HE SLEPT FITFULLY, in spite of the soothing sound of the running water from the brook. He had many dreams, most of which were disturbing. In one dream Johann was lying on a sandy beach beside Vivien while Maria and the other children were playing in the water in the distance. Johann kissed Vivien and felt himself becoming aroused. She wrapped her legs around his body and began titillating his tongue with hers. Between kisses Johann turned toward the children briefly to see if they were still occupied with their play.

In the dream Jomo, Keiko, and Beatrice began to scream. They pointed in the direction of the lake and started running across the sand toward Johann and Vivien. Behind them, Maria was on her knees at the edge of the water, playing with her figurines. She was oblivious to the huge tidal wave that had formed and was now rushing toward the shore.

Johann broke away from Vivien and jumped to his feet. "Maria," he yelled, running toward her. The girl looked at him as if she had no idea why he was calling her. The wave rose off the top of Johann's dream screen as he stumbled in the sand. He realized in horror that he was not going to be able to save her. "Run, Maria, run," he screamed in desperation just as the towering wave broke upon her.

Johann was trembling and disoriented when he awakened. His heart was still beating rapidly. Johann lay on his mat, listening to the sound of the brook, until he returned to normal. When he was almost asleep he thought he heard a scurrying sound at the edge of the woods, off to his left. Johann sat up and looked around. He saw and heard nothing. Had he imagined the sound? At length he cautiously stretched out and managed to fall asleep again.

Johann was awakened shortly after daylight by the sound of snarls and growls. Sitting up quickly, Johann was stunned to see that five members of a six-legged alien species, each roughly the size of an average dog, were now spread out in a semicircle around his sleeping mat. The dark, furry creatures with the raccoonlike white masks and brightly colored red and blue streaks on their backs and torsos were standing on four rear legs and beating their chests with their two remaining front legs. One of the animals was beside the brook, behind Johann's head, while another one was at his feet. The other three were on the grass between Johann and the thick forest.

Johann scrambled to his feet and prepared to defend himself. The alien creatures dropped down on all six legs and paced for several seconds, snarling continuously, before stopping again to shout, bare their long teeth, and beat their chests. When this pattern repeated a second and third time, Johann concluded that no attack was imminent. No longer preoccupied with the immediate danger, he gathered his wits and surveyed the situation.

On the other side of the brook, three more of the red, blue, and black animals paced the shoreline. When they saw Johann looking at them, they too went into a display routine, shouting and thumping their chests. Nearer to him, immediately behind his antagonists, Johann could discern dozens of the signature masks staring out from the protection of the thick woods. They had definitely come en masse to greet him. But for what purpose?

Two loud whistles emanated from the forest. The displays and snarls around Johann ceased. Moments later, four of the creatures walked out of the forest together, watching Johann warily as they came toward him. These aliens also had six legs, the white mask, and dark black fur, but they were missing the bright red and blue streaks of the slightly larger, warrior class who had been threatening Johann. This new contingent of the creatures approached within a meter of Johann's mat. Then they dropped down on the ground and stared at him as if he were an object in a museum. Moving very slowly to make certain that he wouldn't scare them, Johann smiled, made a gesture of friendship, and sat down on the mat on his knees. In response to his initial movement, the warrior aliens shouted and displayed, but they were quickly silenced by another pair of whistles from the woods.

A minute or so passed without anything happening. Johann, still smiling, gazed at the unusual faces and the dark, penetrating eyes that were fixed on him. He confirmed that the creatures had no nose, and nothing that looked like ears. What they did possess were those three extraordinary forehead indentations that he had previously seen on the infant's face. On each of the animals facing him, the tiny triangular structure in the central forehead cavity was constantly in motion. Johann was musing about the possible purpose of this organ when a third pair of whistles sounded and a kind of murmuring chant swelled through the forest. The warrior aliens on both sides of the brook sat down, and added their voices to the chant.

A line of three more of the alien animals, each walking on its back four legs and carrying a covered object in its forelegs, now came out of the forest. The creature in the lead, who was holding something spherical the size of a baseball in its clawed, prehensile fingers, did not stop until it was only a few centimeters from Johann's mat. Then, with a great flourish, it uncovered a lustrous blue sphere and placed it on the ground. The moment the sphere touched the grass, there was a short, shrill shout from all of the alien animals, followed by complete silence.

The leader of the creatures now raised itself to its full height of a meter or so, with only its back two feet on the grass, and began to speak to Johann in a combination of growls and whistles. At first Johann was distracted by the movement of its four free limbs that added histrionic punctuation to whatever was being said. After several seconds, however, Johann's gaze focused on the creature's face—he wanted to see if there was anything in its expressions that he might be able to interpret. When Johann realized that there was no way that he was going to be able to figure out what the creature was saying, he turned his attention again to the three forehead indentations of unknown purpose.

What does it do with that thing? Johann asked himself as he watched two tiny balls, connected by an elastic line that stretched and contracted, move around inside the right forehead indentation. *Is that a receiving sensor or a transmitting device? Or maybe something altogether different?*

The left forehead indentation was even weirder. Three minuscule, concentric rings, each a different shade of brownish black, filled the cavity. The gaps between the rings, and even the location of the composite structure inside the whole indentation, were constantly changing while the alien animal was speaking.

Johann was so absorbed in his study of the alien's biology that for a few seconds he did not realize that the creature had stopped speaking. The alien leader dropped down on four legs, turned to its attendants, and uncovered the other two objects. Johann could not see them clearly until the animal placed them on his mat. They were Maria's final two figurines, Yasin and the beautiful Sister Beatrice, given to her by the glowing ribbons.

The shocked Johann immediately reached over to pick up the figurines. He did not notice that a new and different chant was now under way among the alien creatures until he lifted his head to look at the leader. "Where is she?" Johann said, with an expression on his face that he felt could not be misinterpreted.

He repeated his question a second time. Both the front legs of the alien leader pointed toward the forest. "Oh please, take me to her," Johann said.

FOUR

THEIR ROUTE THROUGH the forest would barely have been called a path. The warrior aliens led the procession, hooting and growling to scare away anything living that might be in the way. Johann and the alien leader were just behind the lustrous blue sphere, which Johann had already determined was an object sacred to these creatures. It had been covered and returned to its box and was now being carried by the two largest warriors, each of whom had vines wrapped around their shoulders that were strung through rings on either end of the box.

Dozens of colorless, ordinary members of the species scurried through the woods beside and behind Johann and the leader. They chattered to one another in a mixture of growls, hoots, barks, and whistles, creating quite a din as they moved through the undergrowth. Early in the trek, Johann attempted to watch a few of the creatures who were nearest to him. His face and arms became scratched from countless encounters with branches, however, and he decided that it was better for him to pay attention to where he was going.

Deep in the thickest part of the forest, about a kilometer from the brook, the leader of the alien animals was met by a new pair of the creatures coming in the opposite direction. Several times during their interchange the trio looked up at Johann. When this new pair left, scampering back in the direction from which they had come, the alien leader pointed down the path in front of Johann. The light

was so dim in this part of the forest that it was several seconds before Johann saw the large swelling on the ground in
the distance.

As they neared the leaf-and-mud-covered mound,
carefully camouflaged among the trees, the dozens of animals who had been accompanying them formed into lines
on either side of the path and began to chant. The warriors
who had been leading the processional also lined up beside
the path and added their powerful voices to the song. A pair
of mound doors, about sixty centimeters tall, opened at the
end of the path, but none of the alien creatures entered.
Soon the leader, after motioning for Johann to stop, walked
forward, said something while standing next to the blue
sphere and its box, and then led the group in what sounded
to Johann like a cheer.

Two large animals with long, bright streaks of brilliant
red and blue hurried out from inside the mound, picked up
the box, and carried it back inside. Meanwhile the leader,
followed closely by one of the two warrior aliens who had
been carrying the sphere through the forest, returned to
where Johann was standing. Facing Johann, it rose up to its
full height on two back legs, and gestured twice for this
particular warrior to move closer to Johann. While the
leader was speaking in its strange mixture of growls and
whistles, it repeatedly clasped its two middle legs together,
and then pointed at Johann and the warrior. To make certain that the message was clear, the warrior also gestured at
Johann and himself and appeared to be repeating what the
leader had been saying.

After a final, brief exchange between the two alien animals, the warrior passed by Johann's side, tapping him
lightly on the thigh, and made a "follow me" gesture. The
pair of them moved away from the others on a path that led
around the side of the mound. When they departed, the
leader and all the other animals filed through the open
mound door.

The mound was much larger than Johann had originally thought when he had seen it from a distance. Its peak was considerably above his head, and it extended over several thousand square meters of surface area. As Johann followed the warrior alien around the perimeter of the mound, they crossed two more paths, each of which ended in double doors that led inside the mound. Shortly after they crossed the second path, the warrior barked four short commands and two of the smaller, colorless creatures, who had been doing something in the woods, scurried quickly into a small outbuilding also made of leaves and mud and returned with two gourdlike green fruits. The warrior handed one of the fruits to Johann and sat down opposite him on a patch of grass. It knocked the top off the fruit by banging it on a nearby stump and then stuck its fingers inside. When Johann reached into his pocket to pull out his knife, the alien animal stopped eating and watched Johann with rapt attention.

Johann opened the blade of the knife and the alien's eyes widened. The motion in all three of the structures in its forehead indentations increased. When Johann cut through the rind of the fruit, and sliced a piece of the meat for himself, the warrior could not contain itself. It began to bounce up and down on all six legs, uttering both growls and hoots.

Johann cut several more slices, offered two to the warrior, and then, much to its delight, handed over the knife, handle first. The warrior grasped the knife in its right front leg and held it for a few seconds before touching the blade to its left front leg, cutting itself slightly, and then dropping the knife on the ground.

The alien picked the knife up again a few seconds later. For a long time it carefully experimented with the implement, first on the fruit, and then later on the leaves and sticks on the ground around it. Its fascination with the knife was so intense that it paid little attention to Johann.

For him, this close-up view of the alien warrior's first exposure to a standard pocket knife was a singular, epiphanic experience.

Johann and his companion were sitting no more than a meter apart. He had ample time to study the deep, dark eyes, the wrinkles in the white mask, and the variety of motions in all the bizarre forehead structures. This particular animal also had a unique defining mark, a wide, jagged scar on the right side of its face that ran from just below the two tiny, connected balls in the forehead indentation to a spot not far from the edge of its mouth. Johann had not forgotten that his mission was to find and rescue Maria. That was still uppermost in his mind. But as he watched this alien warrior discover what could be done with the pocket knife, Johann felt a powerful surge of delight. At that moment he was profoundly happy to be alive.

Not just on earth, Johann was thinking, *did chemicals evolve to consciousness and intelligence. Our paradigm occurred elsewhere as well, probably many places among the billions of planets and stars. One of those products of evolution has itself created this artificial world, and brought together other similar chemicals, permitting us to glimpse a few of the endless manifestations of the astounding miracle of life.*

AFTER FINISHING THE fruit the warrior alien, still holding Johann's knife in its right foreleg, rolled over on its side and fell asleep. Heavy lids came down over the large eyes and its mouth closed completely. Johann wondered how the creature was breathing until he noticed that the two membranes behind the structures in the side forehead cavities were oscillating in and out with a fairly high frequency. *A kind of gill?* Johann asked himself. *On the forehead?*

Resisting an urge to examine the sleeping alien animal even more closely, Johann decided to stand up and look around. The moment Johann rose, there were shouts and whistles from the forest behind him. Scarface, as Johann had by this time designated his companion, bolted upright on its back four legs, bared its teeth, and snarled. Johann immediately held his hands up in front of his body and backed away. Scarface quickly closed its mouth and mimicked Johann's hand motions, finishing its action with a short burst of whistles and a little side-to-side dance. Johann concluded that he had just witnessed the alien's equivalent of a laugh. He smiled broadly. Another whistle-burst-cum-dance followed.

With slow and careful motions, Scarface now extended the knife handle in Johann's direction. Johann accepted the knife, closed the blade, and returned it to his pocket. Moments later, Scarface dropped down on all six legs and returned to the path around the perimeter of the mound.

Johann heard many alien animal noises as they neared one of the few sharp corners in the mound structure. Around that corner, dozens of the colorless variety of the creatures were engaged in excavating another of the paths that led inside the mound. Simultaneously, a second group was busy near the mound itself, removing the double doors and widening the entrance. Scarface stopped when it reached the path, gestured toward the mound, and then pointed at Johann.

He understood immediately. All this industry and effort were under way to make it possible for Johann to enter their habitat. Suddenly concerned that perhaps the alien creatures had not really understood why he had come with them in the first place, Johann cleared some leaves and branches away from a piece of ground and used a stick to draw a crude picture of Maria in the dirt.

"Where is she?" he said to Scarface.

Johann's alien companion sat on the ground and inspected what Johann had drawn for almost a minute. Then, after a growl and a short whistle, Scarface used its front four legs to wipe Johann's picture out completely. His heart sank. *They didn't understand after all,* Johann said to himself. He looked around quickly and started formulating an emergency escape plan.

Scarface, meanwhile, holding a stick in the fingers of its right foreleg, was meticulously creating a design on the very same patch of dirt that Johann had used earlier. Johann glanced down twice, but didn't look carefully at Scarface's drawing because he was already preoccupied with how and when he was going to exit from the woods. When Scarface eventually touched him, and pointed down at the dirt, Johann was dumbfounded. The alien warrior had drawn another, *much more accurate,* portrait of Maria!

"Yes," Johann exclaimed in surprise. "Yes, that's Maria."

Scarface stood up, still surveying his handiwork. Looking at Johann, the alien animal extended one finger on each foreleg in the direction of the mound.

EVEN THOUGH THE creatures had dug the path deep into the soil and widened the mound door considerably, it was still necessary for Johann to enter their habitat on his hands and knees. Once inside, he found himself in a long, straight corridor that had also been recently widened. Scarface was directly in front of him, hooting and barking at the others who were in the way, attempting to sneak a glimpse of their visitor. Down the corridor beyond Scarface, Johann could not see very much—the interior of the mound quickly became very dark.

Five meters inside the door, Scarface turned to the right through an open portal and Johann squeezed into the large room behind his companion. Although the light here was very dim, Johann eventually could see eight or ten workers still tearing down a few walls and part of an intermediate ceiling to finish what had obviously been a rush expansion job. The rectangular room, perhaps a meter and a half high, five meters long, and three meters wide, had been several different rooms on two mound levels before it was prepared for Johann.

Although he could not stand up, Johann was quite comfortable sitting against one of the walls made from mud and leaf. As his eyes surveyed the room, he noticed, in addition to the many workers, two warrior aliens over against the opposite wall. Between them was the box that housed the lustrous blue sphere.

The workers continued their task at a frenetic pace. Johann, deducing that nothing new was going to occur until the room was completed, pulled his water pouch out of his pack. Scarface and the other two warriors exchanged growls and barks and then one of the others hooted sharply. Within a few seconds two ordinary alien citizens entered the room carrying a wooden tureen full of water. They placed the water in front of Johann, stared at him for a few seconds, and then scampered out of the room. Scarface, thinking that perhaps Johann would not be able to figure out what to do with the elegantly carved ladle that was resting in the tureen, came over beside his visitor. With exaggerated motions, Scarface filled the ladle by dipping it into the water, and then brought it carefully to his mouth. The creature did not drink, however, choosing instead to pour the water back into the tureen and push it closer to Johann.

Johann, amused by the lesson, smiled at his hosts before picking up the ladle, examining its design, and nodding appreciatively. All the alien animals in the room, including the workers, were watching to see what Johann would do next. With a dramatic flourish, he filled the ladle and drank its contents without spilling a drop. Growls, whistles, and alien chatter greeted his success.

One of the warrior aliens beside the box barked twice and the workers returned to their tasks. Johann took a second drink and then pushed the tureen over in front of

Scarface. This action also prompted an outpouring of approving alien noises.

When he was through drinking, Scarface lifted the tureen and carried it across the room to the others. Johann's alien companion stayed with his warrior colleagues while they were drinking and the trio exchanged noises. Johann, temporarily out of the spotlight, leaned back against the wall and tried to relax. *This whole place is absolutely amazing,* he said to himself, his eyes moving from the conversation among the alien warriors to the workers hauling blocks of mud and leaves out the portal. *Where did these creatures come from? And what is their connection to the glowing ribbons?*

These were all questions that Johann could not answer. In time, the purpose of his visit to the mound intruded upon his free-ranging, philosophical meditations and he began to wonder about Maria. *Where is she?* he asked himself. *And why have they brought me in here?*

One of his inner voices counseled patience. To pass the time while the worker aliens finished what they were doing in the room, Johann thought about Vivien and his unborn child. A memory from his childhood, of his father teaching him to ride a bicycle on the paths that wound through the grassy park near his home, evoked a powerful yearning in Johann. The yearning deepened into a heartache and homesickness for a world he had not seen for more than ten years. *My son or daughter,* he said to himself sadly, *may never see the Earth and understand the origin of our species. He or she may be a space child forever.*

Johann's reverie was cut short by a sequence of hoots from the warrior aliens across the room. Scarface returned to Johann's side and the workers, who were now finished, departed into the corridor. Several seconds later, the creature Johann recognized as the alien leader walked into the room on its back four legs. It rose to its full stature, made a short speech, and then shouted. A stream of animals, a few warriors but mostly colorless workers, filed into the room and made a broad semicircle, with an aisle down the middle, behind the leader, who was facing Johann and Scarface. Warriors carried the box containing the blue sphere across the room and placed it beside the leader, who immediately began a chant.

All the other aliens joined the chant, which continued for several minutes. When it was over, the creatures dropped into their sitting positions and stared at Johann. "Stop pulling so hard," Johann heard an indignant voice shouting out in the corridor.

"Maria?" he called, rising up on his knees in anticipation.

The aisle between the aliens began at the portal. Two warriors, each holding a single thick vine in its forelegs, entered the room. Maria followed, one of the vines wrapped around each of her arms. "Johann?" the girl cried, her eyes staring in disbelief.

The two warriors dropped their vines. Maria bolted down the aisle into Johann's open arms. "You came for me," she said, the tears flooding down her cheeks.

Johann hugged her tightly. "I'm so glad you're safe," he said.

The leader began a new chant while Johann and Maria embraced. Then the creatures, still chanting, filed out of the room, leaving only Scarface and the two humans. Johann's warrior friend quietly moved away from them and sat down against the opposite wall.

FIVE

"THE MASKETS CAUGHT me in some kind of net," Maria said in answer to one of Johann's first questions. "I was following a brook through the forest and I came to an open, grassy area. Two of the colored ones, carrying the net, came out of the woods. I tried to run but the maskets were everywhere. Finally I went into the brook. I stumbled on a rock and they threw the net over my head. Then they dragged me away into the trees. . . ."

Johann watched her carefully. Maria no longer seemed to be unduly distressed. Soon after they had first embraced, she had entreated him frantically to take her "home, away from this dark, smelly place." Now she was much calmer. In truth, Johann had his doubts about whether Maria and he would be allowed to leave, but he did not want to frighten her. *No,* Johann was thinking, *it's not likely that the maskets are going to stand idly by while we depart. There must have been some reason that they went to all this trouble to bring me in here. Outside, in the forest or any open territory, my superior strength is an important asset. In this mound, however . . .*

"The net was not really that strong," Maria was now saying. "I tore it in several places before I became too tired to fight anymore." She suddenly stopped. "But how did you find me? They certainly didn't trap you in one of their flimsy nets."

Johann reached into his pack and pulled out the two figurines. Maria's face brightened. "So *you* have them," she

said, taking them in her hands. "Oh, Johann, this is wonderful! You're here and I haven't lost Beatrice and Yasin. . . .
You have no idea how angry I was when Hattie—that's the
masket who has been staying with me; I call her Hattie
because she has a crease that runs most of the way around
her head—took my figurines away from me while I was
sleeping. When I woke up and saw that she had Beatrice
and Yasin, I attacked her immediately. The maskets sent in
those red and blue guys to control me. After that Hattie kept
her distance."

"You call Hattie 'her,' " Johann said with a smile.
"How do you know she's a girl?"

Maria shrugged. "She seems like a girl to me. She's
gentle. She never barks or shouts or thumps herself like the
ones with the colored chests." She grinned. "And she
moves to the other side of the room when she farts or
belches. . . ."

Johann shook his head. Maria rambled on, talking
about this and that. She seemed normal, in spite of having
spent many hours in the alien mound. Johann knew that
talking was good therapy for her, so he mostly listened and
made small talk in response to her chatter. When Maria
started to talk about her figurines again, however, there was
something that Johann wanted to say.

"I found your carved Johann and Vivien while I was
looking for you," he said.

Maria looked sheepish. "I was *really* mad, Johann," she
said. "First at Beatrice and Keiko, and then at Vivien and
you." The girl sighed. "I'm sorry," she added. "I just
couldn't accept that everything you told me about my father was a lie."

"Everything wasn't a lie," Johann said. "Yasin *was* one
of the smartest people that I have ever met."

"But he was a bad man, wasn't he? Beatrice and Keiko
said he hurt a lot of women."

Johann drew Maria to him and hugged her. She started to cry. "It's all right," he said gently. "I'm certain your father would have loved you if he had ever met you."

Maria pulled away and wiped her tears with the back of her hand. "Can we leave now, Johann?" she said. "I'm sick of this place."

Johann turned around and looked at the portal. "Maybe," he said. "Let me see what I can find out."

As Johann stooped and walked toward the portal, Scarface left its position on the opposite wall and came over to stand in the exit. The meaning of the masket's action was unambiguous. When Johann pointed at the exit, the masket Scarface emphatically gestured toward Maria. Outside the portal, Johann could see half a dozen other warriors.

Yes, Johann said to himself, turning around. *It's exactly as I expected. We are prisoners here. But why? What do these maskets want?*

Scarface scurried around Johann and led him to a far corner of the room, where he pointed to a deep hole. *No,* Johann thought, *I don't need to use the bathroom. At least not yet. But thank you anyway.*

Two warrior maskets entered the room, carrying Johann's and Maria's sleeping mats, while Scarface was showing him the toilet. Johann walked over beside the girl. Maria showed a brave face. "At least we're together," she said. "And it's not nearly as dark as where I was yesterday."

TWO LARGE WOODEN bowls full of fruit were brought into the room by a quartet of colorless maskets. After they set the bowls down in front of Johann and Maria, they respectfully retreated to the other side of the room beside Scarface, where, after exchanging a few comments with Johann's masket companion, they watched and waited. They all growled and whistled simultaneously when Johann pulled out his pocket knife and opened the blade. Scarface barked something to the others and then crossed the room slowly, stopping next to the fruit bowl and extending its right foreleg in Johann's direction.

"What does he want?" Maria asked, her face registering her displeasure. She had already started eating an oval red fruit that had no hard outer covering. Johann thought for a moment and then smiled. Holding the knife by the blade, he offered it to Scarface. The masket turned sideways, hooted, and the other four maskets scurried over to have a closer look. Maria looked at Johann as if he had lost his mind.

Scarface was very entertaining. Wielding the knife from either of his forelegs, and once, for effect, from his right middle leg, Scarface peeled several pieces of fruit, sliced them into portions, and distributed the slices both to Johann and Maria and the four fascinated maskets. Near the end of the performance, Scarface singled out one of the onlookers and gestured for it to come forward and try the knife. This shy masket crawled forward a few centimeters on its stomach, and reached out to touch the knife blade with one finger of its right foreleg. It would not, however, take the knife when Scarface offered it.

Johann, Maria, and the maskets all thoroughly enjoyed Scarface's show. The other maskets mixed hoots, growls, and whistles throughout the meal. Johann and Maria laughed out loud several times at Scarface's antics. *Now if Maria's idea is correct,* Johann was thinking, *and the warriors are males and the colorless maskets are females, then old Scarface has just made a significant improvement in his social status.*

Near the end of the meal, before the maskets removed the bowls and the fruit that had not been eaten, a contingent of a dozen maskets came through the portal and busied themselves on the opposite side of the room. They stuck four skinny wood pieces about half a meter tall in the ground, forming a rectangle, and then spent several minutes stomping and smoothing the area marked off by the stakes. When this activity was completed, two warrior maskets with small, sharp sticks in their forelegs began to draw a complex, detailed pattern on the smoothed dirt.

Johann, curious about what was happening, stood up in a crouch and started to cross the room, but it was obvious from Scarface's response that he was to remain where he was and not disturb the working maskets. Soon after the wooden fruit bowls had been removed, the masket leader, two warriors carrying the blue sphere in its box, and a host of colorless acolytes came into the room and inspected the design inside the stakes. The leader made a few growl-and-whistle comments to the two artists and some changes were made. The sphere-carrying warriors then went out the portal, the acolytes all sat down against the back wall, and the leader motioned for Scarface to bring Johann and Maria across the room.

What had been drawn on the dirt was very neatly done, but Johann had no idea what, if anything, it represented. Maria had just asked him a question when the two warriors who had carried the blue sphere returned to the room behind a new, smaller masket with a wide, brilliant yellow stripe that started at the top of its forehead, just above the indentations, and ran across its head and then down its back. This yellow masket was cradling a yellow sphere the size of a large marble in its forelegs. Each of the two accompanying warriors had one of the handles of a huge wooden bowl filled with wrapped objects.

The masket leader greeted the newcomers. After the blue sphere was removed from its box and placed beside the yellow sphere at the edge of the rectangular design, the warrior maskets began uncovering the objects in the bowl and bringing them to the leader, who carefully placed each one at a specific location inside the rectangle. One of the pieces was a wooden representation of a six-legged animal with something growing out of its forehead.

"That must be a tusker," Maria whispered to Johann.

The possible tusker was set down on the design and two new objects were handed to the leader. Both resembled maskets. One had a piece of yellow fruit rind affixed to its head, the other some red and blue coloring on parts of its body. They were placed at nearly opposite ends of the rectangle.

At this juncture Scarface crossed in front of Johann to where Maria was sitting. The masket made a gesture as if it were taking something out of its stomach.

Johann understood. "A figurine, Maria," he said.

The girl looked blankly at him. "Scarface wants one of your figurines," Johann explained. "Give it to him, please."

Maria reluctantly removed Yasin from the pocket in her dress and handed the figurine to the masket. Scarface deftly tossed the figurine to the leader, who permitted his yellow colleague to examine it carefully, and then placed Yasin in a specific location on the floor.

"It's a *map*!" Johann suddenly exclaimed in a loud voice. "Look, Maria," he said. "That must be the bay, there's the pool where we swim, over there is the forest where we are now—"

Johann stopped himself. Every creature in the room, including Scarface, was staring at him. *I must have violated the protocol,* Johann told himself. After a few seconds of silence, the alien leader stood up, there was another short speech and chant, and then the procedure resumed.

The final object in the wooden bowl, by far the largest, looked like a giant anteater with six legs. The piece was heavy and ungainly. The masket leader nearly lost its balance while positioning this new creature on the map.

Now it was the yellow masket's turn to speak. In an excited voice with a much higher pitch than its cousins, it told a story that drew noisy responses from the gathering. Near the end, the yellow masket stepped gingerly onto the map, still talking, and pushed the giant anteater creature across the design until it was virtually on top of the masket figurine with the yellow fruit rind. It then sat down, softly wailing, and listened to the concluding speech of the host masket leader.

During the final speech the leader pointed several times at Scarface, Johann, and Maria. Then a whistle sounded and all the visitors filed through the portal. One of the warriors gave the Yasin figurine to Scarface, who returned it to Maria.

JOHANN HAD GROWN accustomed to the darkness of night in the alien worldlet, but he had never experienced a blackness as complete as it was in their room in the mound after the day was over. He heard Maria moving restlessly on her mat and considered using some of his precious supply of fuel to light his hand torch. Johann quickly dismissed the idea, however, as soon as he remembered the way Scarface had reacted to his knife. *Lighting the torch would bring every masket in the mound in here,* Johann mused. *And I wouldn't be able to extinguish it until all the fuel was gone.*

He put his head down on his mat and closed his eyes. "Are you awake, Johann?" Maria asked him a minute or two later.

"Yes, I am," he answered.

"Will we be able to leave tomorrow?" she said.

She understands our situation, Johann thought quickly. "I don't know," he replied. *Probably not,* he said to himself. *There must have been some reason for that ceremony with the yellow masket.*

Johann found her hand in the dark and squeezed it gently. "I don't think the maskets are going to hurt us," he said. "They could have done that already. . . . I believe we're here for some other purpose. But I don't yet know what it is."

They were both silent for several seconds. "Johann," Maria then said, holding his hand more tightly. "I'm sorry I ran away. I just couldn't face Beatrice and Keiko after what they said about my father."

"I can imagine how you must have felt," Johann said. "And I'm sorry that I was in any way responsible. But you can't run away from problems, Maria. We are your friends and family. You can talk to us about what you're feeling."

"No, I can't," Maria answered with bitterness in her voice. "The others laugh, and you're always too busy with Vivien to have time to talk to me."

Johann felt as if he had been stabbed. "I'm sorry it seems that way, Maria," he said carefully, making certain he wasn't discounting her feelings. "But it's not true. I will always make time for you if it's important."

She squeezed his hand but didn't respond. A few minutes later Maria fell asleep. Johann stayed awake another half hour, creating a mental list of the alterations he would make in his daily routine, if and when they returned safely to the others, so that there would be ample time for him to spend with Maria. He then slept dreamlessly until he was awakened by a touch on his shoulder.

Scarface was standing beside Johann. In the dim light Johann could tell from Scarface's gesture that the masket was attempting to communicate something to him. Johann sat up and started to awaken Maria, but Scarface stopped him with a constraining foreleg.

The masket pushed a water tureen and some fruit over closer to Johann and waited impatiently while Johann ate breakfast. The moment he was finished, Scarface touched Johann again and then scurried over toward the portal. Johann followed in a crouch, then dropped to his hands and knees in the corridor that led to the outside.

Near the mound the masket leader, the yellow masket, and several dozen others were standing in a clearing next to a pile of tree trunks of varying thickness and color that had been assembled during the night. Most were about a meter in length. On a signal from the leader, four of the colorless maskets picked up one of the thicker poles and carried it over to Johann. He took the pole and then looked quizzically at Scarface.

His companion masket grabbed a branch that was on the ground and swung it back and forth through the air before pointing at Johann. At first, Johann had no idea what he was supposed to do. However, when he eventually gripped the pole as if it were a baseball bat, and swung it around like a club, he heard a chorus of approving noises from his audience.

During the next fifteen minutes Johann was brought eight or nine more clubs of differing thicknesses, lengths, and weights. He swung each one of them two or three times before a pair of masket warriors came over and took it out of his hands. Following each sample, a discussion ensued among Scarface, the masket leader, and its yellow cousin. Two of the clubs were eventually set aside. The rest were taken back into the woods.

When this procedure was completed, Scarface approached Johann and touched his pocket. Johann pulled out his knife and handed it to the masket. While Scarface sharpened the end of a small branch, new maskets, both warriors and colorless, came out from inside the mound carrying the blue sphere and its box. From the demeanor of the alien leader and the yellow masket, Johann surmised correctly that another ceremony was about to take place.

Johann heard Maria's protesting voice as she was led out of the mound. She was attached by rope or twine to two of the warrior maskets. The masket Johann immediately recognized as Hattie was walking beside her. Maria was brought over beside Johann and Scarface, who were opposite the rest of the assembled creatures.

"What are they doing *now*?" Maria asked querulously. "And why am I not free to walk on my own?"

Before Johann could answer, Scarface approached them. Using foreleg gestures and an occasional punctuating growl, he communicated to Johann that the maskets wanted Maria's figurines again. Maria protested mildly but handed them to Johann after he reminded her that her treasures would undoubtedly be returned to her later, just as they had been after the ceremony the preceding evening.

Scarface gave the figurines to its mound leader. Then the yellow masket, using a loud, shrill combination of noises, told a story that culminated with the large anteater representation from the night before repeatedly smashing its snout into the wooden replica of the yellow masket. The host masket leader was next on the agenda. It walked into the middle of the group holding both the Yasin and Beatrice figurines in its forelegs. Speaking in more measured growls and barks, it held the Beatrice figurine aloft before placing it on the ground next to the red and blue masket representation. Then the masket leader lifted the Yasin figurine high above its head while Scarface and two other warriors came forward. The warriors were carrying the giant anteater figurine and Scarface had a sharpened branch and a miniature club in its forelegs. These three objects were placed on the ground near the leader.

The masket chief picked up the club and spear in its middle legs while still holding the Yasin figurine above its head in its forelegs. Then it began to hoot and snarl, as it struck the anteater object repeatedly with the miniature club, eventually causing the replica to topple over on its side. With all the gathered maskets shouting, the leader transferred the Yasin figure to its middle legs and thrust the tiny spear against the anteater's side.

The barks, hoots, growls, and whistles made such a din that Maria put her hands over her ears. Suddenly the masket leader dropped the figurines and placed all six legs on the ground. It then scampered over to the lustrous blue sphere and initiated a solemn chant. A minute later, the chant ended and the maskets dispersed, almost all of them returning to the mound.

Scarface brought the figurines back to Maria and gestured toward the mound. The two warrior maskets to whom she was attached started moving in the indicated direction. Maria was frightened. "What are they doing, Johann?" she said. "Why are they taking me back inside?"

Johann had noticed during the important concluding parts of the ceremony that Maria, like a typical eight-year-old human, had no longer been paying close attention. She had been watching other maskets in the assembly, and even looking out into the woods. Since Johann was fairly certain that he understood the meaning of the ceremony, he thought that it was fortuitous that Maria's attention had strayed.

"I think there's something they want me to do for them," Johann said evenly. "After I finish, I believe we'll be free to return to the others."

Before Maria reached the mound, Johann hurried over and embraced her. His quick, unexpected movement caused consternation among the maskets. A dozen warriors had encircled the two humans by the time they had finished saying good-bye.

"I love you, Maria," Johann said.

"How long will you be gone?" the girl asked.

"I don't know—not long, I don't think," he replied.

She hugged him one last time and then followed her two warrior maskets and Hattie back into the mound.

SIX

JOHANN SAT ON a stump in the clearing while the preparations were completed. Scarface supervised a colorless masket artisan who worked continuously with Johann's knife to fashion a sharp point on the end of one of the two poles. The yellow masket also remained out of the mound, talking with its cousins, and personally brought Johann water and fruit just before his spear was finished.

The mound leader, accompanied as usual by the warrior pair carrying the box with the blue sphere, came out again a few minutes later. It felt the end of the spear, and then ordered both the club and the spearpoint touched against the surface of the blue sphere. It did not give a speech, but the masket leader did lead the group in a brief chant before returning to the mound.

Altogether there were eight members of the contingent that set out in the middle of the day. The yellow masket was the leader, followed by Scarface, Johann, and then five colorless maskets, three carrying the thick club, and a pair responsible for the spear. The group moved at a rapid pace. They stopped for lunch at a stream, where the maskets gathered fruit and Scarface indicated to Johann that he should drink his fill. Late in the day they passed through another forest. Scarface briefly disappeared before returning with replacement maskets who took over the carrying job from their five exhausted comrades.

The pace did not slow after nightfall. Johann was sweaty and fatigued when they finally stopped on a beach beside the lake on the far side of the island. With the maskets watching him curiously, Johann refreshed himself with an evening swim before dinner and sleep.

Scarface awakened him before daylight. At dawn they were traveling along the top of a sheer cliff that dropped precipitously to the lake below. Johann stopped to admire a beautiful waterfall that cascaded down the cliff, creating a perpetual shower on the narrow beach at the bottom. Scarface signaled to Johann that they needed to keep moving.

Soon thereafter the yellow masket turned and crossed a meadow, full of flowers and grasses, that extended all the way to the cliff's edge. On the other side of this meadow was the forest that was the home of the yellow masket tribe. The travelers were met at the edge of the forest, in a secluded glade, by half a dozen members of the yellow clan, two with the bright yellow stripes on their backs and heads, and a quartet of the smaller, colorless variety who were virtually indistinguishable from their cousins on the other side of the island.

A long conversation ensued between Scarface and all the yellow maskets. The maskets who had been carrying the club and the spear set them against the trunk of a large tree and listened to the discussion. At length the six maskets who had met them in the glade scampered out into the meadow, each going in a different direction. Scarface came over beside Johann and said something with growls and gestures that Johann did not understand. Then Scarface sat down beside his yellow masket comrade and both of them stared fixedly at the meadow, as if they were waiting for something.

Within five minutes a sprinting masket crossed the meadow and burst into the small glade. While it was explaining something to the pair of maskets beside Johann, a loud, deep, enduring noise, reminiscent of a foghorn, resounded in his ears. The three maskets turned instantly, their forehead indentations alive with movement, and looked out into the meadow along the forest line.

The foghorn sounded again. Johann craned his neck to the side, saw something large and brown in the distance, and then moved closer to the meadow so that the trees would not obstruct his view. The five maskets who had carried the two weapons, meanwhile, disappeared immediately into the woods, and the yellow maskets next to Johann dropped down low, out of sight. Only Scarface had the courage to follow Johann to the edge of the forest.

Johann's first sight of the creature was terrifying. It was much larger than he had expected. His estimate was that it was approximately the size of a small elephant. The creature was also intelligent, for it was purposely frustrating its masket prey by moving agilely back and forth, staying between the masket and its forest home. At periodic intervals the elevark, as Johann started calling it in his mind, would make its foghorn sound and then eject, in the direction of the masket, a baseball-sized clump of slimy material from the round hole below its long snout. When one of these clumps grazed the masket and knocked it down, the frightened smaller creature made a mistake and broke for the woods.

Because the masket attempted to reach the forest on Johann's side of the elevark, he had a perfect view of the kill. Out of the elevark's snout dropped a long, rigid, cylindrical tube, open at the end, that seized the masket and immediately lifted it off the ground. For an instant Johann could see the masket struggling wildly against the powerful muscles at the end of the elevark's tube. That struggle and the masket's pitiful wails ended abruptly, however, when a thick fluid, coming down the elevark's tube, engulfed the smaller creature and rendered it motionless in a few seconds. With a triumphant bellow, shorter and lower than its foghorn blasts, the elevark sucked the unconscious masket up its dripping tube and then slowly withdrew the bizarre protuberance into its snout.

Johann was now standing almost in the meadow, no more than fifty meters from the elevark. He suddenly realized that the creature, whose pseudojaw was moving up and down presumably preparing the masket for the elevark equivalent of a stomach, was now watching him with whatever eyes it possessed. Just above the snout, in the center of its head, the elevark had a large circular disc with four black holes located on the perimeter, separated one from another by ninety degrees. Johann did not have time to determine if this was indeed the organ that provided sight to the elevark, because the creature made its foghorn sound, expelled a clump of slime that fell far short of Johann, and began to move quickly in his direction.

Johann, his heart pumping furiously, retreated into the forest. His masket companions had already disappeared. Johann reasoned correctly that the elevark would have great difficulty moving in the forest, so he stopped hurrying when he was thirty meters away from the edge. The elevark, meanwhile, came to the place where Johann had been standing and stuck its snout into the forest, extending its tube twice and searching around to see if it could grab anything of consequence. Johann noted from his secure position that the tube reached out almost three meters.

The elevark, who had six thick legs the size of tree trunks and a massive body whose underside was a meter off the ground, now squatted at the edge of the meadow and seemed to be peering into the forest with its circular disc. Johann did not move. He could not tell if the elevark saw him. A few minutes later the elevark stood up again, turned around, and trundled back into the meadow.

SCARFACE AND THE yellow masket who had been the emissary returned a few minutes later to the glade where Johann was waiting. Soon thereafter, other yellow maskets arrived, bringing food and water. Johann was surprised to discover how hungry and thirsty he was. As he ate, and stared at his pair of weapons leaning against one of the trees opposite him, Johann realized that the club and the spear would be virtually useless against the elevark.

So what is my least unsatisfactory option? Johann asked himself grimly, using an expression from his system-engineering days back on Earth. *I can't simply quit. For even if I could find my way back to Maria, I have no assurance that the maskets will release her.* He paused, knowing what his next thoughts would be. *And an open battle with that elevark will almost certainly result in a quick and painful death.*

As Johann searched for some way out of his predicament, an image from his teenage years, from a trip he had taken with his school class to the Berlin Museum of Natural History, popped into his mind. He remembered standing in front of a diorama showing native Americans, armed with only spears and bows, harassing a huge mastodon near the edge of a cliff. "That's it," Johann suddenly shouted.

The maskets around him stopped eating and stared at their alien colleague. Johann sat on his knees, picked up a mixture of mud and leaves, and began fashioning an object that looked a lot like the elevark. Scarface came over beside him to watch. The others followed. "We'll wait until it's asleep," Johann said, pushing the crude elevark over on its side and trying to communicate the concept of sleep with gestures and noises. . . .

ALL AFTERNOON JOHANN attempted to explain his plan to the maskets. He eventually cleared a sizable section of the forest floor, created a dirt ramp that abruptly terminated to represent the cliff, and even poured water into the trench below the end of the ramp to simulate the lake.

Johann used every possible communication technique he could imagine, and he thought that the maskets had understood, but when night came and it was time to implement the plan, all the maskets curled up and went to sleep, as they usually did, at different locations around the glade.

Johann picked up the spear the masket artisan had fashioned for him and moved noiselessly to the edge of the forest. Questions were racing through his mind. *What if the elevark does not sleep in the meadow?* he thought. *What if its circular disc is not used for sight?* Johann knew that if either of his assumptions was wrong, there was no chance that his plan would work.

He briefly debated whether or not he should awaken the maskets. *I guess I should find the elevark first,* he answered himself. Johann took a deep breath and then eased out into the meadow to begin his search. He stumbled twice in the unfamiliar territory before deciding to light his torch. Johann knew that the torch would make it easy for the elevark to see him, but he considered it too dangerous to proceed in the dark.

Johann wandered in the meadow for a long time without finding any sign of the elevark. Once he returned briefly to the glade. The maskets were still sound asleep. On his second excursion into the meadow Johann encountered two large piles of droppings that were warm and fresh. Later, while standing still and drinking from his water pouch, Johann heard a peculiar sound just above his hearing threshold. The noise was off to his right, in the general direction of the cliff. Johann moved slowly in that direction, stopping often. When the sound became louder, and Johann convinced himself that what he was hearing was coming from some kind of an animal, he extinguished his torch. After his eyes had adjusted again to the darkness, Johann moved cautiously toward the sound. At length he was able to make out the outline of a large hulk lying on the ground.

The creature's loud snores made it easy to locate from any direction. At one point Johann approached within five meters, close enough that he could ascertain its sleeping position. The elevark stirred, breaking its snoring rhythm, and Johann felt a surge of fear race through him. He stood absolutely still as the elevark relocated its huge mass and continued sleeping.

Three times Johann walked back and forth between the cliff and the sleeping elevark, both to measure the distance and to make certain there were no obstacles that might cause him to trip. Twice he dropped down over the side to a ledge, half a meter wide, where he hoped to stand when the charging elevark hurtled over the cliff. Standing on this ledge, Johann noticed that he could barely hear the noise of the waterfall. He climbed back up to the meadow and walked along the rim of the cliff, beyond the end of the safety ledge. He could no longer hear the waterfall. Johann smiled to himself and made a mental note. He now knew for certain how to find the ledge when he was retreating.

He told himself he was ready. Johann took a long, slow drink of water, put the spear in his right hand, and started walking warily toward the elevark. When he heard a guttural growl close to his right ear, Johann's heart nearly leaped out of his body.

It was Scarface and the yellow masket. They were carrying the wooden club. Johann took the club in his left hand and then waited several seconds for his pulse rate to slow down. Gesturing to the two maskets to stay behind, Johann moved closer to the elevark.

From its silhouette Johann could tell that the creature had rolled over while it was sleeping. Its head was now facing the opposite direction. He circumnavigated the elevark and crept up close to the head and snout. The creature's snores were so loud they hurt Johann's ears. The smell of its breath was disgusting. Measuring his distance carefully in the darkness, Johann summoned all his strength and thrust the spear forward into the circular disc just above the snout.

Fluid burst out of the disc, some spurting on Johann. He turned to run, just as he had planned, as the elevark, bellowing ferociously, awakened and bolted upright on its feet. Seconds later, when Johann was certain he was on a correct course, he began to shout at the top of his lungs. The enraged elevark, still bellowing, thundered after him. Johann shouted again and raced toward the cliff.

Johann had assumed he would be able to outrun the huge elevark. He was wrong. The giant silhouette was actually closing the distance between them. It emitted its foghorn noise and one of its clumps flew by Johann, narrowly missing him. A second clump hit him directly in the back, knocking him to the ground. Johann rolled over quickly and saw that the elevark was almost upon him.

At that moment an unbroken stream of hoots, barks, and whistles emanated from a position about twenty meters to Johann's left. The elevark slowed its charge, turned its head and snout, and altered course toward the continuous masket noises. Johann scrambled quickly to his feet and saw a darting movement where the masket sounds had been.

The elevark sounded its foghorn and discharged a series of clumps in the direction of the fleeing masket. Seconds later, it extended its fearsome rigid tube to the ground and grabbed its prey. Masket wails split the night, sending shivers down Johann's spine. He raced over to where the elevark was holding its captive aloft. Using all the strength he could muster, Johann struck the tube with the wooden club. The elevark bellowed as its tube recoiled and released its prey.

Johann was already running, and shouting as he ran. The elevark was now after him again. Between the bellows and the foghorn noises, Johann did not have the presence of mind to listen for the waterfall. He had to trust that he was heading in the right direction.

He dodged one elevark clump but a second one knocked him down again, just as he reached the edge of the cliff. Johann crawled frantically over the side and pressed himself against the cliff face. His feet came to rest on the solid ledge as the elevark hurtled over the side, its bellow fading away as it slowly accelerated downward toward the narrow beach.

Johann sat in a crouch on the ledge for several minutes. He could not believe it was over. When, at length, he pulled himself back up to the meadow, and took a few steps on his trembling legs, Johann realized how utterly exhausted he was. He sat down and took a drink from his water pouch. A few minutes later, artificial daylight returned to his alien world.

Johann walked to the edge of the cliff and looked over the side. There, far below in the fine spray from the waterfall, he could see a brown mass lying motionless on a stretch of sand. Hearing barks and whistles behind him, Johann glanced back into the meadow. A group of yellow maskets had come out of the forest and were now standing in a circle around something. They moved aside to let Johann pass when he approached.

Scarface was lying unconscious on the ground. Without any hesitation, Johann bent down and picked up his masket friend whose courage had undoubtedly saved his life. He carried Scarface toward the forest, accompanied by a growing contingent of noisy yellow maskets.

SEVEN

SCARFACE REGAINED CONSCIOUSNESS before the elaborate yellow masket ceremony was completed. Johann's masket friend had been anesthetized by the fluid in the elevark's tube, but was not otherwise hurt. Johann was impatient during the long ceremony. He was pleased that the yellow maskets were so grateful to him for destroying their nemesis; however, what he wanted most was to return quickly to the other side of the island and be reunited with Maria.

A yellow masket warrior accompanied Johann and Scarface as far as the beach beside the lake. When they were alone, and had finished the lunch provided by the yellow maskets, Scarface waded out into the water and attempted to communicate with Johann with an unusual combination of gestures and growls. It took Johann five minutes to realize that Scarface wanted a swimming lesson.

Johann's first impulse was to dismiss Scarface's request as ridiculous. But as he stood watching his alien companion floundering in about forty centimeters of water, and looking at him with those deep, dark, curious eyes, Johann realized that he had been provided with an opportunity for another unique experience. *Besides,* Johann said to himself, *this creature saved my life. I can certainly take a little of my time to teach it to swim.*

Johann waded into the tepid lake and grasped Scarface by the front two legs. They eased out into water that was only waist deep for Johann but would have been over the masket's head if it had been standing upright on its back two legs. Johann then put both forelegs in one of his huge hands and lifted Scarface's furry torso with the other, so that the masket's body extended along the surface of the water.

When Scarface was more or less floating, Johann grabbed both of the masket's back legs and moved them back and forth in a rapid motion. "Now kick," he said simultaneously, knowing full well that the masket had no idea what he was saying. Three times Johann repeated this routine, alternately moving the back and middle legs when he said "kick." Scarface finally understood. The next times that Johann said "kick" while he was holding the masket's forelegs with both his hands, all four of the other legs immediately began the kicking motion.

Scarface was eager to learn, and adventurous to the point of being foolhardy. Several times in the ensuing hour the masket swallowed a large amount of water, and made a terrible cackling sound that must have been its way of coughing. Once, Scarface's body shook and trembled so much that Johann, who had pulled the masket completely out of the water and thrown it over his shoulder, was afraid he might have drowned his friend.

The lesson was ultimately successful. By the time they left the beach, Scarface could do a passable dog paddle, and was able to swim underwater with his entire body submerged for ten seconds or so. Being that close to Scarface for such an extended period of time had taught Johann some other things as well. Although he had not yet figured out the exact functions of each of the three extraordinary forehead organs, Johann had learned how to recognize certain kinds of masket facial expressions, and had convinced himself that the creatures possessed a guileless honesty that was admirable. He was more certain than ever that Maria would be released upon their return.

Scarface apparently had some kind of natural biological system that measured time very accurately. Late in the day, the masket hurried Johann so that they reached a clearing beside a stream in time for Scarface to dash off into the adjoining grove and pick some fruit for their dinner. Only a few minutes after Scarface returned, with the two of them sitting together and sharing the fruit, the masket suddenly put what it was eating on the ground and pointed up with both its forelegs. Two or three seconds later the artificial daylight vanished.

Scarface was asleep soon thereafter. Johann stretched out beside the stream, his hands behind his head, and gazed up at the dark, distant ceiling. His first thoughts were about Vivien, Maria, and how his life might be changed by the child that would soon arrive. But these more personal thoughts were soon pushed away by the overwhelming questions that Johann knew he could not answer.

Who or what created this artificial world? For what purpose? Why are the maskets, the tuskers, the nozzlers, and the elevark all here? What are the ribbons, and what is their relationship to all these other creatures?

Johann still remembered vividly, even though it had taken place more than eight years before, both the glowing ribbons and the pattern of lights in the sky the terrible night that Beatrice had died. Only moments before the white Beatrice had arrived in the brilliantly white hovercraft, and beckoned him to bring the infant Maria and join her, that pattern had indicated that their spherical spaceship was en route to another world, a real planet somewhere, one with large twin moons. Had Johann misunderstood the pattern? Had it been simply a rich symbolism that was not meant to be taken literally?

He recalled a wonderful evening when a pregnant Beatrice and he had sat together, holding hands and very much in love, on the beach below their cave. They had been talking about God, Beatrice's favorite subject, and she had been chiding Johann because he had admitted that he had never been able to believe wholeheartedly in a personal, Christian God. Why not? she had asked.

"The concept does not make logical sense to me," he had answered, "and is unable to provide answers to reasonably simple questions. How, for example, could a merciful, caring God have permitted you to be raped by Yasin and to conceive a child from that violent act?"

"Sweet Brother Johann," Beatrice had said, touching her hand to his cheek and using the appellation of the Michaelites, "even after all this time you still don't understand. God is not required to make logical sense to you, nor to answer all your questions. He has given you a brain by which you reason, and a heart with which you feel. God loves all your attributes, but knows that you believe in Him mostly with your heart."

The vivid memory of Beatrice awakened powerful emotions that Johann usually suppressed. His mind turned away from his endless string of unanswerable questions and he replayed the last two eventful days of his life. He recalled the moment the elevark clump knocked him to the ground, and his instantaneous thought that he was about to be killed.

Johann stood up quietly and walked over to where Scarface was sleeping. He bent down and stroked the fur on the masket's head and back. *I don't know what you are, or where you came from,* Johann said to himself. *And certainly not why you risked your life for me. But Beatrice would not be puzzled. She would not torment herself with all these infinite questions. She would simply say again, as she did every night, thank you, God.*

WORD OF THEIR success reached the red and blue maskets before Johann and Scarface returned. A huge celebration was already under way in the assembly area outside the mound. A tumultuous masket cheer greeted their arrival, followed by a boisterous chant. The masket leader, along with three representatives of the yellow maskets, made room for Scarface and he was even allowed to hold the lustrous blue sphere during a special chant.

Maria was brought out of the mound and freed of her masket escorts. She embraced Johann and told him that she wanted to go home immediately, but he informed her that they were going to stay at least until the end of the ceremony.

Scarface was the star. Using all the props available (he again borrowed Maria's Yasin figurine, which she relinquished without protest), the masket told the story of the death of the elevark. Johann suspected that perhaps Scarface was embellishing or exaggerating a fact or two, but since he was not able to interpret literally the masket's complicated, mixed language, Johann couldn't tell for certain. What he did know, however, was that at no point in his telling of the story did Scarface ever use the red and blue masket figurine. Had he omitted his role altogether? Was personal modesty another feature of these extraordinary creatures?

Even though he knew he was violating the accepted protocol for a masket ceremony, Johann stepped into the central area following Scarface's presentation and asked for the red and blue masket figurine. With hundreds of alien eyes upon him, Johann made an unsuccessful attempt to explain how Scarface had diverted the elevark and saved his life. Fortunately, one of the yellow maskets present had heard the complete story, and came forward at this juncture to extol Scarface's courage and role in the death of the elevark. When the yellow masket was finished, the burst of masket noises was deafening. Scarface was allowed to hold the lustrous blue sphere again, as well as the smaller sacred stone of the yellow maskets.

The assembly broke up and Johann left with Maria.

They followed the path through the masket woods and arrived at the clearing beside the bank where Maria had originally been captured and Johann had first seen the maskets. They stopped to have a drink of water.

While they were resting, Scarface, by himself, came out of the woods. The masket tried to say something but Johann couldn't understand. At length, Scarface extended a foreleg, which Johann took, and led his human friend downstream to a place where the brook formed a small pool. Maria followed them. With a great flourish, Scarface dove into the water, paddled for three or four strokes, submerged for a few seconds, and then climbed out of the water beside them.

The dripping masket pointed at himself, then Johann, and extended its two forelegs as high in the air as it could reach. After Scarface repeated this action, Maria commented, "What in the world is it doing?"

"You wouldn't understand," Johann said.

He reached in his pocket and pulled out his knife. Carefully opening the blade, and holding it in his hand, Johann gave the knife to Scarface. Next he pointed directly at the masket, then at himself, and raised his two long arms as high as he could.

The masket appeared to be stunned. Johann repeated the set of gestures, took Maria by the hand, and began walking upstream. When he turned around Scarface was still staring at the knife in his hands.

IT WAS LESS than two hours by the shortest route from the masket woods to the cave area where Johann and Maria lived. He was eager to see Vivien, and several times Maria had to ask him to slow down. When they stopped for their last drink at the pool where Vivien and he had spent their wedding night, Johann was tempted to talk to Maria to make certain that she had drawn all the correct conclusions from her experience. As he looked at the girl, however, Johann thought he could already see a change in her demeanor. *Now is not the right time for a parental lecture,* he told himself.

Johann started shouting before they came down the final slope behind their cave. "Hello, hello," he yelled. "We're back."

He was not disturbed that there was no immediate response. It was, after all, about midday, and it was entirely plausible that one of the two adult women might be out gathering food while the other was down at the beach supervising the children.

All the mats were in the cave in their normal places. The fire was not burning, which was unusual, but it was still smoldering as if it had been used the previous day. Johann told himself that perhaps Vivien had been too busy that morning to rebuild the fire.

Johann and Maria hurried down to the beach, both of them shouting. They didn't find anyone. "Where could they be?" Maria asked innocently.

"We've been gone so long," Johann said, counting the days in his mind, "maybe they decided to come look for us."

"But would they have taken little Jomo with them?" Maria asked astutely. "It would be hard for them to go very far with him along."

Johann stood on the beach and gazed out at the bay. A chill started spreading through his system. He fought against the negative feeling and smiled at Maria.

She was looking along the shoreline. "What's that, over there?" she said, pointing at a portion of the beach on which the sand was compacted and covered with ridges. They both moved over to examine the area more carefully.

"It looks as if a boat has been here," Johann said.

Neither of them said anything for several seconds.

"Maybe the others came," Maria said. "Ravi, Anna, and their children."

Johann brightened. "In that case," he said, "they would have left a note. . . . You look around here, while I go up and check the cave."

Questions were flooding into Johann's mind as he started up the path. *But why didn't they wait for our return? And why would they leave the mats?*

He whirled around when he heard Maria scream. Johann raced down to the beach to find the girl nearly hysterical. "What is it, Maria?" he said. "What's the matter?"

She pointed over at some bushes to her left, just inland from one end of the beach. A long blue tentacle, its claw still intact, was lying on one of the bushes.

THE

GROTTO

ONE

AT FIRST, JOHANN counted the days. He kept the tally on a rock wall at the other end of the cave, opposite where the children used to sleep. Maria now slept close to him, near the fire, much as she had done during the years they were alone on their previous island.

Johann clung desperately to the idea that Vivien and the others had been reunited with Ravi, Anna, and their children, and that soon someone would be coming back for them. At least once each day Johann would walk along the beach and stare out at the bay and the lake, searching for a boat. A few times he thought he saw something far off in the distance, but when he called Maria, and requested that she look with her younger eyes, she always told him that nothing was there.

Maria didn't seem to mind that Johann and she were alone again. When he asked her if she missed the other children, her immediate response was "not really." Nevertheless, as the days passed Maria grew restive and moody. Johann knew that she was feeling lonely. Her face brightened immediately when he suggested that perhaps he might carve some figurines to represent all her former playmates.

Using Sister Nuba's knife, which had been among the personal articles that had been left behind when the others departed, Johann made a new set of figurines for Maria. Along with all the humans, he included an elevark, a tusker, and the two different kinds of masket. Maria specifically asked him not to carve a nozzler.

After Johann had finished all the new figurines, Maria was a different child. She threw herself wholeheartedly into her fantasy play, creating imaginative sagas that sometimes lasted for several days. She attempted to involve Johann in her stories, but he didn't participate with any enthusiasm. To comfort her, Johann would sit on a rock, not far from where Maria was playing on the beach, and appear to be listening to her endless excited chatter. In actuality he spent most of this time thinking about Vivien and his unborn child, or Sister Beatrice, or even his youth and childhood in Germany.

When the number of days since they left the maskets reached sixty, Johann stopped keeping the tally on the wall. With that act, he relinquished his belief that anyone would return for them. His depression deepened. *I will never see Vivien again,* he told himself. *Or my child, if he or she exists.* Johann's only release came from his morning swims, which became longer and longer. After exercising, with his body in a state of peaceful exhaustion, Johann was no longer plagued by feelings of hopelessness.

One morning, when he returned from an hour swim, Maria was waiting for him on the beach. She had taken off her necklace with the amulet and was holding it in her hands.

"Johann," she said cheerfully as he emerged from the water. "I've forgotten what you told me about this man on the amulet. I know that he was very special to my mother. But what was he like, as a person?"

Johann took slow deep breaths, as he always did just after a swimming workout. He gave Maria a puzzled look.

"I might want this Michael as one of the characters in my new game," Maria explained earnestly. "So it's important."

Johann sat down on the sand beside the girl and took the amulet. He stared for several seconds at the carving of the young man with the curly hair framed by nuclear flames above and behind him. "Back on Earth," Johann said slowly, remembering his many conversations about Michael with Beatrice, "Michael Balatresi was a religious leader and a prophet. He believed that God wanted humanity to evolve into a higher organism, where each individual would subordinate his needs and desires to the common good of this higher, collective being. Michael formed a special order, of which your mother was a prominent member, to become what he called the circulation system of that higher organism, to distribute the resources . . ."

He stopped. Maria was looking at Johann as if he were speaking a different language. "I don't really understand any of that stuff," she said. "What I wanted to know were simple things. Was this Michael guy tall or short, skinny or fat? Was his hair really this curly? Could he run fast, and did he have a good smile?"

Johann shook his head and erupted in laughter. "Of course," he said, pulling Maria to him and giving her a wet hug. "I'm sorry, Maria," he added, "I once promised your mother . . ." He paused again. "But all that is probably irrelevant too. . . . Yes, Michael's hair was really curly, he was tall but not as tall as I am, his body was lean and lithe, and he had a magnificent smile. . . . But Maria, I never once heard anybody discuss whether or not he could run fast. When we see Vivien and Nuba again, we'll have to ask them."

"Thank you, Johann," Maria said. "You've been a big help."

Johann turned the amulet over in his hands, to the back side where the name Maria was inscribed. "You do remember, don't you, who carved your name here on this amulet?"

"Of course," she said, taking the necklace with the amulet and putting it over her neck, "it was you, Johann, just after Mother gave it to me." She turned to go.

For an instant Johann was transported back to that sorrowful moment over eight years earlier and a tumult of emotions threw him into confusion. Again he heard Beatrice's voice saying, "Take care of her, Johann, as if she were your own."

The voice was so clear that Johann looked around quickly, hoping that perhaps the white Beatrice had miraculously returned. Nobody was there. The voice had been inside his head. Johann stared down at the sand beside his feet and felt the profound emptiness that usually signaled the onset of one of his depressions.

"No," Johann cried out loud, angry at himself for wallowing in loneliness and self-pity. He shouted at Maria.

"What is it, Johann?" she said, stopping and turning around.

"How would you like to do something different today?" he said with forced enthusiasm. "Why don't you and I take a trip to visit Scarface and our other masket friends?"

"That would be great," she said.

BEFORE THEY DEPARTED, Johann and Maria both left notes, explaining that they would be back by nightfall, on the back of pieces of bark. He left his near the fire in the cave; Maria placed her note on a tree sprig near the beach. As they climbed the slope behind their cave, Johann realized that they had not once been away from their cave and beach area for more than ten minutes since they had first returned and found the others missing.

Johann was in a good mood when they stopped at the waterfall for a drink and some fruit. "I bet the maskets will be glad to see you," Maria said. "You're their hero." Johann feigned embarrassment and walked hand in hand with her out into the meadow.

Their next break came when they reached the clearing beside the brook. Maria refilled her pouch with the fresh water. "I was so angry with myself when I came here the first time," she said. "How could I have been so stupid to run away without my water pouch?"

They were making a lot of noise. Johann expected that at any moment a masket delegation would come out of the woods and greet them. After they had refreshed themselves, Johann and Maria headed into the trees along a small path.

"Do you think you can find the mound?" she asked.

"I'm not sure," Johann replied. "I paid more attention the second time I was here, when I came back from the yellow masket territory with Scarface, but there were so many twists and turns along the way."

After they had been walking in the woods for about five minutes, they turned right, onto a new path. Johann glanced around and stopped. "I have another concern," he said. "What if we never find the mound, and lose ourselves here in the woods?" He pulled out Sister Nuba's knife and made a mark on the tree. "I hate to injure a living thing, but I would not want to be lost here after dark."

When Johann turned back around to look at Maria, she was gone. She had wandered off the path a few meters into the undergrowth. "Look at this, Johann," she said, bending down to pick up an oval brown fruit that was on the ground. "There's something inside."

In the dim forest light they could barely see the white markings deep inside the fruit. Johann carefully cut around the shell, removing only a small piece at a time. Inside the oval was a tiny, dead baby masket.

"I wonder what happened," Johann said out loud. He turned around slowly with the fruit in his hand, anticipating the arrival of an adult masket.

Maria had moved twenty meters to the right among the trees. "Here's another, Johann," she shouted. "And another."

During the next fifteen minutes Johann and Maria found eight more baby maskets, all dead, inside brown oval fruits lying on the ground. Some had barely formed and could not even be identified as maskets. Two of them, however, had matured fully and had all the characteristic features of the adults of the species. Johann and Maria did not find a single embryo that was alive.

"Why do you think they're all dead?" Maria asked as they walked along. "Do you think maybe they were sick?"

Johann simply shook his head. He had no idea.

They located the masket mound without undue difficulty. Both of them were surprised that there were no maskets working anywhere in the vicinity, and that the assembly area was in a disordered state. But what convinced Johann that something was dreadfully wrong was the fact that the mound doors at the end of each of the entrance paths were all standing wide open.

"Hello there, you maskets," Maria called, turning around to grin at Johann. "Hello, hello," she repeated.

"I don't think there's anyone in there," Johann said after several seconds of silence.

"How could that be?" Maria asked. "This is their permanent home. There must be someone inside."

They both yelled again but there was no reply. At Johann's suggestion, Maria crawled into two of the entrances and examined some nearby rooms. From one she brought out a bowl and a ladle. "You're right," she said. "Nobody's home."

Johann and Maria retraced their route through the woods. By the time they reached the clearing, Maria had created in her mind a once-yearly ceremony where maskets of all colors came together, leaving their mounds empty, to celebrate something special. She liked her idea, especially since the maskets were so fond of pomp and circumstance. *But that doesn't explain all the dead embryos,* Johann said to himself. He feared a less optimistic explanation for the empty mound.

Thinking about the tiny maskets dead in their oval brown shells made Johann cringe. *And my unborn son or daughter,* he thought, noting to himself that he had never told Maria about Vivien's pregnancy. *Where is he or she? Are Vivien and the child even alive?*

The gloom that had accompanied Johann for days was returning. He had thought that a visit to the maskets might give him a lift. Instead, he now had additional evidence that all was not right in their artificial world.

JOHANN WAS FAIRLY certain what he would find, but wanted to confirm his expectations. He didn't tell Maria the specific reason for their trek, only that they were going to take an overnight camping trip. Johann underestimated the girl's memory. She knew they were in tusker territory before they reached the clearing where they had encountered a dozen of the animals a month before. Maria was thrilled at the prospect of seeing them again.

"They're my favorites, Johann," she said. "The maskets are cute, of course, and I never saw that elevark thing you killed, but I like the tuskers the best."

They walked around until Maria's feet hurt and she started to complain. They did not see any tuskers. *More importantly,* Johann said to himself, for he did not want to disturb Maria with the conclusions he was reaching, *we have not seen any sign that tuskers have recently been present. The meadows where they were grazing are now overgrown. And all the droppings are old.*

The next day, on the way home, passing through a meadow with beautiful flowers, Johann and Maria nearly stepped on another of the dirt mounds that housed the long, skinny, multilegged creatures that looked like nails. After asking Johann's permission, Maria dug into one side of the mound with her hands. She found what appeared to be a nursery compartment, with hundreds of eggs in neat little vestibules, but not a single living, moving creature. Johann considered this discovery to be additional evidence to support his inchoate theory.

That night, after Maria fell asleep, Johann lay on his back and considered the possibilities. *Someone or something is removing all the fauna from this island,* he said to himself. *Maria and I may be the only ones left. All this must be part of some general plan. But orchestrated by whom for what purpose?*

For the umpteenth time since his arrival at the artificial worldlet now more than nine years ago, Johann was frustrated by his inability to either understand or control his destiny. He heard Sister Beatrice's voice in his head. "Don't analyze everything all the time, Johann," she said sweetly. "Just accept and trust in God."

Johann was not in a pleasant mood. "Bullshit," he said to himself out loud.

TWO

IN HER FANTASY games with the figurines, Maria had developed an explanation for where the tuskers and the maskets had gone. "They're on the far side of the island, Johann," she said, "in yellow masket territory. A huge celebration is occurring. Who knows? Maybe that's where Keiko and Beatrice and the others went also."

Johann thought the chances were remote that all the animals in their proximity had suddenly migrated to another part of the island. But Maria kept pestering him until he agreed to go on another trek with her. "Besides," she said with an impish grin the evening before they were planning to leave, "I've never seen the place where you killed the elevark."

Johann noted to himself that the existence of the solitary elevark on their island was additional proof that they were in a managed situation, a zoo of some kind. *But who are the zookeepers?* he wondered. *And where are they?* He went to sleep imagining a fabulously advanced benign species who would soon show up to rescue Maria and him, just as they had all the others.

When daylight came Johann was already down at the beach, limbering up for his morning swim. Maria was still sleeping. Everything was ready for their journey to begin right after breakfast.

Johann swam out of the bay and into the main body of the lake. He turned to the right, following the shoreline, and covered about two kilometers before he turned around and headed back. Johann thought he saw an object of some kind, at the limit of his vision, when he was roughly halfway home, but he dismissed his sighting as a trick his old eyes were playing on him. By the time he reentered the bay, he had reached his state of exercise nirvana and was nearly oblivious to everything around him.

When Johann stopped swimming and stood up to walk onshore, he saw the raft immediately. He blinked his eyes twice, confirming that there was indeed a wooden raft sitting on the beach, and hastened out of the water. "Vivien," he cried expectantly, looking in all directions. "Is that you, Vivien?"

There was no reply. Johann, totally confused by the silence, now yelled for Maria. Again there was no immediate answer.

"We have taken her away," a voice said from the bushes closest to where the raft was grounded. "But don't worry, she is safe."

Johann spun around and felt his muscles tense. A dark-skinned man of medium height, who appeared to be about fifty, stepped forward from the bushes.

"Who the hell are you?" Johann asked.

"Greetings," the man said without smiling. His hair was unkempt and his beard, mostly gray in color, was full. He was wearing blue shorts but no other clothing. "I have come to make your transition as easy as possible. The child is waiting, on a raft like this one, just outside the bay."

Johann's mind was exploding with questions. He stared at the man for several seconds, trying to organize his thoughts.

"Maria is out there, by herself, on a raft?" Johann exclaimed, pointing toward the lake.

"She is in no danger," the man said. "The adoclynes are with her."

"The adoclynes!" Johann shouted. "*What* is an adoclyne?"

The man answered evenly, in a monotone, as if Johann

had asked the time of day. "The adoclynes are the reigning species in this world," he said. "The rest of us are their subjects."

Johann moved forward threateningly. "Look, buddy," he said, "I don't know what's going on here, but if you have harmed Maria in any way, I will personally tear you limb from limb."

The man suddenly darted to his right, out into the water. He turned around and faced Johann again when he was waist deep. "They warned me that you might be violent," he said.

"*They?*" shouted Johann, following the man into the water. "Who are you talking about now?"

The man slapped the water with his open palm three times. "These are the adoclynes," he answered, as six blue tentacles with claws emerged from the water almost simultaneously. Moments later three turquoise heads with oval gray bulbous eyes appeared on the surface next to the man.

Johann was dumbfounded. He stood at the edge of the water, agape, as one of the nozzlers moved closer to him.

"You'd better move back," the man said. "Those claws can inflict quite a wound."

Johann stumbled backward. The man slapped the water and the nozzler stopped advancing. Instead, it turned its forward eyes toward the stranger and waved its pair of tentacles in some kind of pattern. The man made a few signs with his hands and fingers and the nozzler submerged.

Johann could not believe what he was seeing. "Did you just *talk* to that damn thing?" he asked.

The man nodded. "The adoclynes and I worked out a primitive means of communication four years ago. We have been improving it ever since."

Johann was completely overwhelmed. He sat down on the beach, still staring at the man and the six lofted tentacles. "Well, I'll be damned," was all Johann could think of to say.

• • •

THE MAN'S VOICE was absolutely devoid of emotion. His face showed no expression. He waded over next to the raft, talking continuously to Johann. "Everyone else is with the adoclynes," he repeated. "You and the girl are the only ones left. . . . If you'll climb on the raft, I'll take you to her."

Johann gazed fixedly at the stranger, trying to stifle his anger and frustration. Who was this man? Where had he come from? Why did he look vaguely familiar?

"Did Maria take anything with her?" Johann asked during one of the rare moments that the man was not talking.

He did not respond. He didn't even indicate that he heard Johann's question.

"Does Maria have her clothes and other personal things?" Johann said.

"Only those little figurines," the man finally said. "She was playing when we found her."

When you seized her, Johann said to himself, imagining how frightened Maria must have been. *But how do I know this character is telling the truth?* Johann wondered suddenly. *What if Maria escaped and this is all some kind of trick?*

"If you really have Maria in your custody," Johann said, "then I will come with you. But you must show me some proof of your claim."

The expressionless man nodded and slapped the water. Two of the turquoise heads of the adoclynes appeared immediately. Johann watched the man's hand movements and the responding motions of the blue tentacles. After several seconds, the two nozzlers swam off toward the entrance to the bay.

"It will be a few minutes," the man said. "You have time to gather up a few things. . . . But you won't need your mats. And the adoclynes don't allow fire in the grotto."

When Johann returned to the beach with a pair of

bundles on his shoulders, the man was again standing in waist-deep water beside the raft. He pointed along the shoreline in the direction of the cove where Maria liked to play. "Look there," he said. "You will see the girl."

A raft similar to the one next to the man eased into view, coming around a bend in the shore over a hundred meters away. Maria began yelling and waving her arms. Johann heard his name but could not understand anything else she was saying.

His reaction was automatic. He dropped the bundles on the sand and dove into the water, starting to swim toward Maria. He had only taken a few strokes when a pair of nozzlers grabbed his shorts with their claws.

"You will not be allowed to talk to her until we reach the grotto," the man said as Johann treaded water, surrounded by the two nozzlers. "You will travel there with me, on this raft."

Already Maria's raft was headed out toward the lake. The girl was still yelling at him, but Johann couldn't distinguish any of her words. He quickly concluded that he had no option except to comply with the man's instructions. Johann swam back to the beach.

The simple raft, made from light wooden logs, was easily large enough for the bundles, Johann, and the strange man. It was pushed rapidly through the water by three of the nozzlers, whose six claws were attached to the back end. The raft on which Maria was riding alone remained a couple of hundred meters in front of them.

After they left the bay, the two rafts headed out into the open water of the lake. Within an hour, nothing but water could be seen in all directions. Early in the voyage Johann attempted to talk to the man with him, but almost all his questions were ignored. The man would not indicate how he happened to be inside this artificial world, or what he knew (or didn't know) about the adoclynes. All he would say was that the two rafts were en route to "the grotto."

At one point, Johann expressed his concern that Maria might be hungry. After first accepting some berries and fruit from Johann, the man leaned over and slapped the water. When a nozzler head appeared a few seconds later, the man spoke to the creature briefly and then placed the food in its claws. The nozzler, holding the food aloft, rolled over on its side and issued three short, bass blasts from its pulsating organ that looked like tiny pearl clusters. After a quick response from an adoclyne near Maria's raft, Johann watched the elevated claws, carrying the food, head rapidly in her direction.

Since there was nothing to see and Johann's companion discouraged conversation, Johann decided to stretch out on his back, using one of the bundles as a pillow, and close his eyes. As he relaxed and started to fall asleep, he was again struck by the feeling that he had seen the man on the raft with him before. Searching idly through his memories of his years at Valhalla, before he and the others had left Mars in the hatbox-shaped spacecraft, Johann recalled the Asian scientific team that had never returned from its expedition to recover core samples of the Martian polar ice. *Could this man have been part of that group?* he asked himself.

Johann remembered when he and his colleagues had found the dead, frozen body of the only female in the Asian team, a Dr. Won from Korea. The other three members of the team presumably perished in those labyrinthine caverns underneath the ice, but their bodies were never located. Could it be . . . ?

Johann forced from his memory a picture of the small conference room where Narong and he had greeted their scientific visitors. He could not quite reconstruct the faces in the room, but when his companion on the raft broke a long silence by calling Johann's attention to what appeared to be a mountain-sized, pointed rock on the horizon, Johann suddenly recognized the voice.

He opened his eyes to look at the man. "The grotto is

located at the bottom of that rock," the man said, still pointing.

Now Johann also remembered the face. "You're Ismail Jailani, aren't you?" Johann said excitedly. "We met briefly at Valhalla. I'm Johann Eberhardt. I was the director of the facility there."

The man stared at him, blinking intermittently, for several seconds. Then a puzzled frown spread across his face and he looked away. "Ismail Jailani," he said very slowly. "Yes, yes, I am Dr. Ismail Jailani."

He turned back to face Johann. His face was again expressionless but his body was trembling. He appeared to be looking beyond Johann. "Please do not hurt me," he said in a timid voice. "I am a professor at the University of Kuala Lumpur. I have a wife and three children. I would like to return to them—"

At that moment one of the nozzlers accompanying their raft emitted another pair of bass blasts. Dr. Jailani put his hands over his ears and his face contorted in pain. "Yes, yes, I understand," he shouted. His hands pulled away from his ears and went into motion. "I'll do what you ask," he said. "Just don't hurt me again."

Before the startled Johann could say anything, a sheath of brown seaweed landed on the side of the raft, dropped by a nozzler claw. Dr. Jailani crawled hurriedly over to the seaweed and began ripping it apart and stuffing pieces in his mouth. "Thank you, thank you," he said. "I was so very hungry."

Johann reflected a moment and then approached the man, who continued to eat with frenetic intensity. "Dr. Jailani," he said in an even voice, "I have plenty of food in my pack. Would you perhaps prefer to eat some fruit or berries?"

The man did not reply. When Johann touched him on the shoulder and called his name again, Dr. Jailani spun around, seaweed dangling from his mouth and a wild look in his eyes. "No," he said in a loud voice. "I don't want your food. . . . And stop calling me that stupid name. Just leave me alone and let me eat."

Johann retreated to the other side of the raft. As he moved, he noticed the pair of turquoise heads with a total of six gray eyes no more than ten meters away from where Dr. Jailani was eating. *Were you watching us that entire time?* Johann wondered. *And could you understand any of our conversation?*

THE TWO MEN did not talk to each other again during the time that the pair of rafts drew inexorably nearer to the gigantic, pointed rock in the middle of the lake. From time to time Dr. Jailani muttered to himself, or slapped the water and had a conversation with the adoclynes, but whenever Johann looked across the raft at him, Dr. Jailani averted his eyes.

In the bottom center of the rock was a large, dark opening shaped like an arch. Johann watched Maria's raft approach this archway and then disappear from view. Several minutes later his raft also entered the world inside the rock.

At first Johann could not see anything in front of him but darkness. Turning around, and looking back at the light beyond the opening through which they had passed, Johann observed that the rock ceiling was at least ten meters in height, and that the archway was wide enough for roughly three rafts similar to theirs to traverse at the same time. The canal on which they were riding now divided, and the nozzlers guiding their raft took the right fork, down the narrower of the two canals. At this point there were no more than ten or twelve meters separating the rock walls on either side of Johann.

The canal was also turning slowly, causing the light behind them to fade away. However, in front of them it was no longer dark. High upon the left rock wall, just beneath the ceiling, Johann saw the first of the light sources that provided dim illumination inside the grotto. It was a strange light, teeming with movement. As the canal meandered inside the rock, these light sources appeared at widely spaced intervals, some larger and brighter than others. Straining his eyes, and wishing that age had not reduced his visual acuity, Johann concluded that nests of some kind, inhabited by glowing creatures, had been placed in eyries hollowed out of the rock to provide light to this otherwise dark world.

When they had first entered the grotto, the only sound that Johann had heard was the sound of the raft slipping through the water. As they penetrated deeper into the interior, however, occasional bass blasts from the steering adoclynes reverberated off the walls. The lighting increased as well, for the density of the glowing nests became greater near the heart of the grotto.

A narrow boat with sides, resembling a canoe, squeezed by the raft going the opposite direction. It was carrying stacks of seaweed sheaths as well as crude baskets containing fish and other sea creatures. The nozzler claws and the familiar blue tentacles were attached to the rear, the only indication of the boat's method of propulsion.

Johann watched the boat until it had cleared the back side of the raft, where Dr. Jailani was busily slapping the water and gesturing with his hands. When Johann finally turned around, and looked again in the direction they were moving, the raft was approaching a major canal intersection, in the center of which was a large, transparent dodecahedron mounted on a slowly rotating base plate.

As the raft drew closer and the dodecahedron turned to present an optimal view to Johann, his immediate astonishment was so great that he nearly lost his balance and fell from the raft. Inside the dodecahedron was a glowing ribbon, or at least a faithful representation of one, complete with changing boundaries and tiny particles drifting from side to side within its structure.

Johann continued to study the ribbon as the raft entered the traffic flow moving clockwise around the dodecahedron. After perhaps half a minute, the motions of the ribbon began to repeat, convincing Johann that what he was seeing was simply the work of skillful artisans and not a *real* ribbon somehow imprisoned in the unusual structure.

Pushing aside his desire to speculate on the meaning and purpose of the encased ribbon, Johann focused his attention on the circular pool surrounding the rotating structure. Four canals, separated from each other by ninety degrees, emanated from the intersection. Small, curious watercraft were everywhere—moving with the raft around the dodecahedron, heading in and out of the intersection, and standing at what appeared to be a nozzler dock or marina a hundred meters down one of the canals. Many of the craft were carrying cargo, but Johann had no idea what most of the items were.

The noise was deafening. Each of the adoclynes guiding Johann's raft, plus most of the rest of the nozzlers in the intersection, issued periodic blasts, creating a terrible cacophony that was almost painful. Dr. Jailani kept his hands over his ears the entire time.

Three fresh pairs of nozzler claws suddenly appeared on the back side of their raft and an instant later the old ones vanished. As Johann and Dr. Jailani entered a new canal three-fourths of the way around the dodecahedron and left the rotary intersection behind, the noise abated. Johann noticed immediately that the traffic was very sparse on this branch of the canal system. He suddenly thought about Maria, whom he had not seen since her raft entered the grotto, and turned to ask Dr. Jailani a question.

The man was on his knees at the back side of the raft, facing away from Johann. He was conducting what was obviously a serious conversation with a trailing nozzler whose tentacles and claws were elevated half a meter above the canal surface. Johann chose not to say anything and instead simply watched the amazing communication for a minute or two.

The canal on which they were traveling split into two parts. Their raft took the left fork, an extremely narrow, poorly illuminated passageway with a very low ceiling. A few hundred meters farther along, this tributary turned to the right and then widened into a pool. Maria's raft was already in the pool, drifting back and forth next to a thick seaweed gate under which the canal water continued to flow. Maria greeted Johann with a joyful shout and started peppering him with questions from afar. Johann returned her greeting and then, when the two rafts were much closer together, informed the girl that he didn't know any more than she did.

"That man must know," Maria said angrily, pointing at Dr. Jailani. "He's one of them. He tricked me into the water so the nozzlers could grab me."

Dr. Jailani acted as if he had not heard Maria's comments. He waited until the two rafts were in contact before speaking. "You will continue from here without me," he said. "The adoclynes will take you to your destination. . . . You may join the girl on her raft now."

"Where are we going?" Johann asked.

"You will be with the others," Dr. Jailani replied in his monotone.

"Why are we here? What is going to happen to us?" Johann said.

Dr. Jailani ignored his questions. He picked up one of the two bundles and leaned over to place it on Maria's raft. Johann grabbed the other bundle and stepped carefully across the narrow strip of water between them. Maria threw her arms around him.

Dr. Jailani's raft moved away immediately. "The others know all the rules," he said. "They will explain them to you. Do not violate the rules or the adoclynes will punish you severely."

Two nozzler claws holding dead sea creatures that Johann had never before seen dropped their contents on Dr. Jailani's raft. The man's face brightened, the first exhibition of emotion from him that Johann had seen since they had entered the grotto. Dr. Jailani picked up the new food and began eating with gusto. He never looked again at Johann and Maria as his raft disappeared around the corner.

THEY HAD NO time to talk. Less than a minute after Dr. Jailani departed, one of the nozzlers who had been guiding Maria's raft broke the surface, rolled over on its side, and began blasting with its clustered pearl organ. It made two loud, long sounds, and then paused. Three shorter blasts followed. An answer, two quick, sharp bass noises, came immediately from the other side of the seaweed gate. The adoclyne near Johann and Maria next emitted four more blasts in this order: short, long, long, short. At the conclusion of the set the heavy seaweed gate opened in the middle and the two sides pulled back against the rock walls. Johann and Maria's raft passed through the open gate, which closed behind them only a few seconds later.

There was even less light in this section of the grotto. The narrow canal wandered slowly to the right, passing a large open room cut into the wall. Two nozzlers were resting on the lip of the room, their turquoise heads lying on the rock floor and their segmented carapaces partially beneath the surface of the canal. Inside the room Johann and Maria could see a dozen of the adoclynes, a few moving slowly around propelled by wave motion in the hundreds of cilia beneath their bodies. It was the first time that Johann had ever seen one of the creatures completely out of the water.

The nozzlers steering their raft and one of the two hanging on the lip of the room exchanged a few blasts before the latter slid into the water and started swimming toward the raft. Maria cringed and huddled against Johann as one of the new nozzler's tentacles elevated, moved slowly over the boat, and dropped its claw gently down on Johann's head. Although his heart was pumping furiously, Johann exhibited no fear. With a surprising deftness, the adoclyne picked up and let drop several hairs near the back of Johann's head. Its curiosity satisfied, the creature retracted its tentacle and claw into the water, said something to its colleagues with three bass blasts, and swam back toward the room where it had been resting.

Johann and Maria started hearing a mixture of new and different noises they could not identify as their raft approached another canal intersection. In the middle of this much smaller junction, into which four canals, again separated by ninety degrees, emptied, was a solid rectangular block elevated half a meter above the surface of the water. Two huge nozzlers, facing in opposite directions, were sitting on the block. One of these nozzlers turned toward Johann and Maria's raft and made two short sounds. Before any of their guiding adoclynes could reply, a long foghorn blast burst from the canal on their left. Johann recognized the sound immediately and goose bumps formed on both his arms. While he was trying to tell Maria that the foghorn noise could only have come from an elevark, a chorus of barks, hoots, and whistles issued from the canal on the right.

"The maskets," Maria said excitedly. "They're here too!"

Johann could barely hear her, even though they were standing next to each other on the raft, because of the terrible din that had now erupted. What seemed like dozens of different animal sounds, including more barks, hoots, and an occasional foghorn blast, flooded the canal intersection, making it impossible for Johann and Maria to talk, or for the nozzlers to communicate. One of the two adoclyne sentries extended a tentacle toward a small black object in the center of the block and immediately thereafter a loud, shrill whistle could be heard above all the other multifarious sounds.

Johann and Maria's raft eased toward the center of the intersection pool and then stopped altogether. Less than a minute later, with all the noises still continuing, the water in the canal that they had just traveled began to churn with the presence of nozzlers. They were swimming breathtakingly fast, and they were into the intersection and down the canals on the left and right in a matter of seconds.

The alarm whistle terminated, allowing Johann and Maria to hear more distinctly the other animal sounds, which had now changed character and seemed to be charged with pain and fear. Both the loudness and the frequency of the noises coming from the two canals diminished rapidly. What could be heard was only an occasional plaintive cry or wail.

The nozzler police swam back through the intersection less than a minute after silence was restored. Immediately after they departed, a nozzler sentry again looked toward Johann and Maria's raft and emitted two bass sounds. One of their steering adoclynes responded with a similar set and the raft moved away from the sentry block, heading for the canal directly opposite the one on which they had entered.

Even in the dim light Johann could see the fear in Maria's eyes. He took the girl in his arms and gave her a consoling hug. "What's going to happen now, Johann?" she asked in a soft, whimpering voice.

"I don't know, Maria," he replied. "But if Dr. Jailani is to be believed, I think we'll soon see Vivien, Sister Nuba, and the children."

"Then are we all prisoners of the nozzlers?" she asked.

"I guess so," Johann said.

Meanwhile their raft moved slowly along the darkest, narrowest canal they had yet encountered in the grotto. The ceiling here was so low that Johann dropped to his knees to avoid scraping his head against it. Soon thereafter they heard what both Johann and Maria were certain was the mournful wail of a young human child.

"That can't be Jomo," Maria whispered as the sounds became louder. "I have heard his cry many times. . . . This one is different."

The narrow waterway split into two parts and their raft followed the canal to the right. The child's cry reached a maximum at the junction and then dropped off rapidly as they wound through the rock. A few minutes later the raft pulled over against one of the walls and stopped.

Maria saw the tiny opening, barely wide enough for a single adult human, long before Johann did. Since the raft was no longer moving, they both concluded that they were supposed to disembark. Maria entered the tiny passageway first. Johann followed, struggling to squeeze through with the two bundles in his arms. As soon as both of them had their feet on the rock floor, their raft departed.

Once Johann became temporarily wedged between the walls on either side of the path. After he freed himself, Maria and he both laughed. "You see," she said, "there are some advantages to being little."

The voice they heard immediately was music to their ears. "Maria? Brother Johann? Is that you?" Sister Nuba said.

"Yes, Nuba," Johann boomed, his excitement raising his voice by several decibels. "We're coming."

"Sister Vivien, children," they heard Nuba shout. "Come quickly. It's a miracle. God has answered our prayers. Maria and Brother Johann have arrived."

Vivien was waiting for him when Johann squeezed through the final gap. He held her body against his for what seemed like an eternity.

THREE

THE JOY AND excitement of the reunion lasted for several days. The children had forgotten the unpleasant circumstances associated with Maria's previous departure and were eager to renew their friendship. Maria regaled Beatrice, Keiko, and Jomo with tales of the maskets, sometimes embellishing the facts with her precocious imagination. Vivien and Sister Nuba told Johann how the nozzlers had grabbed the children while they were playing in the bay and the other details of what had happened to them since their separation. When Vivien referred for the first time to the "mystery man" who could somehow communicate with the nozzlers and had helped them get settled in the grotto, Johann explained who Dr. Jailani was and the reasons why the Malaysian scientist had originally come to Valhalla. Johann also told them that he suspected Dr. Jailani had been part of the adoclyne plot to kidnap Maria, although he admitted that he had no hard evidence to corroborate his accusation.

Johann was delighted to learn that in spite of the difficulty of their living conditions, Vivien's pregnancy, which was now in its fifth month, continued to be normal.

"I must have been created to be a mother," she laughed. "I have never had any problems, not even with labor or delivery."

"I really can't see that much difference," he said, patting her stomach affectionately. Johann grinned. "Except maybe your breasts are a little larger."

The first few days, when everyone else was asleep, Johann and Vivien dragged the seaweed mats provided by the adoclynes over against the opposite wall and made love with a quiet, subdued passion that amused Vivien.

"You don't have to be *that* gentle, giant Johann," she said with a coy smile after their second time together. "I assure you that your child will not be injured even if there's a little more vigor in your lovemaking."

Vivien, Sister Nuba, and the children had already developed a daily routine before Johann and Maria arrived. Because the glowing lights in their room always remained at substantially the same level, there was really no explicit way to gauge the passage of time. The only external events that occurred with any regular frequency were the deliveries of food and water by the adoclynes, which came approximately every eleven hours (a consensus estimate from the two women), and the appearance of the nozzler cleaner who emptied their crude toilet and collected their garbage between every sixteenth and seventeenth food delivery. The food, mostly seaweed with an occasional piece of meat from an unknown sea creature, came wrapped in a bundle tied to a rope pulley that ran along the top of one of the rock walls on the side of the tiny passageway between their room and the canal. The water arrived in a similar fashion, in a long cylindrical bucket hanging from a seaweed rope.

"But why is it necessary for them to send us water?" Johann asked. "Why don't we just fill the bucket from the canal?"

"One of the rules," Sister Nuba informed him, "is that we must stay completely inside our room here. Dr. Jailani was very explicit. Even the passageway is off limits."

"But that's ridiculous," Johann protested. "What if we want to take an extra bath or need some more water for some other reason?"

"The water allocations are really quite generous," Vivien said. "And they have made it obvious that they do intend for us to follow their rules. The children disobeyed us soon after we arrived," Vivien added, "and one of the nozzler patrols caught Jomo kicking his feet in the canal. He was pinched on the shoulder, enough to make him bleed, and Dr. Jailani showed up no less than an hour later. He made it clear that a repeat incident would have much more painful consequences."

"I think that the nozzlers don't want us to see what is happening on the canal," Sister Nuba suggested.

"What are the other rules?" Johann asked.

"Only one other of any major consequence," Vivien answered. "When the cleaning nozzler arrives, with or without Dr. Jailani, we are all to stand against the far wall, and not interfere in any way with the performance of its duties. Dr. Jailani said this rule is for our own protection. Cleaning our toilets and taking away our garbage, he informed us, is assigned to juvenile adoclynes who might interpret anything we do as hostile."

The women used the food deliveries to define and divide up their day. The sound of the food and water moving along the pulley was the morning alarm. Vivien and Sister Nuba woke the children, fed them breakfast, and then spent two or three hours in what Nuba creatively called "oral schooling." After school was exercise and games. Even though they had brought no toys with them, the adult women and the three children used their imaginations to make up games that required a minimum of props. A small lunch, saved from the morning delivery, was followed by a short nap, "religious discussion," and then free play. The next food and water delivery started the dinner preparations. After dinner was a story period, which lasted until it was time for bed.

Johann and Maria's arrival upset the routine somewhat, but by the third or fourth day they too had accepted the established regimen. The existence of Maria's new figurines, however, became a major source of contention during the games and play periods. Maria, well aware of the fact that she possessed the only desirable toys, quickly took control of the children's activities. She meted out rewards—playing with one or more of the figurines—according to her own caprice. Within a few days, she had purposely driven a wedge between her nemesis Beatrice and the other children.

Several days after their arrival, Johann was helping Vivien and Sister Nuba strip the inedible parts off a spherical sea creature when the disconsolate Beatrice came over to them with tears in her eyes. Across the room, Keiko, Maria, and Jomo were engaged in animated play with a tusker, an elevark, and one of the two maskets. "She won't let me play," Beatrice said angrily. "She says I can't even touch her toys without her permission."

Vivien pointed at the cache of small rocks against a nearby wall and suggested that Beatrice could play a game of checkers with either Johann or Sister Nuba, since all three of them were not needed in the dinner preparation.

Her mother's suggestion did not mollify the girl. "I don't want to play checkers," she yelled. "It's boring. I want to play with the figurines."

Johann crossed the room to the other children. "What's the problem, Maria?" he said evenly. "Why can't Beatrice play with you?"

"She won't follow the rules," Maria replied.

"You always *make* the rules," Beatrice shouted bitterly from across the room. "And *my* creature always dies first."

Maria started to respond but Johann quickly reached into the middle of the group and snatched all the figurines. "I'm sorry, children," he said, "but this game is over for today. I'm going to keep these toys until we can determine a fair way for everyone to play with them."

Maria's eyes flashed with anger. "They're *my* figurines, Johann," she said. "You gave them to me."

"Yes, I did, Maria," Johann said. "But we're in a different situation now. I can't make any new ones, and none of the other children have equivalent toys. You must all share these somehow."

Maria didn't say anything but her eyes indicated she was not happy with his decision.

THE NEXT SCHEDULED day for their adoclyne hosts to clean the toilet and take away the garbage was the seventh day after Johann and Maria arrived. While the children were playing a blindfold tag game invented by Johann and Sister Nuba, the two women were explaining to Johann in detail what their nozzler visitor would be doing.

"Do you think we would even *have* a toilet if Dr. Jailani couldn't communicate with them?" Vivien asked.

"We have no way of knowing," Johann said. "But I'm reluctant to give that guy credit for anything."

"You're too hard on him, Johann," Vivien said. "It's obvious he's been traumatized and brainwashed. The same thing might have happened to us under similar circumstances."

"I doubt it," Johann replied. "We might have succumbed to their power, but I can't imagine any of us deliberately helping alien creatures against members of our own species."

"Maybe he doesn't see it that way," Sister Nuba said. "Maybe Dr. Jailani believes he is actually making things less unpleasant for us. Imagine what might have happened if we had been confronted by the adoclynes without anyone to interpret."

The gory picture of Kwame and the nozzler with whom he struggled to the death appeared in Johann's mind and he recoiled involuntarily. "You may be right, Nuba," he said, "but I still think—"

Johann was interrupted by a pair of bass blasts coming from the direction of the canal. "They always signal us first," Vivien said. "That gives us a minute or two to move into our proper positions."

The children came over and sat next to the adults. Maria was the last to arrive. She looked at Johann with a quizzical expression, shrugged, and sat down casually between Sister Nuba and him.

A whirring noise was heard. Before the cylindrical brown waste container actually appeared, dangling from the rope pulley, Sister Nuba had informed Maria in detail what was going to happen. By the time the adoclyne appeared in the opening between the rocks, every human eye in the room was turned in that direction. This particular nozzler was indeed smaller than most Johann had seen. As it entered its tentacles and claws were retracted and coiled against the turquoise front segment, beside and below the three linear bulbous eyes. The creature trundled awkwardly into the room, its forward motion coming from the flow of hundreds of reedlike cilia, twenty centimeters long, that maintained contact with the rock floor. The nozzler stopped for a moment, the fluid motion in its oval eyes suggesting that it was watching the humans, and then moved toward the brown container that was hanging from the pulley apparatus.

A second pair of bass blasts shook the room a few seconds later. Both the first adoclyne, now holding the container aloft in one of its elevated claws, and all the humans turned toward the passageway where another, much larger nozzler was standing. Except for Maria, the children scrunched up closer to the adults as this second creature entered the room.

"We've never had *two* of them before," Sister Vivien leaned across and whispered to Johann. "This must be in your honor."

Or maybe Dr. Jailani didn't want to show up anymore, Johann thought, *now that he has been identified by me.*

The second adoclyne moved across the floor with less clumsiness. It took a position in the room halfway between the humans and the juvenile nozzler, who had by this time removed what looked like a large wooden scoop from the container and had started cleaning out the hole on the opposite side of their room. Johann watched the creature work with considerable fascination. It held the scoop in one of its claws and extended its tentacle deep into the hole. The scoop was slightly larger than a human hand and held a sizable quantity of material. The adoclyne worked continuously for five minutes or so, half filling the brown container. It had nearly finished its task when Maria announced that she was bored and suddenly stood up and walked away from the wall.

The response was instantaneous. A loud blast from the larger nozzler caused the working adoclyne to drop the scoop on the rock floor and extend its tentacles and claws in a defensive posture. "Come back here, *now*," Johann shouted at Maria, angry with himself for not having kept his arm around the girl. The adoclyne guard moved slowly in Maria's direction. She ran into the corner where the children had been playing earlier, a peculiar smile on her face, and bent down to pick up the elevark figurine. The nozzler, meanwhile, rapidly uncoiled and raised its two tentacles with the fearsome claws as it altered its path to head for Maria.

Her smile waning, Maria dodged over to another corner. The adoclyne came after her. Shortly she was trapped with her back against the wall. As the nozzler aimed its extended claws for her head and face, she put up her hands for protection and then bolted toward Johann and the others.

Maria screamed as the blue tentacles suddenly surged forward and wrapped around her waist. In seconds she was lifted a meter into the air, her feet kicking uselessly, and then pulled toward the nozzler's washboard mouth, which was now open with its knifelike teeth exposed.

Johann shouted and stood up, but the adoclyne restrained him by placing its other tentacle, bent around so that Johann was not threatened by the claw, forcefully against his chest.

Maria's screams continued unabated. The nozzler brought her within a few centimeters of its mouth before lofting the tentacle holding her high in the air, almost up to the ceiling. The creature held her there for several seconds, shaking her from side to side, before depositing her gently on the rock floor near where she had been sitting next to Johann. Maria lay in a crumpled heap where she had been placed.

The larger adoclyne returned to its position in the center of the room and emitted a pair of blasts. Its juvenile companion returned to its work. No more than two minutes later the two nozzlers connected the brown container to the pulley system and ambled through the opening in the rocks. Maria was still trembling when Johann came over to comfort her.

AFTER THE EVENT everyone, including Maria, realized that the nozzler's intention had only been to scare her. Nevertheless, the girl's fright did not immediately subside after the incident. For several days she refused to sleep anywhere except with her mat pressed against Johann's. She also had bad dreams several times, and woke up screaming. Each time she told Johann that a nozzler was tormenting her in her dreams.

Johann tried unsuccessfully to understand what had prompted Maria to test the rules. Each time he confronted her with the question Maria simply shook her head and said, "I don't know." The third or fourth time that he tried to elicit some different answer from her, Vivien gently intervened.

"You're making yourself miserable," she said to Johann, after leading him out of earshot of Maria. "She has no idea *why* she did it. And it's not even pertinent anymore."

Johann argued that unless the reason for Maria's unto-ward behavior could be understood, there was no certainty that another, similar incident might not occur. Vivien shook her head and gently caressed her husband's cheeks. "Dear, dear Johann," she said. "Even after all your experi-ence you still can't accept that human actions, especially those of children, cannot always be logically explained."

Her words struck a resonant chord in Johann's memory. Beatrice had made similar comments to him years before, telling Johann that he was reducing his own enjoyment of the mysteries of life by subjecting everything, even complex emotions, to rigorous analysis.

"Why would you expect that you could understand something like love?" Beatrice had said once. "After all, you're not God. You're only a single human being."

Johann heard what Vivien told him, and knew that she was convinced of its truth, yet his mind refused to accept most of what she was saying. *The most outstanding attribute of a human being is the ability to think,* he said stubbornly to himself. *Logic and analysis are nothing but thought refined to its highest level. Surely we are meant to apply our greatest talent to all the problems we encounter.*

AS THE TIME for the next adoclyne cleaning neared, Maria's anxieties became quite pronounced. Even Sister Nuba, who was usually optimistic about everything, was deeply concerned about what Maria might do when the nozzlers returned.

"Even if Maria stays beside us the entire time," Sister Nuba said, "simply seeing them again will surely bring back the terror of her last experience. And if she tries to run away, and we have a repetition of what happened before . . ." She didn't finish her thought. All three of the adults knew that Maria's fears would not diminish if she had frightening en-counters with the nozzlers every eight days.

"But what can we do?" Vivien asked. "We know they always come precisely on schedule. . . . Maybe if we had some way to contact Dr. Jailani, he could explain—"

"Suppose we empty the toilet ourselves," Johann suddenly interrupted. "The waste container arrives in the room before the nozzlers. What if I just took the scoop and was already at work when they showed up? They are intelligent creatures. They would figure out what was going on."

Both Vivien and Sister Nuba thought Johann's plan was dangerous and foolhardy, but they were unable to talk him out of it. When the bass blasts signaled the arrival of the adoclynes, the trembling Maria was seated between the two women against the wall. Johann was standing next to the terminus of the pulley system, waiting for the arrival of the brown container.

Johann had already placed three huge scoopfuls of material in the container when the first nozzler came through the opening. With a smile and a flourish, Johann leaned over and stuck his long arm into the hole with the scoop in his hand. The alien did not hesitate. It immediately issued a triple blast, which was repeated by its companion farther back in the passageway. It was less than a minute before the shrill alarm whistle resounded through the grotto.

"I think the police will be coming," Johann said to the others, attempting to remain calm. "Just sit still, and let me do the talking."

The two adoclynes who had come to clean their quarters moved just inside the room and stood against a wall beside the passageway. Soon the clanking of carapace segments from creatures hurrying through the narrow opening could be heard above the constant sounding of the alarm. Moments later, four of the largest nozzlers that Johann had ever seen poured into the room, one after another, their tentacles and claws all fully deployed. For maybe twenty seconds the four nozzler police discussed the situation with the two members of their species who had the cleanup duty.

"Look," Johann said during this time, pointing at the container and holding the scoop over his head. "I have been cleaning our toilet *myself*."

He dropped down on his knees and started to stick the scoop back into the hole, but his arm was seized by a tentacle and shaken with such force that Johann dropped the scoop. A tentacle from a second adoclyne pinned his other arm to his body. Across the room, the children began to cry.

Upward pressure in the tentacle wrapped around his chest forced Johann to stand up. He was being pulled toward the passageway. Two of the nozzler police were standing between Johann and the others. "Don't worry," he said bravely. "I'm sure—"

He was silenced by the whack of an open claw against his cheek. The sting was sharp, and blood began to flow down his face. Johann stopped resisting the pressure and headed for the narrow pathway between the rocks.

A new series of blasts from the direction of the canal preceded the relaxation of the tentacles wrapped around Johann's upper body. "Ouch," he heard Dr. Jailani say as the man tried to hurry from the canal to their room. When he entered their living area, he looked at Johann with a totally blank stare.

Nevertheless, during the next hour Dr. Jailani, still without showing any emotion, patiently communicated with everyone in the room, both humans and nozzlers. When he understood the situation, Dr. Jailani informed Johann that the adoclynes had essentially convicted him of an egregious rules violation, punishable by a temporary exile from all members of his species. He, Dr. Jailani, had been able to explain to the nozzlers that there were some extenuating circumstances in this particular case, and that Johann's action had been motivated by a desire to protect one of the human children. Johann would not be taken away from his family *this time*, Dr. Jailani said, but if there were any more similar violations of the rules, Johann would be removed from all human contact permanently.

Without waiting for any questions that Johann might have, Dr. Jailani instructed him to sit down on the floor, next to his children. The man then walked immediately over to the opening between the rock walls and summarily disappeared. The four members of the nozzler police filed out behind him. As the emotionally exhausted humans watched, the juvenile adoclyne who had entered their room first cleaned out their toilet under the watchful eyes of the nozzler guard standing in the middle of their living quarters.

FOUR

THERE WERE NO more incidents with the nozzler visitors. When the aliens appeared, always at the expected time every eight days, the humans dutifully sat against the opposite wall as they had been instructed. After each visit, Maria's fear of the adoclynes seemed to diminish a little more. By the time that six or seven cycles had passed, her behavior had returned to normal. Her recovery was undoubtedly aided by the love and care of Sister Nuba, whose patience and selflessness were remarkable.

During this time Johann was not very helpful to Maria. He was enmeshed in his own private struggle against the constraints of their existence. Each morning after waking he would engage in a set of push-ups, sit-ups, and isometric exercises, hoping for the same release of physical tension that he had obtained from the relaxed morning swims that had been part of his life for nine years. The exercises in the room were a poor substitute, however, and rarely softened Johann's increasing irritation with the world around him.

Vivien attempted to improve Johann's attitude by involving him more directly with the child growing inside her. She would hold his hand against her stomach during the baby's more active periods, and describe for him in detail what she was feeling inside her womb when his fingers would sense the thrust and thump of the child's elbow or knee. For a while, Johann's interest in this newest phase of Vivien's pregnancy pushed aside his gloom and depression, but the negative feelings returned, stronger than ever, in the days before he had the first of what became a series of disturbing dreams.

The dreams recurred in a predictable pattern, always just before he woke up. Suddenly whatever Johann had been dreaming would be interrupted and he would find himself in a labyrinth of dark tunnels. At first there would be no sound in this dream. Then he would hear a child cry, far off in the distance. Johann would weave his way among the tunnels, drawing closer and closer to the crying sound. When it seemed that the child must be just around the next corner, a nozzler would appear and block Johann's progress. The creature would advance slowly, its tentacles and claws well forward of its body. Johann would turn around to retreat, the child's cry still echoing through the dream, and discover that he was trapped. Behind him would be nothing but rock walls. He usually woke with a shudder when a threatening adoclyne claw was only a few centimeters away from his face.

Johann never fell back to sleep after having the recurring nightmare. He would lie on his back on the seaweed mat, listening to the sounds of the other humans sleeping around him. Vivien was next to him on his right, Maria on his left. Vivien occasionally emitted a tiny snore that was almost imperceptible, but most of the time her breathing was rhythmic and very quiet. Maria, on the other hand, was a bundle of energy while she slept. She tossed and turned, changed positions frequently, sometimes ground her teeth, and even talked and cried out during the night. She told Johann that she dreamed almost every night, but she never seemed to be able to describe what she had dreamed.

Johann shared his recurring nightmare with Vivien on a couple of occasions. Once he even attempted an explanation of what the dream meant, based on what he remembered from a book on the interpretation of dreams that he had read during his final year at the University of Berlin.

Vivien was amused by Johann's insistence that the nightmare would not go away until he made an attempt to find the child whose cry he had heard during his initial journey into the grotto.

"What in the world could you possibly do?" she said, holding his hands lovingly. "We're prisoners of the nozzlers, Johann, and we are not allowed out of our cell. That child is almost certainly also a prisoner. You don't know where she is and you couldn't help her even if you found her."

Johann continued to insist that he must do something. Every time the dream recurred, Johann concocted, and shared with Vivien, another possible plan for finding Serentha, or whoever the other child might turn out to be. Some of his plans were so farfetched that Vivien, in spite of her affection for Johann, would unwittingly laugh, causing him to become angry.

"You're just frustrated by the inactivity, Johann," Vivien said one morning after listening to Johann's newest plan. "It's completely understandable. You have no control over any significant element of your life." She smiled. "By the way, Dr. Freud, my guess is that the cry in your dreams is as much related to your concern about the fate of your *own* child as that other cry you heard along the canals."

Nevertheless, Johann remained resolute. Eventually Vivien, mostly because she was growing increasingly worried about his mental stability, allowed Johann to persuade her to participate in the first phase of his most logical plan. In return for helping him monitor the adoclyne patrol patterns in their region of the grotto, Vivien extracted from Johann a promise that if he were not able to find a schedule in these patterns, he would abandon, once and for all, his goal of discovering the location and identity of this mysterious child.

Vivien was not unduly concerned about the deal she had made with Johann until she discussed the plan with Sister Nuba, who would of course need to know why either Johann or she was missing from their living area during these monitoring periods. Nuba, who was usually quite soft-spoken, minced no words.

"How could you possibly agree to this?" Nuba replied immediately. "The consequences could be devastating for the children. Their lives are marginally acceptable now, for they don't often think about the bigger picture. But if either of you is caught watching the canal, and removed from our presence, the children will suffer immeasurably."

Johann was furious when Vivien told him that she would not help him with the monitoring. It was the first serious quarrel that the couple had ever had. When the tension between them did not subside after several days (during which time life in their tiny world was unbearable for everyone), Vivien capitulated in the interests of group harmony. In her heart she hoped that they would quickly and unambiguously discover that the adoclyne patrols operated on a completely random schedule.

Johann, on the other hand, had by this time convinced himself that the nozzlers must perform all their duties on a predetermined schedule. Their bringing of the food and water, and their visits to clean out the toilet, were as regular as clockwork. If Vivien helped him verify that the nozzler patrols also followed a predetermined schedule, and there was a significant time period between any pair of these visits, then Johann might be able to do some exploring in the canal system without being caught.

Johann and Vivien selected their monitoring post one night just after the children had fallen asleep. There was a natural spot along the tiny pathway between two rock walls where they could observe the canal clearly with very little risk of being seen themselves. They decided to monitor around the clock, and created, for the children, an imaginative and not implausible explanation for their irregular sleeping and disappearances. The surveillance started immediately, and Johann took the first shift.

The initial results suggested that Johann's conjecture was correct. Two adoclynes swam by the entrance to their area three times between every pair of food and water deliveries. The time period between these nozzler patrols was virtually a constant, at least as far as Sister Nuba, Vivien, and Johann could ascertain from their separate, individual methods of trying to estimate the amount of time that passed between appearances.

Johann was elated when additional monitoring confirmed the regularity of the patrols. He would have two and a half hours to swim in the canals without being noticed. Vivien had decidedly mixed feelings about the results. She was happy to see Johann excited and out of his pervasive gloomy mood, but she knew that the next phase of his plan was full of danger and uncertainty. Vivien confided her fears to Sister Nuba, who counseled her not to show the extent of her anxieties to Johann. Nuba then suggested that the two of them should ask God for an extra measure of strength and courage for the days ahead.

Both Johann and Vivien were awake long before the food and water delivery on the morning that had been designated by Johann as Exploration Day. Vivien had a new worry. "What if," she said quietly while lying in his arms, "the patrol times are different where the child is staying? You'll be caught for sure, and then we'll never see you again."

Johann had already thought about this possibility. "Maria and I heard the cry at the first junction before we reached here," he said. "The cell where the child is living must be in this general area of the grotto. It makes sense that patrols would go by there either immediately before or after they come here."

Vivien could tell that nothing she could say was going to dissuade him. She closed her eyes and pressed against Johann, hoping that she could stop the passage of time. When they heard the familiar whirring noise and Johann started to rise, Vivien took his hand and placed it against her stomach.

"Feel your son," she said. "For good luck." The child obligingly kicked strongly against Johann's fingers.

They had agreed that Johann would leave before the children were awake. Both Vivien and Sister Nuba had insisted that there should be no additional fanfare, that the children would simply be told the same story they had heard during the monitoring period, namely that Johann needed "private time" by himself and that the only available locations permitting any privacy were on the narrow pathway between their room and the canal.

JOHANN EDGED ALONG the pathway until he was out of sight of the room. Then he stood still about five minutes, as he had agreed with Vivien to do, to allow the adoclynes distributing the food in their region of the grotto to complete their deliveries. When he finally reached the canal and sat down on the bank, Johann's heart was pumping furiously and adrenaline was flooding through his system.

He eased into the water slowly, making only a minimal splash, and headed back toward the canal junction where he had heard the cry of the child. Johann swam breaststroke, with his head fully out of the water. As he rounded the first bend that carried him out of sight of the opening that led to their room, he turned around and swam back a little to make certain that he would be able to find his way back. Unfortunately, Johann's aging eyes and the dim lighting conspired against him. He could not even see their opening from this distance.

Treading water in the middle of the canal, Johann realized that there was a serious flaw in his plan. The canals and the surrounding rock walls were nearly indistinguishable, one from another, in this part of the grotto. It would be extremely easy to become lost and not be able to find his way back. Johann knew that what he was trying to do allowed little margin for error. Reluctantly, he backtracked to the opening, turned around, and started counting his rhythmic armstrokes.

It was a long way to the junction. Johann's stroke count had reached four hundred and eighty by the time he swam into the other fork of the canal and began a new count. Already becoming worried about time, he briefly considered turning around and making the effort on another occasion. Performing a quick mental calculation, however, Johann convinced himself that as long as he reached the other room in five hundred or fewer additional strokes, he could still spend fifteen minutes there and return home with enough time to spare.

When his stroke count in the new canal reached three hundred, Johann found an opening and a pathway leading through the rocks that lined the canal. Reminding himself that he had absolutely no idea what, if anything, he might find at the other end of this narrow passageway, Johann squeezed through it very slowly, stopping every step or two to listen for any possible sound. He heard nothing. When the path expanded into what appeared to be some kind of room, Johann hesitated. It was very dark here, the only light being that which filtered along the pathway from the canal.

Johann warily entered the room, straining his eyes to see if he could make out anything in the dark. He kept his right hand on the wall and continued to move forward, eventually making a full circle around the tiny room that was about half the size of the bedroom in his apartment at Valhalla. Johann then edged into the center of the room, using his feet to check for the presence of any objects on the rock floor. Nothing was there. Near the other side, however, he slipped when his foot nearly fell into a hole. Johann reached out to the wall for support and found a flat ledge, at chest level, that was similar to the ledge cut into the wall directly behind the toilet in their cell. After he regained his balance, Johann felt along the ledge and found small, broken pieces of rock as well as something round and flat that he picked up and put into the pocket that Vivien had sewn into his trunks.

After a couple more sorties into the middle of the room, on the last of which he was on his knees, with both hands searching the floor for anything other than rocks, Johann decided to return to the canal. Before slipping back into the water, he examined the round, flat object that he had picked up on the ledge. It was a medallion of some kind, clearly of human origin. On one side was an engraving of a young woman wearing a uniform; on the other was a single character that Johann thought was Chinese. Pleased with his discovery, and mindful that his time was now running out, he eased into the water and began swimming back toward his cell.

After a hundred strokes, Johann had already convinced himself that the room he had visited had previously been occupied by no more than two humans. There was absolutely no evidence of recent occupation. *But who had lived there?* Johann thought. *And why did they leave? And where are they now?*

Johann was pondering these unanswerable questions when a faint child's cry echoed along the canals. He stopped and treaded water to make certain that his mind was not playing tricks on him. No, that was definitely a human cry that he was hearing. Johann turned into his fork of the canal with a surge of excitement. *I'm returning to my place now,* he told himself, *but I'll be back to find you very soon.*

WHEN JOHANN REACHED his living area, the children quickly gathered around and started peppering him with questions. After a quick exchange of glances with the other two adults, Johann told the truth about what he had been doing.

The children were especially fascinated with his story.

Beatrice had an immediate explanation for the empty room. "That's where they'll put one of us if we're bad, and disobey the rules," she said. She turned to little Jomo. "How would you like to live in a tiny dark room all by yourself?" she said.

"Wouldn't like it," Jomo answered, still stroking the wet trunks that Johann was wearing.

The medallion was passed around the room. There was general agreement that the article was proof that some other human being had been living in that room at some time in the past. After Johann had finished his story, and shrugged off Maria's question about when he was going to go "out exploring" again, Sister Nuba approached Johann, looking very serious, and asked if she could discuss something with him privately.

"That medallion belonged to Satoko," Nuba said, when Johann and she were out of earshot of the others. "She was very proud of it. It was given to her when she graduated from nursing school."

Johann's eyes showed his astonishment. "When Satoko was having her mental difficulties, at the village," Sister Nuba continued, "I often spent hours sitting by her side and listening to her talk. She showed me that medallion several times."

"Do you know if she had it with her when she disappeared?" Johann asked.

Nuba shook her head. "No, but nobody ever mentioned finding it among her things."

Johann whistled. "So Satoko may still be alive," he said, half to himself.

Sister Nuba looked over her shoulder at the children, who were playing on the far side of the room. "Let's not say anything yet to Keiko," she said. "Not until we know more."

Johann reflected for a moment. "But we do know a lot already. Either Satoko or someone from Ravi and Anna's family has almost certainly been in this grotto. . . . Unless

Dr. Jailani or someone else picked up this artifact from Satoko's body or from the village."

"That last possibility seems very unlikely to me, Brother Johann," Nuba replied after a brief hesitation. "I prefer to believe that God has sent this medallion as a sign that we are all going to be reunited."

Johann smiled. "You're probably right, Sister Nuba," he said lightly. "Forgive me, but it's just my nature to consider *all* the possible explanations."

THE ENTIRE GROUP participated in the planning for Johann's next sortie, which was scheduled to occur after the food and water delivery the next morning. This time everyone was awake before he left, and Maria even asked if she could accompany him, citing her outstanding swimming ability as her primary qualification. Vivien and Sister Nuba reiterated to Maria and the other children how very dangerous Johann's sortie could be, and how important it was for him to go alone.

Johann's swim to the fork in the canal was uneventful. He turned the corner and began counting his strokes. After he passed the small empty room on his right, the canal turned sharply to the left and then split into two forks again. Johann had not anticipated this. Eventually he took the right fork, telling himself that the other human room was likely to be physically close to their location.

He became concerned about the stroke count as it neared five hundred. His eyes carefully examining the rock walls on both sides of the canal, Johann decided that he would turn back if the stroke count reached six hundred and he still hadn't found anything. Just as he was turning around to head back, he spotted an opening on the right side of the canal. He swam over to the shore and climbed out of the water. He inched forward slowly, listening for any sounds that might give him a clue about what was ahead. He noticed that the light around him was not diminishing significantly, suggesting that whatever was in front of him had its own source of light.

The passageway led to a room of approximately the same size as the room in which Johann and his extended family were living. Five people were sleeping on seaweed mats on the far side of the room. Crossing the room quietly, Johann confirmed that the four together were Ravi, his wife, Anna, and their two children, Eric and Serentha. Satoko was sleeping by herself, a few meters away from the rest.

Johann bent down beside Anna and started gently shaking her.

"What is it, darling?" she said softly, not opening her eyes.

"It's Johann Eberhardt, Anna," he said. "I've come over from another room in the grotto."

Anna's eyes opened and she stared at Johann, blinking frequently, for several seconds. "Oh, my God," she said then. "I must be going mad." She reached out and touched Johann's arm. "Is that really you, Johann?" she asked. "And not some bizarre dream?"

Johann assured her that he was real. Anna rolled over and grabbed her husband's arm. "Ravi, wake up," she said, shaking him vigorously. "We have a visitor . . . and it's Johann Eberhardt!"

When Ravi saw Johann he bolted up from his mat and scrambled to his feet. "What are you doing here? How did you get here?" he sputtered while reaching out to shake Johann's hand.

Johann started giving a brief answer but both Ravi and Anna kept interrupting him with more questions. The general clamor awakened the children and Satoko, who crossed the room to join in the conversation. The girl Serentha, who was the same age as Jomo, started crying as soon as she saw the huge blond stranger. Johann noted to himself that it had indeed been her cry that Maria and he had heard before.

At one point in the confused conversation, Johann told Satoko that her daughter, Keiko, was fine and staying with them in their grotto room. The woman immediately began to jump around and flail her arms wildly through the air, shouting continuously while tears ran down her cheeks. She then unleashed a flurry of questions that made Johann stop completely his discussion with Ravi and Anna.

The scene was complete chaos. Johann, becoming acutely aware of the passage of time, struggled without success to impose some order on the conversation. He had some questions also. He wanted to know under what conditions the others had been brought to the grotto, how long they had been there, and what had been the nature of their interactions with the adoclynes and/or Dr. Jailani. But he was never even allowed to finish one of his questions, much less obtain any answers, because everyone kept speaking at once. Finally, in desperation Johann raised his arms above his head and shouted "Silence" in a loud voice.

Everyone quieted down immediately, except for Serentha, whose steady cry escalated into a terrible wail. "I'm sorry," Johann said, "but I'm in a hurry. I must return to my own living area before the next alien patrol. We don't have time for any more discussion now, but hopefully, I'll return safely and be able to come again. What's important is that we now know about each other and that we've all managed to survive."

Satoko raced over to her mat and retrieved a silver ring that she insisted Johann carry back to Keiko. Rather than argue with her, Johann slipped the ring on his little finger and prepared to depart. Ravi came over and gave him a friendly hug. By the time Johann reached the canal, he figured he was about five minutes late.

He swam fast, with powerful arm strokes and driving frog kicks that propelled him through the water. Johann passed the first fork without incident and was no more than twenty meters away from the entrance to the canal branch leading to his own room when two loud nozzler blasts reverberated off the walls. The blasts sounded very close. Johann pulled as much air into his lungs as possible, visually measured the distance to his branch entrance, and dove under the surface of the water. Stroke after stroke, he moved through the canal completely submerged.

He did not rise to the surface until he thought he was going to pass out. Once, Johann's head glanced off one of the underwater rock walls. He simply changed his direction and continued to swim. When he did finally raise his head out of the water, Johann was certain that he was now in the canal branch that ran by his living area.

Or was he? As he swam, the walls around him suddenly started looking unfamiliar. He began a stroke count, and tried to estimate how far he had come while underwater, but Johann knew that his estimate was probably inaccurate. Besides, he was now becoming fatigued. The combination of the fast swimming at the beginning and the long underwater stretch had worn him out.

He started imagining that he had passed his opening. The anxiety increased as he continued to swim. Johann fortunately saw the passageway to his room just before he decided to turn around and swim in the opposite direction to his doom. As it was, he was barely out of the water when he heard nozzler blasts behind him. He lunged into the opening, banging his forehead and right elbow hard against the sharp rocks on the wall, and managed to be barely out of sight when the adoclyne patrol passed. Exhausted and bleeding from the rock cuts, Johann stumbled into his living area and collapsed on his mat.

FIVE

AFTER HIS NARROW escape, Johann did not argue with Vivien and Sister Nuba when they both insisted that swimming in the canals was foolhardy at best. The two women were also afraid that Satoko's medallion and the ring for Keiko might be recognized by the cleaning nozzlers; they demanded that both items be carefully concealed each time the adoclyne visitors entered their living area.

In spite of Vivien's and Sister Nuba's desire for their family life to return to the routine that had existed before Johann's pair of sorties, the group's existence was irrevocably altered by the knowledge that their friends were also living in the grotto, in similar conditions, not far away. The children's play reflected this fact immediately. Beatrice and Keiko had grown up with Eric and had essentially been big sisters to baby Serentha. At the children's request, Johann used his knife to mark a pair of large rocks with the initials E and S. The two rocks represented Ravi and Anna's children and often became integral parts in the games that were played.

Among the adults, the missing others were the main topic of many late-night conversations. Both Vivien and Sister Nuba told anecdotes from the days when everyone except Johann and Sister Beatrice had been living in the tepee village. Satoko's presence in the grotto engendered a virtual flood of question and speculation. Although Johann had had hardly any interaction with her during his brief visit to the other room, he was repeatedly asked by Vivien and Nuba about her "overall condition."

For Keiko, the knowledge that her mother was alive awakened feelings that had long been suppressed. Her behavior also profoundly changed. For example, never before had Keiko ever indicated that she was jealous of the relationship between Vivien and Beatrice. After Johann's sortie, however, Keiko became more moody, often quarreling with Beatrice. "You wouldn't see it that way if you were *my* mother," she said on two different occasions when Vivien resolved seemingly insignificant disputes in favor of Beatrice.

Because Johann had seen and talked with Satoko, Keiko came to him often to discuss her mother. Sometimes Maria, whose motherlessness had always been part of her bond with Keiko, participated in the conversations. Slowly but surely, as two, three, and then four visits from the adoclyne cleaners passed, a perceptible rift developed in the extended family. Maria, Keiko, and Johann were on one side; Vivien, Sister Nuba, Beatrice, and little Jomo on the other. The seriousness of this rift became obvious one day when another of the petty arguments between Maria and Beatrice escalated into an angry exchange of words between Johann and Vivien.

That evening Sister Nuba, always the peacemaker, identified the dissension in their group as a significant detriment to the children's growth and solicited suggestions from Johann and Vivien on how to reverse the process that had created the problem. Vivien, plagued by heartburn and the hormonal imbalance of the last trimester of pregnancy, was feeling slighted and ignored by Johann anyway. She was in no mood to compromise. Johann, who disliked conversations about emotions under even the best circumstances, offered nothing substantive to resolve the dispute. In a fit of pique, Vivien moved her sleeping mat away from Johann's side. At Maria's suggestion, Keiko pulled her mat into the spot vacated by Vivien.

An unpleasant pall settled over their lives. Maria and Keiko played together, purposely ignoring Beatrice and Jomo. When Johann would not intercede, and force the two girls to play with Vivien's children, the tension in the room became palpable. Comments that would previously have been considered innocent were misconstrued as insults. When the adoclyne cleaners came again, Vivien was sitting with her two children on one end of the wall opposite the hole, with Johann, Maria, and Keiko at the other end. The dejected Sister Nuba sat by herself in the middle, praying that God would give her the cleverness to resolve the growing discontent among the members of her extended family.

JOHANN WAS SWIMMING a competitive race in his dream. In the lane next to him was his archrival during his three years of international competition, Carlo Lamberti from Italy. They were nearing the halfway point in a two-hundred-meter race and Johann and Carlo, in the middle lanes of the pool since they were the top two seeds, were already a full body length ahead of the rest of the field. Johann executed a perfect flip turn, gathered himself against the wall, and pushed off with all the force of his long powerful legs. He broke the water half a length ahead of his rival.

Johann took one breath on each side before he heard his name being called. He glanced over at the adjacent lane and Carlo Lamberti was no longer swimming there. It was Maria, treading water. Suddenly Johann's dream venue was not the international pool in Milano; Maria and he were out in the lake near the island where he had raised her.

She grinned at him. "Wake up, Johann," she said softly. "I need to talk to you."

Johann opened his eyes and the waters of his dream vanished. Both Maria and Keiko were sitting on their knees near his head. He started to say something in his normal voice, but Maria placed a finger on his lips. "Shh," she said. "We don't want anyone else to hear." She glanced knowingly across the room to where the others were sleeping.

Johann sat up on his mat with a puzzled, unpleasant frown on his face. "There's something we want to talk to you about," Maria whispered before Johann could say anything. She looked over at Keiko.

"Uncle Johann, would you take me to my mother? Please, please, please?" the girl said.

Johann shook his head to make certain he had heard correctly. "We have a plan already," Maria said immediately. "One more nozzler patrol will go by tonight. Then there will be plenty of time before the breakfast delivery."

Keiko leaned toward him and touched his forearm. "I have not seen my mother since I was a baby, Uncle Johann," she entreated. "I don't even know what she looks like."

Johann remained speechless for a few more seconds, struggling to find words that would not hurt the little girl's feelings. While Keiko was waiting for his response, two big tears eased out of her eyes and rolled slowly down her cheeks. Johann automatically pulled her to him and gave her a fatherly hug. "Everything's going to be all right," he said.

Both girls misinterpreted his words and actions. "I'll go out to the rocks beside the canal and watch for the patrol," Maria said excitedly. "I'll let you know the moment it's gone." She vanished in an instant.

Keiko pulled away from Johann's embrace and kissed him on the nose. Her eyes were now flooded with tears of gratitude. "Thank you, Uncle Johann," she said simply. "You're my hero."

Johann started to protest, to explain that he could not possibly do what she was requesting, but before he could formulate the words that would sorely disappoint her, he heard what he thought was Beatrice's voice inside his head. *Why not?* the voice said. *What could be more worth taking a risk than reuniting a mother and her daughter?*

Astonishing even himself, Johann began drafting a plan for their sortie, sharing it with Keiko and revising it as they talked. The girl became so excited that it was hard for her to keep her voice down. At one point Johann heard stirring sounds from across the room and thought they had awakened either Vivien or Sister Nuba. Keiko and he sat in total silence until they could hear no more sounds from across the room.

Maria returned long before Johann expected. He hurriedly finished his preparations and walked with Keiko over to the pathway between the rocks. Maria kissed them both good-bye and wished them good luck. "Thank you, oh thank you, Johann," she whispered in his ear. "I knew you would do it."

Keiko went through the passageway first and then waited on the bank of the canal while Johann slipped into the water. He backed up to where she was standing and instructed her to put her arms around his neck. Johann explained again that he was going to swim breaststroke, just beneath the surface. Keiko would be able to keep her head out of the water if she used her legs to kick and held on with her hands just underneath Johann's chin.

At first the swimming was awkward. Keiko seemed to be fighting against him. She also kicked him hard once and choked him twice when she thought she was falling off. Johann stopped, treading water while holding the girl, and patiently explained to her what she was doing wrong. Soon after they started swimming again they settled into a rhythm that significantly reduced Johann's effort.

Johann was attempting to count strokes, but it was difficult under the circumstances. What was certain was that it took him longer to swim carrying Keiko than if he were swimming himself. But how much longer? How much total time did he need to allocate to account for the child on his back? Of course Johann did not know the precise answer. But when Keiko asked a second, and then a third time, if they could stop while she caught her breath, Johann knew that they would not be able to stay very long at their destination.

They found the opening between the rocks without any difficulty. Johann lifted Keiko onto the bank. Although he had asked her to follow him through the passageway and not to say anything until he verified that there was no danger, Johann and Keiko were barely out of sight of the canal when she started yelling, "Mom, it's Keiko! I've come to see you!"

Johann let the eager Keiko squeeze by him at one wide spot in the passageway and she began to run despite the narrowness of the path. Johann heard the squeals of delight before he reached the room. When he came into the living area, Satoko and Keiko were in a full, joyous embrace, both of them dancing with excitement. Ravi, Anna, Eric, and Serentha were standing just beyond them, Serentha in her father's arms and Eric holding Anna's hand. There was not a single dry eye in the room. Even the baby Serentha was crying, although she doubtless did not understand why everyone else was so happy.

TO AVOID THE consternation that had characterized his last visit, Johann took Ravi and Anna aside immediately and explained to them why Keiko and he could not stay very long. He shared with them both his knowledge of the nozzler patrol schedules and the geography of their region of the grotto, as well as his estimates for the length of time it had taken him to swim, with Keiko on his back, between their two living areas. Meanwhile, the overjoyed Satoko continued to shower her daughter with spontaneous embraces and to ask her questions about all the minutiae of her life. Eric walked in circles around Keiko and her mother, taking advantage of any lapses in the conversation to insert a question or make a comment. The curious Serentha, no longer crying, amused everyone at one point by approaching Keiko from the side, running her fingers over her wet clothes, and then hugging her awkwardly.

The time went by rapidly. Keiko was explaining to Satoko what a good substitute mother Vivien had been for her when Johann interrupted their conversation and informed them that it was time to go. He was unprepared for the response. To Satoko, it was unthinkable that she and her daughter, after having been apart for years, would now be separated again after such a short reunion. It was also obvious that Keiko wanted to stay with her mother. Johann's suggestion that it could be extremely dangerous for Keiko to stay in this room provoked such a passionate outburst from Satoko that he literally did not know what to do.

Ravi and Anna both understood that Keiko's presence in their living area, if noticed, would clearly indicate to the adoclynes that the two groups of humans had purposely broken the grotto rules so carefully explained by Dr. Jailani. They tried unsuccessfully to intercede with Satoko, causing her behavior to become even more erratic. After a few minutes Keiko, frightened by her mother's intermittent wails and curses, put her arms around Satoko and told her that she was staying, no matter what Johann, Ravi, and Anna said. The girl correctly pointed out to her mother, who began to calm down, that there was no way Johann could take her back against her will.

Johann was now angry with himself. *You could have predicted this outcome,* he thought, *if you had not been swayed by emotion.* Aware that he was now critically short of time, Johann asked Ravi and Anna how long it would be before their next adoclyne cleaning visit. He promised to return for Keiko before then. Johann did not underestimate the nozzlers. He was certain that any contact with the aliens would result in an immediate realization that one of the children had changed locations. Johann was equally certain that there would be dire ramifications for both human groups following that realization.

He said hasty good-byes, embracing the thankful Satoko and Keiko only briefly, and hurried into the narrow passageway that led to the canal. Moving too quickly along the unknown path, Johann slipped badly in one spot, smacking his shoulder against one of the walls and wrenching his right knee in the process. He was not aware of the severity of his knee injury until he entered the water and started swimming. Every time Johann made a frog kick, the pain in his knee increased.

Johann faced a difficult dilemma. If he couldn't kick, he knew he couldn't swim breaststroke fast enough to return to his living area before the breakfast delivery. If he swam freestyle, he would make it back in time, but he would also make a lot of noise and churn up the water in the process. Originally, Johann had decided that it was safer to be as unobtrusive as possible and swim breaststroke in the canals, since it was likely, based on the way the adoclynes communicated with each other, that their hearing was very sensitive. In his current situation, however, he decided that he really didn't have a choice. He would swim freestyle and hope that the aliens did not hear him.

He made it to the first canal fork without incident. Only a hundred meters away from the branch that led to his living area, however, Johann heard the shrill sound of the alarm that indicated something was amiss in their region of the grotto. Treading water near the center of the canal, Johann fought against panic and searched both walls for a possible hiding place. Over to his right was an irregular part of the wall that created a small alcove. With the alarm still sounding, he swam in that direction. Johann was delighted to discover that because of the alcove's shape he could only be seen if someone or something was very close to him.

A pair of nozzler blasts in the distance were answered by a trio of sounds that were much closer. Johann moved almost to the wall, took a deep breath, and submerged as deeply as he could. He stayed down until he thought his lungs would explode. When he resurfaced, the alarm was no longer audible. Johann convinced himself that whatever crisis had caused the sounding of the alarm had now passed.

Now, however, Johann had another problem. There was no way he could reach his living area before breakfast delivery. It would be necessary for him to remain where he was, spending as much time underwater as possible to avoid being seen, until the adoclynes had finished with their rounds. For fifteen minutes Johann bobbed up and down in the alcove, spending ninety-five percent of his time underwater. Many times he heard nozzler blasts when he came up for a breath, and twice he felt the water swell as if something had moved through the canal very close to him. Finally, after hearing no nozzler sounds for several minutes, Johann, now bothered both by fatigue and the pain in his knee, eased his way out into the canal and started swimming very slowly.

A few minutes later he turned into the canal branch that led to his living area. Johann was within forty meters of his grotto home when a huge nozzler, who had obviously been waiting for him, suddenly rose out of the water directly in front of him and emitted a terrifying pair of blasts. Johann struck the tentacle trying to seize him with a downstroke of his right hand, turned in the water, and started swimming in the opposite direction. By the time he reached the canal junction, he was surrounded by three of the adoclynes.

Realizing that it was useless to resist, Johann allowed the nozzlers to wrap their tentacles around him. They dragged him through the water at an amazing speed. At the sentry intersection, a small raft was waiting. The nozzlers hoisted Johann onto the raft, released him from the re-straining tentacles, and guided the raft through the grotto. A pair of nozzlers preceded the raft, announcing their presence with periodic blasts.

All traffic moved out of the way. Johann's raft passed by the main grotto intersection, where the rendition of the glowing ribbon structure was still in place, and continued until it reached the very first canal fork just inside the entrance. Johann briefly saw the light from outside the grotto and wondered if he would ever see it again. A few minutes later, the raft passed under a raised seaweed gate into a small cul-de-sac and stopped next to an open room cut into the right wall. When Johann didn't move, one of the guiding adoclynes pointed at the room with a blue tentacle and emitted a short blast. Johann then crawled off the raft into the front of the room. He watched as the raft retraced its path. The seaweed gate descended into the water after the raft vanished beyond the entrance to the cul-de-sac.

SIX

JOHANN'S CELL WAS tiny, no more than five meters wide and eight meters from the canal to the back wall. The ceiling was low and irregular—near the back, where there was a familiar hole for wastes and garbage, Johann could not even stand up straight. The back part of his cell was much darker than the front, since the only light came from a glowing nest high on the opposite wall of the canal.

When Johann was first placed in the cell, he found a thick sheath of edible seaweed lying against one of the side walls, as well as a normal seaweed mat for sleeping. Looking around his cell, Johann considered himself fortunate. *After all,* he thought, *they might have executed me. In some ways the nozzlers are more civilized than we are.*

After a quick snack, Johann decided to survey his new realm. There was nothing to see in his cell. He entered the water and swam to the back wall of the cul-de-sac. Johann then turned around and swam back to examine the gate, which was approximately fifteen meters from the back wall. The gate fit snugly in place. He could stick his hands under the bottom, or between the wall and the sides of the gate, but there was certainly no space large enough for him to escape. Johann vainly tried lifting the gate from the bottom, pushing it at water level, and striking it with his fist. For his efforts all he achieved was a slight back strain and a bruised hand.

He drank some of the canal water and noted its fresh, soothing taste. Then Johann returned again to his cell and sat down on his mat. *It could be much worse,* he told himself. *I have food and water. The canal section is long enough and deep enough that I can exercise. The only significant drawback is that I am alone.*

THE ADOCLYNES BROUGHT Johann new food at irregular intervals, making it impossible for him to obtain any accurate measure of time. He learned that the size of the seaweed sheath that was left for him on the lip of the cell was indicative of how long it would be before he was visited again by the aliens. Whenever his cell was cleaned, which was infrequently, the task was performed by the nozzler who brought his food. Watching the cleaning activity for about five minutes was Johann's sole interaction with another living creature. The other adoclynes never even left the water on the visits when they deposited new food on the lip of his cell.

For the first ten days or so of his confinement, Johann's loneliness was manageable. He swam, ate, and slept whenever he felt like it. He allowed his mind to jump from topic to topic without any overall sense of direction. In general, he was not overly discontent with his life.

Soon, however, the purposelessness of his existence began to weigh heavily upon him. Throughout his life, a considerable proportion of his time and energy had always been spent planning for future events and activities. Even when he had been with the family group in the grotto, Johann had busied himself during a part of every day organizing everyone's activities, thinking about what he might do with the children, what he wanted to discuss with Nuba, when he might have some private time with Vivien, et cetera. In his current situation, the future was forever like the present. He had no idea how long his confinement would last, and no way of finding out. Any thoughts about the future seemed useless.

He began to experience extended periods of abject depression. During these periods Johann did not eat, he did not swim, and he did not really sleep. He would sit and stare for hours at the same spot on the wall, unaware of any thoughts except a longing for his emotional pain to be over. At the end of one such episode Johann was surprised to discover that he had been crying. He could not remember what had prompted the tears, or when they had begun.

Johann knew that he would wither away and die if he did not break the cycle of depression. Yet he was powerless against its pervasive grip on him. He tried thinking about Vivien and his unborn child, but his momentary pleasure in conjuring up images of his first son or daughter was destroyed by the realization that he would probably never even see the child.

Johann's bouts of depression did not diminish until after the third nozzler cleaning visit. By this time he estimated that he had been living in his cell for about two human months. Forcing himself to be interested in some element of his life, Johann stared fixedly at the adoclyne, following its every action during its brief stay. From the far side of the room, sitting with his back against the rock wall, Johann carefully examined the undulating motion of its cilia as it walked, the dexterity of the tentacle-and-claw combination as they scooped up the wastes and placed them in a brown container, and the movement in the three linear eyes as the creature worked. Its stance while it was emptying the hole was with its turquoise head mostly facing Johann. The middle eye always seemed to be watching him; the forward eye paid attention to the progress of the work.

When Johann stood up near the end of the alien's activity, the clustered pearls on the side of its head immediately pulsated and two short blasts came through tiny holes that had formed among the pearls. The nozzler temporarily stopped what it was doing and both front eyes focused on Johann. After he sat down again, the creature returned to its task.

Once his visitor was finished, it trundled across the cell

with its right tentacle and claw carrying the container by a seaweed handle. The container was placed in a short canoe and the adoclyne slipped into the water. It issued a sequence of blasts and the seaweed gate was raised. The nozzler and the canoe passed under the gate, which closed immediately, and Johann was left by himself again.

Johann's curiosity and fascination with the nozzler had lifted his spirits. During those few minutes he had been watching the alien, he had been glad that he was alive. Johann stood up and paced around his cell. *I do not want to lose this feeling,* he told himself, *and sink again into an abyss of gloom. What can I do to fight against my feelings of purposelessness?*

He entered the water and began swimming laps between the gate and the wall at the back of the cul-de-sac. During this long, lazy swim Johann concluded that the only way he could infuse his current life with any sense of meaning was to create some kind of project or task for himself, the completion of which would become his goal and temporary reason for living.

While eating strips of seaweed from the new food that had been delivered, Johann, fully aware of all the limitations of his circumstances, considered what kinds of projects he might undertake. *Somehow I must make it meaningful,* he thought, *otherwise I run the risk of deluding myself. The best project would be something both interesting in itself and useful if I were ever to be released from this cell.*

He listed several options for himself, including reviewing all he had ever learned about science and engineering, conducting a geographical survey by making mental maps of Mars and Earth, and creating an autobiographical chronology with all the major highlights of each phase of his life. Although the last activity had promise, Johann realized quickly that his memory had not stored data with time tags, or other chronological references, and that there was really no way he could accomplish the task. At length he decided that he would assess all the major relationships in his life and see what he could learn from reflecting upon his past interactions with other people.

He spent a few hours the next morning thinking about the proper order for his assessments. Should he review the relationships based on their significance in his life *(and how do I decide,* he wondered, *if Sister Beatrice or my mother was more important in my life?)*? In chronological order? According to some other arrangement? He eventually concluded that since he had no time constraints, the order was irrelevant.

Johann's decision to undertake this project dramatically changed his perspective on his solitary life. In his own mind, he now had something meaningful to do each day. He enjoyed his food again, felt invigorated after swimming, and even laughed out loud at times when recalling specific vignettes from his life. As the days passed, and Johann realized how close he had come to capitulating to his most pessimistic feelings, he repeatedly thanked the nozzler who had cleaned his cell for having rekindled his passion for life.

Johann's immersion in the nuances of his involvement with other people was a new experience for him. An engineer by training and predilection, most of his thinking energy had always been directed toward understanding concepts and working out solutions to problems. People and feelings, both theirs and his, had usually been just variables or parameters in what he was trying to comprehend. Unfettered by time constraints or a directed search for answers and solutions, Johann found himself, for the first time, occupied with *what* he and others had done and felt in a given situation, instead of *why*.

One of his earliest realizations was how utterly devastated his father must have been by the family's financial failures during the Great Chaos. Previously, he had understood that the collapse of his father's accounting business had irrevocably transformed Johann's relationship with his parents, and that almost overnight he had become the parent and they the children. But he had never taken the time to try to imagine what his father must have felt during this transformation, and how hard it must have been for him to have become financially dependent upon his only son. For the first time in his life, Johann shed tears of empathy for his father, and chastised himself for all the cruel and unkind things that he had said about him.

He saw new facets in every relationship he examined. Now, with no certainty that he would ever again have any association with another human being, Johann treasured these memories from the past. His uncle Hermann's nobility seemed almost legendary from this distance. Banished from his sister's and nephew's life for his sexual orientation, Johann's uncle had nevertheless come to his family's rescue when their lives were in dire straits.

Johann winced when he thought about his friend and coworker Bakir. How he had let him down! If Johann had only taken a moment, all those years ago, to imagine what Bakir was feeling during those terrible days of persecution, and to think about how difficult it must have been for the proud Turk to ask Johann for help, the result would have been completely different. There was no guarantee that Johann could have ultimately prevented the deportation of Bakir and his family, but at least Bakir would not have undergone all that additional horror believing that his best German friend had deserted him.

Of all the people on his list, only Maria's father, Yasin al Kharif, produced memories that were overwhelmingly negative. Johann now saw quite clearly what a mistake it had been for him to bring Yasin to work at Valhalla in the first place. Even though Yasin's intelligence and engineering skills were superb, they should have been irrelevant when weighed against his sociopathic behavior. Johann realized now that he had made a devil's bargain for which he had later paid a terrible price. Without Johann's decision to employ Yasin at Valhalla, it would not have been possible for Yasin to appear later as the interloper who transformed Johann and Beatrice's extraterrestrial island paradise into an unmitigated hell.

Johann could not spend much time thinking about Yasin. Feelings of raw hatred for the man, emotions Johann had purposely suppressed for Maria's sake, boiled out of Johann when he recalled the events that had led to Beatrice's humiliation and death. *He deserved to be murdered,* Johann thought, surprised that after all these years he felt no contrition for his action.

For a long period Johann focused on the three women who had been his intimate companions for extended intervals in his life. His girlfriend in Berlin, Eva, had been tremendous in bed, inventive, uninhibited, and possessed with an overwhelming desire to please. Johann had thought that their sexual rapport might have been a strong enough basis upon which to build a marriage. Fortunately, the circumstances in Johann's life had allowed him to postpone the wedding until it became apparent that Eva and he had little else in common.

Vivien was a marvelous friend and companion, and as good a lover as Eva. Vivien's sense of humor and her general positive attitude were her strongest attributes—it was virtually impossible to be grumpy or gloomy around Vivien. Johann's love for Vivien was steady, unwavering, and comfortable. It had never consumed or possessed him. Only once in his lifetime had he experienced that kind of passion.

Whenever Johann started thinking about Beatrice, his heart always skipped a beat. He recalled reading somewhere that in each person's life there is never more than one "grand and passionate romance." In Johann's mind there was no doubt that Sister Beatrice, raised as Kristin Larsen in Edina, Minnesota, the United States of America, was the grand and passionate romance of his life. From the moment that he first heard her magnificent voice, practicing "O Holy Night" in the new Michaelite church on Mars, until she died in his arms in a cave inside this bizarre and still un-explained alien worldlet, Beatrice had fascinated Johann and touched him in ways that no other human had.

It had certainly not been love at first sight. In fact their early encounters, when she was the Michaelite bishop of Mars and he the director of the Valhalla facility that sup-plied water to the human colonies on the red planet, had been tinged with friction. Sister Beatrice's certitude had annoyed Johann. Her declaration that the strange, glowing ribbons of particles both of them had seen were angels sent from God, and her unwillingness to consider any other possible explanation, had irritated him.

Yet even then, in those early days on Mars, Johann said to himself as he walked around his cell, *there was a definite elec-tricity in the air every time we were together. I didn't recognize it at the time, and she was so consumed by her devotion to God and her work that she never would have admitted it. . . .*

Then suddenly they were a pair, a man and a woman separated from all other human contact, living on an island paradise inside a spacecraft created either by God's angels or by some advanced extraterrestrial species. Johann experi-enced a love beyond anything he had ever imagined. And it was not unrequited. Beatrice loved him too, as a woman loves a man, but she was not yet far enough removed from her Michaelite vows of chastity to allow herself to consum-mate their very human love affair.

Alone in his cell, reliving the memory of the happiness of that first hundred days with Beatrice was too much for Johann. A flood of tears burst from his eyes. "Oh, Beatrice," he said out loud. "How I miss you! How I adored you!"

Johann sat down on his mat, put his face in his hands, and sobbed. He could not have told anyone exactly why he was crying. As a montage of poignant images poured into his mind—Beatrice singing to him on the beach, Bea-trice finally kissing him like a woman and not a priestess, Beatrice forlorn and dejected after having been raped by

Yasin, Beatrice radiant and expectant, patting her stomach swollen with Maria, and Beatrice wan and dying, entreating Johann to take care of her child—Johann's sobs continued unabated.

When his eyes were nearly swollen shut from weeping, Johann jumped up and ran to the front of his cell. "Beatrice," he shouted in his loudest voice. Her name echoed off the walls. "Beatrice," Johann shouted again. "I need you. I still love you. Please help me."

He listened until the final echo was gone. Then he collapsed upon his mat and fell asleep.

JOHANN EXTENDED HIS project of assessing the relationships in his life until it included almost everyone of any significance that he had ever known. As he reflected on his interactions with others, he began to discern definite patterns in his own behavior and to construct a composite portrait of himself. There were elements of this portrait that Johann did not like. He resolved that if he ever had the opportunity again to enjoy the company of other human beings, he would pay more attention to what was important to *them*, he would not so quickly discount their feelings and opinions, and he would allow himself to experience a full range of emotions without subjecting every inchoate feeling in himself to rigorous analytic scrutiny.

By this time six more adoclyne cleanings had occurred and Johann was certain that the time for the birth of his child had passed. He wondered if the baby was a boy or a girl, and remembering Beatrice's plight, he hoped that Vivien had had an easy childbirth. Beatrice's voice in Johann's head told him that he could pray for the well-being of his wife and child, but Johann told the voice, out loud, that he couldn't "be a hypocrite."

In fact Johann now talked out loud most of the time he was awake. He didn't feel as lonely when he heard the sound of his voice. He even spoke to the nozzlers when they came to clean his cell. At first the aliens suspended their work when Johann said anything, and made threatening gestures with their tentacles and claws. But eventually they learned to accept the rambling of the giant human with the long beard, now naked because his original shorts had become shreds, who paced about his cell during their visits.

As time passed Johann created other projects to fill his waking hours. He usually selected two or three people from his earlier life to be his imaginary associates. His colleagues were allocated space in his cell where they could work on the assignments he had given them. During his geography project, for example, Sister Beatrice was assigned responsibility for the Americas, Yasin for the Middle East, and Narong for Southeast Asia. Johann gave each person's report when the assignments were complete, altering his voice and delivery to be consistent with the speaking style of the person who had performed the task.

He learned early in his confinement that if he ate a lot of food and drank gulps of canal water just before sleeping that he was much more likely to have dreams. Johann cherished these dreams, for they were usually full of other people, some familiar and some unknown. As the length of time he had been alone passed one human year, it became his regular practice first to swim vigorously to tire himself, and then to eat a big meal before stretching out on his seaweed mat. That sequence produced the most vivid dreams.

Beatrice was often present in these dreams. Johann saw her in many forms, in the blue robe with the white stripes that she had worn as the Michaelite bishop of Mars, in her glowing whiteness as she had been during his brief sojourn in Whiteland after Maria's birth, in the simple island costumes she made by hand (both from the period when they were chaste companions and later, after Yasin's death, when they were lovers), and in several new manifestations. Beatrice and he had extensive conversations during the dreams. Often Johann would continue to converse with her after waking. He would walk around his cell, gesticulating with his arms to buttress a particular point he was making, or alternatively he would sit reflectively on his mat, nodding from time to time, listening to her voice inside his head discoursing on some subject.

Johann used these conversations with the ghosts of his past and his many projects to chase away the demons of depression. "I will endure," he said quietly to the adoclyne cleaning his cell one day. The alien did not even look at him. It simply retracted the scoop from the hole in the rock floor and emptied the contents into the container. Johann took three steps away from the wall, toward the nozzler. It stopped what it was doing, without dropping the scoop it was holding in its elevated claw, and both the two forward eyes looked at Johann.

"Do you understand?" Johann said passionately. "No matter how long you keep me here, I will continue to survive."

Satisfied that he had at least captured the creature's attention, Johann stepped back and sat down against the wall on his mat. The adoclyne continued to watch him for several seconds, then shifted its body weight and plunged the scoop back into the hole.

SISTER BEATRICE WAS dressed in her bishop's robe and headpiece. She was lecturing Johann on some arcane religious subject. Even in his dream, Johann was not listening to her words that closely. He was watching her eyes and the expressions on her face, thinking to himself how very beautiful she was.

Then, suddenly, he could no longer understand anything she was saying. It was if she were speaking some strange new language. Johann tried to interrupt her, but

Beatrice continued to smile and speak in the weird tongue he had never heard before.

In the dream Johann stood up and walked toward her. As he did so, Beatrice began to change color. The blue in her robe and headpiece, and even her skin, became a pure glowing white. Johann raised his hands to protect his eyes from the overwhelming light.

"Johann," he heard her voice in his dream, "wake up. I am here beside you."

He thought he was hallucinating when he opened his eyes. Standing beside his mat in the cell, no more than a meter away, was the glowing white Beatrice who had been his companion in Whiteland.

Johann closed his eyes again. The background glow was still present when he turned his head in her direction. *Could I possibly still be dreaming?* he asked himself. He sat up on the mat and opened his eyes hesitantly, his body trembling from all the adrenaline that was flooding his system.

"Is it really you?" he said. "I'm not simply imagining that you're here with me?"

The white Beatrice smiled. "I am here, Brother Johann," she said, extending her hand toward him. Warily he leaned forward and took her hand. The shock of the touch overwhelmed him. Johann closed his eyes and tried to remember what human touch felt like. Was it like this? Johann didn't think so, but he couldn't be certain. He turned her hand over in his. *This is similar to human touch,* he told himself, *but not quite the same. Unless I have forgotten.*

The glowing Beatrice was still smiling patiently when Johann reopened his eyes. He looked out toward the canal. "How did you get here?" he asked. "Is the gate still open?" He started to stand up.

"That's not important, Johann," she said, motioning for him to remain seated. "I've come to explain what is going to happen to you."

He relaxed on his mat, transfixed by the apparition in

front of him. *Her voice is perfect,* he found himself thinking. *Her face, her eyes, everything is Beatrice. But the smile is not quite right. What is she? Who is she?*

"Listen carefully," she was saying. "We have only this brief visit before all the changes start to occur."

Johann tried to force himself to focus on what Beatrice was telling him, but it was impossible. He could not stop the questions that were pouring into his head. And he could not stop staring at that magnificent face, the one he adored above all others.

He heard her say something about bathyspheres, the bottom of the lake, and a long sleep during a period of acceleration. When it was all over, he and his family, including Vivien and their son, Siegfried, would be at their promised planet with the twin moons. . . .

"What did you say?" Johann asked, suddenly very alert. "Did you say *my son,* Siegfried?"

The white Beatrice smiled again. "Yes, Brother Johann," she said. "Sister Vivien and you have an adorable, healthy baby boy. By the time you wake up—"

Johann's emotions exploded. *"Yes!"* he shouted, standing up abruptly. "I have a *son!"*

He stepped quickly forward to embrace the bearer of these joyful tidings. The glowing figure lost its shape for an instant, pulled away from his outstretched arms, and re-formed into Beatrice a meter farther away. Everything happened in a fraction of a second. Johann stared in disbelief and awe.

"I must initiate all physical contact," the glowing Beatrice said pleasantly. "If I'm not properly prepared, the strangeness may overwhelm you."

Johann stared at her, dumbfounded.

"Please sit down and let me continue," she said.

Johann meekly followed her instructions.

"You will be asleep for a long time," she said, "many years by human measure. You will be taken to a new world, a planet not unlike the Earth, that orbits a star similar to the Sun in this neighborhood of the galaxy. On this new planet are other living creatures who have evolved naturally. They are not incompatible with human life, but it is not certain—"

"What about the nozzlers?" Johann interrupted her. "The ones that are keeping me a prisoner. Will they be there on that new world?"

"No, Brother Johann," the white Beatrice said. "They are going to another destination. Your last contact with them will come when they transport you to the bathysphere."

"Good," he said emphatically. Emboldened by her answer, Johann launched a whole series of questions at once. Who or what had built this spherical spacecraft? Were the glowing ribbons of particles the masters of everything onboard, including the nozzlers? And what were the ribbons anyway, advanced extraterrestrials or God's angels, as she had insisted while she was still living? And finally, since he had watched her die, and buried her himself, what was she? A ghost, an angel, or something else altogether?

When he was finished with his flurry, the glowing Beatrice nodded her head and laughed discreetly. The slight laugh reminded Johann of precious moments Beatrice and he had shared together. The instant heartache took his breath away.

"I see you're as curious as ever, Brother Johann," she said. "I can provide answers to a few of your questions. However, I will not answer them all. . . . It is never necessary for us to have all our questions answered."

Beatrice paused and continued to smile. "In some sense I am still living, Johann, and from your perspective might be considered part ghost and part angel. In truth, what I am is beyond your ken, to use that excellent Scottish expression in its fullest meaning. . . .

"The ribbons are indeed the masters of this spaceship, and were responsible for its creation, but their relationship with you, the nozzlers, and everything else onboard is not easy to explain. To define them as either God's angels or advanced aliens does not do them justice. What they *are* should not be constrained by the limited imagination of the human mind."

Johann's puzzled expression prompted another gentle laugh. "There you go again," she said, "analyzing and scrutinizing everything. Hasn't being alive taught you anything yet? Thinking is only one of humanity's extraordinary attributes. Feeling is an equally unique capability. In our short time together, isn't there something of emotional importance that you would like to discuss?"

Johann no longer had any doubts that the apparition with him was the real Beatrice. Her laugh might not be exactly the same as he remembered, but her outlook on life, her words, and even her earnest expressions were a complete match for the woman he had known and loved. *She is essentially Beatrice,* he told himself, suspending his disbelief and forcing the analytical questions out of his mind.

He looked across at his beautiful visitor. "Come closer, please," he said softly. "I would like to see you better."

She moved across the cell until she was standing only half an arm's length away. Johann stared at her glowing figure for almost a full minute, basking in the joy and adoration he was feeling. "Thank you for coming," he said softly.

"You're welcome," she answered gracefully.

Johann started to speak again but before he could say anything, tears rushed into his eyes and down his cheeks. He stood again in silence, attempting to compose himself. The trickle of tears became a torrent.

"Dear, dear Brother Johann," Beatrice said, reaching up and touching his cheek with her right hand.

"I have never stopped loving you," he said falteringly, "with every fiber of my being. Even now, as I look at you, I know the joy of that love and I am thrilled by its power. To have been alive, and to have experienced that kind of love, makes all the pain of life meaningless and insignificant."

"I know that you love me, Brother Johann," she said. "And I feel fortunate to be the object of such worthy affection. As I have watched you keep your promise to take care of my daughter, Maria, I have realized again what an honorable man you are. . . . I loved you too, Johann, and I love you now, which is why I have been able to make this visit."

Her smile was radiant. "There are so many kinds of love. God's love, for example, is of a transcendent quality . . ."

As Johann listened to her melodious voice, and watched the soft and loving expressions on her glowing face, he felt a peace and contentment so deep, so rich, that his entire being seemed to be in perfect harmony with the universe. He didn't ask any more questions. Johann simply listened to what she was saying, and he couldn't have been happier. Beatrice talked about God, Maria, and the concept of life as a never-ending process that is constantly renewed. They made love to each other through their eyes and words.

All too soon, Johann heard the white Beatrice say that it was time for her to go. "Would you do one more thing for me?" Johann asked, after thanking her again for coming.

"What is it, Brother Johann?" she asked.

"Would you kiss me?" he said.

"I think I could manage that," Beatrice said, smiling again.

During the moments he was waiting Johann thought that the surface of the glowing Beatrice became more clearly defined. When she finally leaned toward him, their lips touched for no more than ten seconds. It was the most extraordinary event of Johann's life.

THE LAST APPARITION

ONE

JOHANN AWAKENED, AS he usually did, about half an hour before sunrise. Being careful not to disturb Vivien, who was sleeping on the mat beside him, he grabbed a pair of clean trunks from the neat stack against the wall and put them on. Standing up, his head almost scraping the roof of the wooden hut, Johann crossed the room in three strides. In the far opposite corner of their small, one-room home, he bent down in front of four large open shells. Beside them was a hollowed-out wooden jar containing dozens of small, smooth stones. Johann took one stone from the jar, dropped it in the shell on the far right, and then quickly counted the number of stones in each of the shells.

Twelve hundred and forty-seven days, he thought to himself as he gently opened the door and went outside. His moccasins were beside the door. He slipped them on and walked down the path toward the outhouse beside the creek. Scanning the sky in the dim premorning light, Johann saw the usual clouds hovering over the front range of the western mountains. To his left, the sky was clear over the ocean, and the surf, which at high tide reached the sandy shore about two hundred meters from the edge of their village, was very gentle. Only an occasional small wave broke against the beach.

The weather will be good today, Johann thought idly, exiting from the outhouse and moving upstream on the path beside the creek. *Our harvest will not be interrupted by wind or squalls.*

By the time Johann started climbing the hill that began behind the pool at the bottom of the creek cascades, the light had increased considerably. He stopped after a few steep switchbacks in the path and took a drink from the cool, refreshing water beside him. He was already a hundred meters above the village. Stretching out between Johann and the ocean were the five simple huts, the irrigation system that had been constructed to divert the water from the creek, and the grainfields and fruit orchards, to the east of the village, that had been planted soon after the arrival of the human contingent in this new world. From Johann's coign of vantage everything looked orderly. He surveyed the small domain with justifiable pride, since he had been the chief architect and engineer of all the critical elements.

Johann climbed rapidly up the next set of switchbacks, reaching a broad, grassy plateau a few minutes before sunrise. He paused briefly to follow the course of a large, reddish leaf that was floating downstream in the creek. After watching the leaf accelerate across the top of the cascades, and then bounce and tumble, in a matter of seconds, into the large clear pool far below, Johann turned to the east.

Sunrise was his favorite time of the day. He loved to watch the stars fade and the two moons dim in the west. During the first few months after their arrival, Johann had thought that perhaps by studying the arrangement of the stars, and comparing it with what he remembered of the night skies over the Earth and Mars, he might be able to figure out exactly where their new planet was located. Unfortunately, his memory did not contain an accurate enough reference map of the heavens from his previous planetary homes for him to complete the comparison. All he had been able to conclude from studying the stars was that he and his eleven human colleagues were almost certainly less than twenty light-years away from the Sun, a fact that he had deduced independently from the length of time they had spent sleeping during the acceleration of their old spherical worldlet.

Making detailed observations of the motion of their new sun, the large twin moons, and the night stars had provided him with additional important information, however. Johann knew that their village was located near the equator of the planet, that the year here was three hundred and ninety-seven days long, and that the local day was approximately one hour shorter than it had been on Earth.

He also had developed a wealth of knowledge about the phases of the two moons and the ocean tides they controlled. In addition to the practical value of this information (such as the amount of light that would be available on any given night, and when especially low tides would allow them easy access to the rich food sources of the littoral), it pleased Johann that he had been able to create a lunar calendar with accurate predictions of both lunar and solar eclipses.

According to Johann's calculations the twin moons, each slightly smaller in the night sky than the Moon had been back on Earth, were full together every fourteen hundred and forty-nine nights. He and his friends had never yet witnessed this phenomenon, which they called double full moon night, since its last occurrence had been a hundred and twenty days before the drone shuttle had deposited them on the planet. Now, Johann was full of anticipation as only eighty-two days remained before he and the others would see the most breathtaking astronomical display their new planet offered—two great moons rising simultaneously in the east, roughly fifty degrees apart, and flooding the land below with reflected light in their dance across the heavens.

Each morning Johann ascended the steep path from the village to the plateau and followed the creek for another kilometer to where it broadened into a beautiful small lake approximately the size of a soccer field. The terrain on the far side of the lake rose abruptly on all sides and was forested with strange, squat plants, more like bushes than trees. A trio of streams dropped into the lake from the surrounding hills, replenishing it with fresh water that eventually overflowed into the creek that ran beside their village.

As Johann neared the lake, a pair of six-legged furry creatures, one brown and one black, interrupted their play beside the water. Even though Johann had seen members of this species before, both during his morning swims and on his occasional exploratory excursions, he was still fascinated by their extraordinary round faces, which were divided in half from top to bottom by a protruding ridge containing three small, dark holes of unknown function. On either side of this ridge were the two long crescent eyes, running up and down the face, inside of each of which was a white object, like a ball, that rolled the full length of the crescent. The creature's tiny mouth was below everything else, near the point of what might have been called a chin. The mouth looked as if it might have been added as an afterthought.

The behavior of these animals reminded Johann of chipmunks or squirrels on Earth, but these were larger, some of them the size of a small dog. The first few times Johann or one of the other humans had encountered one of them, they had broken into a frenzied chatter and scurried away. Now the animals had become more familiar with the odd, bipedal creatures who lived by the ocean, and no longer bolted when a human suddenly appeared.

The pair of furry creatures remained where they were during the first part of Johann's morning swim. Each time he stroked past the spot where they were playing, he noticed that they were watching him intently. Once, one of the pair swam into the pool in Johann's direction, with only its face out of the water; however, two black and white brothers or cousins, somewhat larger, quickly showed up and their chorus of chattering shouts caused the adventurer to leave the pool immediately. All of the creatures were gone when Johann finished his swim half an hour later.

Johann walked back along the banks of the creek, whistling occasionally. At the top of the cascades he stopped and looked down into the village. He could see Ravi, Vivien, and Anna in the region around the community kitchen, already preparing breakfast. Siegfried and Serentha were walking together down on the beach, scavenging for food in the morning low tide. Beatrice stood ankle deep in the gentle surf, fifteen meters away from them. To the east, the first few bundles of grain from their harvest were neatly stacked on the lowest slopes of barren Black Rock.

Just as Johann started to descend, what appeared to be a moving bundle of grain caught his eye. He blinked and tried to focus his aging eyes on the path that wound up the western flank of Black Rock. When he confirmed that there was indeed a bundle of grain near the top, slowly ascending the slope, he started running immediately along the plateau.

After a few minutes Johann realized that he would not catch up with whatever he had seen until after it had crested the ridge behind Black Rock Promontory. Johann stood still, catching his breath. What he felt was more sorrow than anger. *So now you have become a thief,* he said to himself. *Your mother would be sorely disappointed.*

SIEGFRIED GREETED HIM soon after he came down the switchbacks. "Father," he said, "we are missing another bundle of grain. They came across during the night—"

"I know," Johann interrupted his son. "I saw someone climbing the path up Black Rock."

"Who was it?" Siegfried said, his anger visible. "Jomo or that asshole Eric?"

"I couldn't tell," Johann said. "Besides, it doesn't matter. They're all thieves by association."

Siegfried's eyes narrowed. "That's the *third* time they have stolen food from us. When are we going to do something about it?"

The strength of Siegfried's outrage instantly reminded Johann of an incident from his own youth, when he too was sixteen and idealistic and saw the world in terms of blacks and whites. *That was years and years ago,* he thought, pushing aside the memory of his anger after the Bauer brothers had purposely destroyed Heike's bicycle. *On a different planet called Earth. In a country named Germany.*

Johann put his arm around his son. "And what exactly do you think we should do, Siegfried?" he asked. "Attack them at night? Steal their children?"

"Please do not mock me, Father," Siegfried said, his feelings hurt. "You said yourself that it's not fair for us to work so hard and for them to reap the benefits of our labor."

"I'm sorry, son," Johann said. "You're right, of course. But it's not clear what we should do in this situation. . . . Their crops are a mess. When I examined them from the hills last week, their grain looked sparse and desiccated. . . ."

"Oh, there you are," Vivien said, coming up the path to greet her husband and son. Her shoulder-length hair was all gray now, and she walked with a slight limp, but her face was as fresh and smiling as if she were still a teenager.

She greeted Johann with a hug and a brief kiss. "I guess Siegfried has already told you?" she said. After Johann nodded, Vivien added, "What I can't understand is why they would *steal* from us. Why couldn't they simply ask us for help?"

Because Maria has too much pride, Johann thought. *And the others will not argue with her.*

When Johann offered no response, Vivien decided not to pursue the matter for the moment. The three of them walked in silence toward the kitchen, a partially covered wooden shed in the center of the village. Ravi, Anna, and Beatrice were standing together next to a crude, charred pot suspended over an open fire. Steam was rising from the container.

Johann glanced down the path at the three who were waiting and sensed from their body language that a group meeting had already been arranged. His good mood of an hour earlier had been shattered by the discovery of the theft. Now what he was feeling was the same sorrowful heartache that usually accompanied his thoughts about Maria. *I don't want to talk about this right now,* Johann said to himself, abruptly leaving the path and heading toward the ocean.

"Where are you going?" Vivien asked.

"I would like some scruffles for breakfast," Johann replied, without stopping or turning around.

"Siegfried and Serentha picked up three or four dozen already this morning, while you were out swimming," Vivien said.

"I want *black* scruffles, from the hollow," Johann said.

"Be careful," Vivien shouted after a moment's pause. "The tide is coming in and Beatrice saw a pair of sperdens just before you came back."

THE CREEK, TWENTY meters wide and half a meter deep between the ocean and the pool at the bottom of the cascades, formed the western boundary of their domain. Beyond the creek to the west, thick undergrowth, with many strange vines, covered the slopes of foothills that were an extension of the front range of the western mountains. Rarely did Johann and his extended family cross the creek, and then only at low tide to play on the white sand beach in front of the lovely, isolated cove a slight distance away.

Their fields and orchards were on the opposite side of the village. Starting the same distance behind the high-tide point as the village, they covered an area of roughly twenty thousand square meters. Their northern boundary was just before the steep hills that Johann climbed every morning when he went for a swim. On the east, the fields approached the flanks of the bare dark volcanic outcropping they called Black Rock.

The switchbacks beside the cascades were the only path up the northern hills. A second inland path out of their village area slowly climbed the black volcanic rock and ended up near the point of the promontory, overlooking the ocean. It was upon that path that Johann had seen the bundle of grain earlier that morning.

The hollow, the only place where Johann had ever found the black scruffles that had become his favorite food in his new home, was a deep, wedge-shaped cut into the bottom of the enormous expanse of rock that jutted out into the ocean below Black Rock Promontory. The hollow faced the ocean directly. During an average low tide, the water depth at the entrance to the hollow was only a couple of centimeters. Johann and the others often waded down the shoreline and entered the hollow, harvesting the delicious black scruffles or simply sitting on the black sand at the back of the hollow and enjoying being surrounded by the immense cliffs of black rock.

At mean high tide, however, the hollow was an altogether different place. Then the average water depth at the entrance was at least two meters, and no location in the hollow was safe from the turbulent bursts of water and spray that resulted from the ocean waves crashing against the rocks.

But the biggest danger when the hollow was filled with water was not the possibility of being suddenly driven against the sharp rocks by an onrushing wave. Living in the offshore waters of their new planet were huge long-necked serpents that the humans called sperdens. Unrivaled masters of the ocean, these great green and black animals, whose necks sometimes rose out of the water so high that they towered even over Johann, looked like a bizarre combination of a giant eel and a duck or swan with flippers instead of webbed feet.

Fortunately, the humans had arrived at this planet during the annual mating rite of the sperdens and had thus been spared any tragic confrontations with these denizens of the deep. On their very first night, sleeping on the beach not far from where their pilotless shuttle had left them before it departed, they had all been kept awake most of the night by choruses of ululations and wails coming from the ocean. One of the moons had been nearly full that night. Johann and his friends had been able to see the long necks swaying in rhythm as they swam, two groups of half a dozen each merging into one, and some titanic battles, punctuated with sharp, frenzied cries, as pairs of the animals engaged in combat. From that first night forward, none of the humans had ventured more than waist deep in the ocean, and only that far if none of the green and black necks had been recently sighted.

Johann was not worrying about the sperdens as he waded through the surf toward the hollow. In fact, he was not even thinking about the black scruffles that he had come to collect. He was trying to determine what to do about Maria and her accomplices.

Almost mechanically he bent down in shallow water a few meters inside the entrance to the hollow. As the water ebbed away, he thrust his powerful right hand into the black sand and scooped up a large volume of material. Deftly sorting through it with the fingers of his left hand, Johann picked out three of the black, ruffled, wormlike creatures about the length of his index finger and dropped them into the front pocket of his shorts.

He repeated this process over and over, slowly moving

deeper into the hollow as the tide came in. While his pockets were filling with the wriggling scruffles, Johann thought about Maria, particularly the changes he had witnessed in her since they had awakened from their long sleep in the bathysphere. Johann hoped that somehow this careful examination of all the historical events would give him some insight on how to deal with the latest crisis.

The apparition of Sister Beatrice in his cell in the grotto had correctly foretold the future. Only a few days after her visit, Johann and all the other humans had been gathered up by the nozzlers and taken to a platform far out in the middle of the lake. There they had been divided into groups of two and herded in pairs into small, thick-walled, spherical constructions. Before being placed in a bathysphere with Maria, Johann had had the pleasure of seeing Vivien and his infant son, Siegfried, for a maximum of two minutes.

Maria had been frightened and had clung to Johann. From the layout inside their dimly lit submersible, which was furnished only with two hammocks, each a size that matched one of the two of them, it was obvious that they were supposed to lie down. She had refused to crawl into her hammock until Johann set an example for her and gently coaxed her to do what he was doing. When they were both lying in their hammocks, they were enwrapped by dozens of pieces of tiny twine, some of which were sharp and pierced the skin. Johann's last memory, before waking up with a long gray beard and an enormous tangle of gray hair, was of Maria whimpering and asking for his help.

When they awakened, Maria was already a woman. During her long sleep she had obviously been properly nourished, and somehow cleaned, for Johann's first reaction to her naked body was one of shock. After they dressed in the simple clothes that had been laid out for them beside their hammocks, they immediately joined the others on the surface of the lake and were transported back to the large floating platform. In only a matter of minutes the drone shuttle had appeared and landed on one end of the platform. Everyone except Dr. Jailani and Sister Nuba had been loaded inside, and they had been flown across the lake, down a dark tunnel, through what appeared to be an airlock, and then out into space. An hour later the shuttle had hurtled through the atmosphere of their new home planet and deposited them where their fields and orchards would later be planted.

There had been no problems with Maria during the first several months after their arrival. She had taken part eagerly in the building and planning activities, performed her assigned duties without complaint, and had been generally pleasant to everyone, including her erstwhile adversary Beatrice. As time passed, a romantic relationship had begun to develop between Beatrice and Eric, Ravi and Anna's son. Both were then physically in their early twenties and their attraction for each other was completely natural. For some reason that Johann could not fathom, however, Maria had been definitely bothered by their budding relationship. One evening, while everyone was eating together, Beatrice, laughing about some comment Eric had made, leaned over and kissed him on the cheek. Maria, who was sitting next to them, expressed her disapproval verbally and then left the dinner gathering altogether.

Johann had followed Maria but she would tell him nothing about what was troubling her. Later that night, Vivien had suggested that Maria's biological urges were also at work, and that she was perhaps distressed because her particular choice for a mate and the father of her future children was already taken. At first Johann had been confused by what Vivien was telling him. However, later in the conversation, when she made it clear that she believed Maria's prime candidate for her husband was none other than Johann himself, he became indignant and accused Vivien of unreasonable jealousy.

Because of Vivien's comments, however, Johann was not totally startled a week or so later when Maria made an awkward attempt to seduce him one morning after they had been swimming together in the clear lake on the plateau above their village. Johann was caring and considerate in his responses, and explained carefully to Maria why he could not become her lover and her husband, but his rejection devastated the young woman, who thought it was her birthright to claim whatever she wanted from him.

From that time forward, Maria was a changed person. She antagonized Vivien at every opportunity and flew into fits of rage when the older woman patronized her. Maria also vindictively seduced the hapless Eric, claiming him as her mate and completely humiliating Beatrice. After Johann interceded, and chastised Maria both publicly and privately for her untoward selfish behavior, Maria forced Eric to leave the village with her and to establish a new home a couple of kilometers to the east, on the other side of Black Rock Promontory. The schism among Johann's group became permanent when Keiko, who had become Maria's best friend, eloped with Jomo to join Maria and Eric the night after Johann and Vivien tried to counsel the young couple to wait another year before marrying.

Roughly a year later Johann had made a trek to the East Village to try to negotiate the return of the two young couples. His visit had ended with a quarrel between Maria and him, and no resolution of their problems, but he had been able to meet and hold Eric and Maria's infant daughter, Stephanie. He had also learned that Keiko was pregnant. Poor Satoko, mentally destabilized by all the conflicts, had asked for and received Johann's permission to move to the East Village to assist her daughter.

And what have we learned from all this? Johann asked himself, emotionally exhausted after the lengthy recollection. He was still sifting the sand for the black scruffles even though all his pockets were bulging and the hollow was becoming dangerously full of water. He heaved a heavy sigh and headed for the hollow entrance.

We have learned, sadly, that human nature is invariant under a locale and situation transformation. He laughed at himself and his awkward mathematical phraseology. *Or rather, what we are is more important than where we are or how we are living.*

Just outside the hollow a pair of sperdens were swimming about twenty-five meters away, watching Johann warily. The water at the entrance was now knee deep, seriously compromising his freedom of movement. One of the sperdens arched its graceful neck so that it was facing its partner. Johann imagined that the clucking sounds they were exchanging were some kind of conversation. Staring back at the sperdens and exhibiting no fear, he waded along the base of the rock toward the village.

TWO

JOHANN COULD NOT fall asleep. He lay on his back, trying to think about something other than the crisis facing his little clan. The group meeting had been contentious. Siegfried and Beatrice had insisted that the thieves must be punished. Since everyone had agreed that Maria was almost certainly the individual making the decisions in the East Village, there had been a consensus that the punishment should be directed at her. During the heated discussion that had ensued about the kind of action that would be appropriate, first Beatrice, then Siegfried and Serentha as well, had accused Johann of being "soft" on Maria because of his special relationship with her.

"She has never, *ever*, been forced to be accountable for her actions," Beatrice had said to Johann with rancor. "She has not had to live by the same rules as the rest of us. . . . Even now, you are still making excuses for her. It's not our fault that their crops are poor. And it certainly does not justify their thievery."

During the meeting, nobody, not even Vivien, had defended him against the accusations that he showed favoritism to Maria. What had troubled Johann the most, however, was that his own son, Siegfried, whom he loved beyond measure, explicitly suggested that all of them, even Vivien and he himself, were less important to Johann than Maria was.

Johann squirmed on his mat as he recalled Siegfried's bitter words. *He is still young,* Johann told himself, *and has not learned to control what he is saying when he is emotionally aroused.* But the disquiet he was feeling would not go away. Because of the depth of his attachment to Maria's mother, Johann knew that there was a modicum of truth in what Siegfried and the others had said.

Johann changed positions, rolling over on his side facing Vivien. He opened his eyes for a second and saw that Vivien was watching him. "Heavy is the head that wears the crown," she said, smiling warmly.

"I'm not the king," Johann replied.

"But you are our leader," she said. "Everyone acknowledges that. All the conversation today was aimed at helping you make a decision."

Johann was silent. Vivien leaned over and touched him gently. "Siegfried came to talk to me tonight, while you were walking on the beach. He felt he handled himself poorly in the meeting. He wants to apologize to you, but he doesn't know how."

" 'I'm sorry' would be a good start," Johann said.

"That's not good enough for Siegfried," she said. "He is a perfectionist, like you. He wants the apology also to convey how much he respects, admires, and loves you."

Neither of them said anything for a while. Johann was thinking about his teenage son, a beautiful young man, already almost two meters tall, with his light brown skin and blue eyes, and a full head of his mother's rich black hair. *He toils ably beside me in the fields without complaint,* Johann thought proudly. *Already he is stronger than Ravi. Soon he will surpass me.*

He glanced across the hut to where Siegfried had slept the first two years after their arrival in this new world. Johann remembered the night he had been awakened by noises he could not at first identify, coming from Siegfried's mat. Johann had watched and listened for several seconds, without moving or saying anything. The next morning, after talking with Vivien, they had informed Siegfried that the time had come for him to become more independent, and to move into his own hut. Johann and Siegfried had built the hut together, for the boy did not want to move into the one abandoned by Maria and Keiko. Johann remembered their working together as one of the high points in his relationship with Siegfried. He had been impressed both by the boy's intelligence and by his self-discipline.

"Johann, are you still awake?" Vivien said for the second time.

"Umm, yes," he said. "I guess I was drifting."

"There was another reason that Siegfried came to talk to me," she said. "It's important, but it could wait until morning if you . . ."

"No, no," he said. "Go ahead."

"Siegfried and Serentha want to marry," Vivien said. "He's concerned about your reaction. He asked me to talk to you—"

Johann sat up on his mat. "That's absurd," Johann said. "The boy may be physically sixteen, but he's only really lived for three years. How can he possibly know what he wants?"

"There aren't a lot of options," Vivien replied, "as I tried to point out to you when Jomo and Keiko came to talk to us. If Siegfried doesn't marry Serentha, what's he going to do? Beatrice is his half-sister. B would probably be willing but I would hate to see another conflict like—"

"Yes, yes," Johann said, lying back down. "We ought to be able to learn from our mistakes. I doubt if Siegfried would want to wait until Stephanie is a woman, and it's unrealistic to assume other options might show up. So I guess we have no choice."

"He would like your blessing," Vivien said.

"He will have it when he asks for it," Johann said. "Which shouldn't be tomorrow, incidentally. There's something else I must do first."

"So you have decided?" Vivien asked.

"Yes," Johann answered. "I will go over there alone, without carrying any grain or fruit. I guess all of you convinced me that taking food to them might be misinterpreted."

"Are you certain you don't want Siegfried and Ravi to go with you?" Vivien said.

"That would look too much like a war party. And Eric and Siegfried have always antagonized each other." Johann reflected for a moment. "No, I'll go alone, right after my swim in the morning."

JOHANN REACHED THE East Village by the middle of the afternoon. He made no effort to conceal his coming; he was in fact whistling as he walked down the path toward the meager fields to the west of the three ramshackle huts that formed the village.

Eric was standing in the path on the edge of the fields. He was brandishing a long, thick wooden club. "You're not welcome here, old man," he shouted when Johann was within earshot. "Turn around now and go back where you came from."

Johann made no comment and did not alter his pace or his direction. "I'm warning you," Eric then said, "don't come any closer."

Although Eric was much younger and quicker than Johann, he was a man of ordinary size and strength. Biologically nearing sixty, Johann remained an awesome physical specimen, with muscles that were nearly as imposing as his height. His daily exercise regimen and regular manual labor had kept him in great shape. There was no way that Eric by himself could have prevented Johann's entry into the village.

When Johann drew closer to him on the path, Eric stepped forward and lunged awkwardly with the club. Johann dodged the blow and struck Eric hard across the back with his hand and forearm, knocking the younger man to the ground. Immediately afterward Johann stepped on Eric's hand that was still holding the club.

"Don't you ever try something like that again," Johann said matter-of-factly, looking down at the grimacing Eric. Johann reached down and picked up the club, letting Eric go so that he could scramble to his feet.

"Get out of here. . . . We don't want you here," Eric sputtered.

"Well, well," Maria said, suddenly appearing out of the fields, "if it isn't Johann the magnificent. Tell me, oh wise one, to what do we owe the honor of your visit?"

"I came to talk," Johann said simply. "There are some issues we need to discuss."

"Maybe you didn't understand, old man," Eric said now, emboldened by Maria's arrival. He thrust himself into the space between Johann and Maria. "You'd better—"

With amazing celerity, Johann grabbed Eric under the armpits and lifted him off the ground. "You are beginning to annoy me," Johann said as Eric squirmed and flailed. "I suggest you go away before I become angry."

He deposited the flustered Eric on the ground beside the path. Maria did not try to suppress her laughter. She shook her head and looked at her husband. "I can hear Stephanie crying," she said. "Why don't you see if you can give Satoko a hand?"

Eric started to protest his dismissal but decided against it. He walked quickly down the path that led to the village. "So how have you been?" Johann asked casually when Maria and he were alone.

"Comme ci, comme ça," she said, speaking the French phrase he had taught her when she was a young girl. Her eyes were much softer than they had been when Eric was present. "And you?" she added.

"As well as can be expected," he answered.

They stared at each other for what seemed like forever. Johann did not let his eyes wander from hers. He did not dare allow Maria the pleasure of seeing him appreciate her half-naked woman's body, now richer and fuller with her breasts swollen with milk.

"Well," Maria said awkwardly, finally breaking the silence, "don't I at least rate a hug?"

Johann took her in his arms and held her close. Maria's arms moved up his bare back. *I know what she is doing,* he told himself. *This is the child I raised from infancy. I will not play her game.*

"Kiss me, Johann," Maria said, looking up at him.

In one continuous motion Johann leaned down and kissed her on the forehead and then pushed her gently away. "We have a problem to discuss, Maria," he said, as he took her hand and walked toward the village. "It seems someone has been stealing our food. Yesterday it was grain, and last week it was fruit. . . . This is absolutely unacceptable."

MARIA, ERIC, JOMO, and Satoko were sitting on the dirt in front of Johann, who was standing up and rocking the baby Stephanie in his arms. Keiko was nursing Kwame over on the side. "I know that you have been having trouble with your crops," Johann said evenly. "But stealing food from us just creates more problems than it solves."

"We weren't really stealing the food," Maria said coyly. "We always intended to pay you back from our next harvest."

Johann looked directly at Maria. "You know that we would gladly have made an arrangement with you," he said. "I have countless times offered to help you irrigate and replant your fields so that you would have more robust crops. Unfortunately, you have always rejected our attempts to help."

"We're not helpless," Eric said indignantly. "We've just had some bad luck. And we don't want to be dependent upon you. . . ."

"I think that maybe we might be willing to take some

advice, Johann," Maria said. "But we don't want you to do it for us, or even come over here and supervise. . . ."

"Especially if you're going to treat us as if we're stupid," Eric added.

Baby Stephanie started to squirm in Johann's arms so he changed her to a different position. "Forgetting what has already occurred," he then said, "we still have important issues to address. You do not have enough to eat over here, and will not until the tarrier fruit ripens next month. We have plenty over in the West Village, but we could use some help with the rest of the harvest. If you will give us a hand with our work, then we will supply you with enough food to last until the tarrier ripens."

"We're not moving back to the West Village," Maria said immediately, "where you can scrutinize and criticize everything we do."

"Certainly not," Eric added needlessly.

Meanwhile, Jomo slipped over to where Keiko was nursing Kwame and they had a brief conversation. "Uncle Johann," Jomo said a few moments later, "what you are suggesting sounds fair to Keiko and me." He glanced over at Maria and Eric. "But we have a question. Is it all right if all four of us come? Then Keiko could help in the fields while her mother takes care of the baby."

"Certainly, Jomo," Johann said. He looked pointedly at Maria and Eric. "Any and all of you are welcome at West Village whenever you would like to come."

"It will take a day or two to finish up what we're doing here," Jomo said.

"That's fine," Johann said. "That will give us time to prepare Maria and Keiko's old hut for your family."

"We're still not coming, Johann," Maria said.

Johann shrugged. "I understand," he said. "Jomo and Keiko will certainly do enough work to earn plenty of food for all of you. . . . But I still want your commitment that you will not steal again from us."

Eric was about to give an unpleasant answer when Maria stepped in front of him and took Stephanie from Johann. "All right," she said, still treating the subject lightly. "We won't borrow any more food without your permission." She held Stephanie on her waist and touched Johann's forearm with her other hand. "By the way, can I have a couple of words with you in private before you go?"

JOHANN AND MARIA traipsed down the path in the direction of Black Rock Promontory. When they were out of sight of the others, Maria stopped and sighed heavily.

"What did you want to talk to me about?" Johann asked.

Maria was looking at her daughter, whom she was cradling tenderly in her arms. "Eric is such an immature boy," she said at length. "You spoiled me, Johann. You showed me what a man should be like."

"Eric is still very young," Johann said, shifting the thrust of the conversation. "Give him time. It must be difficult for him to suddenly be both a husband and a father with no more life experience than he has had."

"You don't understand, Johann," Maria said, shaking her head vigorously. "I don't love him. I don't want to have any more children with him—what I'd really like to do is give him back to whiny Beatrice. They deserve each other. I never should have interfered in the first place."

"It saddens me, Maria," Johann said softly, "that you are so selfish and have such little regard for anyone else. Do you really think that it's all right for you to toy with people's feelings and disrupt their lives simply to please yourself? Have you forgotten all the things that I have told you about your mother? Why, she would deny herself anything—"

"Spare me another lecture about my perfect mother," Maria said sharply. Stephanie had now fallen asleep. Maria placed the baby gently on the ground and pirouetted, shirtless, in front of Johann. "Look at my body, Johann, and try to tell me that you don't find it attractive. How many children could I produce for you? Three? Five? Maybe more?"

She moved closer to him. "We have spent most of our lives together, Johann. We love each other. It would make perfect sense for me to marry you and give birth to your children. . . . I would not insist on any change in your relationship with Vivien. We could both be your wives, and you could sleep with either of us whenever you wanted. This way you could have the best of both possible worlds. A young, ardent wife, eager to bear you more children, and a barren, older woman, a companion of your own age, with whom you could reflect on the mysteries of the universe."

Johann was speechless for quite a while. Maria's proposition had caught him completely unprepared. He could not deny that she was a beautiful young woman and that he was sexually stirred by the thought of making love to her. Nor could he deny that there was a bizarre kind of logic in Maria's proposal. If their small group was to survive and flourish, they would need to reproduce more, and her plan, assuming Eric and Beatrice would be together again, certainly held promise for a significant number of new children.

But Johann was deeply bothered by Maria's total lack of concern for the other people who would be affected by her proposal. It was clear that she considered the wants and desires of Eric, Beatrice, and even Vivien essentially irrelevant. Maria wanted to optimize her life. Whatever anyone else might feel was of no weight in her decision.

Johann took both her hands in his. "Dear Maria," he said, "you are certainly correct in saying that you and I love each other. Except possibly for your mother, I care more about you than any person I have ever known. And given an entirely different set of circumstances, I would be delighted at the prospect of marrying you and producing many children. But I'm afraid I cannot accept your proposal. Too many others would be hurt, or have their lives diminished, by our actions. It's a question of fairness."

He paused, still holding her hands, before continuing in the same gentle voice. "Your mother's final words to me on this subject were not ambiguous. 'Above all, Johann,' she said to me, 'teach her by precept, and show her by example, the importance of having solid personal values. Without those values, she will never be able to develop her own sense of self-worth, or to recognize that each and every one of us has importance in God's overall design. It is correct for us to do unto others as we would have them do unto us not simply because a great and wonderful teacher told us to behave that way, but also because the universe becomes more harmonious when its creatures follow this simple teaching.' "

Maria's face was soft, and tears were streaming down her cheeks, when Johann finished. "In my heart of hearts," she said, "I knew what your answer would be." She reached up and kissed him on the cheek. "Otherwise you would not be the Johann I love so much."

She let go of his hands and bent down to pick Stephanie up from the ground. Maria took a few steps with her baby daughter and then turned back toward Johann. "In a few minutes I will be angry with you again. Go now, before my mood changes."

THREE

JOHANN PAUSED NEAR the top of Black Rock Promontory to take a drink from the trickling creek that dropped out of the hills behind Maria's village. It had been a long day. He felt mentally and physically exhausted. *I grow old, I grow old,* he mused to himself. *I shall wear the bottoms of my trousers rolled.*

The sun was starting to set behind the western mountains. Desiring a break before returning to Vivien and the others, Johann strolled out along the barren rock toward the ocean and sat down on the edge of the cliff. In front of him, the endless expanse of ocean was broken only by a solitary slender island, a kilometer or two offshore, where he could see the outlines of trees and bushes in the late afternoon sunlight. A couple of hundred meters below him, big waves crashed against the jagged black rocks, sending white spray in all directions.

As the light continued to fade in the west, the stars filled the sky with their splendor, touching Johann with that same combination of joy and awe he had known since he had first examined the clear night sky as a schoolboy. "The stars are your parents," he could still hear his earnest elementary-school teacher Herr Yeager saying. "Every important element in your body, from the iron in your hemoglobin to the calcium in your bones and teeth, was created in the death throes of stars like these and blasted across the galaxy to be present here at that special moment when the Earth first accreted."

Where is Herr Yeager now? Johann wondered, his eyes scanning the moonless sky vainly for some clue, perhaps never recognized before, that would identify for him the Sun that was the home star for his native planet. *And what would Herr Yeager think if he could have known that those same chemicals created by dying stars had made other life, and other intelligence as well, at different locations and epochs throughout our galaxy?*

As his eyes alternately feasted on the star-filled sky and the waves crashing against the rocks below him, Johann thought, as he often did, about the extraordinary sequence of events that had taken him from Germany to Mars to an astonishing spherical alien worldlet and finally to this new planet, located somewhere in the local neighborhood of his Sun, where it appeared it would be his destiny to die. The many amazing scenes from his life swarmed through his mind. He saw again the initial apparition of the particles in the falling snow in the park in Berlin, the ice caverns beneath the Martian polar ice, the endless train of suffering humans during his strange boat ride with Sister Beatrice, the blast from the simulated Hiroshima bomb, Beatrice singing love songs to him on the beach in paradise, the moment that he killed Yasin, Maria's birth, Beatrice's death and astonishing reincarnation as ghost and angel, his masket friend Scarface, the charge of the elevark, the nozzlers and their grotto, and finally, since it was very much on his mind, his scene with Maria that very afternoon.

Overwhelmed by his memories and his feelings, Johann stood up on the edge of the promontory and raised his arms to the heavens. "But what is it all for?" he shouted. "When the last human ever to be alive perishes, and never again does this unique combination of chemicals risen to consciousness grace the glories that nature has created, what will have been accomplished? What purpose will we have served?"

Unaware of the tears now filling his eyes, Johann continued to speak to the sky. "I do not ask all these questions for myself, for I have certainly been shown *my* personal insignificance in the greater scheme of the universe. But do all of us, taken together, not only every human who has ever lived, but also all those who have not yet been born, *also* amount to nothing? Will it have been only a completely random event that for one brief epoch a strange, sentient, bipedal creature dominated a small, insignificant blue planet orbiting an inauspicious stable yellow star in one of the spiral arms of the galaxy?"

Johann paced back and forth along the edge of the promontory for several seconds before raising his arms and invoking the sky again. "And if none of our activities has any meaning whatsoever, how is it possible that I am so filled with anguish at my inability to bestow happiness upon the child that I have raised and treasured? Why do I strive so hard not just to survive, but to understand this amazing universe that surrounds me? And why do I still miss so desperately one single person whom I loved with all my being, who filled my life with a glory beyond anything I could have ever dreamed possible?"

Johann fell down on his knees, trembling. "So tell me God, if You know, and if You exist, how these two completely inconsistent concepts can possibly both be true? How can absolutely nothing human, past, present, or future, have any meaning at all and yet, at the same time, each and every one of us who lives is touched so much by the miracle of our existence that we feel passionately about the importance of our lives and our actions?"

Exhausted by his harangue, Johann fell silent, staring absently at the natural beauty that surrounded him. His disquiet about Maria and, in fact, all his other worries, had temporarily been dispelled. It was one of the rare moments in Johann's life when he was at peace with himself.

He must have sat on the promontory for an hour before he reluctantly decided that it was time for him to return to the West Village and share his news for the day.

Johann stood up, and started walking away from the ocean. As he approached the path that descended to the fields and orchards adjacent to their living area, he turned one last time to look back at the magnificent night sky. Off to his left, one of the twin moons, barely a crescent, had just crossed the horizon. But what caught his attention immediately was a new, glowing light, low in the sky off the end of the promontory, that appeared to be growing and moving in his direction.

A surge of joy and delight energized Johann and chased away the weariness he was feeling. He had no doubt that somewhere in that light headed toward him would be his beloved Beatrice.

THE RIBBON OF particles was so bright, even several hundred meters away from the edge of the promontory, that Johann could see nothing at all except the blinding white light. When the pain in his eyes became unbearable, he looked away, toward the hills, which were now clearly visible themselves in the reflected light. Johann heard a sequence of unidentifiable mechanical sounds behind him and a few seconds later the hills in front of him began to dim.

"You may turn around now, Brother Johann," he heard Beatrice say.

She had never looked so beautiful to him. She was wearing a long, flowing gown that fell all the way to her ankles, just above her bare feet, and a small, sparkling crown on her head. Her blond hair, which reached almost to her waist, was long and full of wonderful curls. In spite of the white glow that surrounded her, Johann could still see the magnificent blue of her eyes.

As always, she was smiling. "So we meet again, Brother Johann," she said, "one final time, on a new and different world."

"One final time?" Johann asked haltingly, still awe-struck by her presence.

"Yes," the white Beatrice said. "This is the last time that I will ever be able to visit you. And I have come for a very special purpose. I cannot stay long and you must listen very carefully to what I tell you, for the survival of every human on this planet is at stake."

Johann forced himself to stop staring at the woman he adored and to pay attention to what she was saying. "There is a terrible danger here on this planet when both moons are full," she said. "Only by taking extreme precautions can any of you survive."

"What kind of danger?" Johann asked, puzzled. "And what kind of precautions?"

The white Beatrice smiled again. "For reasons that you would never be able to comprehend," she said, "I cannot give you any more specifics. In fact, I can only tell you two things: observe the nepps, for in their behavior lie the clues to your safety; also, no land upon which any of you have ever walked is safe."

Johann's mind was exploding with questions. "Are those nepps the furry little creatures up in the hills behind our village?" he asked first.

Beatrice nodded. "But that's the only question I am al-lowed to answer," she said. "Everything else, Brother Jo-hann, you must figure out for yourself."

The glowing bright light, which had been stationed a few kilometers away during their entire conversation, now started moving toward them. "We have only a minute or so left, Brother Johann," the white Beatrice said hurriedly, "and I didn't want to forget to tell you what a big help Sister Nuba has been to me."

"So is Nuba still alive, then?" Johann asked.

"She is like me," Beatrice answered.

She extended her hand in a farewell gesture. Johann

reached out, touched her fingers fleetingly, and felt a tingle run through his body.

"I have never stopped loving you," he said, shielding his eyes from the oncoming light.

"I know," he heard her voice say. Her figure had now been engulfed by the light. "And you have been a wonderful father for Maria, Brother Johann. Especially today. Thanks for everything."

Johann was forced to turn his head away from whatever vehicle had returned to pick up Beatrice. Several seconds later, as the light sped away out over the ocean, he turned around and waved good-bye. In his heart he knew that she could still see him.

EVEN THOUGH IT was very late, everyone in the West Village was still awake when Johann arrived. During his walk down the side of Black Rock, Johann had decided not to say anything just yet about the apparition of Beatrice. He did, however, explain the arrangement he had negotiated with Maria and the others, and that Jomo, Keiko, and Satoko would be temporarily moving back to the West Village in a few days.

As expected, Siegfried and Beatrice both thought that Johann had been "too easy on the thieves," but the other adults congratulated him on having resolved the crisis in a reasonable way. Later that night, as Johann and Vivien lay side by side in the privacy of their hut, Johann was uncharacteristically silent. Vivien rolled over to face him. "I know you so well, darling," she said. "I can tell there's something you haven't told us."

"I had a visit from Sister Beatrice," Johann said at length. "She came to me while I was resting on the top of Black Rock Promontory. She only stayed for a minute or two, told me it was the last time I would ever see her, and warned me that we would all be in extreme danger on double full moon night."

Johann and Vivien spent the next half hour discussing the details of his encounter with the white Beatrice. "Except for Yasin," Vivien said quietly after they were finished, "Maria and you are the only two of us who have seen Sister Beatrice since we parted company in that spacecraft atrium years and years ago. Maria was a baby, and remembers nothing. Yasin of course has been dead all these years. So there is nobody who can corroborate any part of your tale about the time you spent with Beatrice when she was alive, much less these amazing stories about her visits in a resurrected form."

"I know," said Johann reflectively. "I would certainly have a hard time believing in the apparitions myself if I hadn't experienced them. . . . I remember one of my discussions with Ravi soon after we arrived here. . . . He openly asked, in spite of his Michaelite training, if it was possible that my sightings of Beatrice since her death have all been hallucinations born out of some deep, unexplained yearning or guilt. That's why I didn't say anything tonight about this latest apparition."

"Don't you think it's peculiar," Vivien said after a long pause, "that this white Beatrice, as you call her, appears *only* to you, and never to me, who was her best friend, or to Maria, her daughter and next of kin?"

"Maybe. I guess so." Johann rolled over and looked at his wife. "Are you telling me that you *also* have doubts about whether her visits have actually occurred?"

Vivien sat up on her mat. "Johann, once many years ago I saw an apparition of my own, a ribbon of sparkling, dancing particles that formed into an angel in front of my disbelieving eyes. But since that time, I have personally witnessed no more of these miracles. I love you, I am your wife, and I want to believe your stories, but if I am having difficulty with them, imagine what the others, who have no experience at all with these kinds of events, must be thinking? How can we possibly convince them that the danger your white Beatrice mentioned is real? Especially since she was so vague."

"I don't know," Johann said. "That's why I wanted to discuss this whole situation with you first."

They were both silent for several minutes. "Do you remember," Johann then said, "a long discussion you, Sister Beatrice, and I had that night at the church on Mars, about the reality of Joan of Arc's voices?"

"Yes, I do," Vivien answered. "And I also remember you insisted that absence of any explicit proof that what the voices said was true cast doubt upon the reality of their existence. At which point Sister Beatrice gently upbraided you for your narrow view that the scientific method was the only valid approach for determining truth."

"Joan's voices told her," Johann continued, "that she would lead the French to throw off the oppressive yoke of the English, and their predictions turned out to be true. But the result does not prove that the voices existed. An equally valid argument could be made that an inspired Joan fabricated the voices as a vehicle to incite the Dauphin and the French to rally around her and drive the English from French territory."

"Okay," Vivien said, "but so what? I'm not following you. What does this discussion have to do with your visit from Sister Beatrice?"

Johann's features were now animated. "Don't you see?" he said. "Our situation is more straightforward. The apparition of Beatrice has warned me of an extreme danger that will occur on double full moon night. It may be that everyone, including you, believes that my visions of her are a kind of hallucination. But in this instance we will have some kind of proof in only a matter of days. If the danger turns out to be real, then voilà, the apparition must have really occurred. If there is no danger on double full moon night, then my postmortem sightings of Beatrice have probably all been hallucinations."

"This just might work," Vivien said admiringly, after a brief hesitation. "I presume you intend to inform everyone about the visitation, raise the issue yourself about its reality, and ask the group to give you the benefit of the doubt and follow your recommendations between now and the double full moon."

"Exactly," said Johann.

FOUR

AT VIVIEN'S SUGGESTION, Johann waited to mention the apparition of Beatrice until after Jomo, Keiko, and Satoko arrived in the West Village. Both Jomo and Keiko worked very hard, starting before even Siegfried and not stopping until all the rest of the work for the day had been finished. Morale was high on the third evening when Johann decided to tell everyone about the visit from Sister Beatrice and the warning she had given him.

Johann candidly admitted that what he was describing to them might seem bizarre and difficult to believe. He even added, with some humor, that if the apparition had been only a figment of his imagination, they would all know soon enough, in approximately fifty more days. He also told everyone that he was going to take off by himself the next day, to find and observe the nepps, and he both asked their indulgence and requested that they fulfill his normal duties while he was gone.

Early the next morning Johann, carrying the heavy knapsack that Vivien had helped him pack with supplies that he might need for as long as a two-week expedition, climbed the switchbacks beside the creek. He stopped at the little lake for his normal morning swim. While he was swimming he noted to himself that he had seen no sign of any of the nepps for a long time, perhaps as long as twenty days. Johann also realized that he did not really have any good ideas about where the nepps might be—on his few brief excursions into the territory above the lake he had never encountered more than a handful of them at a time.

He began his search by climbing along the side of the broadest and strongest of the creeks that dropped into the lake. The ascent was steep, and after several hundred meters became rocky and devoid of all vegetation. Johann studied the ground for signs of tracks or nepp droppings, which he was certain he would recognize, but after walking all day he had still not seen anything that suggested the presence of the nepps. A disappointed Johann spent his first night with his sleeping mat wedged between two large boulders a few meters to the side of the creek.

When he awakened the next day, Johann decided to retrace his steps and head back toward the swimming lake. Just before he began his descent, however, he heard a peculiar gushing sound, lasting for maybe thirty seconds, in the distance off to his right. Leaving a carefully marked stone on top of the largest boulder he could find, and etching his current location with his knife on a crude map on one of the many pieces of thin bark he was carrying in his pack, Johann headed in the direction of the sound.

The mostly barren ground over which he was traveling became darker and more volcanic-looking as he walked. Based on his general geographic sense, Johann felt certain he was in the Eastern Hills above Black Rock Promontory. He continued to note features on his map, and to leave marking stones in prominent places, so that he would not have to worry about becoming lost.

After nearly an hour of walking on mostly flat terrain, Johann heard the thirty seconds of gushing again, this time much louder, but unfortunately coming from his left, where a steep rock slope blocked his progress. Following some investigation, Johann found a roundabout passage up the rock slope that was difficult but not impossible. However, the three-point scrambling over the boulders tired him quickly. He was quite fatigued when he stopped for lunch.

While he was sitting quietly eating one of the tasty yellow fruits that he and his family called a darben, Johann heard an unusual sequence of sounds, almost a song, similar in tone to the plucking of harp strings but much more rapid and not nearly as melodious. The sequence was followed by another, a variation on the same theme but with a higher pitch and in a slightly different key. As these sounds continued to alternate, first one and then the other, Johann was able to pinpoint the direction from which they were coming. Moving with great care, he edged along the side of the rock against which he had been leaning until he could see a barren pitch of dirt, in full sunlight, no more than ten meters square, in the middle of which were two of the strangest creatures that Johann had ever seen.

At first glance they looked like two giant, segmented centipedes, perhaps a meter long, each with a vertical cluster of long thin reeds attached to its rear segment. These reeds rose thirty or forty centimeters into the air. The larger of the two animals, the one whose song had the lower pitch, was bright red in color everywhere except for the reed cluster, where each of the hundred or so different elements seemed to be a different color. The song of the creature, if that's indeed what it was, was created by both horizontal and vertical undulations of this reed cluster, the individual notes occurring as each element was distended from its equilibrium position. Accompanying the music was a dazzling visual display as well, as the twists and twirls of the reeds produced an astonishing profusion of color.

The other animal was cobalt-blue along the length of its segmented body. Its reed cluster was essentially colorless, but it also was able to produce a song by moving the individual elements to and fro.

As Johann watched, the red creature sang and displayed,

and then took a small step in the direction of the other. At first the cobalt-blue animal backed up after its song, but as the dance continued it began to move forward toward the red aggressor, turning its body slightly to the side.

Just before they reached each other, the red animal suddenly introduced a significant variation into its song, increasing both the number and speed of the undulations in its reed cluster. At this signal the blue partner lay down on the ground and rolled over, exposing its lighter, soft underbelly of powder-blue.

By this time the two creatures had traveled far enough that Johann could no longer see them clearly. When he moved himself to another location for a better view, he accidentally dislodged a small stone, which rumbled down the far side of the rock behind which he was hiding. In an instant the blue creature rolled over and stood up, its reed cluster whirling into action and making a pulsating, repeating, two-beat sound that was much louder than its earlier song. The red animal picked up the same refrain as both creatures faced the spot where the dislodged rock had struck the ground.

Within seconds the area around Johann was full of these alarm sounds. He turned to his right and saw a new, orange creature of the same species blocking his path. Out on the barren dirt square, the red animal was moving toward Johann with its back arched and a long, needle-shaped object extending about five centimeters forward from the front segment of its body.

Johann scrambled to the top of the largest boulder in the vicinity and counted six of the creatures in open view, each looking hostile and making the same two-syllable alarm sound. Since the first noise sounded to Johann like *ack*, and the second like *yong*, Johann began referring to these animals in his own mind as ackyongs.

Several minutes later, when Johann had made no attempt to descend from his boulder and confront the ackyongs, the large red creature Johann had first seen retracted its stinger and called off the siege by silencing its alarm. Within moments all the ackyongs Johann could see were crawling with surprising speed toward a large rock over-hang thirty or forty meters to the right. Johann followed at a distance and watched two ackyongs open and then enter a long, flat shell nested against a rock wall under an overhang. The shell, one of two dozen in a long row under that par-ticular overhang, then closed immediately.

JOHANN SAT WHERE he could see the ackyong shells for half an hour more. During this time he again heard the thirty-second gushing sound, and twice saw one of the shells open and an ackyong edge partially outside. Even though Johann was not moving, the creatures possessed some kind of sensors that recognized he was still present, for both times the ackyong in question sounded its two-beat alarm and retreated back into its long, hard shell.

As fascinating as Johann found these strange new crea-tures, by mid-afternoon he had reminded himself that the primary purpose for his expedition was to find and observe the nepps, and that he had not yet made any progress toward that goal. Marking carefully the location of the ack-yongs, Johann left the area and headed toward the gushing sound. After several minutes of difficult trekking the ter-rain around him changed abruptly and Johann recognized that he had entered a highly active seismic area, like the Solfatara in Italy that he had visited while a student at the University of Berlin. It was thus no surprise to him that the sound he had been pursuing turned out to be coming from a periodic geyser.

The first time he saw the geyser erupt Johann was about a hundred meters away, and his view was obstructed by rocks and bushes. He heard it begin and, moving quickly, was able to see the geyser at its peak, when the ejected subsurface water reached an altitude of sixty meters or so. Disappointed that he had not been able to watch the eruption from start to finish, Johann decided to remain near the vent so that he could watch the next cycle in its entirety.

While he was waiting, Johann examined the unusual landscape in the region. There were holes in the ground out of which fumes and smoke were rising, bubbling hot springs continually pumping water into a creek that ran away from the region, and innumerable open mudpots of different hues and viscosities, in which liquid material oozed and bubbled very close to the surface itself. Around two of these mudpots, which seemed to contain the same or similar material, Johann found many sets of animal tracks. Johann bent down to examine the tracks carefully. Among them he was fairly certain he could recognize the familiar nepp tracks that he had seen so often near the swimming lake.

Johann admired the next eruption of the geyser, but by this time his mind was focused on a plan to conceal himself so that he might observe the nepps the next time they visited one of the two special mudpots. By nightfall he had found a nearly perfect hiding place, no more than fifteen meters from one of the mudpots that had been surrounded by tracks. He stayed awake another two hours after the sun had set, but there were no visitors during that time.

Just before dawn Johann awakened when he heard scurrying sounds plus what was unmistakably animal chatter. At the nearby mudpot, three nepps had gathered. Two were holding a round container and the third was dipping what looked like a crude spoon into the hot bubbling goo and depositing the material into the container. Before they were finished, a second trio of nepps arrived. A brief conversation ensued before the first group departed and the second threesome filled their rectangular container with the thick brown muck.

By sunrise the nepps had all disappeared. Fortunately for Johann, it was easy to follow their tracks. They stayed on the dirt whenever possible and even in a grassy region the recent indentations were easy to spot. Johann had thought that their colony would not be far away. He was wrong. By mid-morning, now almost five kilometers away from the mudpots, he was still following their trail.

He was also climbing in altitude. After a particularly steep half kilometer he emerged onto a great plateau that was covered with tall grasses and surrounded by mountains on one side and thick forests on the other. Here Johann lost the trail of the nepps he had been following. He sat down to eat lunch and to consider what he should do next.

Johann had already reached one conclusion. The material in those mudpots must be very important to the nepps. They certainly would not travel such a long distance without some compelling reason. And judging from the large number of tracks that he had seen around the two mudpots, this gathering of the hot brown muck involved a large number of the members of their colony.

He decided that the only way he could possibly obtain an overview of where he now was, and perhaps gain some insight into where the nepps he had been following had gone, was to climb a portion of what Johann was certain was the beginning of the western mountains. It took him the rest of the day, however, to find a decent path, beside a creek that formed a canyon between tall rock formations on either side. He had no view at all of the great plateau until after he cut through a side canyon, scrambled up a boulder field, and then worked his way back to an overlook that was at least two hundred meters above the plateau. By this time it was already dark and Johann was thoroughly exhausted and disappointed. He reminded himself as he fell asleep that he had already spent three days on this trek and still had no information of any worth.

• • •

THE NEXT MORNING, however, provided a huge bonanza for Johann. From his overlook he could see the entire plateau and even the regions beyond, where the geysers and mudpots were located. Below him to his right, in an area Johann estimated to be at least five kilometers square, was the home colony of the nepps. They lived in hundreds of dirt mounds and underground warrens, like prairie dogs on Earth, and could be seen either scampering about their homes, conversing in groups of three or four, or performing disparate tasks among an orderly set of rows and columns contained by tall stalks of what appeared to be a domesticated plant.

To the left of the colony, on the other side of a small, dense grove, was a large lake at the foot of the mountains. To Johann's astonishment, this lake was absolutely teeming with swimming nepps. To verify that what he was seeing was correct, Johann passed around the side of a small outcropping and found a second overlook just above this lake. There were indeed hundreds, perhaps even a thousand, nepps swimming laps below him. What's more, unless Johann was completely misinterpreting what he was seeing, there seemed to be dozens of supervising nepps around the lake, providing either encouragement or instructions to the swimmers.

What in the world is going on here? Johann asked himself. *Why are all these creatures swimming laps? Is it some rite of their species? Or possibly one of the keys I'm supposed to find?*

Johann stayed in the mountains above the nepp colony the entire day. He moved back and forth between the two separate overlooks, observing the behavior below and trying without success to draw conclusions about what, if anything, it all meant. As far as he could tell, the nepps were either oblivious to his presence or did not care that he was watching them.

Several things that Johann saw struck him as peculiar and unlike anything he had ever witnessed in another biological species at the development level of the nepps. First, they were exceedingly orderly. Each individual apparently had a specific task or assignment throughout the day. At two different times during the day, the lake emptied of swimmers and those nepps who had been swimming laps returned to the central plaza in the colony for a meal served from huge pots to the whole group standing in three long queues. Twenty minutes later, after the meal had been completed, another group of nepps filled the lake and was swimming back and forth under the guidance of the same group of nepps who had overseen the earlier swimmers. The earlier groups that had been swimming had, by this time, either returned to household chores in the colony, or were working among the tall stalks in the fields.

After the sunset, Johann could no longer follow any of the activity in the nepp colony below him. He found a comfortable spot on the overlook and stretched out on his sleeping mat. *Observe the nepps,* he remembered the white Beatrice saying, *for in their behavior lie the clues to your safety.*

And what have I observed so far? Johann asked himself before falling asleep. *That they spend a lot of time swimming. That they have at least one domesticated plant. That they travel a great distance to gather a hot brown muck. That they are orderly. But what this means in terms of our safety and survival is a mystery to me.*

FIVE

JOHANN AWOKE IN the middle of the night and realized he had still established no rationale for why the nepps
collected the material from the mudpots. In fact, at no time
while he had been watching them had he even seen any
nepps carrying the containers containing the muck. The
previous day he had located an accessible shelf, in altitude
halfway between his overlook and the colony, that would
afford him a much better view of the nepps. He had been
reluctant to drop down to the shelf during the day, however, for he felt certain that he would be seen by the animals
and he had no idea how they would react to his presence.

There was ample moonlight a couple of hours before
dawn for Johann to make a safe descent to the shelf. From
there he could see the silhouettes of six groups of three
nepps each, gathered around a leader nepp between the
edge of the fields and the beginning of the mounds. The
whole group of nepps were standing around a huge circular
pot, mostly buried in the ground, that Johann had somehow
not seen the previous day. After some chatter, the trios of
nepps dispersed with their crude spoons and containers,
presumably heading for the geyser region.

Ten or fifteen minutes later, after a specific call from
the leader nepp who had been in the vicinity the entire
time, a dozen or so additional animals came out of their
mounds and stopped in an open work area a few meters to
the side of the pot. They began to tear off the bottom stalks
of the domesticated plant (Johann had already noticed the

day before that the nepps ate only the flowery top part of the plant), clean out its insides, and grind the material into powder with stones. From time to time the leader nepp would inspect each of their efforts.

Not long after dawn, the first group of nepps returned with containers of the brown muck, into which the powder was mixed. Johann, now concerned about being seen, climbed carefully back to his overlook while still watching the activity. Altogether, the morning's effort had yielded five muck containers now thoroughly mixed with stalk powder. The leader nepp tested each mixture carefully, even placing a small portion on its bizarre narrow tongue, and then selected two of the containers to remain on the table in the work area. The other three were unceremoniously dumped into the buried circular pot.

The nepp colony was now awakening. Heads were popping out of holes, juveniles were scurrying about like puppies, morning conversations were under way. Slowly but surely all the nepps were moving in the direction of the central plaza where the vast urns containing breakfast were being filled with food that had been in preparation for half an hour.

Johann, meanwhile, kept a close watch on the nepp who had supervised the predawn activities. This nepp was one of the first to eat breakfast, after which it selected eight others, all of the black-and-white variety, who were larger than the solid-colored animals, and led them over to the worktable area where the two chosen containers were sitting.

While this nepp leader was chattering to its colleagues, the rest of the colony started another ordinary day, one third of the animals heading for the lake to swim, another third going to work in the fields, and the final third returning to the mounds and warrens, probably for domestic duties. The eight black-and-white nepps who had been selected at breakfast, however, walked around the outside of the colony, two pairs of them carrying one container each, the other four with small bags on their backs that were tied around their necks, and headed in the direction of the canyon creek that Johann had followed on his way to the overlook.

Johann scrambled back toward the canyons, certain that whatever this special group of nepps was about to do was of major significance. Fortunately, he arrived at the top of the side canyon just as the eight nepps had turned into it. He followed them from above for about a kilometer, until they disappeared into a group of thick bushes on the shores of the creek. For an hour there was no movement. From Johann's vantage point he could see the entire canyon floor, so there was no doubt that the nepps were still in the bushes. But what were they doing there?

In the middle of the morning Johann heard a familiar sound just beneath him, on his side of the canyon. It was the song with two related variations, and it kept repeating methodically, first one version and then the other, just as it had done a few days before. Johann searched below him until he spotted the pair of ackyongs. Soon a second pair could be heard, then a third. Moving carefully along his ridge, Johann found a spot where he could see the rock overhang that had been directly beneath him. Thirty or more ackyong shells were lined up in a row against the wall. Many of their occupants, however, if Johann's surmise was correct, were now down in the sun on the floor of the canyon, performing their mating dances.

Johann strained his eyes and found seven or eight pairs of ackyongs in the area around the creek, far from their shells under the overhang. The superposition of all their sounds created a gentle symphony far more pleasing than any of their individual songs, and Johann found himself becoming sleepy. Before he closed his eyes, however, he observed that the bushes were stirring and that all the nepps had now gathered at one edge.

Suddenly the nepps all burst from the bushes with incredible speed, even the ones carrying the containers. They raced up the slopes toward the rock overhang where all the ackyong shells were located. The nepps dipped their paws in the hot muck and spread it rapidly around the edges where the two halves of the ackyong shells were joined. Slowly, the shells began to release and open. Other nepps then forced themselves into the shell cracks and pried the shells far enough open that a companion could see inside.

They moved from shell to shell with amazing alacrity. Somehow they knew which shells did not contain a host ackyong. Three nepps entered each of the shells of interest, emerging a few seconds later with an ackyong egg that was immediately placed in one of the bags. Once a bag was full, one of the black-and-white nepps raced away, down the slope with the bag on its back and tied around its neck, headed for the nepp colony.

After three eggs had been removed, the symphony coming from the ackyongs on the sunny canyon floor abruptly changed to the two-beat alarm sound. The nepp thieves had been discovered and the ackyongs were clambering up the slope to confront their adversaries. One bright yellow ackyong was blocking the escape path of a nepp carrying a particularly large egg. Without any hesitation, two of the other nepps screamed ferociously and hurtled headlong into the yellow ackyong, diverting it long enough that the egg-carrying nepp was able to run away. The ensuing battle was short. The surprisingly agile ackyong inserted its formidable stinger in first one nepp, then the other, killing them both instantly.

Three nepps had escaped with eggs, two had been killed, and the remaining three were exposed and surrounded by the angry ackyongs returning to protect their shells. Each nepp now ran in a different direction. Johann could no longer follow all the action on the canyon floor. He heard one animal wail of pain and then, about five minutes later, the double-beat alarm of the ackyongs ceased.

Johann returned to his overlook in a state of confusion. The midday meal at the nepp colony had just concluded, and the normal groups were headed for the lake, the fields, and the mounds. The nepp leader who had organized the expedition was nowhere in sight and there was no sign of the ackyong eggs that had presumably been brought back to the colony.

Johann sat on a flat rock and ate his lunch. His frustration was building. He was observing the nepps, as the white Beatrice had instructed, but nothing he had yet seen was giving him any clues about any safety precautions to be taken on double full moon night.

BEFORE DAWN THE next morning Johann was again down on the shelf below his overlook. The same nepp leader met again with six threesomes who were dispatched to bring back the brown material from the distant mudpots. Again, after ground powder was mixed into the muck, a group of eight black-and-white nepps, two pairs carrying containers and the other four with bags tied around their necks, scampered away from the colony. But this time the group went in another direction, away from Johann. He watched them until they disappeared down a distant slope.

Johann remained on his overlook the entire morning, carefully following the movement of the nepp leader who seemed to be organizing all the critical activities. A few minutes before the middle of the day two nepps carrying ackyong eggs in their bags returned to the colony. The nepp leader received a brief report and then ushered the returnees into the grove that was between the mounds and the lake. The three emerged a few minutes later, with neither bags nor eggs, and were soon joined by another pair of black-and-white nepps, one clearly injured, who probably had taken part in the morning expedition. After another short conversation, the leader nepp crossed over to one of the larger mounds in the colony and entered. Johann did not see the leader again during the day.

As night fell, Johann concluded that he had learned as much as he could from his observations on the overlook. So far, there had been no evidence of any nepp activity at night, at least not until the predawn hours, and the creatures were apparently not concerned about security, for Johann had seen no sentinels posted while everyone was sleeping. He thought that there was a good chance that he could pass through their colony undetected and might discover something that had thus far escaped his notice.

The descent from his overlook through the canyon to the nepp colony was made much easier by the brilliant moonlight. At one point Johann stopped, looking up, and wondered what kind of terror the double moon night might bring that required all the precautions the white Beatrice had mentioned. For a moment, he wondered if it was possible that all his visits from her could really be hallucinations of some kind. *But no,* he told himself, *that cannot be possible. The six months Maria and I spent in Whiteland were absolutely real.*

He entered the nepp colony undisturbed. He walked past the mounds, the central plaza, and along the path toward the lake. Johann then returned and examined the fields and the work area where each of the morning expeditions had been organized. He saw nothing new.

Next he decided to follow the path that entered the grove adjacent to the colony. That was where he had seen the nepp leader take the ackyong eggs. Thirty meters into the trees he heard an animal sound that he did not recognize, a rhythmic whistling occurring about twenty times a minute. At one place on the path the moonlight split through the trees and Johann could see both a small fenced compound in front of him and a sentry, asleep and snoring just to the side of the door.

The door swung open noiselessly and Johann entered

the dim compound. He was immediately assaulted by an overpoweringly foul odor, a stench that smelled like a combination of rotten food and feces. Suppressing his gag reflex, Johann surveyed the area. Against the fence on the left were crude stacked shelves, broken into perhaps a hundred individual compartments by vertical dividers. Roughly half these compartments contained ackyong eggs.

On Johann's right was a large basin. A broken ackyong egg was lying in the basin, surrounded by a colorless fluid that Johann suspected was the source of the powerful stench. He approached the basin and put one finger barely into the fluid. Johann cautiously raised the finger to his nose. The smell was so terrible that he immediately vomited. He then glanced around quickly to see if he had disturbed the sleeping sentry. He had not. The nepp was still snoring.

At the back of the compound was a set of vats of different sizes. All but one was empty. Johann peered into the occupied vat, which was as tall as his waist, and saw what appeared to be hundreds of tennis balls of different colors, each with a dozen or so tiny spikes growing out of its cover. Curious, Johann reached down and picked one up. One of the spikes extended into his hand, stinging him, and he dropped the living ball back into the vat. The creature made a sound like *birtle* and within a few seconds the entire vat was teeming with moving, spiked tennis balls all saying *birtle*.

The noise was sufficient to wake the snoring nepp, but Johann had already raced by the creature before it had gathered enough of its wits to scream. Johann had already planned his escape route. He turned left, out of the colony, at a full gallop and did not stop until he was halfway to the periodic geyser.

THE GROUP HAD sat quietly, only occasionally asking questions of clarification, during the hour that Johann had related his experiences during his absence from the village. Siegfried, Vivien, and Jomo had followed the story with the most interest. Baby Kwame had been something of a distraction and at different times both Keiko and Satoko had left the group with the child to keep him from disturbing the others.

"So what have you concluded from all your observations?" Ravi asked when Johann was finished.

"Very little, I'm afraid," Johann said. "The nepps are a fascinating species, and if I were a biologist I would have hundreds of questions that I would want to answer. But if what I have seen was supposed to help us prepare for the 'extreme danger' of double full moon night, then my trip was a failure."

"That's only forty more days, isn't it?" Jomo asked. Earlier Johann and he had agreed that the work on the harvest was now basically complete and that sometime in the next few days Siegfried would accompany Jomo, his family, and a large quantity of food back across Black Rock to the East Village.

"Forty-two to be exact," Johann replied.

"That doesn't give us much time," Jomo commented, "especially if any of our preparations require much planning."

"There were two instructions that Beatrice gave you, weren't there, Johann?" Vivien said. "Observe the nepps and something else about land you've never walked on."

"No land upon which any of you have ever walked is safe," Johann repeated from memory.

"If we take that statement literally," Vivien said, "then it would suggest that we're all supposed to move up into the western mountains—at one time or another one of us has explored virtually every other accessible region, especially now that you have been in the area around the nepp colony."

Siegfried had not said much all evening. At this point in the conversation he stood up, turned around, and faced the ocean. "What about the island out there?" he said. "That certainly qualifies as a piece of land upon which none of us has ever walked."

"I'm afraid all this is becoming a little farfetched for us," Ravi said at this juncture. Anna and he rose from where they had been sitting and started moving toward their hut. "With all due respect, Johann," he added, "your story about the nepps was indeed fascinating, but Anna and I had doubts about the validity of your 'visitation' before, and nothing you said tonight has caused us to change our minds. We see no evidence of any kind of danger, much less the extreme danger that Sister Beatrice supposedly warned you about."

"Moving ourselves and supplies into the western mountains would be a monumental nightmare," Anna said. "And the island is of course out of the question. Even if we were all excellent swimmers, which we aren't, the sperdens would devour us all before we were more than a few hundred meters offshore."

"I understand," Johann said as he bade good night to Ravi, Anna, and then Serentha. At that moment the image of hundreds of nepps swimming laps in the lake flashed vividly through his mind. *What if?* he started to ask himself.

"We're going to bed as well, Uncle Johann," Jomo said. "Keiko and I spent all day bundling grain, and we're tired. Besides, Kwame still doesn't sleep through the night."

"Thanks for all your work, Jomo," Johann said. "I know it hasn't been easy with my having been gone all this time."

Jomo shrugged. "It hasn't been that tough," he said. "And it's been great to watch Mom with her grandson."

Vivien, Siegfried, and Johann were left alone after the others had departed. "None of them believe that Sister Beatrice actually appeared, do they?" Johann said to his wife and son.

Vivien put her arm around him. "They believe you are a wonderful man—kind, intelligent, thoughtful, and our natural leader. They also think that you are convinced you had a visitation from Sister Beatrice in which she warned you of dangers on double full moon night."

"They love you, Father," Siegfried said, "but you can't blame them for not accepting your story at face value. I was talking to Serentha about it tonight. 'If this ghost or angel or whatever *really* came to give Uncle Johann a warning for all of us,' she said, 'then why wasn't she more explicit about the danger we will be facing. Why did she speak in riddles?'"

Johann shook his head. "Serentha's a smart girl, son," he said, "and her questions are legitimate. As are the doubts of Ravi and the others." He suddenly had a flashback to a conversation about faith that he had once had with Beatrice. "I guess I'm the Thomas in this situation," he added, "the only one who has actually put his finger through the hole in Christ's hand."

Siegfried looked puzzled. Vivien smiled. "I don't think our son's biblical education has been complete enough that he understands the analogy," she said. "But I certainly appreciate how difficult this must be for you."

After kissing Siegfried good night, Vivien and Johann walked slowly toward their own hut. "It will be nice to have your warm body next to mine tonight," Vivien said. "I have missed you."

"And I have missed you too," Johann said. He kissed her and then glanced up at the stars above their heads. "Don't you find it ironic," he said, "that I, who have been all my life so dubious about and critical of all religious and other spiritual experiences related by others, am now asking people to believe that I have had one myself?"

Vivien smiled. "As Sister Beatrice often said, God works in many wondrous ways."

SIX

JOHANN ADMITTED TO Vivien that if he returned from his second expedition to observe the nepps without any more concrete information about what they should be doing to prepare for double full moon night, then he would abandon the activity altogether.

It was raining on the morning that Johann was preparing to leave. Siegfried had returned two nights earlier after having helped Jomo and Keiko carry the food to the East Village. He had reported that Maria was as imperious as ever and that neither Eric nor she thanked him for the food. Siegfried also said that only his promise to his father to avoid unpleasantries at all costs had kept him from striking the truculent Eric.

Siegfried appeared in his parents' hut just as Johann was hoisting his knapsack on his back. "I want to go with you, Father," he said. "Maybe four eyes will be better than two."

Johann glanced briefly at Vivien. "Your offer is appreciated, son," he said. "But there are reasons why I must go by myself. First, you are needed here in the village, to help your mother and the others with tasks that require physical strength. Second, and maybe more importantly, I have become quite familiar with the nepps, and know what I am looking for. It would be just as likely that you would be a hindrance as a help."

Siegfried knew better than to argue with his father. He helped Johann adjust his knapsack and gave him a hug. "Be careful," Vivien said as Johann walked out of the hut into the light rain.

The climb was difficult because of the steady rain. It took Johann almost all day to reach the region of the geysers, fumaroles, and mudpots. Although he was certain there was probably a more direct route to the nepp colony, he was not willing to take any chances on losing his way in unfamiliar terrain. He was acutely aware that double full moon night was now only thirty-six days away.

Johann made a wide sweep around the nepp colony, to avoid being seen in case his rapid flight on the previous visit had branded him as an enemy of the species, and followed the canyon paths back to his overlook. The rain fell throughout his journey and several times he slipped while climbing up rocky surfaces. But by the end of the second day he had reached the position from which he had previously observed the nepps.

The rain stopped just after nightfall. After sleeping a few hours, Johann dropped down to his shelf, expecting to see the nepp leader dispatching the mudpot trios just before dawn. But there was no activity of any kind in the nepp colony before sunrise.

Johann climbed back to his customary overlook as the first rays of sunlight struck the nepp mounds and warrens. The furry, chattering creatures soon emerged from their holes and ambled toward the central plaza for breakfast. After breakfast, the whole colony was addressed by the same nepp leader who had been organizing the mudpot and egg-foraging expeditions during Johann's previous visit.

During his talk, four vats, each carried by three obviously struggling black-and-white nepps, came into view, entering from the path through the grove that led to the fenced compound. These vats were placed on the ground between the work area and the huge circular pot that was buried in the ground. As Johann watched intently, the nepp leader moved out of the colony, on a path leading to the right, followed by several hundred members of his species and the four heavy vats. The whole contingent quickly disappeared from sight and Johann turned his attention to the lake, which was starting to fill with swimmers.

At the lake, something different from what he had previously seen was now occurring. Johann moved around the outcropping to the point on his overlook that was just above the lake. Sitting on the edge of the lake were two more of the large vats. Stretching behind each vat was a queue of nepps. When each animal reached the front position in the line, a swimming supervisor dipped a cup into one of the vats and doused the particular nepp with a clear, slimy material that was subsequently rubbed deeper into the fur by another of the supervisors. Then the nepp was allowed to enter the lake.

Johann surmised that the material in the vats was the same noisome substance from the inside of the ackyong eggs that had made him vomit in the compound on his previous visit. But what he wanted to know was *why* the nepps were rubbing this stuff all over themselves. Was he watching an elaborate rite that he would never be able to comprehend? Or was there something in this process that contained a clue about the "safety precautions" he would need to take for his extended family?

Lunch came and a second group of nepps returned to the lake and went through the same procedure. While Johann was still pondering the significance of this unusual activity, the nepp leader returned with the contingent who had left early in the morning. Johann rushed back to his other observation post, but the only thing he was able to determine was that the vats that had accompanied the excursion were clearly lighter now, for they were being handled easily by a pair of brown nepps.

Johann could not sleep that night. The changes in the

nepp activity during the days that he had been gone suggested that he was witnessing another stage in some process of preparation. If this was true, then everything he was seeing was probably associated in some way with the coming double full moon night. Johann determined that the only way he could obtain any substantive new information would be to somehow accompany the nepps on whatever it was that they were doing away from the colony.

AT DAWN THE next morning Johann was carefully concealed in a group of bushes beside the path that the nepps had taken out of the colony the previous day. As morning came he began to worry. What if yesterday's excursion had been a one-time event? What if the nepp leader took his followers in a different direction altogether this morning? What if he was discovered and attacked?

From his hiding place in the bushes Johann could not see the mounds and warrens of the nepp colony. When he had waited for what seemed like an hour, Johann decided that he had made a mistake and was wasting his time. He had just altered his position in the bushes, preparing to leave, when he heard the sound of nepp chatter heading his way. Johann immediately ducked down, as the chatter increased, and through the branches of the bushes he saw the first of the nepps file along the path.

It was easy for him to tell when they had all passed. The vat carriers were at the end of the procession, moving more slowly than the others. They were clearly struggling with their loads, for the equivalent of nepp grunts and groans accompanied their passage past Johann's bush. He waited several minutes after he could no longer hear any animal noises, and then emerged from his bush and walked down the path, following them.

Johann moved slowly, stopping often, always being careful to keep well behind any nepp chatter that he could hear. Meanwhile, by observing the sun and noticing that the path led mostly downhill, Johann concluded that the nepp group was heading toward the ocean. Constructing a mental map based on his general knowledge of the geography of the area, Johann guessed that the entire procession should reach the ocean, if that was indeed their destination, several kilometers to the west of the human village, in a region that none of them had ever explored because the slopes on the west side of their creek were so precipitous.

Indeed, steep rock cliffs bounded the path on the left as it began to meander beside a small and pleasant creek that dropped out of the hills on the right. The path then entered a phase of sharp turns and Johann slowed his pace, fearful that he might stumble upon the rear of the procession after going around a corner.

Near one of these sharp turns, Johann heard the familiar nepp chatter directly in front of him. Easing forward cautiously, Johann glanced around the corner. About twenty meters away one of the four vats was sitting on the path, surrounded by three black-and-whites, all of whom were lying on the ground in a state of exhaustion with their bizarre tongues hanging out of their mouths. The nepp leader was pacing among them, pointing repeatedly at the vat, and constantly either exhorting or scolding its colleagues. At one point the leader even pushed one of the exhausted nepps over to the side of the vat and raised one of its forelegs up to the closest handle. The black-and-white let its foreleg droop back toward its body, generating what sounded like an angry comment from the nepp leader.

Much later, Johann would ask himself whether what he did next was a stroke of genius or stupidity. Nevertheless, he suddenly emerged from his hiding place and walked down the path toward the nepps and the vat. All the supposedly exhausted black-and-whites scampered into the brush on the creek side of the path. Johann grabbed the handles and picked up the vat, which was full of birtles, and easily hoisted it onto his right shoulder.

The nepp leader did not move as Johann approached. Nor did it try to interfere when Johann bent down to lift the vat. It simply stood in the pathway, eyeing Johann intently, the white balls in its crescent eyes rolling back and forth in constant motion.

Johann smiled and took a forward step along the path. The nepp leader waited only a second or two before shouting something to the others, who began to slink out of the bushes. The nepp leader then gestured to Johann to follow him down the path.

The leader, Johann, and the three trailing black-and-whites soon caught up with the other vats at the tail end of the procession. About ten minutes later, the nepp leader shouted to another group of black-and-whites, who were looking fatigued, and they put down their vat in the middle of the path. The leader then approached Johann and, using a combination of chattering and gestures, requested that he pick up the vat that had just been placed on the ground.

Johann understood immediately. He put the vat he was carrying gently down on the path, and picked up the other one. There was a chorus of approving chatter. The three black-and-whites who had been carrying the first vat, now apparently rested, grabbed it by the handles and lifted it off the ground.

During the next hour, Johann carried each of the four vats one time each. Two of them contained birtles and two contained the terrible-smelling clear slime from the ackyong eggs. At length the path led out onto a mesa about twenty meters above where the ocean waves crashed against a rock cliff. The nepp leader, standing at the edge of the mesa with its back to the ocean, signaled for the vats to be placed beside him. Immediately thereafter, the several hundred nepps formed into orderly rows and columns and became completely silent.

• • •

JOHANN STOOD ON one side of the mesa, away from the nepps and the vats, and looked down at the ocean below. He could see a pair of sperdens in the distance, their long, graceful necks twisting this way and that. When the sea creatures spotted the nepp leader, however, who was close enough to the edge to be easily seen, they began swimming toward the cliff, their ululations apparently signaling for others to gather.

Throughout this period the nepp leader was talking to the other members of its species. Of course Johann had no idea what the leader was saying, but from time to time he did watch what it was doing. Several times the nepp leader pointed at the offshore island, well off to the left of the mesa. It also walked over and thumped the vats several times. When eight of the sperdens were clearly visible in the ocean directly underneath the mesa, the leader called the other nepps forward, one row at a time, so that they could look down upon the fearsome sea serpents.

So what will happen now? Johann asked himself as the final row of nepps came forward to view the sperdens. *And what is this ceremony all about?*

He did not have to wait long for his answers. The nepp leader spoke again briefly and then all two hundred of the nepps came forward, spreading out across the edge of the mesa. They dropped down on their haunches and extended their faces just over the edge. Half of them were between Johann and the vats, but he could still follow the proceedings easily. When all the nepps were in position, the nepp leader and eight of the black-and-whites eased one of the birtle vats to the edge of the cliff, and then pushed it over, dumping hundreds of the tennis-ball-shaped creatures into the ocean water below.

What followed was a terrifying scene. Screaming in high-pitched voices, their necks moving with astonishing celerity first in one direction and then another, thrashing into and out of the water, the sperdens gobbled up all the hapless birtles in a matter of minutes. Johann could tell that the nepps closest to him were all trembling from fright. Some of the smaller ones even closed their eyes and backed away from the edge.

It took several seconds for Johann to realize that the nepp leader was now motioning for him to come over beside the vats. Being careful not to step on the nepps in the way, Johann crossed the mesa until he was beside the nepp leader and the remaining three vats. What followed was an elaborate chatter-and-gesture monologue that Johann missed altogether on the first pass. The patient nepp leader repeated his request, very slowly this time, until Johann finally comprehended that he was being asked to pick up one of the vats containing ackyong slime and pour it into the other vat of birtles. Johann did as the nepp leader had requested, struggling not to vomit from the smell, although he had no idea why he was performing the task.

After another short speech from the nepp leader, this vat too was pushed over the cliff. The ocean was now teeming with the hungry, frenzied sperdens. Johann turned his eyes away at first, not wanting to be sickened by what he considered to be a useless slaughter. But as the frenzied cries of the sperdens began to diminish, and then disappeared altogether, the puzzled Johann dropped to his knees and stared at the ocean below. Everywhere he could see unharmed birtles floating on the surface of the water. The sperdens were not attacking them! In fact, they were moving away.

What is happening here? Johann thought rapidly. *Are the sperdens satiated? No, that couldn't be possible, for some of them were not even here for the first batch of birtles.*

Johann's epiphany came suddenly. His synthesis followed in seconds. The sperdens were repelled by the ackyong slime. The nepps were practicing swimming because they intended, after first covering themselves with the ack-yong goo, to head for that offshore island on double full moon night. *Observe the nepps,* he heard the white Beatrice say again inside his head. *No land on which any of you have ever walked is safe.*

Johann stood up, exultant, completely unaware of all the nepps around him. "Oh, thank you, Beatrice," he shouted. "Thank you for believing that I would be able to figure all this out."

His emotional outburst was so strong, and so sudden, that all the nepps in Johann's vicinity scurried away. Next to the remaining full vat, the nepp leader was watching him curiously. Johann made a few apologetic gestures. The nepp leader then raised its forelegs and motioned to Johann again.

When he was standing next to the chief nepp, the animal made a short chattering speech that brought an immediate noisy reaction from the entire nepp contingent. Several seconds later, the nepp leader dipped its two forepaws into the remaining vat of slime and began rubbing the gooey material on Johann's bare chest. The sudden stench was too much for Johann. He gagged twice and then turned and hurled the contents of his stomach into the ocean water. When he turned back to face the nepp leader, the creature grabbed Johann's hands and placed them in the slimy vat. Johann understood. For the next five minutes, as two hundred nepps watched in fascination and trepidation, Johann and the nepp leader rubbed ackyong slime on every square centimeter of each other's body.

The nepp leader and Johann then walked down a difficult path to a small beach area west of the mesa. Looking out into the water, Johann could see a dozen of the sperdens no more than a hundred meters away. They were eagerly eyeing Johann and the chief nepp. On the mesa above, white balls were actively moving in four hundred crescent eyes.

The nepp leader did not pause. It dove directly into the water and started swimming toward the sperdens. Johann, his adrenaline at its peak level, followed the nepp, even passing it after twenty or thirty of his powerful armstrokes. The sperdens waited, anticipant, until the first wave of the slime odor reached them. They turned their heads, ululating in chorus, and began swimming away. *Yes,* Johann shouted to himself, swimming even faster toward the serpents. *Oh, yes yes yes.*

SEVEN

THEY WERE ALL waiting for him on the shore as Johann took his final strokes in the ocean water, let his feet touch the sandy bottom, and walked slowly toward them.

"Unbelievable," Vivien said, rushing forward to give him a hug.

Siegfried was not far behind. "It worked," he shouted with uninhibited exuberance. "You were right."

Only twenty minutes earlier they had been begging Johann not to go into the water. Four huge sperdens had been swimming directly offshore, feeding on the plethora of sea life filling the ocean. They had also been watching the gathered humans with idle curiosity. Vivien had rubbed Johann's body with the foul-smelling slime, unable to fight back her tears of fear.

"Don't worry," Johann had said with a comforting smile. "I told you, I did this with the nepp leader. The sperdens are completely repulsed by the smell."

They had watched him swim directly toward the sperdens, seen the serpents become agitated and prepare to attack, and had expected the worst. But just as Johann had predicted, when he was almost within striking distance, the uncontested kings of the ocean had swum away, no longer interested in what had appeared to be an exciting prey.

Siegfried was still carried away by his excitement. "Can I try it now, Father?" he said. "I want to know what it feels like to swim in the ocean without fear."

"No, son," Johann answered. "We don't want to waste

the slime. We have barely enough to cover everybody on double full moon night."

They walked as a group back to the village, where dinner preparations had been interrupted so that Johann could perform his demonstration. When they reached the kitchen area, everyone sat down in his customary place. "That was indeed impressive," Ravi said, breaking the silence. "Your observation of the nepps certainly did not turn out to be wasted time."

"We have twenty-six days left," Johann said, still exhilarated from his swim. "That should be enough time for virtually all of us to get into some kind of shape, provided we start right away. I know that Vivien, Siegfried, and Beatrice swim well enough to make it out to the island on their own. What about the rest of you? Ravi, how good of a swimmer are you?"

"Actually, Johann, I'm a terrible swimmer," Ravi said. "I nearly drowned once in India when I was a boy. . . . But that's not the only issue here. There are other considerations."

Johann looked perplexed. "From my point of view," Ravi continued gently, "all that has been established is that there exists a repellent that will keep the sperdens from attacking. But that does not necessarily mean that the correct course of action for all of us is to try to swim out to that island on the night of the double full moons."

"What are you trying to say?" Johann asked. "That you still doubt the apparition?"

"There are many, many unanswered questions," Ravi said, "the legitimacy of the apparition and its prophecy being at the top of the list. But in addition, since you can't talk to the nepps, there's no way you could know for certain that they are preparing to flee en masse when the moons are full. There could be many other possible explanations for the scenes you witnessed. Maybe there is some kind of annual pilgrimage out to the island, for example, for purposes we will never ascertain."

Johann struggled to control himself.

"Then there is the whole question of this 'horrible danger' mentioned by Sister Beatrice in your apparition," Ravi continued. "What could that danger possibly be? We have been living here now for over three years and have not encountered anything, except perhaps the sperdens, that threatens our survival. What is it that is *so* terrible we should all risk a *certain* danger, from drowning or perhaps from other sea creatures that we have not yet encountered, to escape? Is the sky suddenly going to fall on us on double full moon night?"

There was a long, tense silence after Ravi finished speaking. In Johann's head he heard Beatrice's voice. *Tell them it's a matter of faith, Brother Johann.*

"I guess," Johann said somewhat dejectedly, "that the critical issue here is faith. You either believe that my visitation from Sister Beatrice was real, and that her warning should be taken seriously, or you don't."

Ravi nodded. "Anna and I have been discussing this very point since you first left to observe the nepps. For your information, she also is a very poor swimmer, and is afraid of the water. Our daughter, Serentha, as far as we know, has never even put her head under water. We think it would be unlikely, even with help from you and Siegfried and no attacks from sperdens or other sea animals, that we would all survive the swim out to the island and back."

He hesitated and sighed heavily. "Johann, we love and admire you, but after weighing all the factors, including this latest information about the nepps and the repellent slime, Anna, Serentha, and I have decided to forgo the swim and take our chances here on double full moon night."

"I see," Johann said, surprised at the strength of the emotion he was feeling. "And the rest of you?" he asked, looking around the group.

"I will be at your side, darling, wherever that is," Vivien said.

"I'm going with you, Father," Siegfried said.

"I'm afraid I agree with Ravi and Anna, Uncle Johann," Beatrice said. "I feel certain I could survive the swim, but what for? I can't imagine anything happening here that could be that dangerous."

"Then I guess it's settled," Johann said. "Vivien, Siegfried, and I will go into training immediately, and the rest of you will continue with your normal lives."

"I would like to try to make the swim," the normally taciturn Serentha said as the group started to break up. "I just hope, Uncle Johann, that you can teach me enough in the next thirty days that I have a chance." She looked over at her parents. "Is that all right with you?"

"As your mother and I told you last night," Ravi said. "This has to be your decision."

"You must be crazy, old man," Eric said, "hiking all the way over here to try to convince us to swim out to an island to escape some unknown danger a ghost told you about."

Johann had not expected a positive reaction in the East Village, but he could not have been content with himself if he hadn't made the effort. "The slime we have really does repel the sperdens," he said. "I can show you if you like."

"That's not really the issue," Maria said. "We believe that part of your story. It's the rest that seems so preposterous to us. To tell you the truth, when Jomo first told us about your having had another visitation from my mother, we all burst out laughing. . . . Besides, Johann, what you are suggesting is not practical. We have two babies here. How could we transport them safely across the water?"

"I could carry them," Johann said. "One on either side

of my head and neck. I could swim breaststroke the entire way."

"Dear Johann," Maria said, leaning forward, "we all know what a champion swimmer you were. But that was years and years ago."

On another planet. In another lifetime, Johann thought.

He stood up. "Okay," he said. "At least I tried." He glanced over at Maria. "Could I have a word with you in private before I go?"

Maria shrugged. "I guess so," she said.

The two of them walked out of the village toward the ocean. When they reached the sand Johann reached over and took Maria's hand. "Do you remember," he asked, "the night of your eighth birthday, when that ribbon appeared and left you a perfect white figurine of your mother?"

"Yes," she said. "I do."

She turned toward him and put her arms around his waist. "And do you also remember," Johann continued, "when we were surrounded by the nozzlers out in the middle of the lake, and the ribbons came out of nowhere and saved our lives?"

She nodded. "Yes, Johann, just as I remember your always being there for me and being the center of my life until you married Vivien and changed my life forever."

Johann ignored Maria's comment. "Your mother's ghost or angel or whatever it was really did appear, Maria," he said, "right over there on Black Rock Promontory, the night after I left you the last time. If what she told me is true, then none of you will survive double full moon night. After what you have already seen, can you stand there and tell me that you think the apparition could not have happened?"

She took her hands off Johann's waist and looked out at the ocean. "It may have happened," she said wistfully, "but it doesn't really matter."

Maria turned and looked at him again. She certainly was a beautiful young woman. "If I were your wife, Johann, and even the prospective mother of your children, then I would be at your side, soaked in slime, swimming out to your island. But I am not, and never will be. I am trapped in a life with no real hope of happiness. If whatever danger my mother predicted comes to pass, and I should die, then so be it. I am not afraid."

"But what about Stephanie?" Johann asked, not willing to give up. "Surely you must be concerned about her?"

"I don't want to talk about her now," Maria said. She put her arms around Johann's back. "Now grant me one last favor," she said, her eyes filling with tears. "Kiss me please, as a man kisses a woman."

He leaned down and touched his lips to hers. They kissed first softly, then eagerly, before Johann broke the kiss and hugged her tightly. "I have always loved you, Maria," he said.

"And I love you, Johann," she replied.

"No, Serentha," Johann shouted. "You can't stop swimming altogether when you breathe. Otherwise you'll tire yourself out too much. Try to keep swimming while you take a breath."

"She's not going to make it, is she, Father?" Siegfried asked quietly from beside him on the shore of the lake. "It's only eight days more now."

On the far side of the lake, Vivien finished her fifty laps and walked toward them, shaking the water out of her gray hair. "Whew," she said as she came over, "I'm tired, but certainly not like I felt last week."

"You're going to be fine," Johann said, still watching Serentha out in the water. She leaned her head to the side to breathe and swallowed a mouthful of water. She came up coughing and sputtering. "I just can't do it, Uncle Johann," she said. "I don't have enough time."

Johann turned to Siegfried as Serentha slowly emerged

from the water. "You know those dark trees with the large circular leaves in the second section of the Eastern Hills?" he said. "They are the lightest wood on this island. I want you to go over there today, this morning, and bring me back the thickest trunk you can find."

"What for?" Siegfried asked.

"I have an idea for Serentha," Johann said. "But we have to make certain first that the wood is light enough to provide some buoyancy. . . . Since Ravi, Anna, and Beatrice are not going to swim with us, we should have enough ackyong slime to cover a small support."

Serentha was near tears when she walked up beside Johann and Siegfried. Johann put his arms around her. "You're doing great, young lady," he said. "Every day you're getting better."

VIVIEN FOUND JOHANN working on the floor in their hut, finishing the carving of the two cylindrical objects that had one opening on the top and room for two little legs on the bottom. "So that's your version of a papoose?" she asked.

He laughed. "It's the best I could do in the short time," he said. "Any Native American would probably turn up his nose, but I think these will do the job."

Vivien sat down beside him and shook her head. "You still believe that after towing Serentha all the way out to the island on that contraption Siegfried and you made, you will have the strength to go back for Stephanie and Kwame?"

"There is no other acceptable option," Johann answered.

"And what makes you think they'll entrust their children to your care?" Vivien asked.

Johann shrugged. "They probably won't. But how can I ever forgive myself if I don't make the effort?"

Vivien was silent for a long time. "And what if something terrible happens to you while you're trying to help everyone else?"

"That's an outcome I have already accepted in my heart," Johann said. "I have lived a full and amazing life."

Johann had not once stopped working during the conversation. While he was continuing to refine the elements of the papoose, Vivien restrained him with both her hands. "Stop for just a moment, giant Johann," she said, "and give your wife a kiss."

He put down his tools and reached over for her, but she scrambled back toward their mats. "Before we make love," she said, starting to undress, "tell me how you're going to feel if absolutely nothing out of the ordinary takes place on double full moon night."

Johann laughed again. "Like an idiot," he said, grabbing for her leg. "But then nobody's perfect."

EIGHT

THE DAY PRECEDING double full moon night was unusually clear, without a cloud in the sky. Johann checked
the ocean soon after dawn and was delighted to discover
that it was quite calm. All their preparations had been finished the night before. His plan was for the four of them to
leave early, just after breakfast in fact, so that he would have
time to rest before doubling back to rescue the two infants
at the East Village.

Siegfried and Serentha rubbed each other carefully
with the ackyong slime. To reduce the tension, Vivien and
Johann made a game out of covering themselves with the
foul-smelling goo, Vivien even insisting that the area inside
Johann's trunks be drenched with slime for extra protection. During all this activity, Ravi, Anna, and Beatrice
stood by and watched without comment. Only Beatrice
seemed concerned that perhaps she had made the wrong
choice. Ravi, a bemused look upon his face, told the four-
some when they entered the water that he would see them
about noon the following day.

Siegfried acknowledged that he was nervous as he
helped Johann ease Serentha and her "swimming contraption" into the ocean. A long plank of light, buoyant wood
had been tied to the front of her bathing suit, extending
from just under her neck to her hip region, but leaving
both her arms and legs completely mobile. Two long,
thick, sturdy pieces of twine were anchored to the plank

near her armpits and this twine was attached, at the other end, to a belt wrapped around Johann's waist.

They had practiced with the contraption the day before at the lake and everything had worked perfectly. Serentha had trailed Johann by about eight meters and had been able to provide additive thrust when she used her arms and legs. As a test, Johann had swum ten laps with Serentha essentially acting as a dead weight. He announced afterward that pulling her had been surprisingly easy.

There was a herd of seven sperdens just offshore, in the path they were going to take to the distant island. As an extra precaution, Johann rubbed ackyong slime on Serentha's plank as well. He was a strange-looking figure when he started to swim. In addition to the twine trailing from his waist to Serentha's apparatus, he was wearing the pair of papooses strapped to his back and a tight necklace containing two carefully sealed jars of ackyong slime.

The first frightening moment for the swimmers came as they neared the herd of sperdens. As planned, Siegfried was swimming behind Serentha (in case anything happened to her), and Vivien slightly off to the side of the three of them. As it happened, Johann's speed through the water pulling Serentha, at least for the first half kilometer or so, was roughly the same as Vivien's. So they were a closely bunched group as they approached the sperdens.

The serpents could hardly believe their good fortune. They saw four huge animal meals heading toward them, well away from the safety of the shore, and their clucking conversations and ululations changed to feeding-frenzy cries when Johann and his troupe were within fifty meters. One large deep-green creature, its neck already bent down close to the water's surface, raced directly toward Vivien with its mouth open and its powerful teeth exposed.

Vivien was too frightened to continue swimming. Unfortunately, she was also too far away from the serpent for it to sense the ackyong slime. As Vivien treaded water in the small waves, the sperden seemed to be toying with her, making leisurely wide circles around her position and uttering occasional frenzied shouts.

"Swim toward it," Johann yelled.

Vivien shook her head. Her terror would not let her move. Changing direction, Johann swam over beside her and told her to climb on his back. With monumental effort (for he was still dragging Serentha as well), he swam toward the threatening sperden. Once the foul smell reached the equivalent of its olfactory senses, the sperden retreated, announcing with shouts to the rest of its herd that this entire group of humans was rotten.

The swells increased as they entered deeper water. Three times the group had to stop completely for Vivien to rest. Each time Johann supported her on his back while she regained her strength. Halfway to the island Serentha's left arm passed through some kind of stinging nettle. After that she did not use her arms anymore.

Johann was totally exhausted when they finally reached the island. At that moment he could not have even considered swimming back to rescue the children in the East Village. At Vivien's suggestion he found himself a shady place on the sandy beach and took a nap.

"WHERE ARE YOU, Johann?" he heard Maria's voice call in his dream. "I need you."

Sister Beatrice was in the dream as well, wearing her blue robe with the white stripes. She spoke softly to Johann, reminding him that God's angels were protecting him even though he was a nonbeliever. She started to say something else encouraging when Johann was awakened by the sound of nepp chatter.

He opened his eyes slowly. At the far end of the beach, the first contingent of forty or so nepps had arrived. Those who had completed the swim first were greeting the late-comers with exuberant shouts and helping them out of the water.

Johann glanced around and called for Vivien. She emerged from a small clump of trees behind the beach and came over beside him. "How long have I been asleep?" he asked.

"A couple of hours, I guess," she answered. "Siegfried and Serentha are still resting, over there in that grove."

Johann looked up at the sky and checked the location of the sun. "If I leave now," he said, "I can swim easily back to East Village before sunset. Maybe I'll even have time for an hour rest before I start back with the infants."

Vivien sat down beside him and took both his hands in hers. "Darling," she said, "I wish you'd reconsider. You must still be tired and there's no guarantee—"

"We went through all this last night," he said, gently interrupting her. "Nothing has happened to change my mind."

Tears were forming in her eyes as she reached up to kiss him. Their lips touched and Vivien put her hands tenderly on Johann's face. She did not want the kiss to end. At length, she placed her arms around his back and hugged him fiercely with her head resting against his chest. "Should I wake Siegfried?" she asked. "He'll be upset that he didn't have a chance to say good-bye to his father."

Johann pulled away slightly. "No," he said, gently wiping away the tears on her cheeks. "Let him sleep. And stop worrying so much. I promise I'll return, with or without the children."

Vivien sighed and shook her head. "All right, giant Johann," she said, forcing a smile. "I know it's useless to try to dissuade you. But be careful and don't take any chances. My love and my prayers will accompany you."

Johann looked out at the ocean. In the distance he could see another group of nepps swimming toward the island. Behind them was the mainland, with Black Rock Promontory the most prominent landmark. He waded into the water with Vivien beside him. "One more kiss?" she teased.

"Why not?" he laughed.

Johann lifted her up and she wrapped her legs around his waist. They kissed passionately and he put her down in the water. "That was our warm-up," he said. "For our double full moon celebration tonight."

Johann dove into an oncoming wave. He started swimming immediately. "Tell Siegfried I love him," he shouted back at Vivien in between strokes.

THE SWIM BACK to the mainland was indeed easy for Johann. He took his time, alternating strokes every several hundred meters. Twice small groups of sperdens swam over in his direction, looking interested, but both times they turned away after they were close enough to smell the ackyong slime.

About midway through his swim Johann ran into a formation of several dozen animals who were swimming together toward the island. All Johann could see of these bizarre new creatures were their heads, brown, polished spheres with four eyes located on an equatorial line roughly ninety degrees apart. The most striking feature of the floating heads were long, thin, erect protuberances, resembling porcupine quills, on the top hemisphere of each head.

Johann instinctively swam to the side, to avoid the formation. He then watched in fascination as a pair of curious sperdens, approaching too close to the quilled creatures, were each hit repeatedly, and painfully, by twenty to thirty quills fired with considerable accuracy and power by the unusual animals.

So they too, whatever they are, Johann thought to himself, *are leaving the mainland for double full moon night.* He wondered what it could be that prompted the mass exodus of both the nepps and the quilled creatures. He then resolved again to use every wile he possessed to convince Maria to let him take the two infants with him to the island.

Johann's huge body swimming through the ocean water was noticed by the East Village residents long before he reached the shore. Both the two young couples were waiting for him on the beach when he finally finished his swim.

"Well, well," said Eric sarcastically, "look what has washed in with the tide. It's Johann the magnificent."

Johann walked directly up to the two couples. "These carriers are for Stephanie and Kwame," he said, taking the papooses off his back. "Please let me take them out to that offshore island, just in case . . ." He began opening one of the cans of ackyong slime.

Maria recoiled against the smell. "Wow," she said. "What a stink! I'm not surprised that the sperdens swim away from it."

"I have enough here to cover each of the two infants," Johann said simply, looking first at Maria and then at Keiko.

Eric now reinserted himself into the conversation. "But why should they go anywhere?" he asked. "Look, the day is almost done, and nothing even slightly unusual has occurred. Double full moon night is going to be like every other—"

His final words were drowned out by the rumble of scurrying animals and nepp chatter. Down the beach, less than a hundred meters from their village, a large contingent of nepps, perhaps a hundred in all, had burst out of the trees and were scampering across the sand toward the ocean.

"What in the world?" Jomo asked, watching the nepps plunge into the water.

"Those are the animals that Sister Beatrice told me to observe," Johann said calmly. "It was from them that I learned that the slime I have in these jars repels the sperdens."

Everyone watched as the nepps began their swim,

headed in the direction of the offshore island. The sperdens in sight, now accustomed to the fact that all nepp swimmers smelled foul, turned their heads only briefly and then ignored the whole group.

Johann noticed the expressions on the four young people's faces while they were watching the nepps. *At this point anyway,* he thought to himself, *at least the two girls are no longer certain that Sister Beatrice's warning was just a hallucination.*

He walked up closer to the two women. "Look at it this way," he said. "What do you have to lose? Do either of you have any doubt that I am totally committed to taking care of your babies? I would die before I would let anything bad happen to them. . . . You know that, Maria, even if Keiko doesn't. . . . And what if the white Beatrice in my apparition *was* real, and something absolutely terrible is going to happen tonight. How will you feel, as mothers, knowing that you passed up a chance to save your baby's life? Please, please—"

"This is ridiculous," Eric said.

Keiko and Jomo suddenly came forward toward Johann. "You can take Kwame, Uncle Johann," Keiko said. "Just wait a minute while I retrieve him from his grandmother."

She dashed off, leaving the other three of them standing beside Johann. "What about you?" Johann said to Maria. "May I take Stephanie as well?"

Maria turned away and walked down the beach. Johann followed her, as did her husband, Eric. At length she glanced back at both of them. "You *really* believe my mother appeared to you and warned you about double full moon night, don't you?" she asked Johann.

"Absolutely," he replied.

"And what if the warning was false," Maria said. "How could I ever justify to myself exposing Stephanie to the dangers of that ocean swim?" She looked around, at the ocean, the hills, and the sky. "I just don't see any problems,

Johann," she said. "I can't convince myself that there's anything here to fear."

Back down the beach toward the village, Keiko had returned with Kwame. Johann moved back in that direction, eager to begin the process of smearing the ackyong goo on the boy. Jomo and Keiko, in spite of the terrible smell that caused them both nearly to vomit, insisted on rubbing the slime on their own son.

When they were finished, Johann hoisted Kwame's papoose and secured it on his back and shoulders. He then looked at Maria. "It will be sunset and moonrise in a few more minutes," he said to her. "Time is running out. Will you let me take Stephanie as well?"

"I don't think so," Maria answered. She started to add another comment but she was interrupted by Jomo's sudden shout.

"Look, look over there, at the Sun," he yelled. "Something weird is happening."

Indeed their sun, now only two or three degrees above the western mountains, already had its lower right quadrant covered by some kind of dark material that was rapidly spreading across its face.

"What's going on?" Jomo said excitedly to Johann. "That certainly doesn't look like any cloud I've ever seen. Are we having some kind of eclipse?"

Johann barely heard the question. He was staring at the now blackened Sun, slowly dropping behind the mountains. The dark matter obscuring the Sun continued to grow and spread out. *Whatever it is,* he said to himself, *it's headed this way.*

"We must act immediately," Johann shouted at Maria. "Run now, and get Stephanie. Bring her here *quickly*!"

Maria saw the eerie black phenomenon as well and a chill went down her spine. She said nothing, but simply bolted toward the village. She returned with her daughter in about a minute. By that time the blackness had grown to cover a wide area of the western sky. Meanwhile, the twin full moons crested the horizon in the east.

Johann and Maria hurriedly swabbed the crying Stephanie with the ackyong slime and thrust her into the papoose. When the baby was momentarily silent, they heard for the first time the distant chorus of cacophonous noises. "The sounds are coming from that black cloud," Maria said, her voice trembling. "It must be something *alive*."

Johann was already in the water. Maria checked the twine to make certain it was secure and hurriedly kissed both Johann and her daughter. Then, after glancing one more time at the onrushing black matter, she removed her necklace with the carved amulet and stuffed it deep into the papoose where Stephanie was riding. "Take care of my daughter, Johann," she entreated.

Johann churned through the surf with his powerful legs until he was waist deep in the ocean water. Then he plopped down on his stomach and began to swim furiously. The black cloud of onrushing doom now obscured the mountains completely. The chorus of hideous, threatening noises continued to grow in amplitude, echoing through the twilight with a high-pitched *brank, brank, brank* that terrified any living creature who could hear.

Johann was about four hundred meters out into the ocean when the first of the branker scouts reached the East Village. Maria, Keiko, and the others looked up at the giant, loathsome, insectlike creature flying into their living area and began to run toward their huts. The branker pirouetted in the sky, screamed *brank, brank* at another scout hovering over Black Rock Promontory, and the pair descended into the village. Only moments later they held Eric, flailing uselessly, in their combined talons about forty meters above the ground and were flying rapidly in a westerly direction.

Johann saw nothing of this. He was swimming as fast as

he could away from the mainland, the two papooses strapped to his back. It was not until he felt something sharp tearing into his right thigh that he realized he was being pursued.

Being careful to keep the infants' heads above the water line, Johann stopped and treaded water. Hovering half a meter above his head was one of the ugliest creatures he had ever seen. At first glance it looked like a monstrously large fruit fly with a pair of sharp talons descending from the front end of its elongated jet-black body. The branker had a double pair of wings which fluttered so fast as it hovered that some of the time they could not even be seen. The stronger, broader upper wings, attached to the top of the branker's body, were over two meters in length. The lower wings, smaller in every dimension, were attached to the bottom of its body, directly under the upper set.

A huge, black, solitary eye filled most of the branker's head. Under this eye was a gaping dark hole filled with thirty or forty sharp teeth. Its mouth was open continuously and drooling a white viscous material that fell onto the top of Johann's head and made him shudder. The branker suddenly turned toward the mainland, apparently deciding it needed help, and screamed *brank, brank* in a loud voice.

By this time at least three dozen brankers were already scavenging in the East Village. They grabbed everything, not only the human occupants, but also their equipment, food, and anything else that looked noteworthy. Maria, Keiko, Satoko, and Jomo were all now airborne and flying toward the west, each a prize claimed by a pair of brankers looking for unusual prey.

Johann could not see what was occurring on the mainland. But he was acutely aware of his own danger. The branker hovering over him repeated its call for help. Johann kept the creature in his sight and did a kind of back-breast-stroke, moving farther and farther from shore. At length the solitary branker, perhaps irritated because it had not been joined by a mate, flew hurriedly away toward the mainland. Johann immediately started swimming again, as fast as he could, keeping a close watch on the sky over his head.

No more than a minute later a pair of brankers flew out to where Johann was swimming with the infants. Since he was deep in the water, with only his head exposed, the brankers appeared unsure of how to proceed. Suddenly, however, one descended and grabbed each side of Johann's head with one of its powerful talons. Fighting back, Johann pulled the talon off the right side of his face. His effort caused him temporarily to submerge the two babies, who came up sputtering and crying.

The sounds of the infants must have surprised the brankers, for they stopped to conduct a lengthy *brank, brank* conversation while still hovering over the rapidly tiring Johann. Just when they seemed poised for another attack, Johann heard a familiar frenzied cry and two pair of sperdens struck the brankers from both sides. In the melee that ensued, Johann swam away with the children. He didn't see who won the battle. But no more brankers bothered him during his long swim to the island.

JOHANN WAS SO tired that he collapsed on the sand as soon as Vivien and Siegfried had removed the papooses from his back. The children were fine, considering what they had endured. Vivien reached down to give her prone husband a kiss but he had already closed his eyes and fallen asleep. "You are a wonderful man, giant Johann," she whispered.

From the offshore island Vivien, Siegfried, and Serentha had watched the huge cloud of dark material move into the two villages from the west. Of course, they had had no idea that what they were witnessing was a branker invasion. When, much later, an hour or two before sunrise, they awakened Johann so that he could enjoy the spectacular sight of the setting of the double full moons, they listened with rapt attention as he described the horde of flying monsters who had descended upon their world.

"So you don't think that anyone survived?" Siegfried asked.

Johann shook his head. "I don't see how it could have been possible," he replied. "There must have been a thousand of those creatures in the first wave alone. As far as I could tell, they attacked everything in sight."

Serentha began to cry. Siegfried tried to console her. "They didn't believe you, Uncle Johann," she kept repeating through her tears. "And now both my mother and father are dead."

"We don't know that for certain," Johann said. "Let's hope they figured out some way to escape."

As the Sun rose, down the beach on the far end of the island the hundreds of nepps entered the ocean for the long homeward swim. Scanning the water with his youthful eyes, Siegfried found the formation of the quilled heads, already well out to sea, also heading toward the mainland.

"So," Johann said to the others, "are we ready to return?"

Siegfried volunteered to pull Serentha and her contraption as long as Johann would swim behind him in case anything untoward occurred. Vivien helped Johann place the two infants in their papooses, with Stephanie's new necklace carefully packed in her wrappings. There was not much conversation as the preparations concluded. Everyone was thinking about what they would find in their village with a mixture of dread and hope.

Any hope they might have had was dispelled when they were close enough to see the remains of the village. Even from out in the ocean a hundred meters away, the total destruction was obvious. The huts had been ripped apart and demolished, the fields and orchards destroyed. Johann and the others somberly trudged onto the beach and began the process of assessing the damage. A few personal effects were left scattered here and there, apparently deemed unimportant by the rampaging brankers, but there were no signs of Ravi, Anna, or Beatrice.

"They must have been taken away," Johann said sorrowfully, "along with our food, our furniture, and most of our possessions."

He put his arms around the weeping Serentha and called for Seigfried and Vivien to join him. "We must rebuild, of course," he said. "And this site still seems to be the best place. We will begin the day after tomorrow, after we have mourned those we have lost."

Siegfried and Serentha went down to the beach to be alone. Johann and Vivien stayed in the area where their community kitchen had been and played with the infants. After half an hour, Johann removed the necklace with the carved amulet from Stephanie's papoose wrappings and started walking toward the east.

"What are you doing?" Vivien asked gently.

"I must go to the East Village," Johann said. "If by any chance Maria is still alive, I must return this necklace."

HE KNEW WHEN he reached the edge of Black Rock Promontory and gazed down at where the village had once been that there was no chance anyone had been left alive. Nevertheless, clutching the amulet and necklace in his hand, Johann descended into the area and spent several hours searching through the debris.

Just as at their village, the brankers had removed almost everything. But Johann did find one of Maria's handmade skirts, and an outfit for Stephanie. Under a large rock in the middle of the path through the village, he also found a piece of bark on which a note had been hastily scribbled.

"You were right, Johann. Thanks for saving Stephanie. I have always loved you."

THE
BRANKERS

ONE

JOHANN WAS DREAMING about Beatrice. She was wearing her bishop's robe but they were walking along a beach at night, holding hands. They waded out into the calm, tepid water. She turned to him and he gazed at her magnificent blue eyes. He leaned down to kiss her lips.

"Uncle Johann," he heard a vibrant young girl's voice say. "Wake up, Uncle Johann, the sun is about to rise."

Johann tried to stay in his dream and savor his kiss with Beatrice. But it was too late. The waking world had already intruded and he could not recapture the intensity of his dream image. He opened his eyes.

"Good morning, Franzi," he said. She had the same blue eyes as her great-grandmother. "Is it already time for our swim?"

"Yes, Uncle Johann," she said eagerly. She shook her long hair out of her face. "Siegfried and Rowen are waiting down by the creek."

Johann sat up slowly on his mat. He winced at the pain in his back and again, when he stood up, at the ache in his right knee. *Old age is shit,* he thought to himself. *But as far as I know it's better than the alternative.*

Franzi had left the hut to join the others. Methodically, Johann placed one more sand pebble in the rightmost of the shells lined up against the opposite wall. He didn't stop to count the pebbles as he had each day during the earlier years. The number of days he had been on this new planet now numbered over ten thousand, and he was well aware that another double full moon night was fast approaching. After putting on his trunks, he stumbled outside toward the outhouse, a place he now visited at least once every night during the middle of his sleep.

It was a gray, dreary morning with low clouds and a fine mist. The dampness made Johann feel cold. He shivered involuntarily. *Another wonderful attribute of being old,* he said to himself. *Undue sensitivity to thermal variations.*

"Good morning, Father," Siegfried said when Johann came out of the outhouse and joined them beside the creek. "Did you sleep all right?"

"As well as can be expected," Johann replied. He then smiled. "At least I had a couple of good dreams."

The four of them walked along the creek toward the switchbacks. Franzi was in front, her long hair cascading down her back, slipping gaily along and whistling to herself. Johann's grandson, Rowen, a quiet, contemplative young man in his early twenties, was second in the line. Siegfried, whose hair was now completely gray, walked alongside his father.

"The rocks will be slippery this morning," Siegfried said, "so be careful while we're climbing."

Johann chose not to utter the grumpy retort that immediately formed in his mind. Lately it seemed that Siegfried had been treating him more and more like an invalid. True, Johann could no longer work for long stretches in the fields and orchards, but his brain and his hearing were still intact, and his eyesight had not noticeably worsened since their arrival at their new planetary home thirty years ago.

Franzi had already started up the switchbacks, with Rowen not far behind. "I'll bring up the rear," Siegfried said, motioning for Johann to begin the climb. Johann shot his son an angry glance. *I won't slip and fall,* Johann thought but did not say. *I have been climbing up this path for almost thirty years.*

Halfway up the switchbacks, Johann's heart was pumping fiercely and he was feeling a little light-headed. He stopped to rest. "Are you all right?" Siegfried asked.

"Yes, yes, I'm fine," Johann said. "I've just been climbing too fast, trying to keep pace with those youngsters ahead of us."

Siegfried stopped, solicitous. "Is there anything I can do?"

Johann wheeled around. "Yes, you can stop treating me as if I'm helpless. Go on, keep walking, catch up with your son. I'm certain the two of you must have plenty to talk about now that we have a nubile female in our group again."

Siegfried's eyes flashed. "That comment is uncalled for, Father," he said. "You know I have told Rowen that I will not interfere if she chooses him as her first sexual partner."

"That's what you *say*," Johann replied. "But your actions do not support your statements. Your eyes are always following every movement of her body. She sees it. Rowen sees it. That's not exactly the best way to make her feel comfortable."

Instead of answering, Siegfried climbed higher on the path. Johann watched him go and then stretched his right knee, hoping that the ache would go away. *I have become crotchety and sententious,* he told himself as he began climbing again. *Just like most old people.*

IN SPITE OF his age, Johann was still the best swimmer among the four of them. Siegfried had more stamina, and Rowen could beat his grandfather in a sprint, but Johann's effortless stroke and rhythm were still absolutely beautiful to watch.

"I wish I could swim like you, Uncle Johann," the perky Franzi said when they had finished their workout. She was sitting beside him on the grass, her fingers absentmindedly twirling the wood amulet at the bottom of her twine necklace.

"You will someday, if you keep practicing," Johann replied with a smile. He liked this young girl of fourteen.

She had her great-grandmother's positive attitude about everything. And she never treated him as if he were old and decrepit.

"You must have been amazing when you were young," Franzi continued. "Uncle Siegfried told me that you were one of the fastest swimmers on Earth."

"That's a bit of an exaggeration," Johann said, nevertheless feeling pride in the girl's admiration. "But I was certainly better than most."

Johann's mind drifted back in time, to a period sixty years earlier in his biological life. He was remembering being the anchor swimmer for Germany in the 4 x 200 freestyle relay in the European Championships. Johann had barely touched out the Italian swimmer to win the gold medal and there had been a jubilant celebration immediately afterward. For fifteen or twenty seconds he was totally absorbed in his memory, and oblivious to what was occurring around him. When Johann returned to reality, he realized that Franzi was looking at him with a puzzled expression on her face.

"I'm sorry," he said lightly, touching her on the shoulder. "I was just thinking about something that happened a long time ago. . . . We old people do that sometimes. Too many stored memories, I guess. . . . Did you ask me a question?"

"Yes, Uncle Johann," she said. "I asked if I could go with you to collect the ackyong slime. I've never had a chance to go much beyond this lake, and I've always wanted to see the geysers, the mudpots, the ackyongs, and the nepps for myself. Uncle Siegfried said that it won't be much longer until—"

"Of course you can go with me," Johann interrupted. "What a delightful idea. I can't imagine a greater pleasure than spending a couple of days showing you some of the more interesting sights of our world."

BOTH SIEGFRIED AND Rowen were against the idea.
"Father," Siegfried said, "what has happened to your judgment? You know your trip could be dangerous. What if
you encounter a group of the quilled creatures, as we did
sixteen years ago? What if the nepps are not willing to give
you processed slime, and you must harvest the ackyong
eggs yourself? Franzi has no experience with that kind of
situation."

"I'm not stupid, Siegfried," Johann said. "I would certainly take no chances that would endanger the girl. If we
encounter something untoward, we will simply return to
the village. . . . Besides, Franzi *wants* to go. Our existence
here is hardly what a fourteen-year-old girl would call exciting. She deserves a bit of adventure in her life."

"Then I'll take her," Siegfried said. He glanced over at
his son. "And if that makes you nervous, Rowen, you can
come along too."

Johann scoffed. "You two are ridiculous sometimes."
He turned to Siegfried. "Son, you have never established
the relationship with the nepps that I have. Four years ago
when we went together it was obvious that the nepp leader
was not comfortable with you. I am still healthy enough to
make the trip, so I should definitely go. . . . As for Franzi, I
think the nepps will love her. She'll be unafraid, and play
with all the cubs. She'll be an excellent ambassador."

"And what if something happens to you?" Siegfried
asked. "Suppose you pass out, as you did two years ago up
behind Black Rock Promontory. What will happen to
Franzi then? Or worse, suppose you have a heart attack or a
stroke? You are a very old man, Father. Franzi would be in
an impossible situation if you were incapacitated."

"I will make certain before we go that we have very
detailed maps," Johann said in a pained voice. "And Franzi

will know them by heart before we depart. She will be told that if something serious happens to me, she is to return immediately to the village."

Johann stood up. "This discussion is over," he announced. "Sometime next week Franzi and I will visit neppland and, if we are lucky, we will bring back the ackyong slime."

JOHANN AND FRANZI ate their first lunch sitting on a rock only a couple of meters away from the periodic geyser. Her enthusiasm for everything was infectious. Although he was tired from the climb, Johann felt great. He had just explained to Franzi how water pressure builds up underground, when the geyser suddenly erupted, spraying a jet of water sixty meters into the air.

Franzi jumped up and clasped her hands in excitement. "Oh, Uncle Johann," she exclaimed, watching the water rise to its peak far above her head. "I had no idea that it was so beautiful. None of the descriptions have been adequate."

When the geyser had concluded its eruption, the place from which the water had burst forth had become nothing but an unusual hole in the ground. Gathering all her hair in her hands and holding it behind her head, Franzi lay down and stared into the vent. "This is fascinating," she said.

She came back, sat down next to Johann on the rock, and bit vigorously into a piece of fruit. "I want to stay here and see it again," she declared.

"But that will be another hour or so," Johann said.

"Fine," Franzi said. "We'll just eat our lunch slowly and talk."

Johann laughed and shrugged. "As you wish," he said, "but what would you like to talk about?"

Franzi's face suddenly became serious. "Uncle Johann," she said, "I've never been told the whole story about my parents' death, just bits and pieces here and there. You promised me once, when I was ten or so, that when I was old enough, you would tell me the entire story. Am I old enough now?"

Johann reflected for a moment. "I guess so, Franzi," he said. "But it's not a happy tale. Are you sure you want to spoil such a superb day by—"

"Nothing will be spoiled, Uncle Johann," the girl interrupted. "I really want to know. Besides, you have always told me that the truth can free us from our unreasonable fears."

Johann finished chewing the piece of fruit that was in his mouth. "All right, young lady, if that's what you want." He gazed off in the general direction of the ocean, thinking about that terrible, painful day so many years before. Out of his memory came the indelible images that always remain with us when we experience a life-altering tragedy.

"They died on the sixth double full moon night after our arrival here. You were two years old at the time, and your mother was eight months pregnant." Johann heaved a sigh. "I had told both Stephanie and Kwame how important it was that she not be seriously pregnant on a double full moon night, but they ignored my warnings."

He glanced over at Franzi. "Your mother was as headstrong as your grandmother Maria. Fortunately, you seem to have inherited more of the temperament of your great-grandmother."

Franzi leaned over and kissed him on the forehead. "I know, Uncle Johann," she said. "You've told me that before."

"Anyway," Johann continued, "soon after we went into swimming training it became obvious that there was no way that Stephanie, who was a mediocre swimmer at best, would be able to make it out to the island and back. Vivien was also concerned that too much vigorous exercise in the last trimester might cause a premature birth or other complications. . . . I couldn't tow your mother out and back either, for I had started losing some of my strength, and everyone agreed that I would have my hands full taking care of you.

"The brankers had not come the previous two double full moon nights and your father, Kwame, had convinced himself that we would be spared on this cycle as well. I pointed out to him that we knew absolutely nothing about what caused the brankers to come, or not to come, and neither did the nepps. The little guys *always* prepared for the brankers, and it seemed prudent for us to do the same thing.

"Prior to the *fifth* double full moon night, we had discovered a cave complex, actually not too far from here, in the hills on the other side of the volcanic rock. Vivien was unable to swim that time, for she had seriously injured her hip while running from a pursuing ackyong. After great deliberation, we concluded that it would be best if she spent the fifth double full moon night down in one of the caves. Since the brankers did not come at all that cycle, we had no way of knowing if it was a safe haven or not."

Johann stopped and remained silent for a long time. "When the sixth double full moon night arrived, Vivien decided to spend the night in the caves with your mother. The plan *might* have worked. We just don't know because . . ."

Johann's thoughts began to drift again. In his mind's eye he was again swimming in the turbulent ocean, with Franzi in a papoose strapped to his neck, leading what was left of his family out toward the offshore island that represented safety from the brankers. He could still remember Siegfried's shouts, turning around in the water, and discovering, to his horror, that Kwame was no longer behind them and had swum back toward the mainland.

After a long pause he looked at Franzi and heaved a deep sigh. "I'm sorry," he said, struggling with his feelings. "This is hard for me."

"I understand, Uncle Johann," the girl said softly.

"Kwame and I had accompanied your mother and Vivien," Johann eventually continued, "to the cave area and helped them pick out a place to hide. We had left them maps carved on wood that they could read with their fingertips in case they needed to find their way out in the dark. Then the rest of us returned to the village and ate a small lunch before we began our swim.

"It was a stormy day. The waves were much higher than usual. Several groups of nepps and a formation of the quilled creatures were already in the water before us. As planned, I was in the lead with you in a papoose, followed by Siegfried, Rowen, who was only eleven at the time, and then your father.

"You know, of course, that somewhere during the swim your father, without saying anything to the rest of us, turned around and headed back toward shore. When I heard Siegfried's shout and swam over next to him in the water, he was furious. He kept pointing at the Sun, and telling me that Kwame was going to lead the brankers to your mother and Vivien. To this day he believes that both his mother and yours would still be alive if Kwame had not returned to the mainland."

Johann sighed again. "What actually happened in and around those caves that night is complete speculation. The brankers did come, again reducing our village to rubble. When Vivien, Stephanie, and Kwame were nowhere to be seen after we returned from the island, I left Siegfried in the village with Rowen and you and went to search the caves. Where they had been hiding I found only two objects, Vivien's little hat that she sometimes wore as a joke, and that amulet now around your neck, which your mother had placed on a rock ledge.

"So what happened? Did the brankers find your mother and Vivien on their own? Or did your father inadvertently lead them to where the women were hidden? We'll never know. Siegfried, who was very close to his mother, is convinced that your father was responsible for Vivien's death. But there's no way we can ever learn the truth."

AFTER WATCHING THE second geyser eruption, Franzi asked Johann if it might be possible for her to see an ack-yong. "I have heard about them all my life," she said, "and I have these wonderful pictures in my mind. I'd like to know if what my imagination has created is anything like reality."

Johann glanced up at the sky. "Well," he said, "they love cloudless days. And I know there's a large colony of ackyongs living right over there, underneath that cliff face. Maybe, if we're patient, we might—"

"Oh, could we please, Uncle Johann?" the girl said, interrupting him. "It would mean a lot to me."

Again, Franzi's enthusiasm made him smile. There was so much of Beatrice in her nature. He felt rejuvenated when he was around her. "I suppose we're not in that big a hurry," he said. "But you may have to help an old man climb these boulders. I don't do as well scrambling over rocks as I did years ago. . . . And you must promise me that under no circumstances will you take any chances—the ackyongs can be very dangerous."

"I promise, Uncle Johann," she said. Franzi came over and kissed him on the cheek. "I hope we see an *entire* dance," she said excitedly.

"Only if we're very still and completely quiet," Johann warned. "The ackyongs will not mate if they think they're being watched."

The climb to the top of the nearby boulder pile reminded Johann acutely of his age. No longer steady even in a three-point stance, twice he banged his sore knee on a rock. His lower back was in extreme discomfort by the time Franzi and he finally reached a point from which they could see half a dozen potential ackyong mating locations.

But Johann did not complain, even to himself. Franzi's radiant, expectant smile made his aches and pains irrelevant.

Twice, while they were waiting, Franzi started to talk. Both times Johann shushed her immediately. When they had been at their observation post for almost fifteen minutes, they heard the sound that Johann instantly recognized as coming from the vertical reed clusters on the back segment of an ackyong. Franzi's face brightened and Johann reached over and put his finger to her lips.

The sound was answered by a second tone, similar but slightly higher in pitch. Johann and Franzi looked in the direction of the sounds. Backing into the sunlight on a bare patch of ground very close to their boulder was a small green ackyong, its colorless vertical reed cluster undulating to produce a response to a second call from its unseen companion.

As Johann and Franzi watched, the green ackyong exchanged four more tonal sets with its companion and danced six to eight meters backward, leaving room on the dirt patch for the entrance of the most magnificent of these creatures that Johann had ever seen, a huge, bright purple ackyong whose reed cluster was thick with elements and filled with an astonishing array of hues. Franzi's eyes widened as this pursuing ackyong strutted into view.

The smaller green ackyong stopped retreating as the purple creature increased the tempo of its song. A few minutes later, in full view of their human observers, the two aliens lay touching each other side by side on the ground, their reed clusters now intertwined and in constant motion, creating a distinct and original new song that was harmonious even to human ears.

Franzi was uncharacteristically subdued the rest of the afternoon. She hardly said a word as she helped Johann down the most difficult portions of the boulder descent. The two of them enjoyed one more eruption of the periodic geyser and then Johann suggested that they should start traveling again. He had hoped to cover about half the distance between the geyser and the nepp colony, but after they started walking it was obvious that his knees were too sore for such a long trek. Franzi and he stopped no more than an hour away from the geyser.

After they ate their dinner and Franzi spread their mats, side by side under the star-filled sky, she indicated what she had been thinking about most of the afternoon. "When I started my period a few months ago," she said without any introduction of the subject, "you told me, Uncle Johann, that I was now a mature woman and able to bear children. You also stressed to me that for us to survive as a group, it would be necessary for me to mate both with Rowen and Siegfried, in any order I desired, to make certain that there was sufficient variation in the nature of our offspring."

Franzi stopped and looked at Johann. He said nothing. "I think I'm ready to start having babies, Uncle Johann," she said, "but I have some concerns and a few questions. You're the only one I feel comfortable enough to discuss these things with."

"What would you like to know, Franzi?" Johann said gently when he realized she was waiting for him to reply.

"First," she said, "do I have to do anything special to make a baby, or is it enough for me to accept the man's penis inside me?"

"You don't have to do anything special, Franzi," Johann said. "However, the man must deposit his semen—it comes out of the end of his penis and contains the sperm that fertilizes your egg and makes a baby—or you can't conceive the child." He thought for a moment before continuing. "The semen doesn't come out automatically. The man must be what we call sexually aroused first, which means that you will help the process if you kiss him or are generally affectionate in other ways."

Franzi sat for a few seconds and pondered what Johann had said. "Will the man's penis hurt when it enters me?"

she then asked. "When I feel myself down there, it doesn't feel large enough."

"The first time or two you may experience some pain," Johann replied, "both because your partner may not be gentle enough and because you have a thin membrane inside which will break and bleed with the first solid penetration. Once you become more relaxed, you will stretch in the genital area during sex, and will probably find the whole process quite pleasant. Many women do."

A slight frown appeared on Franzi's face. When she asked her next question, there was an overtone of fear in her voice. "Rowen's mother died trying to give birth to a baby, and you have told me that there can be a lot of pain even with a normal delivery. Is there any way of knowing, ahead of time, how hard or easy it will be for me to become a mother?"

Johann pushed aside his painful memories of the deaths of Serentha and Beatrice. *Unfortunately,* he said to himself, *we really have no choice in this situation. If our group is not to perish altogether, Franzi must produce children.*

He leaned over and hugged the girl. "If we were back on Earth, Franzi," Johann said, "there would be doctors, specialists who could examine you and assess your capabilities for having children. They might be able to tell you whether giving birth would be easy or difficult for you. But none of us has any of that special knowledge."

Franzi still looked unsettled. "I do know one good thing, however," Johann added. "Ease of childbearing is supposedly an inherited characteristic and neither your mother nor your grandmother had any difficulties with the birthing process."

Apparently encouraged by this last comment of Johann's, Franzi's face brightened as she played absentmindedly with several thick strands of her long hair. She was clearly thinking now about another serious subject and trying to decide how to talk about it.

"Rowen has never had sex, has he?" she asked suddenly.

"No," said Johann, suppressing his surprise, "he hasn't."

"Has he ever talked to you about it?" she said.

"I have tried twice to discuss the subject with him," Johann said, "but Rowen is shy and very easily embarrassed. . . . We haven't made much progress."

"So because of his experience, Uncle Siegfried would be more likely to know what he's doing? And make it less difficult for me?"

Johann squirmed a bit on his mat. He felt he was being placed in an impossible position, being asked to choose between his son and his grandson. "On the surface," he said at length, "what you said would appear to be correct. But I must point out that I have no firsthand knowledge about Siegfried as a lover. . . . My best advice is that you should choose as your partner the person with whom you are the most comfortable, because sexual intimacy has many emotional aspects that we aren't even considering now."

"But if I did that," Franzi said quickly, "then I would choose *you*, Uncle Johann. You are by far my closest friend. And I can talk to you about anything."

Johann was momentarily speechless. His mind was a jumble of strange and confused thoughts for a couple of seconds. Finally he reached over and took Franzi's hand. "I appreciate your affection," he said, "and you know how much I love you. But there are many practical reasons why I am not a candidate to be your sexual partner. I am now an old man, for example, and there is some doubt if I even have the ability to make you pregnant. During our years here, Vivien and I made love many, many times and she never conceived. That suggests—"

"But Vivien was older too," Franzi interrupted. "Couldn't it have been because of her that you had no children other than Siegfried?"

"Possibly," Johann said after some hesitation. "But we have no way of knowing."

They fell silent. For some reason Johann thought of Maria, and her unusual request to be his second wife. *If I had accepted her offer,* he said to himself, *then life among our group here would have been radically different. There would also be many more of us remaining.*

"Franzi," Johann said at length, "I will admit that I am flattered by your suggestion. But please accept my judgment on this issue. Your choice for the father of your child is between Siegfried and Rowen."

"All right, Uncle Johann," she said.

Johann lay awake for several more minutes, anticipating that Franzi might ask some more questions. When she said nothing for a long time, he leaned down close to where she was lying on her back on her mat. He could tell from the rhythmic movement of her chest that she had fallen asleep.

TWO

THE NEXT MORNING they made the long walk to the nepp colony, stopping for lunch when they were no more than half a kilometer away. Franzi chattered throughout the trip about nothing in particular. She never once mentioned their conversation from the previous evening.

Johann was already thinking about the nepps, and the ackyong slime. On his last visit to the colony, two or three months earlier, he had met the new nepp leader. It had been unclear to Johann, however, even after a long gesture-and-chatter conversation, if the nepps intended to provide any ackyong slime for the four humans. Johann was hoping that they would not be forced to gather their own eggs, as they had sixteen years previously. It had been during one of the encounters with the ackyongs that year that Vivien had fallen, running down a slope, and injured her hip.

Johann and Franzi entered the nepp colony at lunchtime, when the animals were gathered together in the central plaza. Beside one of the queues for lunch, a group of four or five pups were engaged in what appeared to be a nepp version of tag. Franzi joined in immediately, racing after and capturing one of the smaller brown creatures in her hands and then petting its smooth skin with her gentle fingers.

"They're so cute, Uncle Johann," she said, unaware that half a dozen of the larger black-and-whites had quickly surrounded her and were watching her interaction with the pup. Franzi held the trembling animal a few centimeters away from her face and examined its unusual eyes. Both the white balls in its two crescents were in frantic motion, zipping back and forth from top to bottom every couple of seconds.

The nepp contingent around Johann and Franzi moved aside as the nepp leader approached. It said something to the other members of its species and then stopped in front of the humans, perhaps a meter away, and watched Franzi cuddle the pup.

"Perhaps you should put it down," Johann said quietly. "This animal facing us is the leader of the colony."

Franzi stroked the pup two or three more times, bent down, and placed it gently on the ground. The creature looked momentarily confused by the large group of nepps that had gathered. Then, just before it scampered away into the crowd, it rubbed itself briefly against the bottom of Franzi's trousers.

Johann, recalling that his last conversation with this particular nepp leader had been inconclusive, greeted the head of the colony with gestures and then, wasting no time, started pointing toward the small grove of trees inside of which was the fenced compound where the ackyong eggs were stored. In response, the nepp leader changed its position so that it was directly between Johann and the fenced compound. Six additional black-and-whites took up positions near the entrance to the grove as well.

Uh-oh, Johann said to himself. *This reaction looks similar to the refusal sixteen years ago.* Wanting to make it clear that he was requesting processed ackyong slime for only four human beings, Johann used exaggerated motions, pointing first at himself, and then at Franzi, before slowly counting out two more fingers that he held high in the air. He repeated the same motion two more times, believing that he had communicated his message. Just as he finished, the pup Franzi had been holding earlier broke out of the group around them and timidly approached the girl. Bending down immediately with a broad smile on her face, Franzi urged the pup forward until it jumped into her arms and she began to pet it again.

A murmur of what must have been approving voices came from the nepps nearby, but they were silenced quickly by a foreleg sweep from the leader nepp. Franzi, cradling the little pup against her chest and stroking it continuously, walked directly over toward the nepp leader. "There really are only four of us," she said, repeating what Johann had been saying with his gestures. "We don't need that much slime."

Franzi was certainly the youngest female human this nepp leader had ever seen. Perhaps it might have seen Vivien sixteen years previously, when she had helped with the ackyong egg-gathering process, but Vivien had been dressed and acted like Siegfried and Johann, so the nepps had probably not noticed a significant difference. Franzi was clearly different. Already a woman physically, both her shape and her smell differentiated her from Johann and the other human men that the other nepps had met in their lifetimes.

The nepp leader stared at Franzi as the girl continued to talk in a soft, nonthreatening voice, cuddling and stroking the pup she was carrying the entire time. She explained that it would be so much easier if she and her three friends could obtain the ackyong slime directly from the nepps, saving themselves the trouble of harvesting the ackyong eggs and then making the goo on their own. The leader nepp, of course, had no idea what Franzi was saying. However, it was obviously fascinated by the girl, for the white balls in its crescent eyes rolled around continuously and the folds and creases in the rest of its face changed several times, creating a variety of nepp expressions.

For many years Johann, sometimes accompanied by others, had visited the nepp colony once or twice during the weeks preceding double full moon night. This quadrennial visit had always been for the same purpose—to acquire some ackyong slime that would protect the humans from the sperdens during their swim to the offshore island. This historical information was doubtless common knowledge among the intelligent nepps and the current nepp leader almost certainly knew that this new, beautiful human female caressing the pup was adding her voice to the request. Exactly *what* she was saying was not that important.

While Franzi was talking to the nepps, Johann's mind drifted into the past. For some reason he was thinking about his second double full moon night on this planet, when the brankers had fortunately not come. That time, in spite of Johann's objections, Siegfried and Serentha had decided not to train for the swim. Instead, Siegfried had built a small boat for himself and his wife, and had asked Johann if he would try to obtain enough ackyong slime from the nepps to cover the boat's surface area.

That year ackyong goo was in short supply. It had taken all of Johann's diplomacy to obtain ample slime for all their bodies. Only a tiny amount was left over. Nevertheless, Siegfried spattered it around the boat and set off into the ocean with Serentha anyway. The sperdens had not been deterred. They overturned the boat, throwing Johann's son and daughter-in-law into the water.

The sea monsters would have eaten them, Johann remembered, *if I hadn't insisted they douse their bodies before setting out. The boat was a foolish idea anyway, and could have set a bad precedent. What would we have done in later years if we had not been able to acquire enough slime to cover a boat and nobody was in shape to make the swim?*

Johann's attention was snapped back to the present when the nepp leader suddenly moved over directly in front of Franzi. She stopped talking while the leader, standing on its back four legs, extended its two forelegs as high as they would reach and touched the bottom of Franzi's long brown hair. She did not flinch at all, and continued to smile as the nepp played with her hair for a full thirty seconds, stroking it occasionally and even twirling small strands around its jointed fingers. Its curiosity apparently satisfied, the leader dropped back down on all six of its legs and returned to its original location.

Next it made a short speech to the other assembled members of its species. Toward the end of this chatter, four black-and-whites disappeared down the path toward the fenced compound. They returned shortly with a small vat of slime, which they placed on the ground in front of Franzi. The girl gagged when she first smelled the contents, but she managed to force a smile and graciously thank the nepp leader for its gift.

Johann picked up the small vat by its handles, and started to leave the colony. However, the nepp leader's chatter and the response from the crowd of animals told him that his action was inappropriate. While Johann stood still, holding the vat, the leader nepp motioned for Franzi to kneel on the ground. After she understood its request, and dropped to her knees, the nepp leader made a few comments to the others. A long queue immediately formed on the colony side of Franzi.

During the next twenty minutes several hundred nepps filed by the girl, who was still holding and caressing her favorite pup. Each of the nepps touched and examined her long, soft hair for several seconds. Johann, astonished by what was occurring, put the slime vat on the ground beside him and watched the amazing procession. After the last nepp filed by, the nepp leader itself returned to Franzi's side, caressed the full length of her hair one more time, and then with chatters and gestures informed her that Johann and she could leave.

The girl was beaming with delight as she walked down

the path leading away from the colony. Johann was holding her hand in one of his and carrying the vat in the other hand.

TWO DAYS BEFORE double full moon night, Johann, Franzi, Rowen, and Siegfried held a full-dress rehearsal. They rubbed themselves with the ackyong goo, plunged into the ocean, swam through the waves into the proximity of a herd of sperdens (who turned and swam away, as predicted), and then returned to the beach in front of their village. After removing the slime from their bodies, the four of them were relaxed and laughing as they moved toward the kitchen to begin the lunch preparation.

Franzi touched Johann on the forearm just before they reached the village. "Uncle Johann," she said, "may I talk to you? Now, alone?"

Johann looked at the beautiful young girl whose long wet hair was everywhere. "Is anything wrong?" he asked.

"No, no," Franzi answered. "I just want to talk in private."

Rowen and Siegfried agreed they did not need any help making lunch. Since it was low tide, Johann and Franzi crossed the creek, headed west, and sat on the white sand beach in the lovely cove just beyond their village.

They sat side by side, facing the ocean. Johann waited for her to initiate the conversation but soon became impatient. He was thinking about all the things that still needed to be done before double full moon night. "Well, Franzi," he said at last. "What's on your mind?"

She took a deep breath, glanced briefly at Johann, and then looked back out at the ocean. "Do you remember the conversation we had about sex and my choice of partner, the night before we reached the nepp colony?" she said.

"Of course," Johann replied.

"Well, I have made a decision," the girl said. Franzi

shrugged and shook her head from side to side. "Actually, it's several decisions, and they're kind of involved, so I need some time to explain." She glanced back at him. "Please, Uncle Johann, will you not interrupt me until I finish? Because I don't think what I'm going to say makes much sense unless you have heard everything."

"Okay, Franzi," he said. "I'll sit here and listen until you tell me it's time for me to talk."

Again the girl took a deep breath and stared out at the ocean. "Between Rowen and Uncle Siegfried," she said, "based strictly on personal compatibility, I would choose Rowen. It may be because he's closer to my age and I still feel like a child around Uncle Siegfried, but I guess the reasons are not important."

She paused. "However, when I think about being intimate with *either* of them, my stomach becomes nervous and jumpy and I feel very uncomfortable. I know it's silly, but I feel Uncle Siegfried would be judging me, as well as comparing me with Serentha, and I think Rowen would be so shy and inept that the whole experience would be a disaster. I'm sure I could laugh if nothing worked right, but Rowen is so serious he might not be able to take a failure lightly. And he might be so embarrassed that he would not be willing to try again after a failure."

This is amazing, Johann was thinking as he listened to Franzi. *I am witnessing again how acute the feminine intuitive senses are. There is no way Franzi could have acquired this insight by any normal learning process.*

"On the other hand," Franzi continued, "if I were relaxed and comfortable and could guide Rowen, gently, without his knowing that he was being led, then the possibility of a first disaster could be averted. And Rowen would not be embarrassed."

The girl laughed nervously. "So here's my plan. After double full moon night I would like for you, Uncle Johann, to be my first partner and sexual teacher. We don't necessarily even need to have sex. I just want you to show me what to do, in what order, and explain to me what makes a man feel good and comfortable. I know that with you I would be completely relaxed and that you would be a gentle and patient teacher."

Johann didn't know what to say. He stared at her beautiful, smiling face only a hand's width away from him. "All right, Franzi," he said with a nervous smile. "I guess I'll tentatively agree to your plan. But I reserve the right to change my mind."

He hugged her and stood up. "And now," he said, "we must turn our attention to everything we need to do to finish our preparations for double full moon night."

They walked hand in hand, the old man and the young teenage girl, back across the creek and into the village.

LYING IN HIS hut that night, Johann had difficulty falling asleep. In spite of his concerns about the coming double full moon, his thoughts kept returning to his conversation with Franzi. He had long ago acknowledged and accepted that his sex life was over. Still, in the aftermath of his discussion with the girl, he had experienced a couple of twinges of sexual desire that had triggered memories of intense pleasure from long ago. *Perhaps we never become completely nonsexual,* Johann thought. *No matter how old we are.*

He tossed and turned for half an hour before deciding that he would go out for a walk. Some thin clouds were rolling in from the ocean, but there was enough moonlight that he could easily see where he was going. At first Johann had no particular destination in mind, but after he started walking he found himself headed for the makeshift cemetery in the middle of the orchard.

This was not the first time that Johann had wandered into the cemetery in the middle of the night. He liked to be there alone, to immerse himself in his memories without being disturbed by others. *There's no way any of them could understand anyway,* he thought as he stood in front of the larger of the two wooden plaques. *I'm the only one left alive who really knew all these people. Siegfried wasn't even born until just before we left the grotto.*

The first plaque was the same height as Johann. The words carved into the wood were simple and direct. "This memorial commemorates the lives of those who vanished and presumably died during the branker attack on the first double full moon night after our arrival on this planet."

Underneath the statement, listed vertically, were the names of those who had perished on that fateful night. The women were first, and then the men, each group listed in alphabetical order. Johann read the list from top to bottom very slowly. Anna, Beatrice, Keiko, Maria, Satoko, Eric, Jomo, Ravi.

There were twelve of us when we arrived here, Johann remembered. *Enough that we could have survived and flourished. There was ample genetic variation. Two children had already been born. And then in one fell swoop we were reduced to six and our overall chances significantly diminished.*

As he often did while standing in front of the larger plaque, Johann wondered if perhaps by his own actions he might have prevented the devastating tragedy that had occurred so soon after their arrival. *We should never have become divided into two groups. I should have insisted that we all stay together. Then maybe we would not be facing extinction now.*

He read the list a second time, stopping at the name that had dominated his life for so many years. *Maria,* he said to himself. From out of the recesses of his deepest memory came a flood of images of the child he had raised from infancy and, as always, Johann's eyes filled with tears of loss. It had been so many years now since her death, and yet all the pictures in his mind were as crisp and vivid as if they had occurred only moments before.

He remembered Maria's first cry, the sight of her

nursing at her dying mother's breast, dozens of vignettes from their eight years alone together on the island, their frightening and adventurous boat ride at the end of which the ribbons saved them from the nozzlers, the changes in Maria after they found the others and he married Vivien, their shared experiences with the maskets, their life in the grotto, and finally, when she was no longer a child, their disturbing and painful interactions here on this planet.

I loved you like a daughter, Maria, Johann heard himself say out loud. *And not just because I promised your mother I would care for you.* He thought again of the weathered piece of bark on the table in his hut, the bark he carried with him every time he swam out to the island on a double full moon night. It had been her last gift to him. He could barely read the writing now, but he knew the words by heart. "You were right, Johann," it said. "Thanks for saving Stephanie. I have always loved you."

But in the end I failed you, Johann said to himself as he stared through his tears at the five letters on the plaque. *Not on the island, no. There I was an excellent companion and substitute father. Where I failed you was when we joined the others.*

A voice inside his head, the beautiful, melodious voice of the only woman he had ever loved unconditionally, interceded in his interior monologue. "Dear Brother Johann," the voice of Beatrice said, "we have been over and over these issues so many times. When will you accept your own imperfections? When will you allow yourself to forget what you cannot possibly undo?"

Not until I die, Johann answered the voice. *Not until I die.*

He forced himself to walk away from the larger plaque. A few meters away a waist-high monument remembered the three who had died during the branker attack on the fifth double full moon night. Here too the names were listed vertically, from top to bottom, Stephanie, Vivien, Kwame.

Johann's thoughts of Vivien did not bring tears into his

eyes. He smiled, and occasionally laughed, as he recalled their easy years together as man and wife. *You deserved more of my love,* Johann told himself. *But we do not always have the ability to control how much we love.*

Vivien had been adaptable. She had demanded little, made almost no suggestions about how Johann should change, and had supported him in every way, even in his difficult dealings with the adult Maria. *I could not have asked for a better companion,* Johann thought. *You brought joy, laughter, and affection to my life. And gave me my only child, my son, Siegfried.*

The third and final marker in the cemetery was on top of its only grave. On this plaque was inscribed, "Here lies Serentha, beloved wife of Siegfried and mother of Rowen, who died attempting to give birth to a stillborn daughter."

Serentha's death had been especially painful for Johann. Even though his relationship with his daughter-in-law had never been particularly close, her death had reminded Johann vividly of his own inability to save his adored Beatrice many years before. After Serentha's death, Johann had become so depressed that he had even considered suicide. It had taken steady doses of Vivien's love and good humor to restore Johann's normal positive attitude.

So I lived on, Johann said to himself as he stood in front of Serentha's grave. *Another dozen years now. Long enough to know one more charming female with Beatrice's genes.*

He laughed to himself as he recalled Franzi's proposition to him earlier in the day. He tried to picture the two of them together in an intimate situation and his laughter escalated. *Vivien would have had a few hysterically funny things to say,* he thought, *about an eighty-year-old, withered man trying to make love to a fourteen-year-old in full bloom.*

Shaking his head and chuckling to himself, Johann walked out of the orchard. At first he headed back toward his hut, but when he turned and looked up at Black Rock Promontory, he suddenly had an overpowering desire to stand once more on the spot where he had had his last apparition of Beatrice.

He climbed slowly up the path, his heart and mind totally absorbed with the woman who had been the love of his lifetime. When Johann reached the summit, he began speaking out loud, to Beatrice, as if she could hear him. At the very spot where she had last appeared, he gazed intently at the few stars he could see hovering over the ocean and raised his voice.

"Please, please," he said, "let me see you one more time. Send your ghost or spirit or whatever it was one last time, so that I can die a happy man."

Thick clouds were rolling in quickly from the ocean, obscuring the stars and starting even to blot out the twin moons. "It has been so long now," Johann said reflectively, "almost thirty years since your last visit." His desire to see her was so strong that the heartache was overwhelming. "Oh, Beatrice," he shouted. "Where are you now? Can you hear me calling your name? Do you know how very much I still love you?"

He stood motionless, staring out across the edge of the promontory, into the region of the sky from which she had come so many years ago. He waited and waited for a sign. None came. The clouds continued to increase and a few drops of rain began to fall. After more than ten minutes, Johann began talking to Beatrice again, but now in a more subdued and resigned voice.

"There are only four of us left now," he said, "and the odds favoring the extinction of our little group that left Mars have become overwhelming. Your genes, my genes, Vivien's genes—they all seem destined to perish here on this lovely planet. . . . Was that why your God rescued us from the dust storm descending upon Valhalla? So that we could die here, years later, on this faraway world?"

Johann waved his arms at the sky. "None of this makes any sense. You *must* agree with me now. . . . Remember our long arguments during your pregnancy, when you insisted that God's angels had brought us here for some divine purpose. I told you then that everything, including the very existence of our species, was nothing but a random quirk of nature. You became angry with me and even swore that your suffering at the hands of Yasin was somehow part of God's plan."

A shower had begun and drops were spattering on Johann's upturned face. "Don't you see, Beatrice," he shouted again. "There is no plan. Not one made by God, or anyone else. Not for our little group, not for the human species, and not for the universe. We are simply an astonishing physical phenomenon, a miraculous combination of chemicals made by dying stars that have somehow evolved into consciousness. Chemicals capable of asking questions about our origin and destiny."

Inside his head Johann could hear her arguing with him. Passionate, alive, she was telling him that God did not make it easy for humans to have faith. That the very mind He had given them could trick them into thinking He did not exist. The argument was so real, and his feeling of her presence so strong, that Johann started to cry. He caught himself, and burst out in an insane laugh.

"Yes, yes, I understand," he said. "We *do* experience amazing, bewildering, transcendent emotions that we cannot explain. Like love. Without which we would be no different from the robots we have now manufactured on Earth."

He was becoming soaked and started to pace, to stop his shivering. "So I make this pilgrimage as proof of the bizarre contradiction that is humanity, my Beatrice. I hereby proclaim, *simultaneously*," he said with a shouting laugh, "both the absolute meaninglessness of everything and my undying adoration for you."

He shook his head and wiped the water off his face with the back of his hands. "I suppose that when the day arrives that only four humans are left anywhere in the entire universe, and the whole species faces extinction as our group does now, this fundamental contradiction will remain unreconciled."

Johann turned and walked away from the ocean. The rain pelted him as he walked and the black rock beneath his feet was becoming very slippery. He spun around when he reached the top of the path. "Good night and good-bye, my queen and angel." Johann sighed. "I would have been so delighted to have seen you one more time."

Johann was careful on his first few steps down the wet path. But he wasn't paying enough attention several minutes later when his front foot came down upon a loose wet rock. He lost his balance immediately and tumbled head over heels, his head and body banging frequently against the volcanic rock, until he came to rest, unconscious but still alive, about a hundred meters from the edge of the orchard at the bottom of the path.

THREE

JOHANN REGAINED CONSCIOUSNESS some hours later, before it was light. The brief rainstorm had passed and the sky was full of stars. He made an aborted attempt to sit up, but the pain, especially in his right hip and leg, was overpowering. He lay back down, trembling, and realized the predicament he was in.

I will not be able to swim, he thought. *I will not even be able to climb up to the caves. If the brankers come tomorrow I will die.*

He started yelling for help as soon as the sky indicated dawn was coming. Rowen reached him first. Siegfried and Franzi were not far behind. "I cannot walk," he told them. "I think both my right leg and hip are broken."

They carried him carefully to the village and laid him on a mat close to the community kitchen. Franzi gamely fed Johann breakfast, attempting to keep the conversation as light as possible. He called them together after everyone had eaten.

"The three of you must go forward with your plan to swim to the island," Johann said. "For obvious reasons, I will not be going with you. My only request is that you leave me in my hut when you go."

Throughout the day, the other three concocted plots that would not leave Johann alone at the mercy of the brankers. Siegfried thought maybe Rowen and he, between them, were strong enough swimmers that they could tow Johann out to the island. Franzi suggested that if they worked fast maybe they could carry Johann up the hills and reach the caves before the next night.

Johann rejected all their plans as ridiculous. He told them he would not participate in any scheme that increased the risk to any of the three of them one iota. He pointed out that he was not essential to the survival of their group, but that all three of them were. By nightfall the discussions were over. Rowen, Siegfried, and Franzi would leave early the next morning to swim to the offshore island. Johann would be left in his hut as he requested.

Johann had great difficulty falling asleep because he could not find a position in which the pain was not overwhelming. Sometime in the middle of the night, he did manage to doze off for a couple of hours, but it was a light sleep, full of confusing dreams. Many of the major characters of his life made cameo appearances in those dreams, often in situations where they could not have existed in real life. Beatrice, for example, talked with him for a few minutes in the living room of his childhood home in Potsdam, but left suddenly when her pager signaled that she had a call from St. Michael of Siena.

When he awakened, Johann was immediately aware that there was a head lying gently on his chest. Franzi was stretched out perpendicular to the direction of his mat, with her head on the side of his chest and one of her hands in his. Johann stroked her long hair very gently, being careful not to wake her, and wondered when during the night she had come into his hut. Her presence next to him was very soothing and mitigated his pain.

He drifted back to sleep a second time, and was awakened in the morning by the sound of wind and rain pelting against the roof and side of his hut. Franzi had departed. Johann could already see light under his door. Listening carefully, Johann could hear Siegfried's voice above the sound of the storm, but he could not make out any specific words.

Franzi brought him some breakfast a few minutes later. Concern was etched on the girl's usually carefree face. "Are you feeling any better, Uncle Johann?" she said, bending down to feed him.

Johann moved ever so slightly and the searing pain in his right leg made him wince. Franzi saw his expression and struggled not to show her own emotions. She placed a pair of black scruffles in his mouth. "We figured these would cheer you up," she said.

"Umm, delicious," Johann said, forcing a smile. "Almost as nice as the company I had last night."

Franzi grinned. "I didn't think you knew I was here. You hardly stirred the whole time. . . . I hope I didn't bother you."

"Not at all," Johann said. "It was delightful. It's been a long time since I have had someone to cuddle with at night."

"I couldn't fall asleep in my hut, Uncle Johann," Franzi said. "I kept worrying about you. I was afraid . . . anyway, I decided I wanted to hold and touch you one more time in case . . ."

The girl turned away and tears began to flow down her cheeks.

"Come here, Franzi," Johann said softly. "Let me hold you."

The girl leaned over and put herself in Johann's open arms. For a few minutes she wept silently. "Oh, Uncle Johann," she said. "This is so terrible. I love you so much and there's nothing I can do to help you."

"It's all right," Johann said. "Don't worry about me. Just concentrate on what *you* must do today."

He knew what the girl was feeling. *I too have experienced the horror,* he thought, *of being helpless in the face of the death of someone I loved. There is no equivalent agony in our existence.*

He placed his hand under her chin and lifted her face from his chest. Her eyes were swollen and her nose was running. "You are a wonderful young woman, Franzi," he said. "You have made these last years more fun than I could possibly have imagined."

She looked as if she was going to start crying again. "Now go, child," he said. "Just leave the scruffles here beside me. I can feed myself."

JOHANN ATE THE scruffles slowly and pondered the hopelessness of his situation. He moved himself around very gingerly and verified, at least in his own mind, that both his leg and his hip were broken. *I am not afraid of dying,* he thought. *But I will not permit myself to be a burden. If by chance the brankers do not come tonight, I will find some way to die quickly.*

He squirmed on his mat until he again found a position where the pain was not too severe. Then, lying on his back, Johann indulged himself by remembering the best moments of his life. Apologizing in his mind to both Vivien and Maria, he returned in spirit to the days he had spent with Beatrice on their island paradise before Yasin's appearance had shattered the harmony of their perfect life.

She was singing to him on the beach, and he was again enraptured by the sound of her magnificent voice, when his daydream was broken by Siegfried's sudden appearance in his hut. His son was clearly upset.

"The storm is intensifying, Father," he said. "The waves are huge. Franzi is terrified. She doesn't think she can possibly swim out to the island. She wants to go to the caves, by herself if necessary."

Johann shook his head. "The only guarantee of safety is to be away from the mainland," he said. "You know that. Rowen and you must do whatever you can to help her in the water."

"Rowen is frightened also," Siegfried said. "I don't think he'll be much help." He paced about the hut. "And I will need all my strength to make the swim."

Johann studied his son. *He is afraid,* Johann thought. *And not in control of the situation.*

"So what are you suggesting, Siegfried?" Johann asked gently. "That none of you make the swim at all? Surely you know the kind of danger to which that exposes you. We have no evidence that the caves offer any kind of protection. For all we know, the brankers may have such an advanced sense of smell, or something similar, that they can find you wherever you are hiding."

Siegfried sat down beside his father. "Rowen doesn't think the brankers are coming. He constantly reminds me that they skipped two double full moon nights before their last attack. They've only missed one opportunity now. Why should we risk our lives in the storm—"

"That is very dangerous wishful thinking, Siegfried," Johann interrupted, his voice rising, "and I have heard it every double full moon night since our second one here. The truth is we have no idea *whatsoever* what determines if the brankers are coming or not. Here is the record: they came the first time, but not the second. They came again on the third double full moon night, but not on the fourth or fifth. On the sixth they captured Vivien, Stephanie, and Kwame. Then they didn't come the last opportunity.

"There is no discernible pattern in this behavior. We have speculated that perhaps the brankers have several different directions of flight, and don't go in all of them on any single night. Or maybe they don't attack at all on some double full moons. But we know nothing for certain except that if they come, virtually every living creature they find ends up dead."

Johann paused for a moment to catch his breath. Siegfried squirmed without saying anything. "If you are determined to go to the caves," Johann continued, "in spite of everything I have said, then I urge you to leave right away. The climb will be difficult in this weather and you need to spend some time deciding exactly where to hide."

He could stand the pain no more. Johann collapsed on his back on the mat.

"Thank you, Father," Siegfried said, quickly leaving the hut.

The three of them returned in less than half an hour. "We're going to the caves, Father," Siegfried said. "We all wanted to come and say good-bye."

Rowen bent down first and gave his grandfather a perfunctory kiss on the forehead. "For my part," he said, "I fully expect to see you again tomorrow. And then we'll figure out what to do with your leg and hip."

Siegfried kissed his father quickly on the lips and then stood up. He didn't seem to know what to say. "I love you, Father," he blurted out awkwardly, after fidgeting for a while. "I think you're a terrific man."

Rowen and Siegfried left the hut, leaving Franzi alone with Johann. Tears were already streaming down her cheeks. "Dammit," she said, wiping her tears away with the back of her hand. "I told myself I wasn't going to start crying again."

She composed herself and knelt down on the floor next to Johann's mat. She took his hand and kissed it gently. Then Franzi leaned over and kissed him softly on the lips. "You will always be my special uncle Johann," she said. "I hope to see you tomorrow, but if not, I hope that you do not suffer—"

Her voice broke and she turned her face away. Johann reached out to touch her hand. "You have been a light in my life, Franzi," he said. "Please be careful."

Siegfried called, telling Franzi that it was time to depart. She stood up, tried to smile through her tears, and departed from the hut.

THEY HAD LEFT enough food and water within easy reach for Johann to survive for a day. He spent the passing hours allowing his mind to wander from subject to subject, in no discernible pattern, eating a snack or taking a drink whenever he felt like it.

By late afternoon the storm had ceased. The light filtering through the door cracks into Johann's hut was now brighter, suggesting that most of the clouds had also disappeared. Johann did not know exactly what time it was, but he guessed it was only an hour or so before sunset. As he contemplated the possible arrival of the brankers, a cold tingle swept over his body, making him forget temporarily about the pain. His heart began to beat at an increased rate and his breathing became labored.

This must be what it feels like, Johann said to himself, *on the last night on death row in one of those American prisons.* Johann started wondering what it would be like to die. "Like going to sleep and never waking up," a philosophy professor had told him in Berlin.

"There is life after death, whether you believe in it or not," he remembered Sister Beatrice saying to him.

"So what happens to someone like me?" he had asked her.

She had laughed. "You'd probably be classified as a virtuous pagan," she had said. "Dante put you in limbo, along with all the unbaptized children who died early."

But will I see you, Beatrice? Johann suddenly thought. *If so, I would gladly die right now. Or even convert to Christianity. Whatever it would take. I would sell my soul to your devil for one more chance to see your face or hear your voice.*

The light coming through the cracks in the door seemed to be dimming. Had a cloud passed in front of the Sun? Or was sunset and the rise of the double full moons now only minutes away?

Johann lay on his mat with his heart continuing to race. To distract himself, he pictured the cave area and hoped that his three family members were all now safely hidden inside. A distant, unfamiliar sound then shattered his mental image.

What had he heard? At first he couldn't be certain. He lay very still for almost a full minute and then he heard the sound again. It was louder this time. And it was an unmistakable *brank brank*. There was no longer any doubt. The brankers were on the attack.

Waves of fear coursed through Johann's body as the frequency and amplitude of the terrifying branker noises grew louder and louder. Soon the creatures were close enough that he could occasionally hear the beating of their wings. Each time his instincts sent him an overpowering panic signal, Johann took slow, easy breaths, and forced himself to remain calm.

Two or more brankers had landed in the village and were on a destructive rampage. Johann heard what he thought was the sound of first one hut, and then a second, being smashed and broken. The *brank brank* noises were virtually continuous for several minutes, so Johann was surprised when they suddenly diminished and there was quiet except for branker noises in the distance.

Have they gone? Johann asked himself. *Is it possible that for some reason they have left this hut alone and missed me altogether?*

His momentary hope was quickly dashed when he heard a new pair of sounds, first an odd squeal, and then a sound like footsteps just on the other side of his hut. A second squeal from near the door confirmed Johann's worst fears. *They know I'm in here,* he thought, *that's why they have not yet attacked*.

A few seconds later the door was suddenly pushed open and the front part of a monstrous head, most of it a solitary black eye whose moving fluid was contained behind a transparent membrane, thrust itself inside. The branker saw Johann immediately and nearly shattered his eardrums by emitting a terrifying *brank brank*. A similar answering scream from the outside of his hut, near where Johann's head was lying on the mat, was followed by squeals of conversation between the two brankers who were ready to claim Johann as their prize.

The pair of brankers next began the task of widening the doorway, ripping the wood apart with their powerful talons. As he watched them, Johann wondered why they were going to all this trouble when it would have been so much easier to have simply destroyed his home altogether, as they had the others, and then to dig his body out from the debris.

They must want me to remain alive, Johann thought as he watched the hideous creatures at work. *And they must be intelligent enough to know that I could die if the hut collapsed upon me.*

In spite of his terror, Johann examined the brankers as they systematically tore apart the walls of the hut on either side of the door. He noticed that they actually had four additional legs behind the front talons, for mobility on land, and speculated that these comparatively undeveloped, thin, jointed legs were probably folded and stowed next to the body when the brankers were in flight.

When the exterior opening was wide enough that both brankers could enter the hut together, Johann saw a third branker land on the ground not far away. A deafening exchange of *branks* ensued. One of the brankers who had been widening Johann's doorway suddenly bolted and rushed toward the newcomer, who became airborne rather than engage in combat.

When the two brankers were again side by side, they approached Johann with small, mincing steps, almost as if they were enacting some kind of ceremony. White drool was pouring from each of their open mouths. Johann prepared to die, expecting that at any moment the branker talons would begin ripping him apart and putting chunks of his body into those hideous mouths with all the sharp teeth.

Instead each of the brankers slid its two talons under Johann's mat and lifted slightly, to check the weight. Then they picked both Johann and his mat off the floor, backed up through the opening they had created, and laid him temporarily on the ground outside, where he could see the awesome beauty of the twin full moons.

He could also see a dozen or so of the brankers, some flying solo and some as pairs, cavorting in the sky overhead, intermittently screaming their characteristic *brank brank*. One pair coming toward the village from the hills was carrying an animal Johann had never seen before, something large and reddish in color, that was honking in distress as it struggled uselessly against the power of the four talons gripping its body.

Johann's pair of brankers was also studying the sky and conversing in their odd little squeals. After no more than a minute or two, he felt their talons between his body and his mat. Their double wings began to beat furiously and they lifted him off the ground, each issuing a loud, triumphant *brank brank* as it rose slowly into the air. They flew in tandem, one behind the other, with Johann's body just underneath them. The rear branker's talons were extended as far forward as they would go, and were holding on to Johann's thighs. The lead branker had stretched its talons backward and was grasping Johann under the armpits.

Although his fear never really abated, Johann's primary feeling during the unbelievable flight was one of exhilaration. The brankers flew toward the west, their altitude continually increasing. Their speed was astonishing—Johann guessed that they were flying at least one hundred kilometers per hour. Above the hills they flew, then up and over the snowcapped mountains. From time to time, especially when a new pair of brankers carrying some other prize would come into view, Johann's captors would trumpet a series of *branks*, showing their pride in their exotic prey.

The flight lasted almost an hour altogether. On the other side of the mountains was a wide, dense forest, and then a series of lakes. By the time Johann and his brankers had crossed the last of the lakes, they had already begun to descend. The sky around them was now swarming with branker pairs returning home carrying all kinds of booty. Although Johann did not have much flexibility of movement, and any major motion was accompanied by shooting pains from his hip or his leg, he did glance around to see if perhaps any of his other three family members had been captured. He did not find Franzi, Siegfried, or Rowen, but he did see an incredible menagerie of exotic flora and fauna, doubtless gathered from parts of this world to which Johann and his friends had never traveled.

Below them now was a brown barren surface, clearly visible in the double full moonlight, its emptiness broken only by occasional shrubs or other small growth. Scattered around this desert were ten or twelve tall brown mounds, each with a gigantic, thin cylinder rising a hundred meters into the air from its center. Johann noticed that the flight pattern around him was changing. Some of the branker pairs were peeling off and heading in the direction of a particular mound. His deduction that these mounds and cylinders were where the brankers lived was confirmed when his pair abruptly swooped downward, toward a cylinder located in the middle of the group.

They carried Johann directly inside the top of the open cylinder. He was overwhelmed by the activity and the noise that surrounded him. Branker pairs carrying plants and animals were flying this way and that in the crowded airspace. Johann heard hundreds of *branks* and almost as many wails from the wide variety of creatures the rampaging brankers had brought back to their home.

The top dozen levels inside the cylindrical nest each had

individual alcoves, or rooms, separated from one another by a wall that extended to the rim of the hollow center of the structure. These rooms, perhaps twenty of them on each level, completely encircled the nest. Johann's branker pair knew exactly where they were headed. They dropped down four levels from the top and thrust him firmly against the sticky back wall of one of the larger alcoves. One of his brankers next hovered in front of him for a few minutes, removing wall material with its talons and reworking it into something like a rope that it wound around Johann's waist and then secured, on either side, against the wall behind him. Johann was eventually left alone, trapped against the sticky alcove wall like dozens of creatures above and below him.

The brankers had placed Johann in a standing position with his natural body weight on his broken hip and leg. He tried to change his position to relieve the excruciating pain, but he had very little success. His freedom of movement was severely limited, both by the thick sticky substance that was attached to his back and by the rope around his waist.

His pain was so severe that Johann felt certain that he was going to pass out. Fighting to remain alert for as long as he could, he attempted to examine what he could of the branker habitat. The walls on the side of his alcove prevented his seeing any of the adjacent rooms (although he could hear the creature on his left screaming continuously in a high-pitched whine), but Johann could see three levels of alcoves opposite him, forty meters away across the hollow cylinder. He was able to distinguish three ackyongs, two nepps, and one of the quilled creatures among the collection of plants, animals, and odd objects (including a table and hut wall from his village) occupying these other alcoves. Then he lost consciousness.

He awakened when he felt a branker talon on his back, pulling him away from the wall. His pair of creatures had returned and were apparently now preparing to take him to another location, for they had removed the rope around his

waist and were using copious amounts of their drool to reduce the adhesiveness of the wall material.

Once Johann was free of his constraints, one of the
two brankers opened a jar it had brought into the alcove,
and dipped what looked like a rag into the liquid contents
of that jar. The branker rubbed the rag thoroughly all over
Johann's body, starting at his feet. When it reached Johann's
face, the creature was actually surprisingly gentle with the
rag, being careful not to put it in his eyes or mouth.

Johann did not smell the substance with which he was
being covered until the rag was on his face. Then he
thought he understood what was occurring. *I am being per-
fumed,* he guessed, *with something very mild and delicate.* He
inhaled deeply, attempting to recognize the fragrance. *It's
almost a gardenia smell,* he thought, *but very muted and subtle.*

He had just started wondering about the purpose of
the entire procedure when his branker pair took him again
firmly in their talons and gently eased out into the center of
the hollow cylinder. Emitting a carefully coordinated sequence of subdued *branks,* they flew slowly on a descending helical trajectory, down past the bottom of the
alcoves and into the heart of the nest.

At the base of the cylinder, below the alcoves for the
captives and twenty or so levels of branker apartments that
extended vertically for roughly fifty meters, a virtual army
of smaller, talonless brankers were scurrying about on either side of a raised doughnut structure. Inside this thick
torus, sitting or floating in a colorless liquid pool underneath an array of torches providing superb illumination,
was an enormous branker, at least twice the size of any that
Johann had ever seen. Its elongated body was golden, not
black, and its two pairs of wings were a lovely powder-
blue. As Johann and his brankers approached, passing another pair carrying a goat-sized animal with six legs, the
queen branker rose and placed its middle two legs, which
also had talons, on one side of the torus. Johann watched as

the queen accepted with her front talons a large piece of
unknown meat from a dozen of her minions and ripped it
to pieces with the teeth in her cavernous mouth. She then
returned to her position in the center of her torus and focused her attention on Johann.

His brankers flew very slowly back and forth in front of
her huge solitary eye, showing their prize from all directions. Johann thought he could see movement in the blackness behind the transparent membrane, but he wasn't
absolutely certain. What he did see was a surge of white
drool that spilled out of the queen's mouth when she issued
her deeper, louder *brank* of approval.

Her response excited Johann's pair of carriers, for they
burst into a staccato sequence of *branks* and ascended rapidly,
depositing Johann this time in a special, lighted room in the
middle of the branker apartment complex. He dropped
down on his side as soon as his pair was no longer holding
him tightly, so that he would not be forced again to put
weight on his injured hip and leg.

The two brankers stood on either side of him in the
room. Soon there was a crescendo of noise from below and
Johann heard the distinctive *brank* of the queen as she flew
slowly upward in the cylinder. She stopped, all six talons
deployed below her huge body, and then hovered just
opposite Johann's location. His branker pair became extremely agitated. The queen *brank*'d again, in Johann's direction, and his pair flew out into the center of the
cylinder, where they circled their queen twice with great
deliberation. At this point the back third of the queen's
elongated body lifted up, from a joint at her rear, until this
hood stood almost perpendicular to her body. With her
interior parts exposed, each of Johann's two brankers, one
on either side of the queen, approached her very carefully, flying backward. They simultaneously placed their
rears in her exposed area and an incredible, ear-shattering
howl came from all three of them. This shocking noise was

followed by a din of *branks* that resounded off the walls of the cylinder.

When they were finished, Johann's brankers flew back to his side. The queen had now turned in his direction and opened her gaping mouth. Voluminous drool poured out, falling down toward the base of the cylinder. The brankers picked Johann up with their talons and flew toward their queen.

She's going to eat me in one bite, Johann thought as the strongest terror he had ever known surged through his body. Just before he reached her open mouth he held his arms out in front of him and shouted defiantly with all his strength.

"I am Johann," he bellowed.

FOUR

As LONG AS any daylight remained, Siegfried, Rowen, and Franzi continued to trek back and forth from the entrance to the cave to the darkness of their selected hideout. Siegfried kept stressing the importance of memorizing the route completely, and knowing how many steps were between each major junction, since they would be in complete darkness and might have to move quickly.

They were making their final round trip and were halfway between their hiding place and the entrance when they heard the first *brank*. Without saying a word, they quickly retreated to where they intended to remain for the rest of the night.

Even deep in the cave they could still make out an occasional *brank* as the attack on their region began. Franzi's fear for herself was overshadowed by her certain knowledge that her beloved uncle Johann would be helpless against the fearsome creatures. She started to say something but was grabbed forcefully by Siegfried.

The trio sat, motionless and in absolute silence as they had planned, for well over two hours. Franzi's back was bothering her and she had an overwhelming desire to urinate. She touched Siegfried, who was sitting on her right in the dark, and whispered, in her lowest possible voice, "Is it safe now?"

His firm grip upon her forearm gave her the negative answer.

The threesome continued to sit until they were all sore

and miserable. They were unaware that during the time they had been in the cave a solitary branker, discouraged by its inability to find any exciting prey, had been searching the entire area and had picked up the trace of their smell. It had then flown away, to find its partner, and this pair had subsequently canvassed all the cave openings until they had located where the humans had entered. The branker pair, silent except for an occasional exchange of their odd little squeals, had descended one level into the cave by the time Franzi whispered her question to Siegfried.

The brankers did not hear what she said, but they did know, from the strength of the response they were receiving from their olfactory equivalents, that they were growing closer and closer to something that was both alive and unusual. At each junction, the creatures carefully examined each of the pathways, checked the smells, and then continued deeper in the cave complex on a path that would ultimately lead them to the humans.

Siegfried heard the brankers first, their talons and four other jointed legs scraping on the cave floor. As planned, the trio were sitting just inside the door to their little room. They had discussed many times what they would do if a branker showed up. Siegfried, wielding the large club sitting beside him, would distract the creature by engaging it in battle. While he was fighting, Rowen and Franzi would slip out the door and escape from the cave.

The brankers made no attempt to hide their presence. Moving slowly in darkness so black that even their incredibly sensitive eyes could barely see, they moved relentlessly toward where the humans were hiding. When they were just outside the door of the small room, Siegfried picked up his club and moved over to the opposite wall. Franzi was so frightened that she could hardly breathe. The moment the first branker rounded the corner and saw Siegfried's silhouette, it screamed a loud *brank* that was quickly repeated by its partner out in the cave hallway.

Siegfried struck a monumental blow, directly on the lead branker's eye, temporarily stunning the creature.

"Run," he shouted, gathering his strength for a second strike. Franzi, adrenaline saturating her entire body, ducked quickly out the door and down the hallway before the second branker could react. Rowen was not so fortunate. When he raced into the hallway the other alien grabbed him with one talon and then penned him against the wall.

Meanwhile, Siegfried continued his heroic battle. Over and over he managed deftly to escape the lead branker's talons and land another savage blow on its eye. The branker trying to capture him was now filling the cave area with its shrieks. Siegfried did not understand that the creature he was battling was trying to take him alive and was therefore trying not to injure him too seriously. But when the continuing series of blows from Siegfried's club finally caused the lead branker's eye membrane to split open, and some liquid to ooze out, the alien lost its temper.

Howling furiously, the branker attacked with both its talons and ripped Siegfried apart in a few seconds, breaking his body into three pieces in the process. The terrified Rowen, just outside the room, heard Siegfried's death cries and fainted from fear. With Rowen lying motionless on the cave floor, the two brankers had a quick feast on Siegfried's remains.

Franzi, meanwhile, reached the entrance to the cave after carefully counting her steps and making the correct turn at every junction. Outside she stopped momentarily, not certain of what to do, and checked behind her to see if Rowen was coming. She waited as long as she dared. When she heard some noise behind her in the cave, she started to run.

But where should she go? The fact that she could see so clearly in the twin moonlight also meant that a flying branker could see her as well. She glanced around and found a thick group of bushes not too far from the caves. Running at her top speed she approached these bushes, crawled in amongst them, and lay down on the ground. From where she was she could not see the sky. Franzi felt certain that no airborne branker could see her either.

The two brankers in the cave, one of them carrying Rowen, who had regained a sort of traumatized consciousness, proceeded at a deliberate pace to retrace their earlier steps. During their exit, they decided in their conversation of squeals that they would keep Rowen as their personal prey, and head west for home. However, first they would inform other members of their species that there was one more of these exotic animals loose somewhere in the region.

When they departed from the cave, the branker pair secured Rowen in their talons and lifted off in their tandem formation, soaring up several hundred meters before beginning a circular pattern that they repeated six or seven times. While they were flying in circles, both the brankers holding Rowen screamed a continuous string of *branks*, calling to all other members of their species that might be within earshot. One new branker showed up quickly, dove down to the ground to pick up Franzi's smell, and then became airborne again in search of its partner. A few minutes later, after a second pair of their colleagues started flying in their direction, the two brankers carrying Rowen broke out of their circular pattern, increased their altitude, and headed toward the west.

Franzi, lying underneath the protective bushes, had no idea that at least three more of the loathsome creatures now knew of her existence. But she could hear the terrifying *branks* of one pair, who swooped hurriedly to the ground, eager to find her before the other branker returned with its partner. Her trail was fresh and easy to follow. The two new brankers located her hiding place in the bushes in only a matter of minutes. Lying on the ground and trembling, Franzi watched the pair between some twigs while they were deciding how to proceed. When the solo branker who had smelled her earlier returned with its partner, a territorial dispute among the four creatures ensued. Momentarily neglected, Franzi crawled out of the far side of the bushes and began to run.

Immediately there was a chorus of *branks* behind her. All four creatures were airborne and it was a race to see which branker could reach her first. As Franzi ran across a meadow, the fastest branker caught her from behind, placed its talons on either side of her waist, and lifted her off the ground with a triumphant trio of *branks*.

Franzi, her legs dangling in the air, screamed uselessly, her cry giving vent to her fear, as a second branker came up from behind and grabbed her thighs with its talons. The first branker walked its talons up her body, one at a time, until it was holding her under the armpits and the flying formation had stabilized.

Meanwhile the other branker pair, angry that they had not secured this unusual prize, continued to fly beside the creatures carrying Franzi and to voice their disapproval of her seizure with continuous *branks*. Suddenly one of the other pair rushed at the lead branker and it let go of Franzi. She tumbled forward, saw the ground more than a hundred meters below her, and thought she was going to fall.

The back branker held her legs firmly, however, during the fierce midair battle between the others. For the entire two minutes of the raging fight, Franzi was hanging upside down, with her head facing the ground. Eventually the branker who had originally seized Franzi, although severely wounded, won the battle and returned to grasp the front of her body. During the next several minutes of the flight, however, some kind of fluid from this lead branker dripped on the back of Franzi's head.

The brankers carrying her turned left, affording her an exceptional view of the twin full moons, and began to increase their altitude. They rose over the western hills and headed for the snowcapped mountains. Although she was still frightened, Franzi was not uncomfortable. She had already begun to wonder where they were taking her when something extraordinary happened.

Franzi never saw it coming. From out across the ocean, traveling at a fantastic speed, came a glowing ribbon of particles that passed directly over the heads of the flying brankers, pirouetted, and then spread out to occupy the entire airspace toward which the creatures were flying. They *brank*'d, confused, and tried to dive down under this glowing whiteness, but the ribbon extended a part of itself as far as the head of the lead branker, touching it lightly. The lead branker screamed immediately with pain. Moments later the ribbon had surrounded the pair of brankers and Franzi. In their confusion, they dropped her from their talons.

She began to fall. Franzi felt certain that she was going to die. After only a few seconds, however, the ribbon was underneath her as well and part of it had formed into a solid substance, like a cushion, upon which the amazed Franzi rode as the ribbon sped in the direction of their village, now reduced to rubble by the brankers. The ribbon deposited Franzi gently on the beach, next to a glowing bullet-shaped white object the size of a small house. While the ribbon hovered overhead a door opened in the vehicle and Franzi saw that Rowen was asleep in a chair in a small compartment with hundreds of miniature threads wrapped around most of the parts of his naked body.

Franzi glanced at the hovering ribbon and somehow knew that she was supposed to remove her shirt and shorts. When she was naked, a tiny finger of the ribbon extended in her direction and, to Franzi's amazement, made a quick incision in her right buttock, inserted a silver cylinder the size of a small cigar, and closed up the wound, all in no more than one or two seconds, and without causing her any pain. The ribbon extension then gestured in the direction of the vehicle. The dazed Franzi, overwhelmed by what was happening to her, climbed into the other chair in the compartment and was quickly enwrapped by the miniature threads. She was asleep in seconds.

The bullet-shaped vehicle deployed its legs and wings, fired its smaller pair of thrusters, and took off from the beach. It flew in tandem with the ribbon of dancing, sparkling particles until both were well out over the ocean. Then the glowing white bullet turned upward, aimed at the stars, and its larger pair of thrusters roared into action. Once it was outside the atmosphere, and no longer accompanied by the ribbon, the drone vehicle switched to its advanced engine and accelerated into space at a breathtaking rate.

RESURRECTION

ONE

THE IMPOSING CREATURE, holding the small silver cylinder in its four-fingered hand, said good-bye to the woman, closed the door to her apartment, and walked down the cream-colored corridor to the nearest intersection. There the alien being, called the Eagle by the humans inhabiting the giant tetrahedral space station of extraterrestrial origin, hesitated for a few seconds. During those seconds an elaborate conversation occurred between the Eagle and the central intelligence governing the space station. This two-way communication took place in an advanced higher-level language at a phenomenal data rate. The precision and richness of the electronic discussion could not possibly be conveyed in any form as simple as a human language. It is possible, however, to summarize the fundamental information exchanged between the two artificial intelligences and mimic the flow of the conversation.

"The young human named Maria has given me the silver cylinder again," the Eagle said. "She has entreated me to examine it a second time to discover if it contains any information about her ancestors or personal history. She does not accept that I know nothing about the cylinder, or about the events that led to her discovery by Nicole in the octospider zoo inside Rama years ago, just prior to our intercession. Maria has learned, from those octospiders and humans that we have selected to survive, that her parents may not have come to Rama from Earth along with all the other humans. She insists that her life will continue to be meaningless if her origins remain competely unknown to her.

"Does there not exist some way that we can use her passionate obsession with her family background for our own purposes? She is an intelligent and compassionate human, possessing some of the best attributes of the species. Her ancestors had many detailed interactions with the particle beings whose evolution and sociology remain a partial mystery to us. Her silver cylinder may contain data that would be of interest to us, as well as her. It seems remiss on our part not to try to obtain this new data. We have added no new information to the encyclopedia entry for the particle beings for almost a hundred years."

"We have encountered several similar silver cylinders over the past millennia," the central intelligence replied, "and have never been successful decoding their programs, or preventing them from self-destructing when we used invasive techniques. Of all the spacefarers we have cataloged in this segment of the galaxy, only the particle beings have eluded our understanding. The probability that we will learn something new by exposing this insignificant human to the creatures who interacted with her ancestors and created the silver cylinder are vanishingly small, as we discussed several weeks ago when this Maria first gave you the object the particle beings inserted in her mother's body. Nothing has happened since then to change the quantitative analysis that indicated we should not tell her anything."

"I was originally created," the Eagle said, "primarily as an interface for this particular species. My design was optimized to permit me to obtain a deeper understanding of what humans are all about, especially how their irrational, emotional component has played a significant role in their evolution and technological development. I have learned that some special humans, and I am certain this Maria belongs to this group, cannot function properly in their lives if information critical to their perception of themselves is not available.

"What harm would be done if I informed Maria that her ancestors left Earth roughly two hundred years ago, and that since that time her forebears have been part of a grand experiment conducted by a superior alien intelligence, of which we have imperfect knowledge? I could also mention that her parents were rescued from certain death by the particle ribbons on a faraway planet with large twin moons, and then left to be discovered by the octospider species just as it was establishing its colony in Rama. At least this information would answer a few of her questions and might permit her to focus her admirable intelligence and energy on other issues."

"Our overall objective function," the other replied to the Eagle, "shows no significant probability of increase as a result of providing to this young human female the general history of her origins. The only way our endeavor receives a stochastically measurable payoff is if we place her in a situation where she has an opportunity to encounter the particle beings themselves. Only *they* can unravel the secrets of the silver cylinder for her. And as you are well aware from the entries in our historical data base, often these encounters result in the death or permanent exile from their species for the spacefarers involved.

"If you are recommending that we transport her to the spherical spaceship that we have allowed to remain stationed not far from our tetrahedron, then don't tell Maria very much about her background before she arrives there. Detailed knowledge might unduly influence her behavior. We can take her to the sphere and communicate to the particles the nature of her mission. Of course, we have absolutely no control over their response, or her fate if she decides to enter their domain. If she survives and returns from her encounter with them, then we can share all that we know about her family origins."

"I think," said the Eagle, "that this particular human is exceptional and has a high probability, based on what I know of the past encounters between other spacefarers and the particles, of having a positive experience inside their domain. What I propose is to give Maria a brief overview of what we know, and don't know, about her origins, the silver cylinder, and the particles. We can let her decide whether the additional knowledge she seeks is worth risking her life to obtain. If she decides to go, and is permitted to exit from their sphere, she will almost certainly add new and valuable data about the particle beings."

"Your proposal is approved," the central intelligence answered. "If Maria accepts the risks of the encounter, she will carry on her person our most advanced miniaturized remote sensing instruments. Even though the particle beings have always detected, and rendered useless, our information-seeking devices in the past, we have recently made some new breakthroughs that have resulted in sensors that operate at subatomic levels. These may escape their notice. In any case, we agree that if she survives the experience and is allowed to return to the shuttle in which you will transport her, Maria's observations about her encounter will be a major addition to what we know about the particle beings."

"I will speak to her in the near future," the Eagle said, "and carefully explain that we can neither guarantee her safety nor any answers to her questions. My guess is that Maria will still decide the risk is worth taking. In that event, how long will our preparations take?"

"We will have her customized shuttle and the miniaturized instruments ready for deployment in a few days."

TWO

MARIA HAD HARDLY slept all night. She was too excited. She knew that she had just spent the most extraordinary day of her unusual life and that in a few hours, when the Eagle came for her, she would begin an adventure unequaled in all of human experience.

As she lay in her bed she could still see that mesmerizing face in her apartment and hear the words spoken by the Eagle the previous evening. The voice had had an electronic tone, and had seemed to be emanating from somewhere far back in the mouth, but the words had been clear and distinct. "You understand clearly," the Eagle had said near the end of their discussion, "that we have no control over what might happen after you are in their jurisdiction."

"Yes, sir," Maria had replied. "I also know that they might not even grant me an audience, and that even if they do, I may not learn anything about my ancestors. But I still believe this is my only hope. And I can't imagine living my entire life without knowing anything about my family."

The Eagle had then stood silently for a long time in the middle of the living room in her small apartment, dominating the scene both by his size and his presence. Maria had an indelible print of the alien in her memory. The Eagle was very tall, perhaps two and a quarter meters, and shaped like a human being from the neck down. His arms and torso were covered with small tightly woven charcoal-gray feathers. He had four fingers on each of his two hands, which were creamy white and featherless. Below his waist, the surface of the Eagle's body was flesh colored, but it was shiny, like satin, and very much unlike human skin. There were no hairs or feathers below the waist, no visible joints or genitalia, and his strange flat feet had no toes.

The Eagle's face had commanded Maria's attention throughout their meeting. It had four large powder-blue eyes, two on either side of a protruding beak that was greenish gold in color. The feathers on the top of his head were white, contrasting with the dark gray of his back, face, and neck. The Eagle's face was smooth, with only a few feathers scattered here and there.

"Then have you made your decision?" the Eagle had asked at length.

"Yes, sir," Maria had replied without hesitation. "I want to go."

"All right," the Eagle had said, his expression unchanged. "Pack your things. I will return for you in nine hours."

Maria glanced over at the clock, as she had done a dozen times before. It was only thirty minutes until his arrival. She rose from her bed and went to the desk. She thought for a moment, and then started writing three short notes to her closest friends, all members of Nicole's extended family. Maria had deliberately not contacted anyone after the Eagle's surprise visit. She hadn't wanted to explain what she was doing or give anyone a chance to talk her out of her decision.

She didn't say anything in the notes about what she had learned the night before. How could she possibly have summarized the amazing conversation? At first the Eagle had been reluctant to give her specific answers to her questions, but once Maria had explained that there was no way she could make an informed decision based on the sketchy information he had provided, the intelligent alien had been more forthcoming.

"The particle beings are very difficult to describe or classify," the Eagle had said. "First, they are able to reconfigure themselves into an infinite variety of shapes and sizes. Their most common manifestation is as a three-dimensional construct that is glowing white in appearance, shaped like a long, looping ribbon. Inside the structure, whose external surface ebbs and flows, are thousands of tiny sparkling particles that move about in no discernible pattern, drifting freely until they contact the temporary edge of the formation, at which point the particle momentum reverses and the individual mote moves back in the opposite direction.

"In addition, it is impossible to define a single individual among them. The particle beings possess an instantaneous distributed intelligence with internal communications in electromagnetic packets in codes we have not been able to decipher. Finally, they have an advanced system of fault protection that preserves their secrets—any detected attempt by an outside presence to analyze them in detail causes self-destruction."

And these are the beings I am hoping to meet? Maria said to herself as she finished writing the notes. *I certainly was feeling brave last night. I wonder if I would have made the same decision this morning.*

She walked into the living room and placed the three notes in the center of the little table in front of the couch. Then Maria returned to her bedroom, opened and checked the contents of her bag one final time, and sat down on the bed. Her heart was already pounding furiously.

What was it that Nicole said to me the last time we were together? Maria asked herself. *Happiness only comes to people who are willing to take risks.* She laughed nervously. *I guess that's better than Uncle Max's favorite saying. Fools rush in where mortals fear to tread.*

THE EAGLE, PUNCTUAL as always, arrived at Maria's apartment at the appointed time. After exchanging greetings,

Maria followed him through the sterile corridors of the section of the Habitation Module that housed all the humans and the octospiders. When they reached the sealed airlock and gates that separated their environment from others in the module, the Eagle handed Maria a space suit complete with a transparent helmet that would fit over her head.

"Are you still certain that you want to do this?" the alien asked as Maria was adjusting her new clothing and helmet. She nodded.

By some unknown process the Eagle activated the apparatus controlling the series of gates and they passed into another area with similar offwhite corridors. Parked at the first junction in the new region was a small wheeled vehicle with two seats. Maria climbed in next to the Eagle and the doors to the windowless vehicle sealed. "For security reasons, you will not be allowed to see outside the car," the Eagle said matter-of-factly. "You may be returning to your apartments and we do not want you to have any knowledge of the creatures living in your immediate vicinity."

After riding in silence for a few minutes, Maria asked the Eagle where they were going. "To the transportation center of the Habitation Module," he replied, "the place you arrived when you were first transferred here from the starfish. Then we will be transported to the Engineering Module, where the space shuttle that will fly us to our destination is being constructed."

"You are making a special spaceship for me, just for this trip?" Maria asked in astonishment.

"Yes," the Eagle said.

"But why?" Maria said. "Why would you go to all that trouble?"

"We wouldn't ordinarily," the Eagle answered. "Our decision to permit your excursion was based on a complicated objective function in which the primary weighting

was the likelihood of our obtaining any new or character-
izing data about the ribbon culture for our files."

Maria laughed. "I have no idea what you just told me,"
she said.

The Eagle looked at her. "In simpler language, we have
our own reasons for supporting this endeavor."

When Maria and the Eagle disembarked from their
small wheeled car, they were in a large room right next to
the transportation center. Through the huge transparent
window on the side of the room, Maria could see a long
thin passageway, with blinking lights, stretching far into the
distance. At the far end the lights became connected to
each other and to an illuminated sphere, another of the
vertices of the tetrahedron that formed the Node.

Maria remembered the confusion and uncertainty she
had felt the first time that she had stood in front of this
same window, shortly after the shuttles carrying the occupants of the starfish had docked at the Habitation Module.
This time, too, her heart was racing wildly, in anticipation
of the adventure she had decided to undertake. But since
she was not surrounded by others and being pressed to
move forward, Maria took several minutes to enjoy the
spectacular view out the window.

"Is that the Engineering Module?" she eventually
asked the Eagle. Her alien companion had been standing
patiently beside her the entire time.

"Actually, no," he answered. "That particular distant
sphere is the Knowledge Module. But the Engineering
Module is identical in size and construction. And the linear
connector along which we will travel is similar to the one
you are seeing out the window."

Maria glanced again at the large sphere twenty-five
kilometers away. "Is that where Nicole died?" she asked.

"Yes," said the Eagle. "She requested that her last days
be spent learning things that would help her understand

more clearly how human beings, and she in particular, fit into the overall scheme of the universe."

"She was a remarkable woman," Maria said, surprised at the surge of sorrow and loss she suddenly felt.

"Yes, she was," the Eagle said.

"You were with her when she died, weren't you?" Maria said.

"Yes," the Eagle answered simply.

THE TRANSPORTATION CENTER of the Habitation Module was laid out in a circle and was twenty meters tall. On every side of Maria and the Eagle were moving sidewalks leading in different directions, and escalators going up and down.

Maria followed the Eagle down one of the escalators and onto a moving sidewalk. They approached a pair of tracks, on one of which was parked a sleek silver tube.

"Each of the modules is connected to the other three vertices by long linear constructs," the Eagle said. "We use them to move living creatures, equipment, or anything else that needs to be transported from module to module."

The door to the silver tube opened automatically as they approached. Maria and the Eagle were to be the only occupants. A few seconds after they were seated, the tube moved forward. It quickly accelerated to its cruising speed and raced down the corridor. Twice tubes going in the opposite direction whizzed by them, but Maria could not distinguish what, if anything, was contained inside them.

At the transportation center of the Engineering Module, Maria followed the Eagle up several escalators until they reached a docking area where their small shuttle was waiting. The vehicle was round and flat, except for a small bulge in the middle with a transparent window. Maria and the Eagle entered from the underside of the spacecraft. As soon as they were sitting down, seat restraints wrapped around Maria, doors in the side of the Node opened, and their flying saucer edged out into space.

"Even at our high speeds," the Eagle said as they sped away from the illuminated tetrahedron, "it will take several hours for us to reach our destination. I had the designers include a hundred or so selections of human music, in case you become bored. Is there anything in particular that you would like to hear?"

Maria glanced over at the Eagle, who was a passenger in the automatically guided spacecraft just as she was. "I don't suppose you would tell me what else the designers included in this vehicle, would you?"

"No," said the Eagle. "And even if I did, I don't think you would understand any of the technological explanations."

"In that case," Maria said with a wry smile, "I would like to hear something by Beethoven or Mozart. One of the many things Nicole shared with me was her love of fine music."

Beethoven's Sixth Symphony was in the middle of its storm when Maria first caught sight of the polished white ball that was their destination. Her first surprise was how enormous it was. Then she became fascinated by its scattered red decorations, including the polar hood on the top, two red circles that looked like eyes symmetrically placed in its upper hemisphere, and the two distinct red bands, separated by a thin white line, that ran completely around its equator.

As their shuttle drew closer to the habitat of the ribbon culture, aiming for its equatorial region, first the hood and then the two red eyes moved out of sight. Their front window was now completely filled by the whiteness of the sphere, broken only by the red lines in the middle of their view.

"The only opening into their spacecraft," the Eagle

said, "or at least the only one that we have ever observed, is along these equatorial markings. We will cruise near the equator, broadcasting the purpose of our visit in a dozen different high-level languages that we know the particle culture understands, and hope that there is some response."

The alien could sense Maria's anticipation from the set of her body. "Don't be too disappointed if nothing happens," the Eagle continued. "This sphere has only opened once when one of our spacecraft was in its vicinity during the hundreds of years that it has been stationed near us. We have seen it open many times, with our remote sensors, to deploy its own spacecraft or let one back inside, but it always remains firmly closed when any extension of the Nodal Intelligence is in the area."

"Why did it open that one time?" Maria asked.

"It's a long story," the Eagle answered, "most of which you would not be able to comprehend. But what's intriguing is that there were some similarities between that visit and ours. In that previous instance, the ribbons sent out their own drone—"

As if on cue, the deep red equatorial lips of the sphere separated almost imperceptibly for a brief moment and something flew out into space, heading toward the shuttle. Maria's first reaction was fright.

"How do you know that whatever is coming toward us is not a weapon of some kind?" she asked the Eagle.

"In the first place," the alien responded, "that would be out of character with the entire history of the particle culture. Secondly, although you may not realize it, our shuttle has a very high technological level of self-protection."

The craft that was heading in their direction was a red sphere about the size of their shuttle. It circled Maria and the Eagle a couple of times before finally stopping on Maria's side. The red sphere then convulsed and extended a long red hollow cylinder that came to rest against Maria's window.

"Now watch carefully," the Eagle said. "In less than a minute your window will vanish and you will have access to the red sphere through that cylindrical corridor."

The Eagle's prediction was correct. Several moments later Maria's shuttle window disappeared. To her right was a long red corridor that stretched into darkness.

"Now's when you *really* make the decision," the Eagle said. "The ribbons are not going to allow me or this shuttle any closer to the sphere. Unless I have misinterpreted their actions, however, they are inviting you to join them. Remember, Maria, the moment you enter that red corridor, it will almost certainly disengage from this shuttle. From that point forward you will be utterly on your own."

Fear registered on Maria's face for a brief moment. "You don't have to go," the Eagle added. "It would not be cowardly for you to change your mind at this point. Fear of the unknown has been a life-preserving characteristic of your species throughout history. If our shuttle makes any kind of maneuver, I am confident the red corridor will disappear, your window will again be in its place, and that red sphere will return to its home."

Maria looked at the Eagle and then stared for a long time down the strange red corridor in space. She could feel her heart pounding furiously inside her space suit. Taking a deep breath and clutching the small silver cylinder in her hand, she pressed the button that retracted her seat belt.

"Good-bye," she said, standing up. "Thanks for everything."

AFTER HER FIRST three steps into the red corridor, Maria turned around and looked behind her. The Eagle and their shuttle had vanished. The red corridor was now closed and shrinking with each step that she took. Again she felt a powerful rush of anxiety, but Maria forced herself to continue walking forward.

A hundred meters into the corridor Maria saw a white object in the distance moving in her direction. As it drew closer, her trepidation increased. What was coming to meet her looked like two giant, stacked snowballs, riding on a flat white plate with six red wheels. This snowman, however, had no eyes, no ears, and no arms. At least not until it stopped just in front of Maria.

She screamed involuntarily when the snowman suddenly convulsed and extended two white appendages out of the upper snowball, immediately grabbing and removing the helmet to her space suit. For a brief moment Maria expected to die, but when she began to breathe more easily she realized that the environment in the red corridor had been designed for her.

One of the snowman's long, skinny two-fingered arms was now tugging at her space suit. Maria understood. She removed the suit and placed it on the floor of the corridor. Moments later, the external surface of the snowman began to glow and soften. As Maria watched in astonishment, what had been the snowman dissolved before her eyes, first becoming a glowing, formless mass of white containing thousands of sparkling, drifting particles, and then breaking into hundreds of tiny, separate elements, each no larger than a marble. This group of elements spread out into a formation that was approximately Maria's size, and moved in her direction.

Fighting against a powerful desire to flee, Maria held her breath and stood motionless as the tiny particle elements came in contact with all parts of her body and her clothing. She closed her eyes. She could feel the aliens rubbing against her cheeks, her neck, even her eyelids. Then suddenly they were all gone.

When Maria opened her eyes, the snowman was again standing in front of her. Satisfied that she was no longer a remote sensing laboratory, it retracted its arms into its upper snowball and scurried away in front of her. Maria followed, her pulse gradually returning to normal. Occasionally she turned around and noted that the red corridor was no longer shortening and that her space suit still remained at the far end.

When she reached the red sphere, the snowman was standing in its center beside a tall, narrow chamber with a transparent window. There was nothing else visible in the sphere except its red walls. The snowman was pointing at the chamber with an extended arm. Maria entered. Immediately after the door closed, some unseen force propelled the chamber through a hidden door out into space. Maria's short flight ended in less than a minute. The chamber was now standing on a platform just inside the equatorial lips of the huge white spherical spacecraft. The red sphere disappeared from her view as the opening to the outside closed.

So what happens now? Maria asked herself as she stood in total darkness. She didn't wait long for an answer. From behind her, inside the white sphere, a glowing flying white ribbon approached her capsule. It circled her twice in ten seconds, long enough for Maria to examine the characteristic sparkling and dancing particles that were drifting, apparently aimlessly, from side to side inside the ribbon's everchanging external structure.

When the ribbon extended itself and opened her chamber door, lights flooded the area around Maria. At first the illumination was so bright that Maria was forced to cover her eyes. Once her eyes had adjusted, however, Maria saw that she was in a large rectangular white room with very high ceilings. A number of objects were scattered around the room, including a series of large vats with transparent sides, each filled with a liquid of a slightly different color, which were lined up against the wall farthest away.

As Maria tentatively left the capsule, the ribbon transformed itself into the shape of a woman. In the part of the room across from the vats, the ribbon woman demonstrated both the shower and the toilet before simulating eating one of the food cylinders and drinking from a water vessel. Next the particle woman briefly lay down on a sleeping mat in a corner against one of the walls before changing back into a ribbon and flying into the center of the room.

Maria wasted no time. Holding the silver cylinder that had been removed from her mother high above her head, she leaned toward the hovering ribbon. Something like a hand with three fingers formed on one side of the ribbon, reaching down and taking the cylinder from her. Maria felt a brief tingle when a part of the ribbon brushed against her forearm. She then watched with fascination as the cylinder, somehow held aloft by the particle being, was opened along the side by a zipperlike motion, revealing the existence of twenty-six objects inside. One, by far the largest, was shaped like a dumbbell. Except for a small powder-blue cylinder, the other twenty-four objects were all tiny spheres. Ten were black, seven were white, and seven were black with a bisecting white stripe. Each of them drifted slowly in midair inside the body of the ribbon.

The ribbon now moved quickly across the room to where the vats were located. The powder-blue cylinder and the twenty-four spheres were neatly placed on the floor by one extended arm of the ribbon while another dropped the dumbbell into the first vat on the left. The body of the silver cylinder, apparently no longer important, was returned to Maria by still another extension of the constantly changing particle being.

Curious, Maria crossed the room to examine the vats. She picked up the blue cylinder and a mixture of the three kinds of spheres, black, white, and striped, turning them over in her hands before returning them to their locations on the floor. Then she moved closer to the first vat on the left, where the dumbbell had sunk to the bottom. Maria stood there a few moments, waiting for something to happen, until the ribbon attracted her attention by flying almost into her face and then dashing across the room.

The ribbon changed briefly back into a woman and stretched out on the mat. Suddenly realizing how tired she was from all the day's activities, Maria yawned. Not five minutes later she was asleep on the mat.

THREE

MARIA'S DREAMS WERE vivid, but sporadic and confusing. In one episode Nicole was sitting on a throne at the top of her dream screen and Maria was standing below her with other members of Nicole's extended family.

"Life is not about things," Nicole was lecturing to them all in the dream. "It is about the processes and experiences of learning and loving. What we remember most clearly when we confront death are treasured moments with those we have loved and individual instances of piercing insight into the nature of our existence."

In another episode the Eagle was holding Maria's hand. There was a sudden flash of light in the dream and the Eagle vanished, leaving her with an intense feeling of abandonment. As Maria stood alone in a black room, a glowing ribbon came toward her from the bottom of her dream monitor.

"I will not hurt you," the ribbon said telepathically. Maria stood transfixed in the dream, watching the individual sparkling, dancing motes in the apparition's interior drift back and forth from side to side. Suddenly one of the particles transformed into a dumbbell, burst through the external structure of the ribbon, and ominously occupied Maria's entire dream screen.

This disturbing final dream was still in her mind when Maria awoke, groggy, and remembered where she was. Looking around, she noticed that there was no ribbon present in the dimly illuminated room. Across from her, Maria could barely tell that there was now an object in the second vat from the left, but all the others were empty. It appeared as if the twenty-five objects on the floor had not been moved.

Maria drank from the water vessel beside her mat and then ate two of the food cylinders as she crossed the room. She approached the vats, curious about what had happened to the dumbbell and wondering if this oddly shaped growing mass in the second vat might once have been the largest object removed from her silver cylinder. *So what is going on here?* Maria asked herself. *Some amazing technological magic?*

Her questions were only partially answered about an hour later when the ribbon again appeared in the room, apparently coming through the walls, and zoomed over to the vats. As Maria watched, the ribbon removed the mass inside the second vat, which was now about the size of a soccer ball but lumpy and uneven, and placed it in the adjacent third vat.

As the day passed, and the ribbon appeared twice more to move the constantly growing object from one vat to the next, Maria surmised that this mass had indeed once been the dumbbell and that it was being transformed by the chemicals in the vats into a new and different entity. For ten to twelve hours, Maria watched it grow and change shape, but none of its manifestations looked like anything she had ever seen before, or gave any clues to its ultimate identity. Eventually, she became tired and even a little bored. Returning to her mat, Maria fell into a long, deep, and refreshing sleep.

What she saw in the second vat from the right when she awakened was so startling that she blinked twice to make certain she was not dreaming. Something resembling a human figure was standing upright in the vat, still changing and forming as she watched. Maria hurried across the room, her astonishment increasing, and inspected the figure from close range.

Standing inside the vat was a very tall man, with white skin, a well-muscled body, and a salt-and-pepper beard. He was wearing only a pair of shorts. Parts of his anatomy, the eyes, fingers, and toes especially, were not yet human in appearance, but Maria's careful examination of the activity in the vat indicated that it was exactly in those areas of the body that the continuing process of evolution was still the most active. Maria watched for another hour, flabbergasted, as the incomplete eyes and other parts of the body became more and more real.

Once the figure truly looked like a human being, the liquid in the vat began to drain. Simultaneously, the man began to move his limbs, awkwardly at first, but then in a more natural manner. When the liquid had completely emptied from the vat, its door opened and the man walked out into the room.

Backpedaling in fear, Maria kept her eyes fixed on the man who had apparently been created from the dumbbell that had been inside the cylinder removed from her mother.

"Hello," the man said in English. "My name is Johann Eberhardt. Who are you?"

It took a supreme effort for Maria not to faint. She was totally unable to speak.

The man approached her, smiling. "I probably should say, more exactly, I *was* Johann Eberhardt. I am not really a living human being, as you are I presume, but rather a reconstruction of someone who once lived."

"ALL I AM able to tell you," the man said to Maria some time later, after she had recovered from her shock enough to pepper him with questions, "is that I have been created by an information-expansion process that is the inverse of a data-compression algorithm. This expansion process is very similar to that which naturally occurs in embryonic development for virtually all creatures from your home planet."

Although Maria did not understand most of what the Johann was telling her, she listened with rapt attention. "My zygote was the dumbbell," the man said. "Instead of a mother and a placenta, these vats provided the proper environment for the information expansion that resulted in my being here now. A long sequence of complicated chemical interactions inside the vats supplied the raw materials for my growth and development. But what I would eventually become was already contained in the compressed information of that original object, just as the characteristics of the human infant are contained in the genes and chromosomes of its zygote.

"The intelligence that resurrected me has mastered all aspects of data compression and expansion. Stored in my brain, doubtless by them, is information that suggests that they often select living beings and provide them with this unusual kind of immortality for library purposes. These particle beings have the ability to take the life and experiences of virtually any creature that has ever lived, distill its essence by using complex data-compression algorithms, and later resurrect it, almost exactly as it was, for their uses."

Even though Maria heard all the words the resurrected Johann was saying to her, her mind still balked at his explanations. She could not conceive of a technology so advanced that it could store a human being's entire physical likeness, life experiences and memory, and even his personality in an object no larger initially than her smallest toe.

All of Maria's immediate questions to Johann had been about *what* he was, and how it was even possible that he was standing there talking to her. At length she became convinced that she was not capable of truly comprehending how he had been re-created and her focus turned to the reasons she had sought an encounter with the particle culture in the first place.

"All right, Johann Eberhardt, or whatever you are," she said, "let me now tell you who I am and why I am here. My name is Maria and I am currently living at a place we call the Node, a gigantic space tetrahedron built by an advanced extraterrestrial intelligence, but not the same one who is responsible for this sphere and your existence. I was brought here at my own request, for I thought that perhaps I might find some answers to questions about my own origins."

She paused for a moment. The Johann's expression was one of patience. "I was found as an infant," Maria continued, "inside an alien spacecraft that human beings call Rama. Nobody has any idea where I came from or how I happened to be inside that particular spacecraft. The only clues to my background were a silver cylinder that a woman named Nicole des Jardins Wakefield found inserted in my dead mother's buttock—inside of which was the dumbbell artifact from which you developed—and a simple necklace I was wearing as an infant that had my name Maria inscribed on one side. The aliens at the Node said that the silver cylinder—"

"Excuse me," the Johann interrupted, suddenly showing excitement. "May I see your necklace and amulet? It could be very, very important. And tell me everything that you know about your mother, especially what she looked like."

Maria stared at the figure towering over her. She took a deep breath and recited the few things she knew about her mother. Johann nodded several times during her remarks, growing increasingly animated. When she was finished, Maria, surprised to discover that her fingers were trembling, pulled the necklace over her head and handed it to him.

"Yes," he said emphatically. "This is exactly the same one. It couldn't be possible that there would be another like it."

The puzzled Maria looked at the Johann, who was positively beaming, as he gave the necklace back to her. "Young lady," he announced with a dramatic flourish, "this necklace and amulet were originally the property of a woman named Sister Beatrice, who received them when she was ordained as a Michaelite priestess on Earth. It was I *myself* who inscribed the word 'Maria' on the back of the amulet at the time of the birth of Beatrice's daughter, who was indeed named Maria. . . . It is very likely that you and I are relatives."

Maria heard his words but her internal emotions were in such turmoil that she was having difficulty accepting what this smiling giant was telling her. She couldn't think of anything to say. She just stood there, still staring at Johann, tears easing into her eyes.

"Based on what you have told me," Johann said softly, "I believe that you are either my granddaughter or great-granddaughter. Your mother's name was Franzi. For reasons I will explain later, your father might have been my son, Siegfried, or my grandson, Rowen. I don't know which one of them might have escaped—"

Johann was not able to continue. Maria had rushed forward and thrown her arms around him. With a fountain of tears running down her cheeks, she pulled his head down and began kissing him on the forehead, on the nose, everywhere she could find.

"Thank you, oh thank you," she said. "This is the happiest day of my life."

THEY WALKED HAND in hand across the room and sat down together on her mat. Maria drank some water and offered it to Johann. He explained that he didn't need food or water, and was not, in fact, even remotely similar to a human being underneath his skin.

"I am a sophisticated machine," he reminded her, "similar to a member of your species only on the surface. My creators have substituted brilliantly designed engineering subsystems for the brain, the heart, and all the other biological organs that you have. Although my memory contains exactly the same information as Johann Eberhardt's did before he died, it is actually about the size of one of your fingernails and is located here, beneath my armpit."

"But how is it possible," Maria said, still gawking at her companion in utter amazement, "that you are so *human*? You smile, you frown, you show compassion and excitement—how can all those qualities have been built into a machine?"

Johann laughed. "Technological magic, Maria," he answered. "This culture is so much more advanced than humanity that virtually their entire civilization, including their very existence, would be incomprehensible to all except a few members of the human species."

As Maria took another drink from the water vessel, Johann stood up and extended his hand to her. "You're in luck, young lady," he said. "By the time I finish the story I'm going to tell, you will know more about your ancestors than you could possibly have imagined. But for reasons that will become obvious soon enough, I want to tell the tale over there, near the vats."

They walked back across the room. Pseudo-Johann stopped near where the other objects in the cylinder had been neatly arranged on the floor and picked up the seven white spheres. "I'll start with a quick summary of my childhood, adolescence, and early adult years in Germany, on the planet Earth," he said, dropping the white spheres in the vat on the right, which Maria noticed for the first time was slightly separated from the rest. "In a way, my background is a prologue, because the *real* story of your ancestors starts on Mars, where I had gone to manage a large processing plant that converted the polar ice into water. . . ."

"WITH THE ENTIRE Martian infrastructure rapidly falling apart, there was every reason to believe that a fierce global dust storm might be the final blow in the destruction of human civilization on Mars. . . ."

Maria had listened attentively to Johann. His story had been fascinating. She had temporarily forgotten about the white spheres developing in the vat behind her. The last few times she had looked, they had not substantially changed. Each of the spheres had grown to the size of a softball, without any definitive form she could recognize, and had then apparently stopped growing.

"Never for a moment, as I drove out to the plateau in the rover that Martian morning," Johann continued, "did I think that I would *myself* become a passenger on that alien spacecraft that had been constructed on Mars. Needless to say, my life was about to undergo what a mathematician would call a gigantic step discontinuity."

Johann laughed. "There is always change, Maria," he said. "But sometimes change is so profound that it separates our lives into distinct phases, with almost no connection between the two parts. That's the kind of change that took place when I boarded what looked like a large hatbox sitting on the Martian plain."

He glanced over his shoulder at the vat behind them. "Ah," the Johann said with a smile, "nearly perfect timing." Maria also looked at the vat. Inside were seven human figurines, roughly twenty centimeters tall, fully dressed, with extraordinary detail in their faces.

"Don't you try this," Johann said, sticking his arm into the vat and retrieving the figurines, "or you will feel terrible pain. The liquid in this particular vat would eat through most biological cells from the Earth in a matter of seconds. But it's perfect for this particular purpose."

He dried the figures on his shorts and then stood them upright. "Here," he said to Maria, "are seven of your ancestors, just as they looked on the morning we departed from Mars. From right to left, we have Sister Vivien in her Michaelite robes, Anna Kasper—"

"Wait a minute." Maria interrupted him. "I'm lost. I thought you said *eleven* people left Mars on that spacecraft."

"That's correct," Johann said. "For reasons I can't explain, only re-creations of your relatives were included in the silver cylinder that was inserted in your mother. There are no representations of Brother Jose or Sister Nuba, the two Michaelites in our contingent who remained celibate."

"So that makes nine," Maria said, thinking out loud.

"Plus me, plus Sister Beatrice," pseudo-Johann added, "for a total of eleven." He took a few steps and picked up the powder-blue cylinder. "This is Sister Beatrice," he said, "always a special case, just as she was in real life."

"All right," Maria said. "Now I understand the arithmetic." She bent down and examined the figurines one by one. "From what you have told me," she said, "this must be Fernando and Satoko, the other Michaelite is Brother Ravi, and these two are Kwame and Yasin. . . ."

FOUR

INITIALLY JOHANN HAD difficulty making any progress in his story because of Maria's frequent interruptions. She was continually asking questions about exactly *how* she was related to each of the individuals represented by the figurines.

"If you'll just wait," the resurrected Johann said, displaying a surprisingly authentic irritation, "all your questions will be answered. You can't possibly appreciate how unique you are, the sole survivor of all these people represented here, as well as both Beatrice and Johann, unless you hear the story of what happened."

"All right," Maria said, realizing that her impatience was once again out of control. "I'll try to listen better."

"Now," Johann continued, "none of us had the slightest idea what was going to happen after that gigantic sphere, exactly like this one, swallowed the spacecraft that had carried us away from the surface of Mars. We might have all panicked had it not been for the calm certitude of Sister Beatrice, who was completely convinced that God's angels were our rescuers and therefore nothing untoward could possibly occur. . . ."

Maria restrained herself as Johann explained how Beatrice and the actual human from whom he was reconstructed were separated from the others. He summarized the main events of the next eight years fairly quickly, drawing liberally from what Vivien had told him after they had been reunited. He limited himself to describing the key milestones in everyone's lives and omitted almost all the details of his passionate love relationship with Beatrice. Each time Johann would talk about a specific character, Maria would reach down and pick up the figurine for that person, adding to the verisimilitude of the images she was forming in her mind while Johann was telling the story.

Maria found Yasin both fascinating and repugnant at the same time. "So you believe," she said during a short hiatus in Johann's tale, "that the ribbons *purposely* brought him to your island because Sister Beatrice and you had not mated? Why would they do that? They must have observed him, and known what he was like."

"My resurrection has added to my knowledge only a tiny set of information about the beings who have brought me back to life," Johann said. "I know nothing of their value systems, or of their motivations. What I do know, however, is that the *actual* Johann was certain that Yasin's appearance was not coincidental. He definitely believed that Yasin was sent to the island by the extraterrestrials governing the sphere as part of an additional experiment they were conducting on the humans they had rescued."

Pseudo-Johann paused and sighed in a very human manner. "But I was never able to convince Beatrice of that fact," he said wistfully, "not even after Yasin raped and impregnated her. She was still sure that God's angels were responsible for everything and there was some purpose for even the most heinous deeds. Beatrice was as incapable of pessimism as she was of guile."

Johann fell silent for a few seconds. As Maria looked at the emotions registering on his face, she found it impossible to believe that she was listening to a machine and not a real human.

He suddenly stood up. "That reminds me," the Johann said. "I'd better start Beatrice on her development. She takes longer than the others. And while I'm at it, since you clearly have more interest in *who* your ancestors were than the story of their lives, I might as well fill out the cast of characters and the alien menagerie that accompany the rest of my tale."

He scooped up all the rest of the spheres, both the black ones and the striped ones, and tossed them in the right vat where the first group of white spheres had been placed. Then Johann walked down to the fourth vat from the end of the array and gently dropped the powder-blue cylinder inside.

"This is probably a good place for a short break," Johann said to Maria upon his return. "After these have developed, you'll be able to meet all your ancestors and we can construct your family tree." He smiled. "Then maybe you'll let me tell the rest of the story."

MARIA LAY DOWN on her mat while the spheres in the vat underwent their billions of chemical reactions that would change them into the figurines the Johann would use to illustrate the rest of his story. As she lay there, Maria kept telling herself, over and over, that what was happening to her was real, and not some bizarre dream or hallucination. Even in her extraordinary life, nothing had occurred that was even remotely as amazing as everything she had experienced from the moment she had arrived at this sphere.

I am having a conversation with a resurrection of my grandfather or great-grandfather, she told herself. *These particle beings, for some unknown reason, using an advanced technology no human could ever understand, have chosen to preserve him for posterity. They also have compressed additional data to expand into figures that represent the people and creatures who played key roles in Johann's life.* Maria smiled. *And this is either all true or I have become completely crazy.*

She must have dozed off, for when she heard Johann calling, it seemed as if only a few minutes had passed.

"Come over here," he said, "and you can meet your whole family. I've set up an alignment that will make everything easier for you to understand."

On the floor across the room, Johann had arranged all the human figurines, including the ten that had developed from the black spheres, into rows and columns. "Although I still believe it's putting the cart before the horse, I'm going to introduce you to everyone first," he said. "Then later on, as the story unfolds, you will learn more about the personalities and characters of each of your ancestors."

He motioned for Maria to come over beside him. "Back there, in the first row," Johann said, "are the original group of your relatives that left Mars, minus Beatrice and Johann, each of whom are represented in this schematic matrix by a small piece of fabric torn from my shorts. The piece next to Yasin is, of course, Beatrice. The fabric on the right side of Vivien is Johann.

"On the far left in the top row are Fernando and Satoko. Coming forward from them, in the next row, is their daughter, Keiko. Moving across from Fernando and Satoko we find Kwame, then Vivien, then the piece of fabric representing me when I was alive. One row in front, on Kwame's side of Vivien, is their son, Jomo, who married Keiko. . . ."

It took Johann almost an hour to explain to Maria all the complicated interrelationships that made up her family tree. Of course, part of the time was spent answering her questions, to which Johann inevitably replied, "If I had told you the whole story first, as I suggested, then these questions wouldn't be necessary."

Eventually Maria had everyone straight and Johann continued with his tale by handing her a figurine of a nozzler, which had developed in the vat from one of the striped spheres. "This is the creature," he said, "that frightened the wits out of your namesake, the first Maria, when we were crossing the lake. It's a shame that it doesn't move, for only then would you have a true picture of how terrifying it and its friends were when they surrounded our little boat."

Each time that an alien animal played a major role in the story, Johann handed that particular figurine to Maria. Understating his own heroism, he told of his battle with the elevark that prompted the maskets to release the first Maria. Since each of the developed replicas were exactly one-tenth scale, Maria had some sense of the enormous size of the elevark.

"So you would have been killed by this creature," she said, holding the elevark in her hand, "if that masket friend you called Scarface had not diverted it at the last minute?"

"Yes," said Johann. "It was an astonishing act of selfless bravery by Scarface. Partially because of that event, in subsequent years the actual Johann often reflected philosophically on the similarities and differences among the many alien creatures he had encountered during the odyssey that was his life. We human beings, from my point of view, are chemicals evolved into consciousness by a unique process. Yet other chemicals have evolved into similar consciousness along entirely separate paths, and share some of our basic values. Is it possible that there are some overarching maxims governing the entire process? Do life and intelligence occur a certain percentage of the time due to high-level truths or natural laws that we human beings have not yet discovered?"

The Johann was suddenly silent. Maria did not say anything for a while. "Was the real Johann as deep a thinker as you are?" she asked at length.

Johann laughed. "I believe I am a resurrection of the real Johann," he said, "or at least a very close approximation thereof. Of course I have no way of knowing if the actual Johann had thoughts like those I just expressed. But judging from his life and varied experiences, it would make sense that he would have developed an extraordinarily broad view of the universe."

THE JOHANN TOLD the story of the family's stay in the grotto and their subsequent transport to the planet with the twin moons. While he was building dramatically to the description of the branker attacks on double full moon night, he gave Maria the nepp, ackyong, and sperden figurines.

"Yipes," she said, placing the newest creatures beside the nozzler, the masket, and the elevark. "Now I understand why you referred to this group as the menagerie."

"And here is the most fearsome alien of all, the branker, the animal that was responsible for the death of almost all your ancestors, including me. Imagine if you can," he said, holding the branker figure over her head, "thousands of these filling the sky, terrifying every living creature with their piercing calls, *brank brank brank*."

It was not difficult for Maria to imagine the fear that the brankers must have engendered. But based upon Johann's story, she could not understand why anyone ever stayed behind and did not swim with him to the offshore island.

"To be fair to them," the Johann said, "I should point out that the others had serious reservations about whether the apparitions of Beatrice that I reported really took place. After all, nobody else ever saw her, not even her daughter. 'Why does she come to you alone,' Ravi asked me several times, 'and not to all of us? Then it would be much easier to verify that the apparition did indeed occur, and is not some kind of yearning hallucination that exists only in your mind.' "

When Johann finished the story of the final double full moon night, including his being eaten by the queen branker, Maria felt a powerful sadness. "And I am the only one left," she said softly. "After all these years, and all the incredible adventures, I am the only remaining member of this extraordinary family."

"That is correct," Johann said.

A flood of emotions, most of which she could not understand, engulfed Maria. "Could you leave me here alone for a little while?" she asked the Johann. "I would like to think about everything you have told me."

Johann crossed behind her to the other vats. As Maria looked at the faces spread out on the floor, and heard again in her mind the stories from their lives, she felt amazingly small. "Thank you all," she whispered humbly. "For your perseverance, your courage, your unwillingness to accept defeat. Without your heroic efforts, I would not exist."

It was then that the epiphanic thought burst into her mind. *I am an absolute miracle,* she thought.

"THIS," THE JOHANN said, handing to Maria a beautiful female figurine dressed in a blue flowing robe with white stripes down the side, "is Sister Beatrice, dressed in her bishop's attire just as she was the first time I met her on Mars."

"She's beautiful," Maria said, examining her carefully before placing her gently on the floor among the others.

"Ah, but her external beauty was only the beginning," Johann said. "She had an internal beauty that far surpassed what could be seen on the outside. Never did I, or Vivien either for that matter, ever meet another human being who was so fundamentally good.

"She was the perfect Michaelite priestess. Sister Beatrice never thought of herself even *before* she was ordained. And after she joined the order, she was an example for everyone else. She was a wonder to behold."

Maria looked at the admiring smile on Johann's face as he gazed down at the figurine. "You loved her very much, didn't you?" she said.

The Johann looked up slowly. "That would be an understatement," he said, his emotion reflecting in his voice. "I adored her, both as a friend, and as a woman. She was by far the most significant person in my life."

"And did she love you?" Maria asked.

Johann hesitated before answering. "Yes," he said, "as much as she could. But her love for me was subordinate to her love for God and the family of man."

The Johann fell silent. As Maria watched him, his eyes staring at the faraway walls as if he were a normal human being remembering special moments from his life, she was again overwhelmed by the awesome capability of the technology that had resurrected him.

"So did the two of you ever decide who was right?" Maria asked.

"What do you mean?" Johann asked.

Maria pointed at the ribbon that had just appeared in the room and was flying slowly toward them. "Is that one of God's angels, or simply an advanced extraterrestrial creature?"

Johann didn't answer for a while. "From a true human perspective," he said finally, "I guess Sister Beatrice and I were both right. The ribbons, in their different manifestations, have all the attributes that people normally ascribe to angels. But they are also extraterrestrials in the literal sense."

He shrugged. "You know, maybe it doesn't really make any difference *what* they are. That they exist at all is what is important."

The ribbon was now almost directly over their heads. As always, Maria could not stop watching the motion of the sparkling, dancing particles moving to and fro inside the glowing, changing structure.

At that moment the Beatrice began to walk toward them in a gracious, flowing movement. Her face broke into a magnificent smile as she approached Johann and Maria.

"As you have seen," the Johann said, "none of the other preserved figurines have been endowed with any of the characteristics that made them human. But Beatrice's smile, the wondrous blue of her eyes, and the grace of her body movement have all been retained for posterity. And one more thing—"

The ribbon reached down and touched the Johann, interrupting what he was saying. He stared intently at the ribbon and then turned to Maria. "Your time is up," the Johann said. "The shuttle that will carry you back to the Node is waiting outside."

Maria glanced back and forth from the ribbon to Johann. "It *talked* to you," she said incredulously. "And you *understood* it?"

Johann laughed again. "Yes," he said. "But that should not surprise you. I am not an *exact* resurrection of the Johann who was your grandfather or great-grandfather. I have been given some additional capability."

Maria looked at the ribbon again. "But I'm not ready to go yet," she protested. "I have so many more questions."

"You really have no choice," Johann said.

Maria shrugged. The ribbon remained in place, hovering over both of them. When Johann didn't say anything else, Maria bent down and picked up the Beatrice figurine. "May I keep this?" she said. "She's so beautiful."

Johann nodded and started walking across the room. On the far side, around a corner, the upright capsule with the transparent window that had been Maria's space vehicle a few days before was waiting for her. Its door was open.

When they reached the capsule, Maria turned to the Johann. "Then I guess this is good-bye," she said with difficulty. She gazed up at the re-creation of the man who had been her grandfather or great-grandfather and forced herself not to be sad. She walked over to him and put her head against his chest and her arms around his back.

"Thank you," she said. "Thank you so much."

He hugged her silently for several seconds and then gently pulled away. Johann took the Beatrice figurine from Maria's hand and held it at eye level.

"I haven't been completely honest with you," he said. "I loved Beatrice with a passion beyond any feeling I ever experienced in my life. She was beyond my wildest expectations as a friend, a companion, and a lover. I never really recovered from her death."

Maria was astonished to see tears running down the Johann's cheeks. "She also had the most beautiful singing voice I ever heard in my entire life. The first time I heard her sing, just before Christmas on Mars—"

The figurine in his hand, no more than a meter from Maria's face, opened its mouth and began to sing. " 'Oh Holy Night, the stars are brightly shining. . . . It is the night of the dear Saviour's birth. . . . Long lay the world. . . .' "

Goose bumps swept up Maria's arms and tears spontaneously flooded her eyes. She could not believe that any human being who had ever lived could possibly have had such a beautiful voice. She stood and stared, trembling and stupefied, as the tiny Beatrice continued her song.

" 'Fall on your knees. . . . Oh hear, the angels' voices. . . . Oh Night, Divine. . . . Oh Night, when Christ was born.' "

Maria and Johann both wept silently and separately until Beatrice was finished. Then Maria collapsed into Johann's arms, allowing her sobs to give vent to the myriad of emotions that were overwhelming her.

"So beautiful," she said softly. "So unbelievably beautiful."

Johann squeezed her tightly. She reached up and gently wiped the tears off his face.

"You must go now," he said softly.

"I know," she said.

He handed her the Beatrice figurine, which Maria lovingly cradled in her hands. Waving good-bye, she backed into the capsule. An instant later the equatorial lips of the giant sphere parted slightly and Maria's chamber hurtled out into space. The red sphere and the red corridor were still there. The Eagle and the shuttle that looked like a flying saucer were parked on the far side of the red corridor.

Maria's space suit was lying at the end of the red corridor. Placing the Beatrice gently on the floor beside her, she put on her suit and helmet. After checking her equipment and adjusting it, she picked up the figurine and walked right through the end of the red corridor into the shuttle.

Maria mechanically put her seat belt around her.

"How was it?" the Eagle asked pleasantly.

Maria could not answer. There were no words she could find that could do justice to what she had experienced. She simply nodded her head up and down.

The Eagle noticed the figurine in her hand. "What's that?" he said.

Maria stared at her alien companion. "A miracle," she said at length. "Another of the miracles of life."

ABOUT THE AUTHOR

GENTRY LEE has been chief engineer on Project Galileo, director of science analysis and mission planning for NASA's Viking mission to Mars, and partner with Carl Sagan in the design, development, and implementation of the television series *Cosmos*. He is co-author of *Rama II*, *The Garden of Rama*, and *Rama Revealed*. **Double Full Moon Night** is a sequel to his novel, *Bright Messengers*. He lives in Frisco, Texas.